I0541240

# STREET LIFE IN PARADISE

*Book #2*

# STREET LIFE IN PARADISE

*From The Secret Diary of Eddie Ocean*

E. O. TEST

Copyright © 2016 E. O. Test
All rights reserved.

ISBN-10: 0985305029
ISBN-13: 9780985305024

Sea Angel Publishing

# AUTHORS NOTE

Disclaimer: This is a work of fiction. The characters named in this story are fictional and their actions should not be assumed to be true depictions of anyone's character or behavior. Any incidents herein are fictitious.

I'd like to dedicate *STREET LIFE IN PARADISE* To all the readers of my first book *CROCODILE ISLAND,* especially those of you who have left such kind and enthusiastic reviews online.

Also a special shout-out to my entire extended family, especially The Hatley Clan for inspiring the 1974 short story *Crocodile Island* that became the first chapter and title of book #1 in *The Eddie Ocean Series.*

Finally, a special thanks to Judith Sipes for providing her beautiful paintings for my interior. The black and white reprints do not do her artwork justice.

# CONTENTS

# PROLOGUE
## *El Muerte*

\* The following events were taken from the memoirs of a man named Carlos Romero (a/k/a *El Muerte*). In order to maintain a chronological flow I have included these events as a prologue to Book #2 of my secret diary.

Carlos Romero was confined at *Fortaleza de la Cabaña* Prison, Havana, Cuba in April of 1961. The following events took place precisely two years after his capture during the failed Bay of Pigs invasion by Brigade 2506.

## APRIL 19TH, 1963

"Come take this one away!" the captain of the guard ordered as he walked toward the unconscious man chained by the wrists to the dungeon wall.

"Put *El Muerte* in his place!"

The prisoner hung limply from the stone wall like a scarecrow, arms spread wide, legs buckled, and chin resting upon his chest. With an expression of disdain, the captain of the guard examined the man's battered face as blood poured from his mouth. Then he leaned in closer and pressed the lit end of his cigar against the man's cheek. From across the room I saw a wisp of smoke rise from his burning flesh, but the prisoner did not stir.

"Are you still with us, comrade?" the sadistic captain asked, scowling at the unconscious man.

He took another puff to keep the snuffed cigar lit and then leaned in even closer to examine the perfect circle that he had branded into the man's left cheek.

"Yes, this one is finished. Prepare *El Muerte*." The captain walked to a wooden table in the center of the room and sat down to wait. He leaned back in his chair and blew a thick cloud of grey smoke toward the ceiling. From the opposite side of the dungeon, where I sat chained to a steel autopsy table, I watched the captain with hatred. The captain noticed my hostile glare and turned his attention to me.

"Are you enjoying the show, *El Muerte*? Are you enjoying the anniversary celebration of your great defeat at the Bay of Pigs? Now it is your turn to play the star role in our little drama." Beads of sweat formed on my forehead and trickled down my face as I fought back my fear.

A short, fat, sweat-soaked man named Garza stood next to the unconscious prisoner. He was the captain's chief interrogator. Garza had worked me over several times before but could never break me. The pudgy little man used his sleeve to wipe blood from the jaws of a set of long-handled tongs and then walked over to the captain and placed the instrument of torture on the wooden table. Garza's sweat-soaked green coveralls were spattered with blood.

"Garza, you are only good at putting them to sleep. We need them awake! Awake so they can feel the pain." The captain was unhappy with Garza's torture techniques.

"Captain, these dissidents are weaklings! They faint like little girls as soon as I touch them, sir!" said Garza.

"Well, maybe the Russian will have more success than you did, Garza!" The captain took a puff from the fat cigar, and it glowed bright red in the dimly lit dungeon. Disgusted with his accomplice, the captain blew a cloud of smoke toward Garza's face.

"You need to learn finesse, Garza. You are too heavy-handed. Maybe the Russian can teach you finesse."

Through a small, barred window cut in the center of the heavy metal door to my right, Garza spoke to the guards in the hallway outside. There was a rattling of keys as the door opened, and two prison guards hustled into the concrete-and-stone dungeon to unshackle the unconscious man hanging from the far wall.

"Is this one still alive, Garza?" one guard asked the interrogator as they dragged the limp body by the arms toward the open door.

"He might be dead. I don't know," Garza said.

The captain was angry. "We don't know if he's alive or dead. Just get him out and prepare *El Muerte*."

"But sir, should we take this one to his cell or outside to the morgue?"

"What does it matter? He is useless to me now—we took his tongue out. Just put him in his cell for now to see if he is dead."

Two guards left, dragging the limp man's body by his arms, and the two remaining guards unlocked my chain from the table. I was shackled at the ankles and wrists with interconnecting chains. Guards on each side of me lifted me up from my seat by my biceps, and I shuffled over to the table and stood glaring down upon the captain. He squirmed uncomfortably in his seat before rising and stepping several feet away from me. I flexed my biceps and scowled at the nervous guards who held me. Even though I was securely shackled, I believe they sensed that they would have trouble restraining me if I chose to fight them.

"Sir, we should get *El Muerte* secured—secured to the wall."

"Yes I see that," said the captain as he drew his Russian-made 9 mm semi-automatic pistol.

"*El Muerte*, I have a special surprise for you today." The captain motioned with his pistol for me to move toward the shackles pinioned to the bloodstained stone wall.

My smirk became a smile as I recognized fear in the captain's eyes and the beads of sweat forming around his mouth.

*You will never break me, you sadistic bastard!* I kept that thought to myself because I was looking down the barrel of his pistol.

I resisted for a moment and, as I had suspected, the guards could not budge me. They leaned in hard to push me toward the wall, but I just laughed at their futile efforts.

"Get him over there and fasten the chains, quick!" ordered the nervous captain as he chambered a round.

I knew the captain would have no problem shooting me dead if I gave him an excuse, so I relaxed my biceps and shuffled forward. My smile disguised the fear that was starting to overcome me. Then, as the cold steel shackles were clasped shut around my wrists, my smug smile suddenly turned into a scowl of disgust as I noticed the severed tongue lying at my feet on the bloodstained cobblestone floor.

"What's wrong, *El Muerte*—cat got your tongue?" asked the captain as he kicked the tongue closer to my feet while laughing at his own sadistic joke.

"You will not break me, you sick bastard!" I rattled the chains that restrained my arms and tried to spit at the evil man, but my mouth was too dry.

"It is true, *El Muerte*: I have not had much luck breaking you. But today you will have a new playmate. I think you might like him better than Garza. I think you might like Nikko very much. He's Russian."

My real name is Carlos Romero, not *El Muerte*, and I was born in the year 1932 to upper-middle-class landowners in western Cuba. My family had farmed our land for three generations. From years of hard farm labor, I grew from a small, frail boy into a tall and strong man. It was in 1950 that I went to Havana to attend college. Two years later I graduated from the University of Havana with a degree in agriculture and returned home to take over the family business.

Five years later, in the summer of 1957, a series of events shattered my world and changed my life forever.

That summer, just after my twenty-fifth birthday, Communist rebels came down from the Sierra Maestro Mountains to confiscate our family farm. The well-armed guerillas rounded up my family and our six employees and encircled us, as we stood huddled in the front yard of our modest wooden farmhouse.

The leader of the guerillas was a small, thin man with a mustache, who was wearing a black beret. He stepped forward holding a pistol and spoke. "We are here to reclaim the land! All the lands of Cuba belong to the Cuban people!"

"Yes, commander, and we are Cuban people," my father protested.

"No, you are not the Cuban people. You are the bourgeoisie oppressors of the Cuban people! You are a land baron, and you must leave this land and leave this country."

"I will never leave my land," my father declared.

"Very well, then. You shall remain here as part of it." The little man walked to my father's side and pressed the pistol into the gray hair at his temple.

"No, please, I beg you, sir! No!" wailed my mother as she dropped to her knees, pleading for mercy.

Before I had time to react, the evil little commander looked down at my mother, smiled, and then pulled the trigger.

*Pow!* One shot blew out the opposite side of my father's head, spraying his brains across the yard. The old man's body dropped and convulsed for a moment before becoming flaccid, lying motionless on the ground as a pool of blood formed under his head.

"You little coward!" I screamed, and charged the commander.

"Look out, Ernesto!" warned a rebel soldier.

I tackled the little bastard from behind, and he was knocked off his feet and driven hard, face-first, into the ground. His beret flew off his head and spun through the air like a Frisbee as his pistol dropped to the ground beside us. I grabbed the gun and aimed at the back of the commander's head, but before I could fire off a round I was clubbed with the butt end of a rifle stock and knocked unconscious.

The rebels held back the rest of my hysterical family and the angry farmers as I lay bleeding on the ground. They dumped my body into the back of an army truck, where two guards sat holding rifles, and then they forced my family to get into the truck with me. I was told that my weeping family was forced to watch from the truck as the Communist soldiers buried my father's body in a shallow, unmarked hole. Then we were driven to Havana. Somewhere along the journey I regained consciousness and found myself hogtied with a rope.

"Lucky for you Commander Ernesto did not regain consciousness until we had departed from your farm!" a guard said to me and pointed his rifle at my face. The guard made it clear that the vindictive little dictator would have put a bullet in my brain for assaulting him if he had come to his senses before we left for Havana.

In Havana, a not-so-generous offer was made to the surviving members of my family: Sign over to the Cuban government the deed to our farm and leave Cuba, or die in prison. Penniless, we flew to Miami, Florida, to start a new life. We survived in America by cleaning houses, doing handyman work, and I also tended bar at night.

One night while tending bar, I learned from some newly arrived exiles that our once-productive Romero family farm had been turned into a commune and populated by peasants brought in from the cities. The city dwellers had no idea about how to farm, and soon the once-productive land went to ruin, becoming a withering expanse of pestilence, weeds, and rotted fruits and vegetables.

Cato's Communist regime continued to confiscate and redistribute property and businesses across Cuba. Skilled citizens were forced from their occupations and fled the country. Many more were imprisoned. The once-vibrant nightlife and growing economy of Havana collapsed as unskilled people took over industries that they had no knowledge of, and soon the middle class disintegrated.

All the people suffered except for the ruling elite and Cato's sizeable military forces.

The middle classes became impoverished, and the poor had even less than before. The sins of Batista were repeated tenfold by the Communists, and Cuba became a ghetto island. Food, energy, and vital services were now in short supply. The dictators began rationing goods as prices inflated dramatically across Cuba, and the black market became the only reliable source of goods. Much of the resources of Cuba were spent domestically on the military and on spreading the Communist revolution across Africa and into Central and South America.

On a daily basis, people attempted to flee the island-prison, and many died on rafts and inner tubes as they attempted to escape from their Communist oppressors. Those caught trying to escape were killed or imprisoned. Long prison sentences were handed out to Cubans who dared to even criticize Rafael Cato or his revolution.

In Miami, I joined a paramilitary group of Cuban exiles called the Brigade of 2506, who hoped to reclaim Cuba and install a democratically elected government. I trained with these exiles during the day and tended bar at night.

## APRIL 17ᵀᴴ, 1961

With the assistance of the CIA and the American government, I, along with over 1,400 fellow Cuban exiles, invaded Cuba in a clandestine attack that is now commonly known as the Bay of Pigs Invasion.

The battle lasted for three days before Cato's troops gained the upper hand and routed our outgunned fighters. Wounded in the battle and feeling betrayed, I surrendered and was imprisoned by Cato's troops. They held me without trial for over a year in *Fortaleza de la Cabaña* prison in Havana, and I suffered in the deplorable conditions of Cuba's inhumane prison system. Others were sent to labor camps. Despite the torture, I knew I was one of the lucky ones. Hundreds of Brigade 2506 fighters had been summarily executed without trial between April and October of 1961.

On April 7th, 1962, along with 1,178 other men, I was convicted of treason and sentenced to thirty years in prison. For two years, Cato's instruments of torture scarred my body from head to toe. To survive the brutality, I devised a way to endure the pain by using self-hypnosis.

First I would visualize my father's execution by Commander Ernesto. My anger gave me the will to survive, to stay alive so that some day I could seek my vengeance on the Communists. Next, I would go into a trance and leave my physical body to visit with my father in heaven. When successful, I never felt the pain of torture until later, when I came out of my trance and transformed from my zombie state back into Carlos Romero. The guards began calling me "*El Muerte*," the dead one.

"Bring in the Russian. Call in Nikko," ordered the captain of the guard.

A razor-thin young man slipped into the torture chamber just before the heavy steel door slammed shut behind him. He looked like a homely teenage boy. His wispy, snakelike body seemed to slither forward rather than walk. Probably because of his short legs and long torso, he reminded me of a weasel. The young man moved on an angle, clutching a large glass jar, which he held tightly to his right side. He was turned slightly, as if he wished to conceal the jar from my view. I could see the brass-colored lid but not the contents of the jar, and I turned my attention from the jar to the young man's face.

"*¡Ay, coño! ¡Muy feo!*" I said under my breath.

The man's face looked inhuman. A long, hooked nose accentuated the narrowness of his ghost-white, pockmarked face, giving it a hawk-like look. The ugly birdman's grotesque features even disturbed the hardened Cuban prison guards, who looked away from him. Like a crab, he moved sideways across the room toward me and stopped less than three feet away, still turned at an angle.

"So you are *El Muerte! El Muerte* the zombie! They say you cannot be broken, *El Muerte!* We shall see." The Russian spoke Spanish but with a heavy accent.

He hid the jar from my view and said, "My name is Nikko. I have brought with me my prized collection. I wish to share its beauty with you."

Nikko turned to face me head-on, and the right side of the Russian's face became visible for the first time. *¡Ay coño!* The Russian's right eye was lifeless, and a bluish film covered the dead eye's socket. His hair was as shiny and black as a crow's wing and was slicked back with oil. A long, jagged scar extended down from his greasy hairline and continued down through the lifeless right eye and across his cheek before ending just above his quivering, sweaty, upper lip.

"Ay, mother of God!" This time I spoke out loud, startled by the hideous man's face. My dismay brought a smirk to the Russian's thin, quivering, sweaty lips.

"Do you like my pretty face? You might like these even more, *El Muerte!*" The Russian held the jar out for me to see.

"*¡Ay! ¡Usted es loco!*" I gasped in horror.

I could not believe what I was seeing. The large glass jar was packed with eyeballs floating like pickled eggs in a clear fluid. The gallon-sized jar was filled to the brim with orbs of various colors; some had thin, wispy optic nerves still attached to the back of the eyeball.

"Aren't they beautiful? I like the ones with the nerves attached the best. They remind me of pretty little jellyfish." He gave the jar a shake to make the eyeballs dance up and down.

"Do you recognize anyone, *El Muerte?* Some are Russians, but most come from Cuban dissidents, Bay of Pigs fighters just like you. You might recognize some of your comrades in there." He moved the jar in a circular motion this time, to make the eyeballs swirl around, a morbid parade of orbs behind the glass. I looked away and stared down at the severed tongue on the floor.

"Well, fun time is over, *El Muerte*. We must get down to business." The Russian's heavy foreign accent somehow made him even more terrifying.

As I have explained, due to my ability to disregard physical pain, the Cuban prison guards had nicknamed me *El Muerte* (the Dead One), but English speakers and Russians called me the Zombie.

The Russian leaned in close, examining my eyes. "Very nice eyes. Clear, dry, and healthy—very good eyes," he said.

Then the captain spoke to me. "*El Muerte*, are you ready to give up some names? Will you identify your CIA contacts before things get messy? This is your last chance!"

The creepy, psychotic Russian frightened me far more than any Cuban interrogator ever had, but I remained resolute.

"*Bese el culo, Capitán Mariposa!*" I closed my eyes and yelled with false bravado.

I could not give them what they asked for even if I had wanted to. I didn't know the names of the CIA operators who trained us in Guatemala because the spooks all used code names.

"Very well. Nikko, please begin," said the Captain.

"Okay, wait, captain! Viper, Mustang…Raptor!" I screamed out in fear.

"You told us those names before, *El Muerte*. We want their real names, their God-given names, not code names!"

"Do not fear, captain. I have never failed to break a man. We will soon have those names."

The Russian placed the jar of eyeballs on the wooden table and then began removing tools of torture from the inside lapel of his black leather jacket. He placed the instruments in a neat, straight line and arranged them in order of size.

"By the look on your face, I don't think your zombie devil magic will work this time around, *El Muerte*," said the captain, who was thoroughly enjoying the horror show.

The Russian took the smallest instrument from the table. It was a small stiletto with a white, ivory handle. He pressed a button, and a pointed, razor-thin blade shot out. "Let me introduce you to Baby," said the Russian, as he pointed the knife at my left eye.

*Mother of God, be with me!* My silent prayer was always the prelude to my trance.

"Hurry, Nikko. *El Muerte* is turning zombie on us!" said the captain.

That was the last thing I heard before vanishing into myself.

Keep calm and zombie on!

*Chapter 1*

# DISASTER AT SEA

## MONDAY, DECEMBER 24ᵀᴴ, 1973, 10:00 PM

Ever vigilant, Melon Dog stood in the bow of the *Watermelon* boat sniffing the chilly night air, wary of some unseen danger lurking ahead in the darkness. A stiff breeze out of the Northeast ruffled the dog's thick fur coat as he turned to look at me with troubled eyes. His uneasiness was palpable.

"Speak to me, dog!' I called out to him. He didn't respond but returned his worried gaze to the dark sea, stretching endlessly before our small sailboat.

Since leaving the Whatchacallit Indians, I had lost my sixth sense, the ability to communicate with animals. Even Melon Dog had gone silent ever since we had left the Indian village. Now fatigue brought on by three days of sailing solo was beginning to overwhelm me. *Sing to keep yourself awake, dude.*

"You better watch out
You better not cry
You better not pout…I'm telling you why…."

My attempt to ward off sleep by singing was futile. My eyes began closing involuntarily every few minutes as I steered the boat across the choppy, black water of the dark North Atlantic Ocean on this cold and moonless Christmas Eve in 1973. There was only one thing on my mind: sleep, sleep, sleep…wonderful sleep.

My mind clouded over, lost in a fog of illusions and dreams. Thoroughly exhausted, my thoughts tacked back and forth between reality and the task at hand and a dreamland of strange visions.

*You're off course! Check your heading, dude.*

My eyes were burning, and the compass looked blurry. I wiped condensation off the glass dome as I checked my heading.

"North by 12 degrees. That's good."

Instead of adjusting my bearings to compensate for wind and drift, I felt my eyes close again, and I began daydreaming: *What I wouldn't give to be a child lying in bed right now. How many children across the world are lying sleepless in bed, waiting for Santa Claus?*

I smacked myself on the cheek. *Calculate your point of aim, idiot!* The strong northerly flow of the Gulf Stream helped propel the boat toward our destination, the Port of Miami. With the favorable wind and current, I hoped to make landfall by dawn on Christmas morning.

"Hey, dog! I'm exhausted! Can barely keep my eyes open…need to get some shuteye. Take the night watch!"

When I called out to him, Melon Dog turned his head toward me and barked. It was an uneasy bark, followed by a whimper.

"Don't worry, mutt. If you're lucky, Santa will air drop some doggy biscuits when he flies over us on his way to Miami." My reassurance seemed to lift the dog's spirits. The collie's ears perked up, and he looked toward the sky as if he understood my silly, sleep-deprived whimsy.

We were sailing the *Watermelon* northbound along the western edge of the Gulf Stream, which put us within the international shipping lanes. In order to avoid a collision with a large ship, we needed to be on constant lookout for other vessels. After throttling back to slow the *Watermelon*, I put her on autopilot and then spread my bedroll out above deck. My wristwatch indicated that it was 10:33 pm; I switched to the alarm mode and set my cheap Timex to wake me at 12:30 am.

"Two hours' sleep should recharge my batteries, dog."

Sleep came as soon as my head hit the pillow, but in short order the cold wind chilled me to the bone. I awoke trembling violently. My eyes still burned as I squinted to read my watch. Ten forty-five. *Wow, I got twelve minutes of sleep!*

I sat upright, clutching my knees to my chest, shivering. Sleeping inside the cuddy cabin would have been much more comfortable on this blustery night, but I did not want to go below deck without another human on board acting as a lookout.

Rising to my feet, I struggled to straighten my stiff, aching body and make my legs move and staggered toward the door of the cuddy cabin, tempted to go below deck.

*Bad idea, Eddie Ocean. Accidents happen quickly. You might not hear the dog bark. You might not get out in time.*

The structure of the cabin acted as a windbreak and helped to shield me from the chilly north wind. By repositioning my bedroll just below the ship's wheel behind the cuddy cabin, my sleeping arrangement was greatly improved. *Why didn't I think of sleeping behind the wall before?*

My brain, impaired by sleep deprivation, was unable to readily solve even the simplest problem.

*Ahh, much better on the leeward side! Duh, ya think, dude? Your brain is mush, dude…you need sleep.* Soon I was fast asleep, and a vivid dream came to me.

In my dream, Captain Rubio, the old sea captain who had sold me the *Watermelon*, was standing over me and smiling as I lay at the helm, curled up in the fetal position. The dream was one of those eerily realistic envisagements, the kind of dream that, when you recall it later, confuses you because you aren't sure if you're remembering an actual event or merely a dream.

Rubio looked down at me and smiled. He waved to me, as if to say goodbye, and then he went toward the bow, where Melon Dog was standing guard. As he left my side, Rubio seemed to drift away, not walk. Rubio's body was translucent, ghostlike, as he drifted about the boat inspecting the rigging. He trimmed the mainsail and then stood at the mast, looking up to the top for a moment before drifting over toward the bow of the boat.

Rubio stopped at the bowsprit and hovered next to Melon Dog. The collie's frantic barking interrupted my dream and woke me from my deep sleep. Groggy, I had trouble clearing my head as I sat upright to see what was the matter. The brightly glowing apparition of Rubio began to grow dim. My eyes were open, and I was not asleep. As I watched him standing next to Melon Dog, waving goodbye, the old man began fading into the darkness. Rubio's soft brown eyes conveyed a deep inner peace to me.

*Don't worry; soon we will all be at peace.* It was the sound of Rubio's voice inside my head; it comforted me.

*Thank you, Eddie!* the old man said. He seemed to be very happy as he turned to look ahead into the darkness.

*Thanks for what?* A wreath of mist swirled counterclockwise around Rubio, and suddenly the apparition vanished from sight.

*I'm awake now, so how can I still be dreaming?* Confused, I stood up at the helm and took the wheel. Now the dog stood alone at the bow and began barking hysterically.

"Calm down, dog. That wasn't Santa. That was captain Rubio," I said, my mind still cloudy. I looked out into the darkness and realized that Melon Dog was not barking at the apparition of Rubio. He was looking at something up ahead of the boat.

*That's a giant Christmas tree!* The gigantic, lighted tree hovered above the ocean in front of our boat; its lights twinkled through the mist against the black sky.

My mind refused to clear. What the heck...?

I stared dumbly at the sparkling, giant, triangular-shaped object looming tall just off our bow.

*What is that Christmas tree doing out here in the ocean?* Only after taking a deep breath of the cold salt air did I became fully cognizant and realize what the object was. It was not a Christmas tree!

"Holy crap! That's a ship—a freighter—bearing down on us fast!"

The string of lights running up from the deck to the top of the ship's superstructure formed a huge triangle that resembled a lighted Christmas tree.

Melon Dog kept barking his alarm as the huge ship raced straight toward our little 26-foot sailboat. A surge of adrenaline and the cold air helped me fully regain my senses. I slammed the throttle forward, but that was a mistake because instead of gaining speed, the engine stalled, and the boat slowed. Frantically I tried to restart the engine. She was turning over but not firing up. As I continued to crank her over, I could only watch in horror as the ship grew larger, bearing down on us with alarming speed. We were positioned for a head-on collision!

"Come back here, dog, quick!" I called the dog to get him off the bow as I turned the boat westward toward shore, hoping to get out of the ship's path. Powered by sail alone, we were not moving fast enough, and the boat's motor still would not start.

"Please start!" I yelled at the *Watermelon* and kicked the wall of the cuddy cabin. Finally the motor started up but then sputtered and stalled out again. Now the giant freighter loomed high above us just a few hundred feet off our starboard beam. The huge container ship must have been either empty or carrying a very light load because the bulb of the ship, the part of the hull that protrudes from under the front of the bow, was well above the waterline. When fully loaded, a ship's bulb is usually submerged well beneath the surface of the water, but the bulb on this freighter was coming at us like a medieval jousting lance.

"We're going to be rammed, dog. Prepare to jump overboard!"

I had no time to grab a life vest! The ship's bulb sizzled through the foaming sea, closing fast and throwing a huge wake that was at least 10 feet high. The ship towered above us. I had to look up now to see the tip of the freighter's bow. The huge steel bulb was twice the size of my boat, and it plowed through the water like a submarine running at the surface, preparing to ram us. I ran to the bow of the *Watermelon*, and Melon Dog followed me.

"Jump, dog!" I yelled and dove into the Atlantic Ocean with the freighter only 100 feet from our starboard gunwale.

With my arms extended over my head, like an Olympic swimmer, I hit the surface and knifed through the water, kicking my legs hard in an attempt to get as far away from the ship as possible before surfacing. When I came up for air, I turned around just in time to see the bulb of the ship strike my little boat amidships. She exploded on impact like a watermelon being dropped off a two-story balcony.

"No! No!" My call of grief and despair was cut short. The ship's 10-foot-high wake was coming at me like a mini-tsunami. I filled my lungs with the cold, salt air and held my breath as the wave hit me hard, cresting over me and driving me below the surface.

At first I was propelled away from the ship's hull like an underwater body surfer, but then a strong suction reversed my direction and began pulling me back toward the ship.

*I'm getting sucked into the props!*

The thought horrified me; I imagined being ground into hamburger by the twin, 20-foot screws.

The intensity of the suction increased. By spreading and extending my arms and legs, I hoped to resist the suction, but it did no good, and I was drawn in like a ragdoll doing underwater cartwheels.

*I'm being sucked into the propellers.*

*Whump...whump...whump...**Whump**.*

The pounding sound of the propellers grew louder as the massive ship sucked me in like a baitfish being swallowed by a giant Goliath

Grouper. Hoping to make myself a smaller target, I pulled my knees up to my chest and held my legs like a kid doing a cannonball dive.

*Swoosh.* Suddenly I was "spit out" and pushed away from the stern of the ship.

Miraculously, the blades of the propellers had missed me, and the prop wash was propelling me away from the freighter. The cavitations of the two giant props created a jet stream of bubbling water shooting out from behind the freighter. I came out of my cannonball position and once again was cartwheeling head-over-heels underwater. The giant propellers had not killed me, but now I was drowning.

*Get to the surface!*

The suction of the prop wash finally released me. Disoriented, I fought hard to swim to the surface, and just before I lost consciousness, my head and arms broke free, exploding out of the water. I began reaching for something, anything to grasp but grabbed only air. With a gasp I exhaled and then breathed in deeply. The cold night air on my face had never felt so wonderful as I treaded water and gulped in oxygen. The hulking, southbound ship was speeding away, and it disappeared into the blackness, leaving me bobbing up and down in its wake on the surface of the vast, cold, Atlantic Ocean.

"*Santa Maravilla.*" I read aloud the lettering on the stern of the ship just before it vanished into the dark.

*Santa? How ironic—a visit from Santa on Christmas Eve! They don't even know that they hit me. I wasn't even a speed bump for that megaship.*

In the dim light, pieces of my wooden boat were barely visible, littering the surface of the ocean. I swam toward a large green chunk of debris; it was the wooden transom of the *Watermelon*. After climbing onto the flotsam I saw her name, *Watermelon*, painted in yellow on the shattered green transom. Even after being destroyed and torn to pieces, my beloved little vessel had left me a chunk of her to use as a life raft.

"I'm sorry, little boat. I should have never fallen asleep. Please forgive me."

I placed my palm on the lettering beneath me and said, "So sorry, Captain Rubio. I promised you I would take care of the *Watermelon* boat, but now she is lost."

My apology to the old Cuban sea captain was cut short by a weak bark in the distance.

"Dog, where are you?" I called out into the darkness.

There was only silence.

"Melon Dog—where are you?" I called out again.

From the darkness off to my right, a weak bark was barely audible. I dove off the raft to swim toward the sound. Ahead in the blackness, the glow of two eyes became visible, and I swam toward them. Melon Dog was barely keeping his head above water as he doggy-paddled over to meet me. He was weak and tiring rapidly. By pulling his collar, I got him back to the transom/raft, and with great difficulty hoisted him onto the piece of wreckage. The dog's sharp nails scratched my chest and arms badly as he scrambled to get up onto the raft. Saltwater stung my open wounds. His sharp little claws shredded my white linen shirt.

"Ouch, dog! Those giant propellers didn't chop me to pieces, but you seem determined to finish the job," I whined as I climbed aboard the raft and lay down next to him.

The scratches were the least of my worries; we were drifting helplessly on the dark, open sea, being propelled north by the 4-knot Gulf Stream current. I removed what was left of my shirt and dabbed the deep scratches on my chest with pieces of the cloth. My entire body began shivering; the biting cold of the stiff breeze was painful. The feeling was like being poked all over with red-hot needles.

By lying on my side in the fetal position, I was able to cradle Melon Dog so that we shared each other's body's heat. The spooning position helped to keep us both warm for a while, but it was no use. My body began to go numb, and I was starting to fall into a sleep from which I knew there would be no awakening.

"Dog, I'm freezing to death. I've got to go back into the water."

I slid off the raft and into the ocean. The 74-degree Gulf Stream water felt like a warm bath compared to the 45-degree air temperature. While holding onto a transom cleat, I submerged all but my head and one arm into the warm water. The dog seemed comfortable enough, protected by his thick fur coat. He was lying on his belly with his head resting on his paws, his snout only inches from my face as he stared at me with sad and worried eyes.

"Don't worry—we always find a way out of every mess that I get us into." I tried to comfort the dog.

My attempt to be optimistic belied my thoughts: *I wonder if our luck has finally run out this time, little dog.*

I put my face below the surface and opened my eyes. The salt water stung at first, but below me I saw thousands of glowing lights that resembled underwater stars. I gazed in amazement at the underwater universe.

*Those lights must be coming from squid. They rise up from the depths at night—come up from over a thousand feet deep. They look beautiful!*

My fascination with the underwater display was cut short when I realized that the squid brought more than a light show—they brought danger.

*This is not good! The water below me is full of squid...and squid are bait!*

The black ocean was alive and busy with life just a few feet below me. What other creatures lurked throughout the water table all the way down to the bottom, 1,100 feet below?

I stuck my head under for another look. Sure enough, illuminated by the bioluminescent glow of the squid, dark, torpedo-shaped forms moved swiftly among the flashing lights.

*Those might be sharks! Where there is bait, large predators are sure to be found nearby!*

By getting out of the water I would be safe from sharks, but then I would surely freeze to death, so I continued to cling to the side of the raft, hoping for the best.

## TUESDAY, DECEMBER 25TH, 1973

To my great relief, the sun rose, providing much-welcomed sunlight. I took a peek below to check for sharks. The glowing lights of the squid were gone, and I saw no other creatures below me. *All clear—yahoo!*

After climbing up onto the raft I looked toward the west, but we were too far from the coastline to see land. I wondered what our position was after drifting all night. We had been due east of the middle Florida Keys, somewhere off the coast of Islamorada, when the freighter struck our boat. She must have been sunk just after midnight, which meant that we had drifted north for over six hours. My calculation was that we were now probably just due east of the upper Florida Keys.

"We're most likely near Key Largo. Lots of fishermen live there," I said to Melon Dog, who looked up forlornly before returning his stare to the ocean.

My hope was that some fishermen would find us, but the fact that it was Christmas morning dampened my hopes.

*There will probably be fewer fishermen than normal out on Christmas morning.* I kept that thought to myself.

The sun rose, and its warm rays were a welcome relief from the cold night. Lying on my back, I spread my arms and legs out like a snow angel and soaked up the warmth of the sunshine.

"Are you thirsty? Me too," I said to the dog.

*We won't last long without water.*

That Christmas Day, three freighters passed to the east, but I could not draw the attention of the crew. Far to the west, I saw a couple of small recreational fishing boats in the distance. Precariously, I stood up on the wobbly raft and waved my arms.

"Hey, over here!" I screamed.

The boats were near shore and too far away. They didn't spot us. We were desperate for water, but nothing could be done. Christmas Day, 1973 was the longest day of my life. Christmas night arrived as the sun began to set in the western sky.

Once again the night air was chilling, so I slipped back into my warm ocean bath. Even the moderate 74-degree water would eventually lower my core body temperature below 98.6 degrees, but thirst would surely kill me before hypothermia did. My loose-fitting linen pants were causing a drag in the current and making it harder for me to hold on to the raft, so I took them off and put them over the dog like a wet blanket. Now the only clothing I wore was my tighty-whitey underpants and my black rubber croc-chewed dive fins, which I used as shoes.

Christmas night was not completely dark; there was a sliver of moon that hung like a sickle in the eastern sky. It provided a little bit of light, and I could see the look of despair in Melon Dog's eyes as he whimpered sadly, suffering from pangs of thirst.

"I'm thirsty too. Wish I could do something for you, dog."

Soon I saw bright city lights in the distance to the northwest.

"Hey, dog, that's Miami. We've almost drifted home, but I have no way of getting you to shore." The dog gazed longingly toward the inviting, warm lights of Miami.

After midnight I fell off to sleep in the water. To keep me from sinking as I dozed, I had lashed my right arm to the cleat on the raft with cloth strips from my torn linen shirt. Suddenly something woke me. Something had bumped my thigh, bummed it hard! The moon was high overhead now, and its soft light glistened on the surface of the ocean. Coming toward me, a large dorsal fin cut through the glistening sheen in a frenzied zigzagging pattern.

"That's a shark! Make room! I'm coming back onboard!" I called to the dog as adrenalin surged into my veins, causing gooseflesh on my arms and the hackles on the back of my neck to rise.

With not enough strength left in my arms to pull my body up onto the raft, I was forced to kick my legs violently on the surface of the water to help lift me aboard. The splashing caused the sea water to glow below me as the disturbance caused millions of plankton to phosphoresce. The commotion also excited the shark, and it circled back, swimming fast, this time on a beeline toward me. Ten yards away, the dorsal fin disappeared below the surface as the shark sounded. The killing machine was diving below the surface; preparing to attack me from beneath.

Before hauling myself onto the raft, I took a final glance down and could see the shark rising up from the depths below me, mouth agape. The horrific look of his black, dead eyes provided me with a surge of strength, enough to clear the surface. I pulled my legs up onto the raft as the shark's head exploded out of the water! His hideous, dissociated eyes disappeared, rolling back into his head, covered by a protective film as he snapped his jaws shut.

*Pop!* The loud, hollow sound was frighteningly powerful.

The shark's razor-sharp teeth had barely missed my left foot, and now the hungry predator sounded again, passing below the raft. The beast swam with an excited, jerky motion and came back around, as Melon Dog and I lay side-by-side, wet, shivering, and terrified. We watched the determined shark make ever-tightening circles around our unstable life raft.

*Blood drops from my cuts probably attracted that shark.*

I had just finished thinking that thought when two more fins appeared at the surface. In the dim light I could not identify the species of these sharks, but that didn't matter; they were big, and they were hungry.

Now a trio of oceanic predators began investigating us by bumping into the raft. One shark thrashed its tail, creating a small wave that washed my pants from the unsteady raft and into the sea. The white pants drifted at the surface, reflecting the soft moonlight for a few moments until, with a splash and a swirl of water, a shark grabbed them and dove below the surface. The brave little collie growled and attempted to bark at the sharks, but the only sound he could muster was a weak, pathetic squeak. We were both suffering badly, severely dehydrated. For a split second I considered jumping into the ocean to end my agony.

*A slow and painful death is imminent…but three hungry sharks will quickly put me out of my misery.*

Luckily I regained rational thought, and after about ten minutes, the sharks finally gave up and went off to hunt elsewhere.

The bright lights of Miami were now due west of us, and the skyline of the city illuminated the western horizon. Melon Dog did not look well, he was dying of thirst, and so was I.

"There are hundreds of fishing boats in Miami. One might find us in the morning. We might get lucky, dog. Don't give up on me… not yet," I said, but this time Melon Dog did not even look up to the sound of my voice.

Water, water, everywhere, but not a drop to drink

## *Chapter 2*

# TOO YOUNG TO DIE

To the west, the crescent-shaped sliver of moon drifted slowly down from the black sky and disappeared below the horizon. Melon Dog and I watched as the bright meniscus departed, taking with it the last scintilla of light. Now we drifted on the sea surrounded by infinite darkness. Thirsty, cold, and alone, we were lost in a world where there was no boundary separating the black sky from the black ocean. We seemed to be adrift in outer space. As I lay on my back, gazing toward the heavens, a sprinkling of stars suddenly peeked out from behind the heavy cloud cover. I searched the heavens for a recognizable constellation.

"We are alone. Even my good friend Orion isn't keeping us company tonight," I said to the dog.

Dawn was approaching, and the stars began to fade as the eastern sky lightened.

"We made it through another night, dog." My encouragement to the dog belied my thoughts. Without fresh water, we won't last another day.

The night sky and the vast ocean began their familiar chameleonic color changes. On the eastern horizon, the infinite coal-black void of outer space lightened to dark shades of purple and now became distinguishable from the black seawater. Twice during the long, cold night, I had stopped Melon Dog from drinking saltwater. Now he was at it again, bending down at the edge of the raft, trying to quench his thirst from the ocean.

"Saltwater will make you sick, dog…it'll kill you!" I grabbed him by the collar and pulled him back to the middle of the raft, where he lay forlornly, licking the wet, salty surface of the broken transom.

*It's the day after Christmas. Surely there will be some fishermen out to sea today…out on the ocean trying out their new fishing gear.*

My attempt to remain optimistic was failing by the minute. The reality of our dire situation and imminent death overcame me and angered me.

*Great Wanaka, why did you call me into your service? Why did you ask me to travel to Miami to save the boy named Luca? Why—why, when you knew my fate was to suffer and then die of thirst out here on the ocean? We will not last another day without water!*

I was becoming delirious.

"We are too young to die!" I screamed at the ever-lightening sky above.

My loud, angry outburst roused Melon Dog. He attempted to lift his head but was too weak, and his head dropped back down with a thud.

I had barely finished my rant when a flash of light caught my attention. The rising sun had reflected off the glass windshield of a distant boat.

A fishing boat was trolling the edge of the Gulf Stream and moving in our direction, approaching us from the north.

Fishermen who venture offshore are always on the lookout for floating objects. Flotsam, as well as patches of Sargasso weed, attract the much sought-after dolphin fish or mahi-mahi. Luckily for us, such was the case on this beautiful winter morning. The fishing boat slowed and then suddenly turned southeast and began speeding in our direction.

"The fishermen have spotted us!" I began waving my arms as the boat continued toward us.

The boat looked blurry in the distance. It seemed to glow and was surrounded by a bright aura. The intense sunshine reflecting off the glass window blinded me as if a mirror had reflected the light, and I had to look away.

*Please don't be another mirage. Please be real.* I returned my eyes toward the boat, and then suddenly the boat stopped.

"Why are you stopping?" I called out.

The boat turned and began slowly moving to the west, apparently no longer interested in the distant floating object that was us.

"Where are you going?" The boat was too far away to see what the fishermen were doing.

"Why have they stopped?" My question was answered when behind the stern of the boat a billfish began leaping from the water and violently shaking its head. Then the big fish began to run to the north and went "greyhounding" across the surface of the ocean. Now it was apparent what had happened. When the boat accelerated toward us, a blue marlin had been enticed into striking one of the high-speed trolling lures.

"Damn! They've hooked a marlin! It must be huge!" Because I could identify the billfish from such a distance, I knew it was a big one.

We watched helplessly as the boat pursued the leaping northbound marlin. The fishing boat disappeared into the distance as the fisherman followed and fought the mighty blue marlin.

"How much more bad luck do you have in store for us!" I yelled at the heavens. "Will you ever give us a break?"

Melon Dog appeared to be sleeping, but he was not. He was lapsing into unconsciousness. I lay down beside him, looking at the dark clouds above, and prepared myself for death. I began to drift off into my final, eternal sleep. *This is the end, dog. There must be something we can be grateful for.*

I began to recall my wonderful life, a life filled with enjoyable experiences. Beginning with my childhood, memorable events crossed my mind, playing out before me like an old black-and-white super-8 home movie. I was slipping into a state of semi consciousness when the ending to the movie flickered behind my closed eyelids. The sudden ending roused me for a moment, and I opened my eyes. *I'm not dead.*

"Thank you for a wonderful life," I said and rolled from my side onto my back, looking up at the dark clouds roiling above. "And thank you for this cloud cover blocking the relentless sun," I murmured.

We could not have borne another minute of the scorching hot sun.

I patted the dog's head. "Goodbye, dog." Melon Dog appeared to be sleeping and did not respond to my mumbling. The clouds above began to look like human faces gazing down on me. Men with black beards and women with long, swirling dark hair hovered above. They appeared to be having a discussion as their faces changed shape and became distorted. *Those are just clouds, dude; you're hallucinating now.* The faces turned angry and grew dark before losing their human appearance altogether. Then an angel appeared in the form of a mermaid. She hovered over us just below the dark roiling clouds offering a colorful bouquet of flowers.

By Judith Sipes 1

With neither a flash of lightning nor a crack of thunder, the heavens opened up. Ice-cold raindrops the size of marbles began falling from the dense, black clouds above.

"Thank you!" I called out and opened my mouth as wide as my cracked lips would allow. Melon Dog lifted his head and began to lick the fresh water running across the surface of the raft. I could not catch enough water in my mouth to quench my thirst.

"Yahoo!" After screaming with delight, I took off my rubber shoes and began collecting the rainwater in them and drinking in the heavenly liquid, shoe full after shoe full.

"Here, dog." I placed a shoe containing half an inch of rainwater in front of Melon Dog, and he lapped it up in short order; I gave him another. We both began to feel revitalized. The hard, heavy rain became gentler, but it lasted for hours, providing us with plenty of water and shielding us from the hot sun. Without a way to collect and save the water, I realized that the rainfall was only a temporary reprieve from our death sentence. We still needed to get to land, but now my mind was much clearer and my body rejuvenated.

The rain and ominous dark clouds drifting above the Gulf Stream were a mixed blessing. They brought us lifesaving rainwater, but they also kept the recreational fishing boats close to shore. The small craft that I was counting on to find us were not venturing out into the Gulf Stream due to the heavy rain. Many small boats remained near shore to the west, and to the east two large ships and then an oceangoing tugboat pulling a long barge passed by. Night began to fall. With our thirst quenched, pangs of hunger now overcame us.

The heavy cloud cover remained throughout the night, providing an insulating blanket that kept the air temperature from falling as severely as it had during our previous nights at sea. After midnight, sharks returned to circle our raft. Thankfully the cool air was bearable, and I was not forced by the cold to go into the warm water.

With my arms wrapped tightly around Melon Dog, we both fell into an uneasy sleep. That night a horrible nightmare haunted me. In my dream sharks were eating me alive! The hungry sharks ripped off both of my legs and my right arm, leaving just my head and torso with only my left arm attached. My effort to swim to shore was futile because swimming with only one arm caused me to spin around in circles, unable to make any forward progress. To make matters worse, I was not bleeding to death and so could neither die with dignity nor save myself. I was left all alone, paddling in circles for all eternity, as my screams of horror and rage went unheard and unanswered.

"Why do you leave me alive to suffer? Why did you leave me with only one useless arm?" With my only hand raised toward the sky, in my dream I pleaded for mercy.

The voice that answered me was not real. It was just part of my nightmare.

"You have to play with the hand you're dealt!"

Mercifully I woke up intact when Melon Dog licked my face.

*Chapter 3*

# ESCAPE FROM CUBA

*The following passages were taken from the memoir of Carlos "El Muerte" Romero in 1974.*

## APRIL 1963, *FORTALEZA DE LA CABAÑA* PRISON, HAVANA, CUBA

My torture session ended, and I found myself back in my prison cell, lying on the floor in a pool of my own blood. Searing pain enveloped the sides of my head as I came out of my hypnotic trance. My temples felt like they were on fire; my flesh was burning. I reached up to cover my ears, and blood pooled in my cupped hands. Confused, I looked around my prison cell and recalled the Russian torturer, Nikko, pointing his stiletto at my eyes just before I went into the trance.

"I can see!" Ecstatic, I cried out in relief that Nikko had not added my eyeballs to his grotesque collection. I closed my eyes and rubbed them with bloody hands. *Yes! My eyes are intact.*

A guard outside of my cell door heard me talking to myself and alerted his comrades, "Garcia, come here! *El Muerte* is awake! *El Muerte* is alive!"

I rose to my feet and lowered my hands from my eyes; now the blood covering my eyelids dripped down onto my cheeks and ran down my face. The sight of me joyfully laughing as I stumbled around my cell with blood dripping out of my eyes and pouring out from the sides of my head must have been terrifying to the guards.

"*Ayyyy, coño!* The zombie is crazy! *El Muerte* has used his devil magic to survive once again! He has returned to us from the dead!" The sound of heavy boots slamming onto the concrete floor filled my cell as other guards came running to my door to get a look at me. They took turns peering through the small window in my door.

"Mother of God, he bleeds from his eyes and his ears, and it only makes him laugh! *El Muerte* is *El Loco!*" Horrified by the sight of me, a guard turned away from my window in disgust, but a friendly face replaced his mask of horror; it was Garcia.

"Garcia, I still have my eyes!" Again I laughed with joy.

Garcia smiled, "*Sí,* you are alive, *El Muerte!*"

"Why did the Russian spare my eyes, Garcia?" I asked.

"Nikko said that your eyes were no good to him. Your eyes showed no fear. He said that the eyes of a zombie are dead eyes. Your dead eyes would spoil his collection of eyeballs—eyes that are full of fear—so he cut off your ears instead."

"What? My ears?" For the first time I realized where the blood was coming from, and again I cupped my hands over my ears. My ears were not just bleeding; they were gone. Only bony holes remained. I was horrified.

"Nicky the Knife said your ears would be a fine gift for a lady friend. His Russian girlfriend collects human ears."

"That bastard! I will kill that Russian bastard!" My anger was tempered by the fact that I still had my eyes. *It could have been much worse, amigo!*

"Here, *El Muerte,* take these." Garcia passed two dirty washcloths through the window. Garcia was one of the few prison guards who was not sadistic. He showed me respect for some reason, and at times, when no one else was around, he even displayed acts of kindness.

"Thanks, Garcia." I covered my scalped temples with the rags to stop the bleeding.

"*El Muerte*, try to be awake at two tonight," Garcia whispered through the hole.

"Why?"

"Something might happen at two o'clock. Just be ready."

Garcia left me wondering what might happen.

The pain began to ease a bit now that my wounds were not exposed to the open air. I lay down on my cot, pressing the cloths to my head and staring at the ceiling. *They have mutilated my body. That means I will never leave this prison alive!* It was well known among the prisoners that if the Communists maimed you, like cutting off some fingers, you would never be permitted to be seen by the outside world. The dastardly deeds of the torturers could not be put on display for the free world to see. My sentence was no longer thirty years. Now it was life!

Having no clock and no alarm, I seldom knew the exact time of day. But on this night a loud explosion woke me from my sleep. Another explosion followed, and screaming voices filled the prison hallways as I stood at the door looking out from the small window. Guards were running past my cell through thick, gray smoke that was pouring down the hallway toward my cell. I pressed my face into the window opening, attempting to get a better look at what was happening outside. Suddenly the door was being opened, pushing me backward. It was Garcia.

"Garcia! What's happening?" Garcia stood at my open door with a ring of keys in his hand. The smoke now filled the entire cellblock, and visibility was poor.

"Go to the north end!" Garcia ordered as he ran to the next cell and unlocked the door. Garcia was releasing the political prisoners.

"What's happening out there, Garcia?" I didn't want to run blindly into a mass execution in the prison courtyard.

"I'm a member of the underground. I'm with the counter-revolution. Members of Brigade 2506 have come from Miami to rescue dissidents and take you to Florida! Go to them, *El Muerte!* Go *pronto!* The boats will not wait!" Garcia disappeared into the smoke, and I ran down the hallway with dozens of other desperate men.

We crossed over a pile of rubble and then climbed through a large hole that had been blown through the prison wall. In the open courtyard, a running gun battle was in full force. The man running next to me dropped to the ground, shot dead. Over twenty of us made it out of the prison that night and to the seawall on the north side of the fortress. With bullets flying overhead, we dove off the stone seawall and into the water of Havana Harbor. Bullets followed us; the hot lead sizzled into the sea all around me, and the saltwater burned my open wounds. The pain almost made me pass out, but I kept on swimming. Men were waiting in speedboats; some were returning fire toward land, as others were busy plucking dissidents from the harbor.

I was pulled aboard a cigarette-style racing boat. Two similar boats were moving slowly nearby, also rescuing swimmers.

"Welcome aboard, brother!" a middle-aged Cuban yelled to me in Spanish, but I could barely hear him. The holes in my head were filled with saltwater.

Soon all three boats were racing away out to sea. The roar of the powerful engines must have been deafening, but to me they sounded muffled and distant. I began to wonder if I was going deaf.

Suddenly three men with AK47s ran to the starboard gunwale and opened fire, shooting blindly into the darkness. What are they shooting at? I wondered. Then the black night exploded as a blindingly bright searchlight flashed on and grew larger as it raced toward our boat. On radar, our captain had spotted a Cuban gunboat stealthily stalking us under cover of the darkness.

"We can outrun the gunboat!" our captain called out and dropped back into the wake of a faster boat up ahead. Now all three speedboats that had previously been running three abreast formed a single line, and men stood at the starboard gunwale of each boat, unloading on the Cuban vessel. The barrage of machine gun fire from the fully automatic weapons extinguished the searchlight and discouraged the gunboat from pursuing us farther.

"He's turning back!" The captain yelled above the roar of engines.

In Miami, I was taken to the hospital and treated for several days. In addition to my open head wounds, I was suffering from severe malnourishment. After convalescing for three months at home, I resumed working with the resistance in Miami to undermine the Communist regime in Cuba. We were determined to rescue as many fellow political prisoners from Rafael Cato's dungeons and labor camps as possible and to overthrow the dictator.

Soon, with the covert help of the CIA, we were making monthly runs into Cuba to raid the ports and wreak havoc before returning to Miami. Sometimes we were able to rescue political prisoners, and each time I went to Cuba, my secret wish was to find and kill Nikko, the Russian torturer they called Nicky the Knife.

~

Thirteen years later, off the east coast of Florida:

## WEDNESDAY, DECEMBER 27ᵀᴴ, 1973, 5:50 AM

On a dark winter night, Katarina and I were returning from Cuba with three political prisoners we had rescued from a Communist labor camp in western Cuba. Seven miles off the east coast of Miami, we passed an object adrift on the ocean.

"Stop, Carlos! Turn around! There is a man on a raft." My niece, Katarina pounded her fist into my shoulder as I drove the boat at full throttle toward Miami.

"No, Katarina, we must get back before light! We cannot be spotted by anyone—especially the Coast Guard!" Even though we had the support of the C.I.A. and the U.S. government, our operation was clandestine. If we were caught, our American allies would deny helping or even knowing about us.

" I said stop! A man on a raft was waving to us!" Katarina grabbed the dual throttles and pulled them straight back. The sudden deceleration of the boat threw us both against the instrument console.

"*¿Estás loca, mujer?* Are you trying to kill us?"

"Get out of my way!" Katarina pushed me to the side and took the controls. Whenever she got like this, I knew there was no stopping her. She turned the boat and went back to search for the raft.

"I think there was a dog out there, too," she said.

"A dog? Woman, you are *loca*!" But she was right! When we found the raft, a young *gringo* and his dog were lying on it. The man was either dead or unconscious, and the dog was in bad shape, too. We took them aboard our boat. "I thought you said he was waving to you, Katarina. He's dead!"

"Yes he was waving…and standing up. I saw him standing."

"Well, now he looks dead. What are we going to do with them? We can't take them to the safe house."

"We will put them on the beach so someone will find them, and then we will get our people home before daybreak," she said.

"Okay, but we must hurry, Katarina. It's almost light!"

"Hey, the guy just moved!"

You'd be surprised at what you can live through.

*Chapter 4*

# DÉJÀ VU ALL OVER AGAIN

## WEDNESDAY, DECEMBER 27ᵀᴴ, 1973, 5:50 AM

**M**ercifully, my vivid nightmare of being dismembered by sharks was ended by a lick from Melon Dog's wet tongue and a distant rumbling sound. After waking, I reached down and felt for my legs. *Thank God I'm intact. That dream of being eaten alive by sharks was horrifying!*

It was just before dawn but still very dark. The rumbling sound was growing louder and seemed to be coming toward us from the east.

"Listen! That's a boat!" I said as I sat upright. The boat was approaching at high speed.

"That's a racing boat. A high speed rum-runner," I said as the distinctive sound of a cigarette boat roared out from somewhere in the darkness.

The speedboat was approaching fast, making a beeline for Miami. Now the sound of water could be heard slamming against its hull. I visualized a long, narrow boat cutting through and jumping over the three-foot waves.

"She's really hauling ass!"

With great effort, I rose to one knee on the unstable raft and looked into the predawn darkness. By the sound, I could tell the boat was very close now and about to pass us to the north. The distinctive, deep-pitched roar of the engines told me that she was indeed a large, oceangoing racing boat

The powerful engines became deafening as the boat pounded through the choppy ocean and suddenly flashed into view. The boat was illuminated just enough for me to make her out in the darkness. She had a black hull and was over 30 feet long. The cigarette boat surged and bucked across the ocean's surface, running at full throttle and sending up a rooster-tail spray of water behind her. For some reason, the captain had not turned on his running lights, and by the time the boat was visible to me she was no more than 20 yards away.

"She's running dark. Hold on, dog!"

Balancing myself on one knee, I placed my palm flat down on the raft. Beneath my hand I saw the letter W of the name *Watermelon* painted on the shattered transom.

"This is it. This is goodbye, little boat. Our last chance—either we're rescued now, or we will die before dawn. Hold me up one last time."

Painfully I rose to my feet and began waving my arms and yelling as the cigarette boat flashed past in the darkness.

"Over here! Over here…. Damn, she blew right past us, dog! She's heading for Miami. I hope she saw…"

Before I finished my sentence, the wake of the speeding boat struck our raft. My feet flew out in front of me, and I felt myself falling backward. A hollow thud echoed through my head, and then everything went black.

After a few moments, I found myself weightlessly floating among fluffy white clouds. My thirst, hunger, and pain were gone.

"Hey, I know this place. I've been here before. I love it here! This is the afterlife. It's déjà vu all over again!"

Without a care or trouble, I enjoyed a lovely walk through the mist. Billowing white clouds surrounded me, constantly changing shape. Sometimes faces formed in front of me and gazed curiously as I floated past.

"Am I dead?" I asked the hoary face of an old, bearded man.

The face did not answer but became distorted and lost its shape and vanished in the mist. A bank of clouds changed into a beautiful landscape of mountains and valleys, inviting me to float through scenic passages. Cool mountain air refreshed me and was exhilarating as I came off the mountainside. Below, a tropical island with palm trees and a white sandy beach beckoned me.

Suddenly a large, fluffy cloud took the form of a white horse. The horse stood directly in front of me, blocking my path, and then the sound of steel drums playing island music came from every direction.

"Hello, horse. Am I dead?" I asked.

"Hello, Eddie. I'm your gift. I'm here to keep you company."

The movement of the horse's mouth was greatly exaggerated when it talked, like an animation. It wore a black leather bridle. The horse's voice was gentle and surprised me.

"Huh, how about that—a talking horse! You look like you came directly from TV...from a television show, like the famous Mr. Ed," I said.

"No, I'm not from your world, Eddie. I'm from the world of spirits...animal spirits. My name is Hanna."

Now I realized that the horse was female, a mare. She was tall— 16 hands, maybe—and she was beautifully groomed. Her body and head were pure white. A long, flowing, golden mane hung from her crest and covered her neck down to the withers. Her perfectly arched back dipped slightly before rising to merge with her well-rounded crop. Her legs were long and powerful. A thick, flaxen-colored tail arched up majestically behind her rump.

"You are beautiful. Your conformation is perfect," I said.

"Would you like to ride me bareback?"

"Sure. Got nothing else to do."

I swung a leg up and over the gentle arch of her back and mounted Hanna. Beneath me, she was very responsive to my cues, and I rode her hard right there on the beach, just at the water's edge. She galloped and bucked beneath me, sending up a spray that got us both wet and salty. My exhilarating ride was finished when Hanna reared up and whinnied. I dismounted her and flopped on the beach, fully spent.

"Wow! That was something!" I said.

Hanna was heavily lathered. She said, "You are an excellent rider, Eddie."

"And you are an excellent mount. Do you want me to brush you down, Hanna?"

"No, I like being ridden hard and put away wet. My veterinarian says that shows that I have low self-esteem."

"Low self-esteem? Why? Anyone would be proud to have you as their horse Hanna!"

With my back pressed into the warm beach sand, I spread my arms and legs wide and looked up at the fluffy, white clouds drifting above us in the clear, blue sky.

"I've been to this heavenly place before, Hanna. I never want to leave this place again," I said.

"Oh, but you must leave, Eddie. Your ancestors are calling out to you from the heavens. Do you hear them? They are calling you into service. You must return to Earth...return with Melon Dog. Together you and the dog must find Luca and save the boy from a terrible fate."

"The ancient spirits give me too much credit, Hanna—and too much responsibility. Everything I touch turns to ruin. I will stay here instead. I will stay and take care of you."

"I was sent to look after you, Eddie, but only temporarily. You are near death now, and my job is to keep you alive until you are rescued. My task was to preoccupy your mind and to keep your spirit alive inside your body...to help you survive your ordeal and to tolerate your pain and suffering. Now my job is done."

"I'm not leaving. I'm staying here." Like a spoiled child, I rolled onto my stomach and clutched the powdery white sand in my hands, hoping that I could anchor myself to the beautiful beach.

"Before you are allowed to rest among your ancestors in this after-life, you must first return to Earth and fulfill your service to the ancient spirits."

The gentle music of the steel drums ceased, and Hanna reared up, pawing at the sky, and let out a loud whinny that echoed across the island. "I'm being called home, Eddie. Take care of yourself. Go save the boy and his dog."

"Wait, Hanna—don't leave me."

My plea was ignored, and Hanna rose off the ground and began galloping toward the heavens. The beautiful horse grew small as she ascended and raced through the blue sky above me. She slowed to a canter and then stopped altogether; standing atop a large cumulus cloud, she looked down upon me. Her tail and mane changed from white to black as she began to meld into the darkening clouds.

By Judith Sipes 2

"Wheeeee!" She reared up on her hind legs and pawed the air one last time.

The bridle and bit were gone from Hanna's mouth, and her supple lips quivered as she called down to me from the heavens.

The warm, soft, powdery sand beneath my back turned rock hard, cold and wet.

"Where am I? Oh no, please! Not back on the raft! Hanna, take me with you, damn it!" Anger overcame me. Excruciating pain returned, filling my head. Above me the sky turned black again. I reached over and felt the soft fur of Melon Dog lying beside me as pain shot through my body like jolts of electricity.

"Wheeeee!" Hanna's white body began to swirl and converge with the large cumulus cloud upon which she stood. The clouds merged together, forming a huge cumulonimbus that began to grow dark and menacing. The last part of Hanna that I could still recognize was her mouth, from which came a bright flash and a resounding crack of lightning.

"Hanna, come back for me."

Her lips quivered as the deep rumble of thunder emerged from her open mouth, a mouth that grew larger until it became a black hole in the swirling dark cloud. My agony was too great, and I looked away from the dark hole before slipping back into unconsciousness.

Never look a gift horse in the mouth.

*Chapter 5*

# JACKSON MEMORIAL HOSPITAL

In the darkness, two shadowy figures moved about above me, their bodies' silhouettes against the early morning sky. The sound of gentle surf lapping against the fiberglass hull of a boat aroused me from unconsciousness. *Am I on a boat?* Then I heard voices.

"Now what, Katarina? We should not have stopped for him!"

"Shut up and help me get him to the beach. We must hurry." The pair of silhouettes bickered angrily, unaware that I had regained consciousness. One voice was that of a woman.

"It's almost light, Katarina! We need to get to the safe house before light!"

"Shut up, *El Muerte*! Take the poor guy ashore! I'll bring his dog."

Like a sack of potatoes, I was slung over the powerful shoulders of a man and carried off the boat and onto a sandy beach. The man dumped me down on my back in the soft sand.

"Ouch—my head. Where am I?" The drop jarred me. My head ached. I was disoriented and too weak to move.

"He's awake, Kat! He just spoke!"

"Be gentle, Carlos! Cover him with this." Now I could see the bow of a boat in front of and above me. The boat had nearly been beached and stood just offshore in very shallow water. Standing on the bow was the dark silhouette of a shapely young woman. She threw a beach towel toward the man, and then she went out of sight. The man covered me with the towel and then ran into the gentle surf until the water was up to his waist and began pushing the bow of the boat away from land.

"Someone's walking on the beach, Carlos! Get into the boat now!" said the woman.

"Okay, go! *¡Vámonos, Kat!*" he called out.

The roar of the boat's powerful engines was deafening as it backed off the beach and turned around before speeding away into the dim, pre-dawn light. The loud roar hurt my head, and I closed my eyes in pain until I felt a warm tongue lick my face. With my eyes open again, I saw Melon Dog standing over me with a look of concern in his eyes.

"Hello, dog. Where are we? Have we been rescued?" With my head throbbing, I tried to sit upright, but everything began spinning, and I must have passed out.

The next time I woke, I felt the softness of a white cotton pillowcase beneath my head, and I turned my head to breathe in the fresh scent of the clean, bleached sheets that covered my body. A soft mattress beneath my body had replaced the hard, cold, wet wreckage of my *Watermelon* boat, and it felt like a bed of fluffy white cirrus clouds.

*I've died and gone to heaven again!*

Someone covered me with a warm blanket.

I feel like a newborn baby. Never has a blanket felt so soft...so good. I touched a corner of the blanket to my cheek.

"Hey, he's coming to, Jimbo. This guy's in bad shape. He needs an IV. Start a D-5 Ringers drip," said a medic. The man's bearded face was visible in the glow of the early morning light. Daybreak had come, and I was alive! The medic opened the doors to an ambulance.

"I'm still alive!" I whispered wonderingly.

"Yeah, kid. We're taking you to Jackson Memorial. We should be there in less than ten minutes."

"What a co-winky-dink! I once worked there for a short time." I was light headed and giddy now. "Did you give me a sedative? I feel like I'm floating on a cloud."

"Hell, no. Are you kidding me, kid? You probably have enough drugs in you to put down an elephant."

Light-headed and dizzy, my mind was still in a dreamy state, and suddenly I began laughing for no good reason. "Isn't life wonderful? Isn't it wonderful to be alive?" I said rhetorically and pointed up at the clear, azure morning sky above.

"Sure, kid—life's just wonderful, a real picnic. You're the tenth overdose that we've picked up since midnight," said a medic. My inappropriate laughter seemed to annoy the medics, who apparently thought I was high on drugs.

"Whew-whee! This kid's sure high on something, Jimbo."

"What did you take, kid?" asked the clean-shaven guy.

"Nothing. No food or water for days, in fact. Hey, just look at that sky up there; can you believe it? It's so beautiful! I swear I can see straight into heaven."

You've never really lived until you've almost died.

The paramedics wheeled me into the Emergency Room of Jackson Memorial Hospital, where a tall, dark-haired nurse met us.

"Eight hundred and three...eight hundred and four..." I stared up at the glass bottle and watched the next drop begin to form inside the drip chamber.

"What is he saying?" The nurse asked the paramedics.

"He's counting his IV drops. The kid's delirious. Might be high on drugs. He was found passed out...sleeping on the beach under a beach towel."

The nurse began examining me.

"He has a large bump on the back of his head," she said.

The IV fluid was starting to rehydrate my body and bring me down from my light-headed bliss. The return to reality brought discomfort and a severe headache. Then the agonizing pain of my sunburn made my body feel like it was on fire.

The dripping fluid no longer mesmerized me, and I began to look around the room, examining my surroundings. "I know this place—Jackson Memorial Emergency room. Hey, where is Melon Dog?" I asked a medic.

"We had to leave the dog at the beach. No animals allowed in the ambulance. Company policy."

"What? We gotta go get him!"

"Don't worry. A nice elderly woman said she would watch him for you," the bearded paramedic told me as his partner stood nearby giving the nurse a report. Then a doctor came to my bedside.

"So kid, they found you passed out on the beach...sleeping it off, eh? What did you take, what are you high on?" asked the doctor.

"Nothing, Doc. I was floating on a raft...shipwrecked for days. Some boaters put me ashore. I think I hit my head."

After a brief examination by the emergency room doctor, I was informed that due to dehydration, hypothermia, and a possible concussion, they needed to do a CAT scan and then admit me to the hospital for observation.

"No, I can't stay! I have to find my dog."

"If you have a subdural and leave the hospital, you might be dead before lunchtime, son," said the doctor.

"But I have no money and no insurance," I told the doc.

"Worry about that after you recover, kid. With your electrolyte imbalance and head trauma, you might slip into a coma and die."

The doctor's dire prognosis and my hunger caused me to reconsider. From somewhere behind me, the hum of a microwave oven and the smell of cooking food drifted out from the staff lounge.

"Mmm, it smells good in here. Doc, you mentioned something about lunchtime. I guess I'll stay if you insist." My hunger convinced me to acquiesce to the doctor's medical advice.

The Emergency Room doctor smiled. "Smart choice, son. Good luck," he said and then walked away as the nurse took over my care.

"Mr. Ocean, if the CT scan is clear, you will be allowed to eat something. You will get lunch in your room after the test." She stood beside me reading my chart, and then she inserted the doctor's examination report into an aluminum binder.

"Orderly, take Mr. Ocean to X-ray, please." She shoved the chart under the mattress of my gurney and walked away. A guy dressed in white clothing and white shoes wheeled me down the hallway and into an elevator.

After my scan, the orderly took me to the fifth floor and into my room. I shimmied over from the stretcher and onto my bed just as a young nurse came into the room. The other bed in my room was empty but looked as if it had been slept in. The orderly began stripping the bedding from the empty bed.

"Hi, nurse. Where's my roommate? Not dead, I hope?"

"No, he was discharged earlier this morning. Looks like you've got the place to yourself for now. Open up," she said as she held a thermometer in front of my mouth.

Here I am for the second time in my life lying in bed and being nursed back to health by a pretty young girl after nearly dying on the high seas.

"It's déjà vu all over again," I mumbled despite the thermometer beneath my tongue.

"Déjà vu? Oh, so have you been a patient here before?" asked the nurse as she removed the glass thermometer and took a reading.

"No, but I've been in the same predicament before. Getting rescued at sea, and then having a pretty girl take care of me."

She smiled and placed the thermometer into some clear liquid. "Well, you're a feisty one, Mr. Ocean. That's a good sign. I'll be back with your lunch in about fifteen minutes. Get some rest."

As the nurse left, I couldn't help but think of my long-lost love, Little Hooters. *Little Hooters…I wish you could be my nurse once again. Wish it were you taking care of me…like you did in the Whatchacallit Indian Village.* I closed my eyes and imagined Little Hooters' smiling face leaning down to kiss me.

*My sweet Little Hooters; my love… I miss you every day. I'll never forget you.* Dreams of Little Hooters came to me as I dozed off.

"Here is your lunch, Mr. Ocean. Sorry to wake you." The nurse aroused me from my light sleep and rolled a tray table over to my bed.

"Thanks, I'm hungry."

"People downstairs are asking me about you. The rumor is that you once worked here at Jackson…in radiology," she said as she pressed a button to elevate the back of my bed.

"That's right—about a year ago. Worked here for about a year, but the medical field isn't for me. I like to be outdoors, especially on the ocean. Left the hospital…bought a boat…got my captain's license," I said in between bites of food.

"Well, you sure have a fitting name for a sea captain, Eddie Ocean. They say that you lost your boat in some kind of an accident. Is that true?"

"Sadly yes, ma'am," I said just as a loud voice came over the intercom.

"Nurse Whacker…Nurse Whacker…report to the nursing station."

"That's me. I can't believe they're paging me again."

"Must be nice to be so popular," I teased.

"I'd like to hear more about what happened to you sometime, Eddie."

"Sure, anytime," I said and took a bite of the gummy mashed potatoes. "Mmm, this hospital food is better than I remember it."

"Really? You like that mush? You must be starving!"

"I am, and this grub sure beats a poke in the eye with a sharp stick," I said as I gleefully scooped up the last glob of gooey mashed potato.

Nurse Whacker glanced at me askance, as she nervously rearranged the food on my tray table and then asked, "I'm off at three-thirty. Are you up for a visitor later on, Eddie?"

"Sure. See you later, and thanks for this delicious food." I noticed that Nurse Whacker had stopped calling me "Mr. Ocean" and was now using my first name. *I think you like me, Nurse Whacker!*

The young nurse was clearly pleased. She giggled and walked to the doorway, but before leaving she turned, smiled, and said, "See you later, Captain Eddie Ocean."

Nurse Whacker came back to visit me at 3:41 pm.

"Hi, Eddie. Hope I'm not being too forward by asking to visit with you. Administration frowns on employees fraternizing with patients, but you're scheduled to be discharged tomorrow morning, and I might never see you again. I really want to hear your story before you leave."

She seemed nervous now as she stood beside my bed with her hands behind her back, looking down at her feet and rocking from side to side like a little girl.

"No bother. Your company is welcome, since my TV doesn't seem to be working." *Damn, that was kind of rude. She's only welcome because I have no TV to watch?* Nurse Whacker didn't seem offended by my thoughtless remark.

"Some of the people in radiology say you are a bit of a celebrity here in Miami. They say that you traveled with some Native Americans to South Beach and that an article was written about you and your Indian friends. They say the story was written up in the Miami *Post*." She appeared to relax and gain confidence as she took the chair beside my bed and gazed up into my eyes.

"Yes, that's all true."

Nurse Whacker had changed out of her nurse's uniform and into her street clothes. She wore a silk blouse with a print of a green iguana surrounded by colorful tropical foliage. Her bell-bottom denim jeans fit tightly around her hips and thin waist. She looked even prettier now. She had let her long, thick auburn hair down so that her beautiful mane was no longer pinned up beneath the goofy nurse's cap. Now she smelled like grapefruit and citrus, not antiseptic alcohol wipes. What I liked most about Nurse Whacker was her cheerful demeanor. Her warm smile and positive attitude lifted my spirits.

After swinging my legs over the side to sit upright on the edge of my bed, I said, "Yes that's all true—about the newspaper article. My Indian friends and I never knew that we made such a splash! In fact, earlier today some of my old friends and co-workers from the hospital paid me a visit, and they did treat me like some sort of a celebrity. It was awkward…but the truth is, I'm homeless and destitute. Everything that I own, except for those rubber Kroc shoes, is at the bottom of the Atlantic Ocean."

"Rubber Kroc shoes?" she repeated with a puzzled expression.

I pointed down at my rubber shoes sticking out from under the bed next to my bare feet.

"Those are my shoes. They're actually chewed-up dive fins. A giant croc chewed off the flippers and put all those holes in them. Those shoes are all that I have left. All my belongings went down with my *Watermelon* boat. I don't even have underpants…can you believe it, someone in the E.R. must have thrown away my dirty tightey-whiteys. Some celebrity, eh? I don't even have underpants, just this ugly hospital gown!" I extended my arms up from my sides to display my grotesque hospital gown, but she was still looking down at the shoes.

"Those black shoes with yellow polka dots were your dive fins? Hmm, shoes made out of rubber." She bent down to get a closer look at the Kroc shoes sticking out from under my bed.

"Yeah, the croc chewed them up on Crocodile Island."

"Tell me about Crocodile Island."

"I'll tell you that story later. It's a long story. The croc almost killed me!"

"Okay, later."

"Well, I was going to throw the chewed-up fins away, but some fashion designer on South Beach loved them. He started calling them 'Kroc shoes,' so I kept them. Now the shoes are the only possession that I have left in the world."

"I like these Kroc shoes too. They're pretty cool!" She picked one up.

"Well now they also have sentimental value to me. They are the only connection I have left to my old friends the Whatchacallit Indians...and to my girlfriend, Little Hooters."

"Oh, a girlfriend? Do you miss her?" Nurse Whacker seemed disappointed.

"Yeah, I do. But I lost her forever. And to make matters worse, the dog that I was responsible for is running loose in the city...I lost him too! The paramedics wouldn't allow the dog inside the ambulance! They said the dog was staying with an old woman, but that dog won't stay put with an old woman. He's a drifter. He's always looking for adventure, and he's a magnet for trouble."

I realized that I was feeling sorry for myself by whining. "Sorry to be such a bummer, Ms. Whacker. You must think I'm a real loser."

"No. You're a young man, Eddie Ocean. Soon you'll be healthy again. You'll be back on your feet in no time...sailing a new boat across the sea, sailing back to your girlfriend."

"No, I'm afraid I've lost my girlfriend forever. She is destined to marry my best friend, Jumping Jack."

The young woman tried to act sympathetic, but she couldn't fight back a smile. Her blue eyes twinkled as she said, "I'm sorry, Eddie."

Then she looked down to hide her inappropriate smile and faked a serious expression. "Eddie, you're very young and will have many more adventures. You'll meet many interesting people and lots of girls, I'm sure." The girl's optimism and cheerful disposition were very appealing.

We sat smiling at each other, and there was an awkward silence before I said; "The first thing I need to do is find Rubio, the old Cuban sea captain who sold me the *Watermelon* boat. The old man loved that little boat, and I promised to take good care of her. I'm afraid he'll be devastated when he learns what has happened to his boat. When he learns that the *Watermelon* is at the bottom of the Atlantic, I don't know what he'll do."

Nurse Whacker stood up and reached over to hold my hand to comfort me. "Start from the beginning, Eddie, before the accident. I want to know everything about you." She released my hand and moved the visitor's chair closer before sitting down again. "Tell me where you grew up," she said as she crossed her legs.

"What? You want my entire life story?"

"Sure. You have nowhere to go, do you? No TV and nothing to do, right?"

"Guess not. Well, I was born near Detroit, grew up in Kentucky, and moved with my family to Roslyn, Pennsylvania when I was around eleven or twelve. Later we moved to South Jersey. Went to school there, then started college in Philadelphia, but six months into college and on the very evening of my twenty-first birthday, my father suddenly passed away from a pulmonary embolism, which was caused by a nasty leg injury. I dropped out of school to go back to work repairing truck tires, big rig tires...needed to get some money together...lived in my sister Karen's basement for a while to save money. The college let me re-enter the radiography program the following year and with full credit.

"As soon as I graduated I drove my 1971 Ford Pinto down to Miami and got a job here at Jackson Hospital taking x-rays and ultrasound images. Worked in radiology for about a year but knew from the start that I didn't want to do medical imaging my entire life.

"My father's sudden death made me realize that life is short. I needed to follow my dream of becoming a sea captain while I was still young and before it was too late, so I worked for a year at Jackson and saved most of my money.

"On April 1st, 1972, I began searching for a boat. Three weeks later—yeah, I remember clearly—it was on April 21st that I met Captain Rubio at the docks in Miami. The old Cuban gentleman had painted his boat to make it look like a floating watermelon. He had a business—transporting watermelons from Homestead, here in Florida, to Nassau. He had sailed that route for many years but was retiring at the age of seventy-nine, and for health reasons he was forced to sell his boat, the *Watermelon*.

"He loved that little boat and would only sell her to someone who would agree to not paint her differently or change her name. Apparently I was the only seaman in Miami who would agree to sail around the pirate-infested Caribbean and Atlantic in a *Watermelon* boat. So the old man and I came to an agreement on price, and I sold my crappy car; then I went to the bank and took out my life's savings and bought his little *Watermelon* boat on April 21st.

"Captain Rubio taught me basic seamanship and how to sail the *Watermelon*. He trained me for one month. Later, I took courses at the Sea School in Ft. Lauderdale and obtained my Merchant Marine Captain's License. That made me a legal, legitimate merchant marine sea captain, and I took over Captain Rubio's trading route. I had been doing the route for about a year and a half now...until the wreck on Christmas."

"But what about the Indians—Native Americans—and the article in the Miami *Post*?" I could tell by her attentiveness that Nurse Whacker was truly interested in my story.

"Well, you might not believe me, but here goes nothing. One day on my return trip from Nassau to Key West, I ran into a giant sea turtle, and it broke my prop. There was no wind to sail the boat, so I drifted to Crocodile Island. I was marooned there. That night on the island, I was attacked by a giant, mutant croc that nearly killed me. That's when my dive fins were chewed into rubber Kroc shoes.

"I was critically injured, but I escaped to my boat and drifted in the Gulf of Mexico...drifted unconscious and near death until I was rescued by three Indians from the Whatchacallit Indian Tribe, a tribe of Native Americans living in seclusion in the Big Cypress area of the Everglades. Those Indians nursed me back to health and adopted me as one of their own. I fell in love with the girl who cared for my injury. Her name was Little Hooters. But fate would not have us remain together."

Silence overcame me as I remembered the look in Little Hooters's eyes as I sailed away, leaving her sitting heartbroken and alone on the beach.

"Ahh, hum." Choking up with emotion, I had to pause to clear my throat.

Nurse Whacker sensed my sadness. "I'm sorry," she said and touched my arm again.

After a brief pause, I regained my composure and continued speaking. "Well, after I regained my health, three of my Whatchacallit warrior friends sailed with me to Miami to trade goods. We had quite a time on South Beach. My Indian friends had never been exposed to modern civilization and the Wasichu's pop culture."

"What's 'Wasichu'?"

"'Wasichu' is their word for white people. Anyway, watching their reactions and interactions with modern Miamians was hilarious. Our whacked-out adventures on South Beach were described in that Miami *Post* article that you've been hearing about. I had a copy, but now it's at the bottom of the ocean with my boat."

"I'm going to look up that article in the archives at the library, Eddie. Go on, I want to know what happened next!" She leaned in toward me.

"Well, when we left Miami to return home to the Whatchacallit village, a dog stowed away on our boat. That's the dog that I was telling you about. I was trying to return him to his master here in Miami, but now he's lost in the streets of the city." I paused and gave her a nervous glance.

"What's wrong?" she asked.

"I'm embarrassed to tell you the next part of my story. Please don't think I'm crazy." I lay back on the bed and stared up at the ceiling, wondering if I should continue.

"You can trust me, Eddie." She touched my arm again.

"Okay, but you were warned." I sat back upright. "The Indians have a sixth sense; they can communicate with animals."

"Like with hand signals and voice commands?" she asked.

"More than that. They can talk to them...both out loud and sometimes with telepathy." I waited to see her reaction.

"Hmm, I've heard legends and myths of Indians doing that. They are very close to nature."

"Well, I can confirm that it's true. For a short time even I was starting to acquire that sixth sense, but I seem to have lost it after leaving the tribe."

"Are you saying that you talked to animals?" Her eyes widened, but she seemed to believe me.

"Yes, I talked to the little collie, the stowaway dog. We call him Melon Dog."

"Did you say...little collie?"

"Yes."

"Is he tan and white and very smart? So intelligent that when you look at his eyes he's a little bit spooky?" she asked.

"That's a perfect description of him." I leaned toward her.

"We have been feeding a little collie at the service entrance to the cafeteria," she said.

"Could it be Melon Dog? Is he okay? He must be scared to death out there all alone," I said.

"No, he's not scared. The dog is accustomed to street life. We've been feeding that dog for nearly a year. He disappeared for a while—that must be when he went away with you on the *Watermelon* boat. People thought he was dead, thought that a car might have hit him, but now he's back again, begging for food. He was here yesterday not long after you were admitted to the hospital."

"Does he have a black collar and silver dog tag?" I asked.

"Yes, he has a silver tag on his collar, but he has always appeared to be hungry and homeless. People in the hospital call him 'Hobo.' He has become our mascot. Everybody loves that dog." She had a bright smile as she spoke fondly of the dog.

"Melon Dog told me that he lives here in Miami with a young boy named Luca. Luca's father is cruel and beats both the boy and the dog. The boy is in danger, and I need to find him. I need to help Luca somehow. The ancient spirits have commanded me to save Luca." I was excited and speaking rapidly now.

"Whoa, slow down, Eddie. The dog told you what? The dog spoke to you? Ancient spirits commanded you?" She gave me a skeptical look.

"That's what I was afraid of. You think I'm crazy, don't you?"

"You've been through a lot, Eddie. You had hypothermia and dehydration, and you lost everything you owned. The mind can play tricks on us when we're stressed out and traumatized. I've seen it before. But I believe you really are concerned about the dog and the boy. Maybe I can help you find them." She stood up beside my bed.

"Yes! You can help me! Go see if Melon Dog is outside the cafeteria. If you find him can you please take him home for the night?"

"I can't have dogs where I live Eddie—but I'll sneak him into my apartment if he lets me." She started to leave to look for the dog.

"Hey, wait—what's your name, Ms. Whacker—your first name? You never told me."

"Patty, Patty Whacker. I'll call your room later to let you know if I've got Hobo with me." She kissed my forehead and left.

The kiss surprised me. *Wow, that girl is forward—confident. She's very direct. I like that...I like Nurse Patty Whacker.*

I swung my legs back onto the bed and then pressed the button to recline my head. I could still feel Patty Whacker's warm lips on my forehead as I started to daydream of Little Hooters, my lost love.

I touched the moist spot on my forehead. *Wish it were your sweet honeysuckle kiss, my beautiful Indian princess. Patty Whacker can never replace you, Little Hooters. No girl will ever replace you in my heart.*

At 5:30 pm my phone rang. It was Patty. She told me that Melon Dog had not been outside the hospital and that she was at home alone making dinner. Patty promised to see me in the morning after coming on duty at 7:00 am.

## THURSDAY MORNING

Nurse Patty Whacker came to my room at 7:20 am, pushing a wheelchair.

"Good morning, Eddie. You're being discharged. I asked for your belongings and was told you have nothing, not even clothes."

"That's what I told you, Patty. I lost everything. The only thing I have now is this hospital gown and my black rubber Kroc shoes."

"A van from the homeless shelter will pick you up, and at the shelter you can get some clothes and food until you can find a job. Do you still have your radiographer's license? Radiology is hiring," Patty said.

"That job is not for me, Patty. I'm going to see if one of the charter boat companies is hiring captains. But thanks for the thought."

She looked disappointed.

"I hoped that you might work here at the hospital again." She handed me some discharge papers to sign.

"I don't think I need to go to the homeless shelter. Willie, the owner of Slick Willie's Trading Post, will give me a helping hand...I hope." I handed her the paperwork. "There you go, Patty."

"Get in. I'll wheel you downstairs," she said.

"I can walk just fine."

"Eddie, it's hospital policy. Get in." She rolled the wheelchair toward me.

I sat down, and Patty Whacker wheeled me to the lobby and the main exit.

"Are you actually going to walk around town in that gown with your butt sticking out the back? Let me get you a set of O.R. scrubs to wear," said the kind nurse.

"No, Patty, you might get in trouble. A guy got fired for stealing scrubs. Slick Willie's is only a few miles away. I'll be fine, but thanks for your kindness. You're a very sweet girl."

"Take care, Eddie Ocean. I hardly know you, but if you don't call on me, I have a feeling that I'll miss you. You know where I work— come see me sometime." She grabbed my face with both hands and kissed me hard on the lips. Then she turned and ran back into the hospital.

I began walking east on 14th Street toward Slick Willie's Trading Post, trying to hold the back of my gown closed, but every once in a while it would pop open in the breeze. Oddly, in spite of all my recent misfortunes, Nurse Patty Whacker had put me in a good mood. I began singing a popular song, an oldie from 1964 called "The Name Game."

Patty, Patty, bo-batty,
Banana-fana fo-fatty
Fee-fi-mo-matty
Patty!

Let's do Whacker!

Whacker, Whacker, bo-backer,
Banana-fana fo-facker
Fee-fi-mo-macker
Whacker!

When I passed by a construction site and had to jump over some rubble on the sidewalk, my butt popped out from the back of the gown. Then some unseen workers perched high in the rafters of the construction project interrupted my happy song.

" Fee-fi-mo-wacker! Look, Harry, he's a real whack job, all right!"

"Yeah, another lunatic just escaped from the insane asylum!" The voices calling down from the rafters of the high-rise construction project mocked me mercilessly.

"Put on some clothes, you pervert." I looked up to see where the voices were coming from and spotted a guy wearing a yellow hard-hat. He flashed me the bird and screamed at me, his face red and distorted by anger. "Pervert!"

Then his buddy called out and pointed to my exposed buttocks: "Hey psycho,

Just say no to crack!"

## Chapter 6

# THE NAME GAME

From their lofty perches high in the rafters above me, the construction workers continued to rain down taunts and insults, so I quickened my pace and hurried down the block to escape their nasty jeers. Once out of earshot, I resumed singing the "Name Game" song.

Lets do Chuck!
Chuck, Chuck, bo-buck
Banana-fana fo-...

My song was cut short by a single, short burst from a siren followed by flashing blue and red lights. Approaching me from behind was a police car. I turned to face the cruiser as it pulled over to the curb and stopped beside me, lights still flashing. From behind the closed window, the officer in the passenger seat looked me up and down. He appeared to be laughing. When the policeman lowered the window, I could hear both officers laughing loudly.

"Ray, get a load of this guy's outfit! Check out those clown shoes!" The men joked about my appearance as I stood on the sidewalk facing the patrol car.

"Hey, pal, who you running from?" asked the cop.

"No one, sir."

"You busted out of the pavillion at Jackson, right? Looks like we got another runaway psycho, Ray—another mental case loose on the streets of Miami. How surprising!"

"Third one this week!" said the driver.

"I'm no runaway. I was legally discharged from the hospital today, officer," I said and walked toward the car.

"Stay back, kid!" The cop stopped me from approaching, opened his door, and got out of the car. "Legally discharged, eh? Sure you were, pal. So that gown is just your normal, everyday attire. Your butt's hanging out in the breeze for all the world to see, kid!"

"Sir, I swear I'm not on the run…just don't have clothing at the moment."

With only three blocks between Slick Willie's Trading Post and a pair of pants, I was about to get cuffed by the cops. My perpetual bad luck continued to plague me.

"It's called indecent exposure, kid. Let me see some ID." The cop stood in front of me, holding handcuffs.

"I lost my wallet, sir. And as you can see, I don't even have any clothes at the moment."

"Well, then, I'm gonna have to take you in till we can ID you."

The cop began to turn me around to apply the cuffs when I looked down at my wrist and noticed my hospital ID bracelet. "Oh, wait! Hey, look!" I held out my arm to show him the ID bracelet. "Look, this is my name and patient number. You can check me out with the hospital! Call the hospital."

The cop leaned over to have a look. "Hmm…Eddie Ocean. Hey, that name rings a bell. How do I know your name? Are you on our most wanted list?" The other cop began to scramble out of the vehicle, and I saw him release a snap on his holstered pistol. He stood on the opposite side of the car with his hand gripping the pistol's butt.

"No, I'm clean, sir," I said.

"Tony, cuff him while I run his name," said the cop standing with his hand covering his gun.

"Hey, Ray, wait! I got it…Eddie Ocean! This is the guy who was in the newspaper."

The cop turned me back around to face him and closely examined my face. "Yeah it's him, the guy with the crazy Indian friends." He clipped the handcuffs back onto his service belt.

"You're the guy who was with them Indians, sailing on that ridiculous-looking *Watermelon* boat…saw your picture in the paper a while back. You *are* crazy but not dangerous, I guess!"

"Yeah, that's me. I'm Eddie Ocean, but I'm clean, officer. I'm not running, just on my way to get some clothes from Slick Willie's Trading Post."

"Okay, looky here, Ocean—you and your Indian friends are obviously whacko, but the last time I picked up a loony tune, I was doing paperwork all day long…complying with all that privacy crap. You look harmless enough. If you stick to the alleys and stay off the main street, I won't run you in for indecent exposure this time. Just get some damn clothes!"

"Thank you, officer." The police officers turned off the flashing lights and drove away.

*Whew, that was a close one.*

I cut down the alleyway and continued toward Slick Willie's Trading Post. In the alley, several homeless people loitered near a dumpster behind an Italian restaurant. As I passed by them, an old woman with long, gray hair and grimy, tattered clothing noticed my backside peeking out of my gown.

"Hey, sweet cakes. Let me have a bite of those sweet buns." The old woman approached me, leering with a toothless smile.

Then a crusty middle-aged guy with drool coming from the corner of his mouth started following me. He walked rigidly, like a zombie from the movie *Night of the Living Dead.*

I quickened my pace, leaving the pair of ghouls behind, and scurried into the entrance of Slick Willie's Trading Post, desperate for some pants.

I greeted Willie. "Hey, Willie, long time no see!"

"Well, look at what the cat just dragged in! Ratfink, Eddie Ocean!" Slick Willie was behind the checkout counter and in a foul mood.

"Willie, I'm badly in need of some clothes, but I won't be able to pay you for a couple of days," I said.

"You want credit? Why the heck would I do you any favors, Ocean? Last time you were here with those savages, you chose to do business with that Yankee catalogue trader L. Lucky Bean, not me."

"I was representing the Whatchacallit Indian Tribe, Willie. Those were not my goods to sell. Bean offered them the better deal."

"You picked the Yankee over me, your honest, friendly, local businessman." Willie scowled.

*Yeah, you're about as friendly and honest as a rattlesnake.* I suppressed my negative thought, still hoping to get a pair of pants.

"I didn't know you took your business transactions so personally, Willie. I apologize. Sorry that I hurt your feelings."

"Get out of my store before I toss you out on your ear!" Willie leaned down to grab something and then came out from behind the counter to threaten me with a nightstick.

Reluctantly I walked outside and crossed the street to go beneath the overpass, where I had met three homeless guys on my last trip to Miami. I remembered that the vagrants had a pile of junk including used clothes that they were trying to sell.

I stood in the bright sunlight gazing into the dark shadows beneath the overpass. "Anyone home?" I called out.

The men were not there, but their pile of junk was still under the overpass. The last time I was in town, that guy with the chronic cough had offered me the pick of this junk pile. *Guess his offer still stands.* I bent over and began sorting through the pile, looking for some clothes, when an angry voice interrupted me.

"Hey kid, what are you doing with our merchandise?" The voice came from behind me. I turned around and saw the tall, clean-cut, homeless guy standing in the sunshine holding a little league base-ball bat. He squinted into the dark shadows beneath the overpass where I stood, holding up a woman's dress.

"Hi—remember me? I'm Eddie Ocean," I said.

"Well, I'll be damned! How the hell are you, Eddie? Never expected to see you again. Saw the article about you and your Indian friends in the newspaper—you were the talk of the town for a few days."

"Well, sir, now I'm flat busted and need some clothes."

"No kidding, you needs some of them thar clothes! When you were bent over that pile of goods with your ass sticking out, I thought I had come face to face with a three-foot tall, red-eyed Cyclops. You won't last long on the streets of Miami dressed like that, kid."

The other two homeless guys I had met on my previous trip to Miami arrived to join us.

The grubby guy with the long coat entered the shadows first. "We don't sell to no transvestites." The vagrant had noticed me sniffing the dress to see if the pile of old clothing was mildewed.

"Moe, this is Eddie Ocean. Remember Eddie?"

"Oh, hey, kid…didn't recognize you. What's with the dress-sniffing? Not that there is anything wrong with sniffing women's clothing…especially undergarments—do it myself."

"I was just checking for mold. I'm actually looking for some pants, Mr. Moe…that's your name, right? Sorry, fellas—I never did get all your names the last time we met."

"I'm John Dumas," said the tall, clean-cut guy. "And this here is my friend Moe Lester." John pointed to the grubby guy with long, dirty hair.

"Pleased to meet you again," I said.

"This guy with the bad cough and soggy bottom is Brownie Shytles," John Dumas said, putting his hand on Brownie's shoulder.

"John, Moe, and Brownie, I got it." I memorized their names and noticed the creepy, wide-eyed guy, Moe Lester, smiling at me.

"How does that dress smell, anyway?" Moe asked.

"Fine...no mold." *Why is Moe wearing that long winter coat?* I wondered. "Moe, aren't you hot in that long coat?" I asked.

Moe stood there with the stupid-looking smile but made no reply. With a weird look in his eye, he reached out, took the dress, and started sniffing it. Brownie answered in his stead, "The pervert doesn't wear anything under that coat, Eddie. He's buck naked...gets plenty of ventilation from down below."

"Nah, come on, Brownie's kidding me, right Moe?" I looked at Moe and realized that Brownie was not joking. Moe stood silently, catatonic-like, with that weird smile, still sniffing the dress. *Does this guy have brain damage?* I wondered as he continued to stare at me in silence.

Like I said, Moe Lester was very scruffy. Long, dirty, tangled hair hung down below his shoulders, and he wore a long, threadbare, heavily soiled trenchcoat. The man reminded me of Aqualung, a character described in a song by the rock group Jethro Tull. When I was in college I owned the Aqualung vinyl L.P. album. The picture of Aqualung on the cover of the album could have been a portrait of the man standing in front of me. Moe Lester, Brownie Shytles, and John Dumas, what a trio of misfits!

Moe broke his silence. "Eddie, no offense, but I got to hand it to ya, you wearing that hospital gown with your butt hanging out while sniffing that dress was classic! Gotta hand it to ya, you look way more perverse than me, kid." *Moe's right. In my condition, who am I to judge them as misfits?*

We huddled around the pile of junk. John Dumas was tall, fit, and fairly well groomed, the only normal-looking guy among the four of us.

Brownie Shytles, on the other hand, was a mess. He was obviously sickly, with a chronic cough. He had cut two holes in a black plastic trash bag for his legs to go through and then tied the top of the trash bag around his waist. *Looks like a big, black plastic diaper. I hope that guy doesn't have TB*, I thought as I watched Brownie cough violently into a dirty rag.

"John, the last time I was here you fellows offered me anything from your junk pile...oh—so sorry—I mean your merchandise pile."

"Sure, Eddie, take what you need. We owe you; those Indian pony drags you gave us are great for hauling our merchandise around town. Help yourself—find yourself some clothes."

Stacked next to the large, disorganized pile of junk were dozens of neatly folded, brand new tee-shirts. I found a medium and tried it on.

"It's a little snug at the chest, but it fits," I said as I examined the lettering on the shirt.

"Looks good," John said.

I examined the graphics on the front of the tee-shirt. I'M WITH STUPID! "Hmm...hey, John why is that arrow pointing downward?"

"Because of a colossal screw-up. That entire stack of brand spanking new tee-shirts was in the dumpster outside of the tee-shirt factory. Some idiot printed them up with the arrow pointing down instead of off to the side." John held one up for me to better see.

Moe piped up. "I think those shirts are great! Angry wives would love to give them to their cheating husbands...don't ya think? I think they're funny! They could have sold hundreds of them shirts...those idiots! But their loss is our gain!"

Brownie agreed, "Yeah John, remember that senator who was running for president a few years back...Senator Gary Hart? He got caught cheating with that hot chick on a sailboat in Coconut Grove. Hart's wife should give Gary one of these shirts as an anniversary present."

The three guys had a hearty laugh, but I didn't get the joke at first. Then it dawned on me, and I understood what Moe meant. The arrow was pointing down at my crotch to the area of the male anatomy that sometimes causes men to act stupidly and gets them into trouble with the wife.

"Ahh, now I get it! That's a good one—good point! You're on to something, John," I said with a chuckle.

"We got the shirts just in time for New Year's. Some drunken guy will act stupidly at the New Year's Eve office party. Then the wife can give him one of these tee-shirts along with the divorce papers," John said.

"That's funny." I said but then realized, *So now I'll be walking around town wearing an "I'm With Stupid" tee-shirt with an arrow pointing at my crotch! Just great, and I don't even have an angry wife!*

"Let's find you some pants, Eddie. I'm the local pervert, and I don't need no competition from you," Moe said as he rummaged through the pile of junk. "Try these." He tossed me a pair of blue cut-off denim shorts.

"They fit perfectly!" I said. "But look at how short they are. These look like hot pants. I look ridiculous, like a male go-go dancer." We continued searching through the pile.

"Here we go—men's dress pants." John tossed me a pair of black pants.

I examined the tag. "These are size 48 and I'm a 32" waist."

"Looks like that's all we got, Eddie," said Moe, as he hit the bottom of the heap.

I kept the denim hot pants to use as underwear and then pulled on the black dress pants. The waistband came up to my chest.

"We could all fit inside this sucker," I said.

By holding the front belt loops pinched together at my chest, I kept the pants from falling down.

"Eddie, I wouldn't share pants with Brownie, if I were you," said Moe, who looked at Brownie Shytles with a taunting smirk.

"Shut up, Moe! At least I'm not a pervert."

"Lay off Brownie," John warned Moe.

"Moe knows I can't help my incontinence. I have Crohn's disease, colitis, irritable bowel syndrome, and some other medical problems that I can't even pronounce. It's not my fault, Eddie. I contracted the diseases in South America, years ago." Brownie Shytles spoke in between hacking coughs.

"Stop the bickering, you losers!" said John.

I needed a place to sleep, so despite all the bickering of my annoying new friends, I asked them, "Do you fellows mind if I spend the night here under this overpass with you?"

"Bad idea, Eddie. This place is only our daytime business location—our street store. We don't sleep here. The cops will run you off at night because this area is in the tourist district. We sleep under the I-95 overpass just outside of Overtown. We call it the Big O Skid Row. About seventy people camp out over there," said John.

"We're about to close up shop and head on over. You can come with us," Moe offered.

"Thanks, Moe, but can I meet you guys there later? I need to stop by the docks and find Captain Rubio. I need to tell him that a freighter sank his *Watermelon* boat. I'm afraid the old man will be devastated by the bad news."

"Sure, Eddie. Skid row is open 24/7. See you later."

I walked to the docks, clutching the front of my oversized pants to keep them from falling off. I pulled the pants up high, trying to hide the arrow that pointed down at Stupid as I walked.

At the marina, I found the dockmaster adjusting some dock lines. "Hello, sir. Do you know how I might find Captain Rubio, the old Cuban gentleman who used to live here on the *Watermelon* boat?"

"I'm afraid you're too late. Rubio passed away on Christmas Eve—well, technically Christmas morning. It was some time just after midnight, they say."

"What—Rubio died?" I was shocked. "What happened?"

"Rubio died in his sleep...heart attack, they say."

*Wait—this can't be right. That means Rubio died right around the time I had the dream of him wandering around on the* Watermelon ... *just before the boat was destroyed.*

"Are you all right, kid?" the dockmaster asked, as I stood dumb-founded by the realization that the apparition might have been Rubio's ghost.

Could the ancient spirits have arranged Captain Rubio's reunion with his *Watermelon* boat? Had they returned Rubio's boat to him in the afterlife on Christmas morning? In shock, I began to mumble my thoughts out loud.

"Rubio is probably sailing his *Watermelon* boat in the afterlife... sailing right now...even as we speak." I spoke slowly, in a low voice, still dazed by the revelation.

"What are you talking about, kid? You must have a screw loose! I just told you that Rubio is dead...not sailing his boat." The dock-master closely examined my face and then my odd, ill-fitting attire.

"Do you need some help, kid?"

"No, sir. Do you know when Rubio's funeral will be?" I asked.

"I was a friend of Rubio's for over twenty years, kid. He always wanted to be buried on the farm in Cuba where he grew up before the Communists took all the land from the Romero family. He wanted to be buried under a special tree that he climbed as a young boy."

"But I thought travel to Cuba was illegal, even for the dead."

"Money talks, kid. Someone with connections to the Miami mob has black-market connections in Cuba and has arranged to smuggle Rubio's body home to his relatives. I heard that the Boss is paying for everything. Rubio's body might already be in Cuba by now."

"Yes, I'm sure he is home by now," I said.

*In the afterlife, I wonder if Rubio is a young man once again. A young captain sailing his beloved* Watermelon *boat.* A sense of relief spread over me.

Maybe it was fate, not my negligence, that had doomed the *Watermelon*? Maybe the Great Wanaka had determined that it was time to return Rubio's boat to him...and it wasn't my screw-up!

"Thanks for your time, sir." I turned to walk away, and my pants fell below my butt, exposing the blue denim undershorts.

"Hey, kid, you don't look so good. If you need some mental help, go to the pavilion at Jackson Memorial Hospital. It's on 12th Street."

"I know where the hospital is, sir. I used to work there," I said as I walked off toward skid row clutching the crotch of my sagging pants.

"Sure you did, kid—probably a brain surgeon, right?"

As I walked toward skid row, the back of my saggy pants slipped down below my butt again and again. They were so large that I gave up trying to keep them up in the back. I no longer cared if my ass was sticking out because the blue denim underpants covered my buttocks.

As I walked, once again I wondered if it was possible that the simultaneous sinking of the *Watermelon* and Rubio's death were truly fate.

Could it be possible that the beloved little boat was returned to the old Cuban sea captain precisely at the moment of his death? Did a Greater Power reunite him with his *Watermelon* boat?

I turned onto NW 14th and walked west toward skid row.

*Or could there be another reason for my shipwreck? Did the ancient spirits take my boat so that I would be landlocked in Miami and forced to concentrate my efforts on finding the boy named Luca? Spirits, are you trying to tell me that I'm not doing enough to find Luca? Is that why you have left me without a boat…without anything?*

I looked toward the heavens and screamed at the sky,

"Did you destroy the boat as punishment for me not serving you adequately?" My angry outburst caused some approaching pedestrians to quickly cross to the opposite side of the street to avoid me.

"Why do you always treat me so harshly?" Again I yelled toward the heavens. I must have looked like a raging lunatic and realized that I was channeling my grief over Rubio's death into anger. When I spotted a police car driving toward me I forced myself to calm down. Inside I was simultaneously heartbroken and seething with anger.

*My current situation is pathetic! No job, no food, no decent clothes…I see no hope or window of opportunity.*

My angry thoughts were interrupted when I recalled the encouragement that nurse Whacker had given me.

"You will be back on your feet in no time, Eddie Ocean," she had said to me.

Patty reminded me that I was young and healthy. She was telling me that I should be grateful for what I had, my youth and my health.

"Patty, you are right!" I said out loud as a truism came to mind and comforted me:

When God shuts a door, he always opens a window.

# Chapter 7

## A NIGHT IN THE PENTHOUSE

### THURSDAY, DECEMBER 27TH, 1973

The city was loud and the streets alive with heavy, late afternoon rush hour traffic as I walked north on Biscayne Boulevard, dodging knots of fellow pedestrians. Buses roared by, spewing gray plumes of diesel fumes into my face as I walked, clutching my oversized pants at the fly and pressing my hand to my bellybutton. The pants caused me to walk with a short, gimpy stride, and despite my efforts to hold them up, the back of my pants kept falling down below my butt.

When I stopped to wait for a traffic light, a man approached me. "Here you go, kid," said the man as he stuck a dollar bill in my pocket.

*Wait, I'm no beggar.* Before I could say it out loud, the traffic light changed, and the man darted across the street.

*Hey, I look like a bum!* Despite my best attempts to keep the pants up, they kept sliding down in the back, causing people I passed to give me a wide berth. *I could use some suspenders!* People avoided making eye contact. I'm sure they were afraid I was going to panhandle. After turning left onto NW 8th Street, I proceeded toward Overtown and the I-95 overpass, where I had been told skid row was located.

On 8th Street, I walked along a stretch of eight-foot-high cyclone fence topped by razor wire. Posted on the front gate of the property was a HELP WANTED sign. I stopped beneath the sign, put my fingers through the fencing, and looked over the grounds. In the middle of the large lot was a trailer that appeared to be being used as an office. THE GARBAGE GUYS was painted in red lettering across the side of the trailer. Six garbage trucks and dozens of green dumpsters were parked around the large, open space. *This appears to be a waste management facility.* I pulled on the gate, but it was chained shut and locked. They were closed for the day. I made a mental note of the location and planned to return in the morning to see what jobs were being offered. My priority was to obtain decent clothing, food, and housing, and for those things money was needed.

"Be patient with me, Great Ones! I will find Luca for you, but first I need a job to survive." My speaking to the sky brought an odd look from a wino who was sitting across the street on a bus bench, sipping from a bottle hidden inside a brown paper bag. I waved to the wino and then continued walking toward skid row. The prospect of a job lightened my spirits.

By the time I reached the ghetto, it was dark. To the west, about one mile ahead of me, I could see the streetlights atop the I-95 overpass, and upon arriving there I found a large open area, littered with trash and small tents, extending to the south of NW 8th Street. Beneath the highway overpass, a concentration of tents and large cardboard boxes covered every inch of the sprawling open area. This was the Big O Skid Row, a small city populated by hundreds of vagrant squatters.

The orange glow of fires burning inside 55-gallon drums illuminated the weary, weather-beaten faces of the people gathered around them. Some people were roasting what appeared to be hotdogs on sticks. Many more were drinking from containers inside brown paper bags.

One group of men stood around a barrel, singing old 1950s doo-wop songs a cappella. The dirty faces of the trio of singers expressed a hint of joy and hope. Their songs seemed to lift the spirits of the desperate, unwashed masses living here. The singing was pleasant to the ear, the glow of the fire pleasing to the eye, and the aroma of the food cooking over the smoky wood fires made me hungry. But as I came closer to the overpass, the offensive, acrid scent of urine combined with body odor overpowered the pleasant aromas, making for a repugnant odoriferous experience.

A crusty middle-aged guy with a long beard was standing off to the side of a fire barrel, drinking whiskey from a small glass bottle. "Do you know a guy named Moe Lester?" I asked him.

"Yeah, I know that pervert. He lives up in the penthouse. Him and his brown-nosing friends live up there...they work for the Boss. That's how they got to live up there in the penthouse."

"Where's the penthouse?" I asked.

"You must be new around here, kid." He lowered the bottle and started eyeballing me like the Big Bad Wolf sizing up Little Red Riding Hood.

"You got to be careful who you make friends with around here, kid. Someone might try to rip you off. You know, we gotta look out for one another...never can have too many friends on skid row."

"I'm just visiting. Seeing some friends here. So where is the penthouse?" The guy looked disappointed that I did not want to make friends and took a big swig of whiskey before pointing to the top of the concrete slope that went up to the I-95 roadway.

"Up on that flattop...where the incline meets the I-95 bridge abutment. That's the penthouse."

"Thanks, mister."

"Hey wait! Want a swig, kid...only fifty cents a swig?" He held out the bottle of cheap rotgut whiskey.

"No, thanks. I'm looking for food, not whiskey."

"Well, come back when you gots a full belly." He took a long drink. "Mmmm, now that's some smooth hooch. You'll like it—only fifty cents!"

I climbed the steep concrete embankment to the penthouse. At the top was a large, flat area just beneath the highway, where four large, heavy-gauge corrugated cardboard containers sat in a row. Each little shack had a blanket hanging down over the entrance that functioned as a door.

"John, Moe, Brownie…anybody home?" I called out their names.

Moe poked his head out from behind a blanket. "Hey, Eddie, you made it here alive." He came out of his little cardboard hut.

"A guy told me that this place is called the penthouse. You guys must be at the top of the skid row pecking order," I said as I looked around.

"Yeah, we are tight with the Boss. Do him favors from time to time," Moe said.

"The Boss? I keep hearing about the Boss. The boss of what?" I asked.

"'The Boss' is short for 'crime boss'…the godfather of Miami, and he's also the overlord of skid row. The Boss coordinates the schemes and the scams, collects and doles out money. He's the brain of our operation. The Boss has connections to the suits and uniforms, so they all leave us alone," said Moe.

I didn't understand what Moe was talking about. I realized I was in a foreign world now and had a lot to learn.

"Let me get you some food, Eddie," said Brownie after emerging from a different box.

"Thanks, Brownie. I'm starving."

Brownie walked to the side of his hut and went to a large hibachi that had a pot cooking on top.

"I had one of those hibachis on my boat…only mine was much smaller," I said.

Brownie ladled hot stew into a bowl, handed it to me, and then gave me a spoon.

"Damn! This stew is delicious. Yum, what's in this stew?" I said as I gobbled up the hot meal.

"Meat, potatoes, carrots, celery, salt, pepper, and a splash of Worchester sauce."

"Brownie, it's delicious! What's the meat?"

"Dog—fresh road kill. A couple of guys saw the poor dog get hit by a car over on NW 27th Street, just east of Biscayne."

"Dog! I'm eating dog!" I almost choked.

"Sure—why let the poor animal go to waste? You just said it's delicious, right?"

"Please tell me that it—the dog, I mean—was not a small tan and white collie." I stared into my bowl, aghast at the thought that I might have eaten Melon Dog.

"No, not a collie. They said it was a big sucka. Like a bulldog… maybe a bullmastiff. We got a lot of meat off his bones."

I was relieved that at least it was not Melon Dog. Thankfully Brownie had told me that I was eating dog meat after I had already finished all but one bite of my stew. I desperately needed the nourishment and did not know if I could have eaten the stew knowing that it contained dog meat, but I had to admit, it was tasty.

John came up the embankment to the penthouse area.

"Hi, John. Look who's here," said Moe.

"Hey, Eddie! Welcome! Make yourself at home. You can bunk down in Riley's shack—he's in jail," said John.

They directed me to one of the containers. It was rectangular, 8X10 and 8 feet tall, and quite comfy inside. I could stand up, and there was a small chair and a bedroll, with blankets on the floor. Two cheap-framed pictures, a black cat with bright green eyes, and a sailboat, were hung on one wall. After inspecting the shack I came back out.

"That's a cozy little hut. If you guys don't mind, I'll crash early tonight. I'm exhausted, and I need to go look for a job first thing tomorrow morning." I said.

"Sure, Eddie. See you mañana," said Moe.

I went inside the hut and lay down on some musty-smelling blankets. The noise from the traffic traveling on I-95 just twelve feet above my head was very loud, but soon I became accustomed to it. Each time the loud humming sound from the tires of an 18-wheeler passing overhead rattled my shack, I tried to guess the destination of the trucker as the sound faded off into the distance. That guy is headed for the Rocky Mountains in Colorado. This one's hauling oranges up to Michigan. Counting the trucks was like counting sheep, and sleep came quickly.

Before sunrise, I came out of my box to find a light, misty rain falling upon skid row down below the penthouse. There was a chill in the morning air. Luckily for us, the overpass acted as a roof and kept us dry. Some people down below were not so fortunate. Many lived in the areas of skid row that were not sheltered by the I-95 overpass. They were the weaklings, those at the bottom of the pecking order, and they were given the least desirable locations. *It seems that even on skid row there are the haves and the have-nots.* Miserable, wet, cold people were covering themselves with plastic sheets and trash bags. I felt sorry for them.

"Hey Eddie, come get some hot java!"

To the side of Brownie's shack, my friends were making a pot of coffee on the hibachi.

"Good morning, fellas. Where do you guys pee?" I asked, but before they answered I noticed John pissing in an area about twenty feet away. "Oh, I see." I walked over to join him.

"Just make sure you hit the down slope. Don't want it running back this way," John said as he pulled up his zipper.

I took out Stupid and relieved myself.

"Eddie, we're going alley-shopping today. Need to collect more goods for our street shop. Want to join us? You might find a better pair of pants...pants that fit you."

"No thanks, Brownie. I need to pay a visit to an old friend before I apply for a job opening over on NW 8th Street."

"Who's your friend? A hot young chick, I bet," said Moe Lester as he smirked and rubbed his grubby hands together like a housefly.

"No, not a chick, just a guy I worked with at Jackson Hospital. They call him the Vampire because he's a phlebotomist. You know— he draws blood from patients at the hospital," I said.

"That's a cool name, 'the Vampire.' I like that," said John.

"His real name is not so cool. It's Uranus Johnson," I said.

"Uranus Johnson! You're kidding." Brownie Shytles laughed. "That name is worse than mine!"

"I'm serious. His father is an astronomy buff. He named each of his seven children after a planet. I'm sure you've heard of Mercury Johnson, the star running back for the Miami Dolphins. Mercury is Uranus's older brother. Uranus's oldest sister is Venus, the star tennis player. Earth, the third-born—another sister— became a drug addict—polluted with heroin and killed in a gang shootout."

"That's crazy, man—he named his kids after planets. Wow!" said Moe.

"The Johnsons live in Overtown, only about five or six blocks from here. I want to ask Uranus to keep a watch out for my missing dog. Gonna ask him to contact a nurse who took care of me at Jackson Memorial, too—then I'm heading over to 8th Street to apply for that job," I said.

"A nurse? I knew it. You probably date two chicks a night, don't you, Eddie! I bet she's hot—a real looker, I bet, right?" asked Moe Lester.

"Yeah, she's real cute and sweet."

"Mmm, mmm! Sure would like to find me a little nursey gal so we could play doctor together," said Moe as he flicked his tongue in and out from his grimy, bearded face like a hairy lizard.

"Shut up, pervert! He's talking about a nice girl," Brownie said before going into his shack and then emerging with a hat.

"Eddie, here, take this cap to keep your head dry. We'll meet you back here later on. *Hasta la vista*." Brownie handed me a Detroit Tigers baseball cap, and then the three men went down the slope to go alley-shopping.

"Come on, you dirty pervert, time to go to work," said Brownie.

"Tell him to shut up, John. I swear I'll punch him in the nose!" Moe said and clenched his fist.

The three stooges walked through the puddles down below, arguing. I watched Moe and Brownie shove each other around like a couple of six-year-old kids until John got in between them to keep the peace. After waiting for them to leave, I put on the baseball cap and went down the slope. Ouch! Something was pricking my forehead. A small pin was protruding from the stitching on the inside of the bill of the hat. I took the cap off but could not remove the sharp little pin.

"Well that sure is annoying!" I said as I touched the sharp pin with the tip of my index finger. By my turning the cap off to the side and wearing it on an angle, my long hair protected my scalp from the pinprick.

*That's better.* So with my cap cocked to the side, the arrow on my I'm With Stupid tee-shirt pointing down at my crotch, and my baggy pants falling off my butt, I went off to apply for a job, but first I needed to visit Uranus so he could help me find Melon Dog. I needed Melon Dog to lead me to Luca.

While we were co-workers at Jackson, Uranus had invited me to a few family backyard cookouts, so I knew where he lived. Within a block of Uranus's home, three young punks blocked the sidewalk and stopped me. One guy was wearing a Miami Dolphins ball cap, and the other two had wool beanie-style caps that glistened with silver beads of water collected from the gentle rainfall.

"What you doing 'round here, Crackah? You be in the wrong hood now, boy. You best jet before me and you shoot the five."

"Don't want any trouble, dude. I'm here to visit my friend," I said.

"Who 'round here be yo friend, whitey? You and your crooked cap and baggy ass pants best jet." The guy flipped the bill of my sideways cap, knocking it off my head.

"Hey, I said I don't want any trouble, dude...just looking for the Vampire." I picked up my cap.

"You know the Vampire?" asked the short guy.

"Yeah, I worked with him at the hospital."

"You know his bro—you know Mercury Johnson, too?" asked the guy with the Dolphins hat.

"Sure. I'm a friend of the whole Johnson family," I said.

"This cracka be all right. This white boy gots soul!" said the third guy.

"The cracka be stylin', too, Ravon. Look at that funky outfit he be wearing," said the little guy as he pointed at the blue denim shorts covering my exposed butt.

I pulled the baggy pants hanging down across the back of my thighs back up to my waist. "Nah, leave 'em down, bro! Those saggy pants be off the hinges. And where you get that slammin' I'm With Stupid tee-shirt...and them badass kicks, too? " he asked and pointed at my black rubber shoes with yellow polka dots.

"The homeless guys that have that street store across from Slick Willie's Trading Post are selling these tee-shirts," I said.

"Cool Whip, we best go over and boost a few of them shirts for the brothers."

"If I were you, I wouldn't steal from those guys. They're tight with the Boss. They work for the Boss," I warned them.

"Well, we got a few Washingtons we can slide their way, then... just to keep the peace. White boy, you tell the Vampire that Cool

Whip, Pee Wee, and Ravon say hey. Now we gonna gets some of them slammin' I'm With Stupid shirts and some big, saggy pants, too," said Cool Whip.

All three guys loosened their belts and pulled their pants down under their butts, exposing bright-colored boxer shorts. Then the guy with the Dolphins cap turned his hat on an angle, and the trio walked away, headed for the street shop in front of Slick Willie's.

A few months later I returned to visit Uranus and found that the streets of Overtown were filled with young guys walking around with baggy pants falling down below their butts. Many wore baseball caps cocked off to the side, and several guys were wearing the I'm With Stupid tee-shirts. The arrow pointed down to where the homies clutched their crotches as they walked with a short, gimpy shuffle, the same stride that I had used months earlier.

It surprised me that I had inadvertently started another new fashion trend. A teenager walked by clutching his crotch with his butt hanging out, prompting me to say a silent prayer. *God forgive me!*

Don't get caught with your pants down.

# Chapter 8

## A DAY IN THE DUMPSTER

### THURSDAY DECEMBER 27TH, 1973

As the misty rainfall came to an end and the sun began to burn through the low-lying cloud cover, the three punks left to go score some *I'm With Stupid* tee-shirts from my buddies. The dreary early morning sky began to brighten, and so did my mood when I recognized the Johnson residence two houses ahead on the left. Walking with my awkward shuffle, I approached the house. A large, black dog began barking at me as I neared. Thankfully, a four-foot-high chain link fence kept the dog penned in on the property.

"Good boy," I said in a soft voice.

The dog barked louder and bared his teeth when I stopped in front of the gate and spoke.

*He looks mean.*

"What do you want, mister?" someone inside the house called out from behind the darkened screen doorway. It was a woman's voice.

I recognized the voice of Uranus Johnson's youngest sister. "Is that you, Neptune? It's Eddie Ocean—Uranus's friend Eddie."

"Come here, Pluto. Come, boy." She called the dog and put him inside the house and then walked over to me at the gate. "Say hey, Eddie!"

"Hi, Neptune. When did you get that Rottweiler?" I asked.

"About eight months ago. We had a burglary when everyone was at work. So Papa got Pluto from the dog pound to guard the house during the day."

The tall, skinny girl had blossomed into a shapely young woman since the last time I saw her. "Wow! You have really grown up, Neptune. When was the last time I saw you—maybe a year and a half ago?"

"I don't know...been a while, though. What brings you 'round?" she asked.

"I came to see Uranus."

"Well, come back in about thirty minutes after Papa's gone off to work, and we can make that happen," she said as she stuck out her bubble butt and did a little wiggle with her hips.

"I'm talking about the Vampire—your brother, Uranus." I must have blushed; she seemed to enjoy my embarrassment.

"He's already gone to work." She looked me up and down with lustful eyes. "Mmm-mmm, boy, y'all filled out, too."

"Well, these ugly clothes are only temporary. I lost everything when my boat sank." Embarrassed by my attire, I held the pants up high to hide the arrow on my tee shirt.

"Don't like that funky outfit much...but what's underneath ain't half bad! I's always thought you was cute, Eddie. Nows you be lookin' more rugged...more handsome...sure do like that long, sun-bleached hair and tanned, weathered face, bro. Whatcha all been doin', anyway?"

"Sailing. I quit the hospital. Now I'm a sailor."

"Where you been sailing to, brother?"

"Sailing between here and the Bahamas...lived with some Native Americans near the Big Cypress Reserve for a while too."

"Well, if you bring your butt back later—say thirty minutes—my offer still stands. A sailor like you should get to know Goddess Neptune up close and personal. Come 'round later, and you might get to see the celestial body of your dreams, Captain Eddie Ocean." She did that little wiggle again.

"I have a job to check out. Maybe afterward I'll stop by for a visit, Neptune."

"I'll be waitin', Captain Ocean."

"Great! Hey, Neptune, in the meantime would you please tell Uranus that I'm searching for the little collie dog that he calls Hobo."

"Sure, no problem. I'll do that right now, Eddie." She twisted her body sideways, turned her head, looked down at her butt, and said, "Hey, anus. Keep a lookout for a collie dog called Hobo—and tell Eddie Ocean if you sees him."

We both laughed out loud. "How did your brother ever survive childhood with that name...Uranus?"

"You know my bro. Nothin' bother the Vampire. He be mister positive. That boy be our guiding light." Her supple lips parted to display a wide, brilliant smile; her dark skin accentuated the whiteness of her teeth.

*The skinny kid has grown into a beautiful young woman, but I sense that all this excessive flirting is really for show and no action.*

"How old are you now, Neptune?" I asked.

"Seventeen last week," she said.

"Only seventeen, girl? I might have to take a rain check before I get to know the Goddess Neptune any better! Like maybe in a year," I said.

"You'll never make it a whole year, Eddie Ocean. The goddess has irresistible, seductive superpowers."

I didn't doubt her. I'm pretty sure she's just play-acting, but best to keep my distance from this little temptress. "Well I've gotta run, Neptune. Don't forget to talk to Uran...I mean the Vampire." *Almost fell into that trap again.*

"Bye, Eddie. Keep that cute butt safe, now." She stared at my exposed blue denim shorts as I shuffled away.

It was 9:30 am when I arrived at the waste management company on NW 8th Street. The HELP WANTED sign was still posted, so I went to the trailer with the sign OFFICE hanging above the door. A rotund, middle-aged woman was sitting at the front desk doing some paperwork.

"Good morning. I'm here about the job, ma'am," I said.

"Hello, son. Do you know what the job entails?" she asked.

"No, but I'm desperate for work. With the bad economy and all the Vietnam vets returning home from the war, jobs are very hard to find."

"I know jobs are nearly nonexistent around here, but this job is almost always open. The longest anyone has ever lasted was one week."

"I'll last—I'll take the job!" I said enthusiastically.

"You look like a sweet kid. Maybe you should keep looking elsewhere," she said.

"Like I said, ma'am, I need to eat, buy myself some clothes, and find a place to live. What could be so bad about the job?"

"Better you see for yourself." She picked up a microphone and paged the foreman over an outdoor loudspeaker.

"Dickey Stroker, Dickey Stroker, please come to the office."

Shortly, a middle-aged black man came into the trailer. "What's up, Betty?" he asked.

"This young man wants the job. Would you show him what needs to be done?" She frowned and looked down at her pile of paperwork.

Dickey took me outside to a row of green garbage dumpsters. He explained the process.

"Dumpsters in need of maintenance are dropped off at this lot." One dumpster had been turned on its side, and we watched a guy with long hair, wearing coveralls and rubber boots, use a pressure cleaner to clean the inside of the dumpster. The smell of rotted garbage emanated from the milky-white sludge that flowed out from the container onto the ground.

"That's not so bad. I can handle that," I said.

"Pressure cleaning is one of the good jobs…don't need another pressure cleaning man," said Dickey. The dumpster was then turned back upright by a forklift operator, and the outside of it was pressure-washed. At that point the container was left to dry in the sun as the guy moved on to the next dumpster in line.

Dickey took me over to a dumpster that had been pressure cleaned and was dry. He pointed out spots on the outside of the container where the green paint was bubbling up.

"That's rust under the paint," he said as he used a screwdriver to chip away the bubbling paint to expose the rust pocket. Then he leaned over and looked inside the dumpster. I followed his lead. The dumpster still reeked of decayed material, even after the pressure cleaning.

"Look in here. See there—yeah right there, and also over there?" He pointed out spots where the gray paint on the inside of the garbage container had bubbled up.

"We need someone to get inside these dumpsters and take a grinder to those rust spots—grind it down to bare metal. Later the containers are spray painted by Jimmy." Dickey pointed to a guy across the lot, spray-painting a dumpster with a paint gun powered by compressed air.

"Now you saw it, do you still want the job?" Dickey asked me.

"Want, no. Need, yes. Yes sir, I'll take the job," I said.

"Can you start right now? If not, and another guy walks in off the street, he will get your job. We are way behind schedule as is," said the boss.

"Yes, I can start now, but can I get paid at the end of the day? I need to buy some work clothes and food."

"We normally pay on Friday—I'll talk to Betty. I think we can get you paid from petty cash. Oh, what's your name, kid?" Dickey reached out to shake my hand.

"Eddie Ocean, sir."

"Nice name. Welcome aboard, Ocean."

I took off my baggy pants, and my blue denim short-shorts drew a few snide comments from my co-workers as I climbed into the dumpster. Dickey handed me a powerful metal grinder that was powered by compressed air. When I began grinding away at the rust spot, the rotten material lodged in the honeycombed rust pocket sprayed out from the grinding disc, splattering my face and arms. The stench was disgusting. I pulled my I'm With Stupid shirt up to cover my mouth and nose as I ground away the rust.

The noise of the grinder was deafening inside the steel compartment, and dusty paint and rust particles choked me. The sun was rising higher in the sky, and its heat turned my dumpster into a steel oven that baked me along with the putrid, stinky garbage stew that splattered out from the hidden, honeycombed rust pockets. It was 11:55 am, and the thermometer below the clock on the outside wall of the office trailer registered a temperature of 79 degrees Fahrenheit. *This is December. How could anybody do this job in the summertime with 90-degree heat?*

Thankfully I heard a whistle sound, and then Dickey told me that I had a thirty-minute lunch break. After climbing out of my garbage can slow cooker, I drank a gallon of cool water. It was wonderful. Not having a lunch to eat, I drank more water to fill my aching belly and sat alone in the shade to rest.

*I'm sure none of my coworkers want to eat around me...not until I've had a long, hot shower. How long can I handle this disgusting job?*

My growling stomach answered that question. *You gotta do it until you find something better, dude!*

After lunch break I went back to work until the whistle sounded again at 4:00 pm. My day in the dumpster had finally come to an end. Dickey came over to me as I was putting away the grinder.

"You can use that hose outside the office to wash off, kid," he said.

"Thanks, sir."

"Well, you made it through the day, Ocean. Are you gonna show up in the morning?"

"Sure, I'll be here," I said.

"Great. Betty has money for you at her desk. See you at 7:00 am. Don't be late."

After hosing off and putting on the baggy pants, I went into the office. "Hi Betty."

"You're still alive, kid." She reached into a drawer and took out an envelope. "Here's your pay. Minimum wage is $1.60 an hour, but we pay the grinder $2.00 an hour cash. No sense in doing the new employee paperwork for a grinder. Nobody has lasted for over a week inside the cans." She scribbled on a pad of paper.

"So let's see, six and a half hours at $2.00 equals $13.00…here is your pay."

She handed me an envelope containing a ten-dollar bill and a five-dollar bill.

"Huh…hey, Betty, this is fifteen dollars."

"Considerer it a tip, kid. Looks like you need a hand up."

"Thank you so much. I really need this cash!"

"I can see that…I like your attitude, Eddie. Maybe Dickey will promote you to pressure washer if you keep doing good work."

"I want to be honest, Betty: This job is only temporary. I plan on getting a job at the docks as soon as possible. I'm a licensed sea captain," I said.

"Well, we're happy to have you as long as you want to stay. Have a nice night, Eddie."

I walked to Overtown and went into a Goodwill store I had passed earlier that morning. It was located at 2111 NW 22nd Avenue. Once inside the store, I began looking for clothing when I noticed one of the young punks who had accosted me on the street earlier. He was doing some shopping of his own. It was the short guy named Pee Wee. He looked about the store with shifty eyes, looking to see where the clerks were before turning his back and bending forward. I sensed that Pee Wee was trouble because the kid had initially been hostile toward me before learning that I was a friend of Mercury Johnson, the football star.

Pee Wee's shifty eyes fixed on me with a nasty glare, but then softened slowly as he recognized me. "Hey, white boy—whatcha name again, boy?"

"Eddie Ocean—and you're Pee Wee, right?"

"Right on, brother. I'm looking for a pair of those saggy, baggy-ass pants, so I can show my off my fine butt to the ladies." Pee Wee was looking at my sagging pants as I clutched them above my crotch.

"Well, that's funny. I'm here looking for a pair of pants that actually fit me so my fine ass ain't hanging out in the breeze."

"I'll take them baggies iffen you don't want 'em…and that slammin' tee-shirt too," said Pee Wee.

"Sure, as soon as I change clothes, you can have the baggies and the tee-shirt."

I found a nice pair of used jeans just my size for fifty cents.

"Hey, Pee Wee, what's happenin'?" Three more guys entered the store and walked over to Pee Wee. I had never seen these guys before. All four young men began picking through a rack of extra-large pants.

After finding three more outfits and a pair of used leather boat shoes, I went into the fitting room and changed my clothes. I threw my blue denim hot pants into the trash and then gave my old baggy pants and the I'm With Stupid shirt to Pee Wee.

"Better wash that shirt before you wear it, Pee Wee."

"Whew! It's ripe, bro…but I'll gets it washed up real good! Ocean, you welcome here in Overtown anytime, my man!"

"Thanks, Pee Wee. Where's the nearest hamburger joint?"

"Go right, then down four blocks."

I left Goodwill with my stomach growling. *I'm starving.*

Up ahead, the golden arches beckoned me, and I was able to walk normally now without tripping over my baggy pants. The smell of the hamburgers drove me crazy, so I quickened my pace.

It was 7:00 pm by the time I got back to skid row. With an aching back and weary arms, I went to bed early but on a full stomach for once.

## 1:00 PM SATURDAY, DECEMBER 29TH, 1973

After working all day Friday and a half-day on Saturday morning, grinding the dumpsters, I got off duty at one o'clock on Saturday with $31 in my pocket. Dickey said that I was doing good work.

Although disgusting, my newfound occupation came with excellent job security, for there seemed to be an endless supply of rusty dumpsters in the city of Miami. As soon as one green monster was hauled away, one more arrived on the lot. As they say:

Garbage in, garbage out

*Chapter 9*

# A DAY AT CHURCH

*Warning: It has been brought to my attention that the following chapter might be offensive to some readers. Any hidden meanings or double entendres reside solely in the perverse minds of some readers, not the author's.*

## SUNDAY, DECEMBER 30TH, 1973

Today is Sunday, my day off. Each morning since my arrival, my pent-house roommates have cooked up some grits and coffee, *but not on this lovely morning.* Brownie emerged from his cardboard box picking at the seat of his pants to find me staring longingly at the cold, empty hibachi grill.

"There's no hibachi today, Eddie. Are you coming to St. Peter's with us?"

"Church? No, I'm faithful, but I'm not much for religion, Brownie."

"Well, it's your loss, Eddie. I'm not Catholic either, but I go to St. Peter's every Sunday."

"Well, why go, then?"

"You see, if I sit and listen to the padre babble for thirty minutes, he gives me a good hot meal afterward," said Brownie as he pounded hard on the side of Moe's box with an open palm. "Up and at 'em, pervert—don't want to be late for church."

My stomach grumbled, and I reconsidered Brownie's offer. "Brownie, I've changed my mind. Let's go to church."

Over fifty skid row residents sauntered in small groups over to St. Peter's Catholic Church. It was about a mile away. While we were walking, John saw a woman he knew. She was walking up ahead of us among a group of five other disheveled people.

"Hey, Ima!" John called out and then jogged forward to catch up to her. The pair stopped walking and stood in the middle of the street talking as we approached them. The young woman was dressed in a very tight-fitting, low-cut black blouse that revealed her ample cleavage, and skin-tight black stretch pants, a very provocative ensemble for Sunday morning. Heavy makeup covered her face, and she carried a small bouquet of flowers. The woman appeared to be in her mid-thirties, and I could see that beneath the gaudy makeup and tacky outfit she was an attractive and shapely woman. When we approached, she turned her attention to me.

"Who's the new guy, John?"

"Hi, I'm Eddie Ocean. What's your name?" I asked her and extended my hand.

"Ima Hooker," she said as we shook hands.

"I kind of suspected as much. Your outfit is very sexy for a Sunday church service. But don't get me wrong—I don't mean to be judgmental. So what is your name?" I asked again.

"That's my name...Ima—Ima Hooker. I know Ima is an odd name; my parents were a pair of cartoonish hippies. They thought the name was funny," she said.

"Oh gosh, I'm sorry, miss," I said.

"Yeah, we lived on a commune in California, and my parents smoked more weed than a Rastafarian, but I think it was the

LSD—the acid—that cooked their brains. They named my brother Fish. Get it—Fish Hooker?"

I was mortified, not at the names but that I had bluntly told the poor woman that she looked like a hooker.

"Oh! I'm an idiot! Please excuse me, Ima! So sorry...."

"Don't be sorry. You're right. I'm a lady of the night. John is one of my best customers. I guess you could say that John is my favorite john." She put her arm around John Dumas's waist, and our band of misfits continued walking to church.

The church compound consisted of several buildings. We went into a large room adjacent to the main cathedral. The structure served as a combination cafeteria and recreation hall and had a kitchen in the back. Out front there was a podium with a microphone and a small mahogany organ off to the right side. Long tables with chairs were set up in rows. We all sat down together on the side closest to the organ. Soon a blind man wearing dark sunglasses walked out from the kitchen area tapping a long cane in front of him. He sat down at the organ. The bind man was very pale, bald headed, and slightly overweight.

"That's my friend Jack Kanoff," said Ima as she got up and went to the mahogany organ to place the lovely bouquet of flowers on its console. The organ player tilted his head back and sniffed the air.

"Is my gorgeous friend Ima Hooker here with us on this beautiful Sunday morning?" asked Jack as he rocked his head back and forth, breathing in the scent of the blood red flowers.

"Yes it's me, Jack. I've got your favorite flowers today, a bouquet of red tulips."

"I know! I can smell them, darling," said Jack.

A priest carrying a bible approached the podium.

"Jack, I'll talk with you at breakfast after the sermon." Ima scurried back to her seat.

Jack Kanoff had a broad smile as he reached out to touch the flowers. He gently stroked the velvety red petals with the tips of his fingers.

"Jack loves it when I put my tulips on his organ, and I enjoy pleasing him," Ima Hooker said.

The murmur of people talking died down, and then silence fell over the room as Jack began playing lovely music; it was a piece by J. S. Bach. When Jack stopped playing, the priest began his sermon. The priest spoke of the evils of greed and how we need to be more generous to our neighbors—an odd message to deliver to a group of destitute people, I thought. After the sermon there was a prayer of thanks, and then the nuns along with a group of volunteers brought food out from the kitchen.

"Yum! Haven't had pancakes for a while," I said as I poured maple syrup on my stack of hot cakes.

Jack Kanoff came over and sat next to Ima. The blind man seemed to find his way around the crowded room with ease.

"Jack, you get around very well," I said.

"Lots of practice," Jack said before stuffing a forkful of flapjacks into his mouth.

"Jack went blind when he was about fourteen years old," Ima told me as she passed Jack a bottle of maple syrup. "Here you go, darling."

Jack spoke while pouring the syrup. "She's right. My parents blamed my sudden blindness on my obsession with playing with my organ. They tried to forbid me from playing with it, but my organ was the only thing that gave me any pleasure in life. Do I smell bacon?"

"Yeah, Jack, there's some on your plate," Ima said.

"Aha!" Jack took a bite of bacon and then continued his story. "Well, the doctors said that my parents' belief that my playing excessively with my organ was causing me go blind was a myth—an old wives' tale. The doctors said it was actually a very rare disease that caused me to lose my sight, not excessive playing with my organ. All the experts agreed that excessive organ playing could have caused my carpal tunnel syndrome but not my blindness."

"Well, you play the organ beautifully," I said.

"If I had the choice—a choice that I could regain my eyesight by giving up playing my organ, I wouldn't take it. I would rather be blind than organ-less," Jack Kanoff said.

After breakfast, Jack left our group and went over to the main Cathedral to play the massive pipe organ for the Sunday Mass. The rest of us walked to a park in Madison Hammock and sat beneath a huge, beautiful banyan tree. We formed a semicircle and sat cross-legged on the grass talking about our lives. I listened as each member of the little group told their story and explained why they were living on skid row.

Moe Lester was first to speak. "I was a school teacher. A student lied about me—accused me of molesting her. So now I'm a registered sex offender and can't find a job. I've lost everything...so now here I am, a bum on skid row."

John Dumas spoke next. "My problem is I have a felony assault rap. Apparently nobody will hire someone considered a violent felon."

"What did you do, John?" I asked.

"Well, you know, I'm used to a-holes calling me 'John Dumbass' instead of 'John Dumas.' Heard it my whole life, but one day I took my son to work, and a guy that I hated said, "Hey, look—a big Dumbass and a little Dumbass." I pounded him to a bloody pulp. Spent six months in jail. Lost my job, my wife, my family—lost everything. What I regret most is being violent in front of my son."

It was Brownie Shytles turn to vent. "Do I need to explain my maladies? Nobody wants to be near me, let alone work with me. The doctors say that my gastrointestinal problems could be fixed by surgery, but I can't afford the operations, and I have no insurance. I need a colostomy, a bowel resection, and some other GI surgeries. Did you know that before my disease progressed, I was a well-known architect?" Brownie stood up and pointed north toward the downtown Miami skyline.

"See that glass tower, the tallest building on the left? I designed it, and the Omni Mall Building on Biscayne Boulevard...designed that one as well. I was on the verge of perfecting a revolutionary flexible building foundation, a design that would make high-rise buildings nearly earthquake-proof. But then I got sick and lost my job. My guts began rotting—rotting from the inside out, and no one could stand to be around me, so I lost my job."

"We like being around you, Brownie," said Ima.

"Well you're all skid row people. You're used to the stench of people, used to the smell of body odor and rotten garbage—used to the malodorous street life," said Brownie.

"Well, thanks a lot. That's not a very nice thing to say about your friends," Ima scolded Brownie.

"Sorry, Ima, no offense meant. What about you, Eddie?" Brownie changed the subject.

"My situation is only a temporary setback, cause by a shipwreck," I said.

"Eddie, that's what everyone says in the beginning. Everybody on skid row thinks their situation is only temporary when they first land here. Then the years fly past and nothing ever changes. Tell him, Ima," said Brownie.

Ima spoke next. "My downward spiral started in high school. With a name like Ima Hooker, no one would take me seriously. I was a joke. My fate was sealed. I got tired of fighting back. Dropped out of high school, ran away...lived on the streets. Thought my life of ill repute was only temporary, but I'm still waiting for my knight in shining armor to rescue me and take me off the street."

We were all distracted when three attractive young coeds wearing University of Miami sweatshirts rode past us on bicycles. The young women stopped a short distance away. They dismounted and locked their bikes onto a bike rack and then began doing yoga in an open grassy area.

"Excuse me. I'll be right back." Moe got up and started walking toward the bike rack.

"Don't do it, Moe!" Brownie called out.

Moe Lester went to the bikes and appeared to be closely examining them.

"Is he trying to steal a bike?' I asked.

"No, it's worse than that, Eddie. Moe is a very sick man."

Moe bent over to put his face close to the bicycle seats. We could see him inhaling and exhaling deeply.

"Oh my God! Is he sniffing the bicycle seats?" I asked in disbelief.

Moe realized that the girls had noticed him messing with their bikes, so he casually walked away and sat on a park bench facing them. He sat there in his grimy raincoat, ogling the young women as they contorted and stretched their fit young bodies. Again the image of Aqualung came to my mind as I watched Moe Lester undress the girls with his eyes. The lyrics of the Jethro Tull Band came to mind. The song "Aqualung" was playing in my head as I watched Moe Lester fumbling around beneath his raincoat.

"Sitting on a park bench Dah Dah Dah
Eyeing little girls with bad intent
Hey Aqualung!
Snot is running down his nose
Greasy fingers smearing shabby clothes
Hey Aqualung!"

When one girl became suspicious and started glancing over at Moe Lester with narrowed eyes, he stopped fidgeting under his coat and looked away, pretending to be interested in the pigeons strutting around near his feet.

Ima stood up, "He's gross! Let's get out of here." We all followed her lead, and on the walk back to skid row, Moe Lester was the topic of our discussion.

"I don't think that Moe Lester is as innocent as he claims to be," I commented. No one replied.

We couldn't get away from the scene of Moe Lester's perversion fast enough!

A man is known by the company he keeps.

# Chapter 10

## IMA'S INTERVIEW

### 6:00 AM MONDAY, DECEMBER 31ST, 1973

My sleep was restless. Nightmares of Aqualung stalking me with a pickaxe had me tossing and turning until I awoke just before dawn. The song "Aqualung" kept playing over and over in my head as I ventured outside, weary and overtired. The year 1973 was ending on a wet and rainy note in South Florida as a cold front brought a steady rainfall that soaked many of the inhabitants of skid row on the morning of New Year's Eve. From my penthouse perch above the tent city, I observed the shivering mass of humanity huddled below.

*Wish I could do something for those poor souls.* My thought was interrupted when Ima Hooker emerged from Moe Lester's shack.

"Good morning, Eddie."

"Hey, what you doing here, Ima?" I asked as I turned to see her.

"Moe Lester got himself arrested again. Happened yesterday, in Madison Hammock."

"Why? What happened?" I asked.

"After we left Moe at the park, he flashed those young college girls—the three girls doing yoga." Ima stood in front of Moe's cardboard shack adjusting her bra. With her hands under her tight-fitting red sweater, she adjusted her ample bosom.

*The bigger the better, the tighter the sweater! Oh no, is Moe Lester rubbing off on me?*

The sight of the attractive young woman made me long for female companionship, and I closed my eyes. My dopey, groggy mind wandered off again, and I closed my eyes and began dreaming of my lost love, Little Hooters, as Ima finished her brassiere adjustment.

"Are you falling asleep on your feet, Eddie?"

"Sorry, just daydreaming. You look very nice this morning, Ima."

"Really? I haven't even put on my makeup yet."

"I like you better without that heavy makeup, Ima. You look younger. So, why did you move into Moe's shack?"

"I felt like having a little privacy, so I checked out of the shelter yesterday. I plan on watching over Moe's place until he gets out of the slammer."

"Well, welcome to the penthouse, neighbor. This is where you get to mingle with the upper crust of skid row society." My fatigue was causing me to act silly. I bowed low with my arm across my waist, and she responded with a graceful curtsy.

"I've got to get to work now, Ima. I'll be grinding and scraping those God-awful dumpsters all day. My job is hell, but it's the only one I could find."

"Okay, see you later, handsome. Happy New Year's Eve!" she called out as I waved goodbye and scooted down the steep concrete embankment.

When I arrived at the Garbage Guys lot, Betty was in the office doing paperwork. She informed me that there was no work for me today. "We should have told you, kid—we don't work in the rain. Can't prime or paint in this weather. Sorry about that—and tomorrow's New Year's Day, so it looks like you got a couple days off, Eddie."

"Darn, I needed the money, Betty—but, oh well, I do have a few errands to run."

My new plan for the day was to visit Rosalina at the Miami *Post* to see if she might help me find Melon Dog, and then go to the marina to apply for a captain's position with Sun 'N' Fun Sailing Charters. My garbage-stained work clothes would not make a good impression on anyone, so I went back to the penthouse to change into nicer clothes. When I returned, Ima was sitting on a chair in front of Moe's shack, sketching the tent city below.

"What happened, Eddie? Did you get fired?" she asked me.

"No. Work was canceled because of the rain. Hey, are you an artist?"

"No, I just doodle. Been doing it forever. When I was a little kid, drawing used to help me escape reality and my insane parents." She squinted her eyes, which made her forehead wrinkle as she intently focused on the tent city below. Then she looked down and scribbled on the inside lid of a discarded cardboard pizza box.

"Eddie, have you noticed how skid row is organized?" she asked.

"It's just a mess of boxes and tents."

"No, not really. See that far right quadrant, where the adults have kids...the ones living in parked cars? They are the families that were just one paycheck short of a mortgage or rent payment. Now look over there. The left quadrant is full of chronic druggies and winos. Stay out of that area. Out back are the mental cases—the end-of-the-worlders; the king and queen of England live among that crowd." She continued drawing with rapid hand movements as she spoke.

"Hmm, I never noticed that before. Hey, Ima, is that a piece of charcoal from the hibachi that you're drawing with?"

"Yeah. You don't mind, do you? Works pretty good."

"No of course not." I said as I walked around behind her to see the drawing.

"Oh my God!" I gasped, shocked by her sketch.

"Is it that bad?" She stopped drawing and covered the cardboard box with her arms.

Ima's charcoal sketch was amazing. She had impeccably captured the soul of the miserable, dreary, rain-drenched people in the tent city below. Her depiction of their weathered, desperate faces brought a tear to my eye.

"Are you kidding me, Ima? You really don't know how good this sketch is? You are an incredible artist!" I moved her arms off the pizza box; I couldn't stop looking at the intricate detail of her work. The emotion and hopelessness of the place that Ima had captured in her charcoal sketch jumped off the cardboard box like a 3D image.

"I've always been told that I suck at drawing...told that I suck at everything...huh, I guess literally and figuratively. Good joke, eh?" She chuckled cynically, but I didn't think it was funny.

"Ima, you've got to come with me today. I need to visit a reporter at the *Post* this morning. I want her to see your sketch." Ima suddenly became very angry and threw the pizza box off the ramp. It sailed like a frisbee before landing in a large mud puddle below.

"I don't want people looking at my sketches. I told you I suck. I know it, and don't need to hear it anymore!" She went into Moe's shack and pulled down the blanket to cover the entrance.

"Hey Ima, I'm sorry! Well...you could come along just to keep me company, not to draw. I need the help of a woman reporter—her name is Rosalina Rossi—need her to help find a lost dog." Secretly, I still hoped to get Ima to draw something for Rosalina. Ima had too much talent to waste.

Ima peeked her head out from the edge of the blanket. "Did you say dog? Lost dog? I love dogs. My parents said dogs are dirty and smelly. They never let me have my own dog." Ima pushed aside the blanket and came out of the box. "Okay. I'll go to help find the dog."

"Got a raincoat?" I asked her.

"No but we can borrow one of Moe's. That crazy old flasher has got a whole collection of raincoats in here." She pulled an old, dirty, threadbare London Fog trenchcoat from a pile of clothes in the corner.

"This one should fit you." She tossed me the coat and then found a pink, plastic raincoat for herself.

I examined the coat. *This London Fog was once top of the line, a very expensive coat. Some executive must have trashed it. Moe probably found it while alley shopping.* I put the coat on, and then we slid down the wet, slippery embankment. Ima laced her arm through mine and said, "Let's go, my darling. Maybe we will find your little lost puppydog."

We arrived at the entrance to the Miami *Post* building at 9:35 am. A burly guard dressed in a blue rent-a-cop uniform stopped us just inside the doorway.

"Can I help you people?" he asked.

"I would like to see Rosalina Rossi," I said.

"Have an appointment?" he asked in a gruff tone as he looked at the visitors' log.

"No, but I think she'll be glad to see me."

"No can do, buster. Need an appointment." He made arm motions, waving us away, back out the door, wanting us to leave.

As I turned to go, I overheard him speak to a sharply dressed guy wearing a brand new London Fog-style raincoat. "Can you believe the trash that wanders in here off the street? Good thing they got me guarding the door. That guy in the grimy trench coat is a pimp, and the woman's his hooker! I can spot 'em a mile away," the wannabe cop boasted to the businessman.

We walked across the street to the west side of Biscayne Boulevard, where there was a phone booth. I pulled a dime from my pocket and called Rosalina.

"Good morning, This is the Miami *Post*. How may I direct your call?" asked an operator.

"Rosalina Rossi, please. She's a reporter on the Entertainment Today section."

"Thank you. One moment, please." After a short delay the operator returned on the line. "Sir, Ms. Rossi no longer works at entertainment. She is now assistant news editor. I will connect you."

"Thanks"

A secretary answered the call and connected me to Rosalina's desk. I explained that we were outside the building but could not get past the guard. Rosalina told me that she would come down to escort us inside, so we walked back across the street and waited on the sidewalk outside the main entrance. From behind the large plate glass window, the nosy security guard gave us the evil eye. A few minutes passed, and then Rosalina came outside to greet us.

"Hi, Eddie. It's wonderful to see you again. I heard the report about your *Watermelon* boat being sunk. Thank God you're okay!" She hugged me and kissed my cheek.

"Thanks, Rosalina. It was a close call—that's for sure. I want you to meet Ima. She's my penthouse neighbor."

"Pleased to meet you, Rosalina," Ima said as they shook hands.

"Let's go inside and talk," Rosalina said.

The guard had a sour expression as we walked toward him. Ima winked and swiveled her hips in an exaggerated motion as she strutted past the grumpy guard.

"I guess anyone can get in here nowadays," he mumbled disapprovingly to Rosalina.

We went into Rosalina's office and sat in front of her desk.

"Eddie, I received a promotion after my story about you and your Indian friends ran in the Sunday paper. People were talking about you for weeks. I owe you one. How can I help you?" she asked as she pushed a stack of papers to the side of her desk.

"You remember the collie on the pier? The one that wouldn't get into your car and then ran away into the city?"

"Of course I remember him."

"Well, after you left, the dog came back and jumped onto our boat—a stowaway!'

"Did you ever find his owner?"

"No. After the shipwreck we were separated, and now the dog is lost, running loose in the streets. We wanted to see if you could help us find him. He belongs to a boy named Luca."

"I would love to help. We could post some flyers at all the newspaper stands. I'll ask the newsstand operators to keep an eye peeled. Do you have a picture of the dog?" asked Rosalina.

"Darn, no I don't...but, hey! Ima could draw his picture from my description," I suggested.

"Eddie, I told you, nobody sees my drawings—nobody!" Ima was angry again.

I turned to Rosalina and said, "Ima is an amazing artist, but she's very shy. She doesn't realize her talent."

In a panicky voice, Ima said, "Talent! Rosalina, I've been told a thousand times how bad I suck. My parents always told me that my doodling was awful and that drawing was for babies and preschoolers, not for little girls."

I persisted. "But, Ima, Melon Dog's life might depend on us getting a good picture of him posted."

Ima squirmed in her seat nervously and began wringing her hands. "I want to help you—you know I want to help—but I don't know if I can. I can't draw in front of other people."

Rosalina stood up. "I'll leave you two alone. If you do decide to draw, here are pencils, pens, and paper. I'm going to get coffee. Anyone else want some?" Without waiting for an answer, Rosalina got up and left the office.

I described Melon Dog as best I could. In about five minutes, Ima finished her sketch but was reluctant to let me see it.

"Ima, the sketch is not going to do any good if no one can see it." I was becoming perturbed by her paranoia. We both sat in silence as she clutched the drawing tightly to her chest.

*Man, this poor girl is really messed up...really damaged. She doesn't have a shred of self-esteem; it must have been stripped away over many years of verbal and mental abuse.*

My train of thought was broken when she suddenly handed me the paper. "Here!"

"Holy crap! This looks like a black-and-white photograph of Melon Dog!" I was impressed.

Ima looked like she was about to cry. "Well, I only had a #2 pencil...no colored pencils." She lowered her head in shame.

"No, no, no! Black and white is fine! This is perfect! The picture is great, Ima. I'm trying to tell you that it's perfect. You even got his eyes. How could you do this when you never even saw the dog?"

"You're just saying that because we're friends, Eddie."

Rosalina overheard the remark as she returned to the office carrying three coffees. "Well I don't know you, Ima, so I'm not your friend, and furthermore, I've been told that I'm very demanding and hypercritical—a perfectionist. So let me see that drawing, Eddie." Rosalina took the paper from me as Ima cringed and slumped in her chair.

"The realism is extraordinary—almost like a photograph of the little dog that I saw on the pier. This looks like a professional sketch, Ima. You must have had some technical training."

"That's what I've been telling her, Rosalina!" I concurred.

Ima perked up. "Are you guys being honest? You're not going to turn this into a big joke on me, are you?"

"Rosalina, you should have seen the landscape of skid row that Ima drew on a pizza box. She used a hunk of charcoal from our grill! It was incredible!" I said.

"Listen, Ima, I'm a very busy middle-aged woman with two grown children and a demanding job. I don't have time to get inside your head and fix whatever it is that's wrong with you. You have an exceptional talent. The newspaper is always looking for a good artist like you. You are one in a million."

"What? Me? One in a million?" Ima perked up.

"I want you to draw this office with me and Eddie sitting here at my desk. This is your one shot—no whining. I need to see if the dog sketch was just a fluke or if you really are as good as I think you are."

I encouraged Ima. "Do it, Ima! This might be your shot to get off skid row." To my surprise, Ima picked up a sheet of paper and went to the far corner of the room. While holding the pencil extended out in front of her, she squinted and looked around the room. Then she began to draw. Her left hand moved rapidly. Ten minutes elapsed as Rosalina and I sat discussing our strategy for finding Melon Dog.

"Rosalina, finding the dog is just the first step. We need the dog to lead us to a young boy named Lucas or Luca. He is in grave danger. The registration number on the dog's tag should lead us to the boy."

"Okay, Eddie, when we locate the dog I will run his registration number. The number from the dog tag will give us the boy's home address." Rosalina scribbled a note.

"I'm done." Ima interrupted us. She stood clutching her drawing to her chest.

"Let's see," I said.

With her right hand Ima had to literally force her left hand to release the piece of paper, and I took the drawing from her. Just as with the landscape of skid row and the portrait of the dog, Ima's artistry depicted the office with the accuracy of a photograph. But there was more to it than just the realism: Somehow she had captured the pulse and personality of Rosalina's office space. How she perceived the shadows and the light seemed to be the key to her magic. She had transferred a living image onto the blank piece of paper.

"Wow! Look!" I handed the drawing to Rosalina.

"This is astounding! Where have you been hiding this girl, Eddie?" Rosalina asked me.

Ima answered, "Mostly at the homeless shelter, ma'am—but I'm over on skid row for now." She finally seemed to believe that we actually liked her artwork.

"The newsroom is looking for a good sketch artist to cover the 'Boss's' big racketeering trial next week. Cameras are not permitted in the courtroom, and Josh needs pictures for his report. He's not happy with the work of the freelance artist he's been using lately. Do you want a shot at that job here at the *Post*, Ima?"

Ima's eyes widened, and her head twirled. She looked up at the ceiling just before she went limp and fainted. Luckily I caught her right before her noggin hit the hard terrazzo floor.

"Eddie, she's not on drugs, is she?"

"Don't think so. Please, get her some water, quick!" I begged Rosalina.

When Ima came to, she opened her eyes and looked up at me, smiling. "Eddie, you are my knight in shining armor."

"You should be thanking Rosalina, not me," I said as Rosalina retuned with a cup of water.

"Thank you, Rosalina," Ima said.

"How old are you, Ima? If you don't mind my asking." Rosalina handed Ima the water.

"Twenty-five." Her young age surprised me. I had taken her to be about thirty-three. She was just a few years older than me. *Street life must be hard on people.*

Rosalina must have had the same impression, as she sounded surprised when she said, "Only twenty-five, Ima? You understand that this job offer is on a trial basis—no pun intended. We'll see how you do, Ima, but if you choke up or are into drugs—or anything else illegal—you'll be back out on the street in a flash."

"With a job I won't want or need to do anything illegal. Never again," Ima said as she stood up.

If your sketches at the trial are even half as good as what I've seen so far, you'll be a rising star here at the Miami *Post*. The whole world will be watching the big trial...the trial of the 'Crime Boss of Miami,' Tony Montana. The whole world will see your sketches, Ima!"

*Damn, Rosalina! Why did you have to go and say that!* But to my surprise, the fact that the whole world might see Ima's sketches did not upset her. She smiled and looked pleased by the comment, no longer frightened.

Rosalina took Ima's sketch of Melon Dog to a copy machine and made a dozen copies.

"Take these and post them around the city, Eddie. Here are some tacks. After these pictures are posted, eventually the dog will turn up."

A picture is worth a thousand words.

*Chapter 11*

# NEW YEARS EVE

## MONDAY, DECEMBER 31ST, 1973

The rain ceased as the cold front pushed south past Miami and into the Florida Keys. The clearing sky brought a chill to the air on New Year's Eve 1973. Ima and I took a long, meandering route home, tacking up the MISSING DOG posters at corner newsstands and on telephone poles as we walked. Rosalina's office phone number was printed on each poster under Ima's sketch of Melon Dog.

At 4:05 pm we arrived home and climbed the slope up to the penthouse. Down below I could see some men stacking old wooden pallets in an open space located well away from the tents and shacks of skid row.

"What do you think those guys are building, Ima?"

"A bonfire. Every year we have a Big O Skid Row New Year's Eve party with a bonfire, music, dancing—stuff like that. The Boss usually brings us some adult beverages."

"But Rosalina said that the Boss is a mobster. She said that he's going on trial."

"Yeah. His real name is Tony Montana. He's a Cuban refugee who came to Miami with nothing but the shirt on his back. He became involved in organized crime and was so ruthless and street smart that he quickly took over the city. He's become Miami's godfather. He's a ruthless killer. But to us street people he's like Robin Hood. I know he isn't truly generous to the poor—or, what I mean, it's not out of kindness. He buys influence and uses us to run scams.

We work for him as lookouts and provide information. We provide cover for his illegal operations. Montana does lots of drug smuggling, loan sharking, insurance scams, gambling, and other racketeering—he's into everything illegal."

"Aren't you worried about covering his trial and drawing him in the courtroom? He's going to see you...he'll see your sketches of him, and you said the guy is a ruthless killer."

"I plan on making him look real good...making his portrait flattering. I wouldn't want Montana as an enemy, Eddie."

John and Brownie arrived and began climbing up the embankment.

"Hi, Ima. What's happening, Eddie?" John asked.

"Well, I got a job!" Ima said and sprang to her feet.

"Of course you do! It's New Year's Eve, Ima! I'm sure you'll have lots of work tonight. Girl, you're gonna be busy, all right!" said John.

John sat down and said to Ima, "Brownie and I had a good day at the street stand selling those 'I'm With Stupid' tee-shirts. We made good money today—so since I got some extra cash, can I make an appointment with you for a date later tonight, babe? We can bring in the New Year with a bang."

"Sorry, John, but I found a real job. I start next week. Gonna retire from the escort business."

"Say it's not true! Eddie, is she serious? What kind of job?" John was upset.

"Yep. Turns out Ima is an artist *extraordinaire*, John. She's gonna work at the Miami *Post* newspaper, drawing sketches."

"No crap! That's just great," said Brownie Shytles. He hugged Ima and then picked at the seat of his pants.

"What's so great about it? I've always been a loyal customer, Ima! What about me? Who will keep me company now?" asked John.

"You'll find a new girl to date. Why not try Tricksy Turner—she's always looking for work? There are plenty girls for you, John, but I'm out of the business, fellas!" I had never seen Ima look so happy.

John stopped his whining as our attention was drawn to two black stretch limos that pulled into the area of skid row near the stack of wooden pallets. The doors opened on the lead car, and some intimidating-looking men wearing sunglasses and dark suits took defensive positions surrounding both vehicles. One guy looked up at us with binoculars. Ima waved to him, and he relaxed his rigid stance when he recognized her. Then a guy opened the back door of the second car, and a man got out. Even from this distance I recognized the frightening face of the Boss Man, Tony Montana.

"That's him, that's the Boss. He's must be out on bail. I'm going down to say Hi. Do you want to meet the Boss, Eddie? He might have a job for you to do," said John.

"No, thanks. Rather not."

John scurried down to ground level and jogged over toward the limos. Montana opened the trunk of his car and began removing things and handing them out to a growing crowd of people gathering around his limo. I could not tell what he was giving away. Later I found out that he was distributing food and bottles of champagne. With two honks of its horn, a delivery truck pulled into the same area, stopped, and then two guys began unloading kegs of beer. They put the kegs into garbage cans and then covered them with ice.

"Looks like there will be some partying going down tonight, Ima," I said.

"Will you be my date, Eddie? That will help keep the drunks off me."

"Sure, Ima. That would be my pleasure."

"I'll help protect you, too," said Brownie as he vigorously picked at his butt in between hacking coughs.

"Thanks, Brownie." Even though the guy was revolting, Ima was always kind to him.

We stood around watching the activity below until Brownie went down to join the party and Ima went into Moe's shack to get ready for New Year's Eve. At ten o'clock some guys used gasoline to start the bonfire. People had been playing music, singing, and dancing since sunset. Many revelers were already plastered, and the fire further riled up the growing crowd.

"I'm ready to join the party—Eddie?" Ima came out of Moe's shack. She was not wearing her usual provocative clothing, and her makeup was less gaudy and more tasteful.

"You look very pretty tonight—more wholesome than usual. You even look younger, Ima," I said.

"Thanks, no need for me to show off my goods anymore. I feel great, like a different girl. Like a new girl!"

"You *are* a sweet girl, Ima. Why did you get into hooking anyway?"

"Why did you get into the dumpster grinding business, Eddie?"

"Okay, I get your point. No choice—you were desperate just like me."

"Let's go party," she said.

We went down to the fire and got a couple of ice-cold beers. A boombox played a funky song by the group War. It was called "The World Is a Ghetto." I put my beer on top of a crate and then took Ima's cup from her and placed it next to mine.

"What's this?" she asked as I took her hand and put an arm around her waist.

"It's called dancing." I began to dance with her, and she did a slow spin. She twirled smoothly beneath my raised arm and in perfect rhythm to the beat.

"You're a good dancer. Very light on your feet," I said.

"Not so bad yourself."

As we danced, I sang the lyrics to the song that was playing.

"Don't you know…that it's true.

That for me…and for you.

The world is a ghetto."

"You have a good singing voice, too. Are you trying to seduce me, Eddie Ocean? Because it's working."

After our dance we sat on milk crates, staring into the fire. The glowing embers and smell of burning wood brought back memories of all the fires and sumptuous feasts that I had shared with the Whatchacallit Indian Tribe in the Big Cypress Preserve. The fire made me miss my Native American friends and think of them. *Those were good people. They not only saved my life, they adopted me as one of their own. What I wouldn't give to have Little Hooters sitting beside me right now.*

"Why the sad face all of a sudden, Eddie?" asked Ima.

"Just missing some old friends—the Whatchacallit people. They are good, honest people. They take care of one another," I said as I noticed a wino steal his friend's bottle of champagne after the fellow walked away to take a leak.

"The Whatchacallits? What's a Whatchacallit?"

"Sorry, Ima. I forgot that I never told you about them. They're a tribe of Native Americans that I lived among. I'll tell you the story some other time. Not in the mood now." I could not get the image of Little Hooters out of my mind as I stared into the fire. In my mind she was frozen in time, sitting alone on that white sandy beach where I had left her.

"I need to stop staring at this fire. Let's dance again," I said.

We had several more dances and drank more beer as the time flew by. Then suddenly everyone was counting down along with the radio DJ, whose voice shouted from the boombox.

"Five, four, three, two, one!" The DJ played "Auld Lang Syne," and everyone sang together and then made a toast with the champagne that the Boss had given to us.

"Happy New Year, Ima. I think 1974 is going to be a great year for you!" I kissed her lips, but she recoiled.

"I'm sorry—I don't like being kissed. I haven't kissed for a long time, Eddie. You're a decent guy; you don't want to kiss a girl like me."

"Tonight you're a new girl, Ima. You are reborn. The year is now 1974, and this is the first day of your new life. A brand new and improved Ima Hooker has been born, and you're a professional woman now—a professional artist. Here's to you, Ima!" I raised my cup and took a sip. Two drunks interrupted us and tried to grope and kiss Ima.

"Happy New Year, babe!"

I pushed them away. "Get off her, a-hole!"

"See what I mean, Eddie? To them I'm good for only one thing."

"Ima, it's getting crazy down here. Let's go up to the penthouse."

We sat outside our boxes for a while, talking about her new career. I tried to build her confidence, but the poor girl was badly damaged. I realized that her healing process would be long and slow.

"The best thing for you now is to get started at work, to get busy right away. Maybe Rosalina has a project that you can start before the trial begins next week. I'll talk to Rosalina about that tomorrow," I said.

"That would be wonderful. I can't wait to get a paycheck and get a room of my own. Can't wait to get off the street and away from those jerks down there." She nodded at the drunks stumbling around the bonfire.

"Well, I need to change my life, too. I need to get out of that dumpster diving job. Tomorrow I'm going to see about a job as a charter boat captain over at Sun 'N' Fun Sailing."

"But tomorrow is New Year's Day, Eddie."

"I know, but the charter boats will be operating. People are off work, and some will want to celebrate New Year's by going sailing.

"Wow, it's already 2:30 am. We'd better get some sleep, Ima."

"Good night and happy New Year, Eddie," Ima said as she went into Moe's shack.

I went into Riley's box and dropped the blanket to cover the door. Despite the noisy, rowdy crowd below I fell asleep quickly, dreaming about Little Hooters. In my dream, she had pretty yellow flowers in her jet-black hair. We were sitting beneath the Australian pines at the Kissing Place, gazing at the stars above. When I kissed her, the sweet taste of honeysuckle flowers was still on her lips. And again that old truism came to mind:

A moment on the lips, forever in the heart.

*Chapter 12*

# MY HORRIBLE BOSS

## TUESDAY, JANUARY 1ST, 1974

The Miami Marina was bustling with activity on New Year's morning. Bleary-eyed, hung-over tourists from the hotels were already in the Tiki Bar drinking Bloody Marys.

"What'll it be, bub?" the bartender asked me.

"Happy New Year. Just coffee for me this morning, sir."

"You get that at the buffet table, kid."

Two thirty-something guys trying to hold down the greasy eggs and sausages that they had eaten from the buffet table were drinking Alka-Seltzer. After getting my cup of coffee, I followed the two guys out toward the docks. The guy in the Guy Harvey tee-shirt stopped short, moaned, and almost puked before taking a sip of the Alka-Seltzer.

The other guy mocked his buddy, "Come on, wussie! We're already late for the fishing boat!" I passed the pair of stumbling drunks and approached a party-boat captain waiting patiently on the dock behind his drift fishing boat.

"You looking for the Blue Heron?" he asked me.

"No, sir. But those two guys coming up the dock behind me might be."

"Oh, brother, this is gonna be another messy, gut-wrenching trip! Once one of those landlubbers feeds the seals, it starts a chain reaction, and they all start hurling over the side!"

The two stragglers were ten minutes late and had delayed the fishing trip, which did not please a dozen sober guys and gals who had shown up early. The other fishermen were pissed off, and I heard a few snide remarks directed at the drunks as they boarded the boat.

The captain laughed when the guy in the Guy Harvey shirt stumbled and grabbed the handrail to keep from falling down. "I feel sick," he moaned.

"Hey, Jimbo, we might not need to use all that frozen chum on this trip. Only thaw out half. These guys will be chumming the water before we even get out to the reef."

Jimbo laughed as he threw off the dock lines. "Already put one block back in the freezer, Cappy."

It was 8:30 am when I located the office of the Sun 'N' Fun Sailing Charters, and they were open for business, so I went inside.

"Happy New Year!" A very short woman with frizzy hair, thick, round eyeglasses, and buck teeth greeted me. She wore a white top that exposed her midriff above a pair of skin-tight blue Capri pants and white sneakers.

"Happy New Year," I replied.

"Welcome to Sun 'N' Fun. Let me show you our fleet." Before I could tell her that I was there to apply for a job, she hustled me out back to the docks. She was jabbering incessantly, and I couldn't get a word in edgewise.

"At the moment, you have your choice between three mono-hulls ranging from 33 feet to 48 feet or three catamarans ranging from 36 feet to 49 feet. Those boats are in port and available right now."

"I can sail any…"

Before I finished my sentence, she talked over me again with her heavy New York accent. "You look like an experienced sailor. Are you interested in a bare-boat charter, or do you require a professional captain? I would guess by the look of you that you are a bare-boater. You look like a sailor, but if not we also provide captains and sailing lessons." The hyper little woman was obviously trying to charm me in an attempt to close the sale, but she only came across as impatient and annoying as hell.

"Ma'am, I'm not here to charter a boat, I'm…"

Again she interrupted me. "What? Not here for a charter boat? Well then, why are you wasting my time?" she turned off the charm as quickly as switching off a lamp and turned her back on me as she walked back toward her office. I followed her until she stopped, turned around, and said, "What do you want now? I don't give free boat shows, mister."

"I've been trying to tell you ma'am, I'm a licensed boat captain, and I've come to inquire about a job."

When she was not pretending to be a nice person, she had an annoying habit of wrinkling up her nose, which accentuated her big buck teeth. "A job! A job! We have no job openings! Why do you think we have a job opening?" She was shouting now and waving her stubby little arms around. I could not decide if she resembled a rat or a rabbit when she squinched up her piggy little nose.

"Well that's what I came here to find out. I desperately need a job, ma'am. My boat was run down by a freighter on Christmas morning, and I lost everything."

"Hey! Are you the guy who was in the newspaper? Were you the captain of that *Watermelon* boat that was sunk by a freighter a few days ago?"

"Yeah, that's what I just said."

"I read the report of your accident, and then I remembered a while back I had seen another article about you and your Native

American friends in the Sunday Miami *Post*. You and your Indian friends were the talk of the town for several weeks. The article claimed that you hang out with a bunch of South Beach celebrities…and those jet setters that live over on Star Island. Well, do you? Is that all true?"

I was about to say, "Not really," but she was calming down now, and suddenly the angry little troll was morphing back into the charming albeit hyper little lady again.

"Well, yes, I do have some connections here in Miami."

Suddenly she was interested in my dilemma and my problems. "Well, now, I can't ignore a fellow sailor who is in need, can I? It's the first rule of the sea, to help a fellow sailor in distress. Perhaps I could take you on as a part-time, per diem back-up captain. It's the busy season and you will get some work, just not full-time. Are your papers all in order? When are you available?" Again she asked questions without waiting for my answers.

"I would be fine with…" I wanted to tell her that part-time work would be just fine, but it was impossible to finish a sentence.

"Come inside. I'll get the information that I need and tell you how we pay. Now…I'm sure some of those fancy friends of yours enjoy sailing, don't they? When you get them to schedule a charter, I want to take some pictures of them on my boats to use in our brochures." The woman seemed to care only about my bringing her the business of rich and famous celebrities. I sensed that she did not really care a whit about my personal problems or me.

"Let me copy your credentials. I'll need your Merchant Marine captain's license, first responder's certificate, and social security card, and such. Oh, by the way…what's your name?"

"It's…"

"Oh, right, I remember now. The *Post* said your name is Eddie Ocean."

"That's right." Yippee! I'd finished a sentence, even if it was only two words!

"So, where's your license?"

"Everything was lost at…"

"Never mind, I can call it in…verify it with the Coast Guard. Just need your social, then. Write it down, please."

"What's your name, ma'am?"

"Oh, I'm sorry, how silly of me. I'm Dr. Jill Hamm. Welcome aboard, Captain Eddie." She turned on the charm again and smiled as she shook my hand. My stomach felt queasy as I sensed that the little shrew was flirting with me.

"Oh you're a doctor?" I asked.

"Yes, but not a medical doctor. I'm a PhD. I have a doctorate in Maritime Sciences." She sucked in her bare midriff and puffed out her puny little chest as she walked over to a wall where several framed documents were hung neatly in a row. She extended her right arm under the documents with her palm facing up like Vanna White presenting a prize on the *Wheel of Fortune* TV show. Proudly she posed for me in front of her doctorate degree.

"Very impressive," I said with a sarcastic tone. She did not seem to recognize my sarcasm; she was too enthralled with herself and her documents.

*I have only just met this nasty little woman, but she is the most annoying and disgusting human being I've encountered in quite a while.*

"Ocean, I'm going to give you a pager—a beeper. You must be on call 24/7. You're not a big drinker or anything, are you?"

"No, not really. I do…"

"We conduct random drug tests, Captain Ocean. I hope that's not a problem either."

"I don't do…"

"Well, anyway, I'll be in touch. Here, take my card."

She handed me a business card that was hard to read because the print was so small. A picture of her homely face and frizzy, Brillo pad hairdo took up all the space on the card. *What, no tiara for the head of this little princess?*

"Doctor Hamm, do you mind if I post a flyer of my lost dog in your waiting room?"

"It is company policy that only information related to the business may be posted on company property, so no, you may not. Anyway, I don't like dogs. Dogs are dumb and smelly animals. I can barely even tolerate cats."

I couldn't get out of the mean little woman's presence fast enough. Working for this spoiled little brat might have me longing for my dumpster job.

Hamm followed me to the door with her big, buck-toothed smile. *Uck! She's flirting again. I need to get out of here. I need a stiff drink.* I left the office and looked across the marina and saw the palm frond-thatched roof of the Tiki Bar. *Hmmm, those Bloody Marys with the celery sticks that I saw earlier looked pretty damn good.*

I decided to stop at the Tiki Bar to get a Bloody Mary before returning home to skid row. A woman had replaced the male bartender.

"One Bloody Mary...extra spicy please," I said to the barmaid.

"You want the breakfast buffet too?"

"No, thanks. I'm short on cash. But if you could put extra celery and carrot sticks in that Bloody Mary, I would appreciate it."

"Sure, no problem."

"Oh, I'll take one of those Slim Jims, too." I put the Slim Jim in my Bloody Mary.

"Hey that's clever!" she said as I took a bite from the stick of spicy mystery meat.

"Tastes real good."

The drink helped me relax and get the nasty little doctor's image out of my head. I finished my breakfast of spiked tomato juice with vegetables and then left the marina.

After walking home, I spent the rest of New Year's Day playing chess with some guys on skid row. We listened to college football on the radio as we played. Everyone was wagering on the games and was either cheering or groaning after each score. I won some money when Penn State beat Baylor 41 to 20 but then lost my winnings and then some later on when USC defeated Ohio State 18 to 17 in the Rose Bowl. Even though some of my hard-earned money was lost, I had a lot of fun on skid row that New Year's Day of 1974.

A fool and his money are soon parted.

*Chapter 13*

# HOBO COMES HOME

## WEDNESDAY, JANUARY 2ND, 1974

Someone pounding on the side of my cardboard box woke me from a deep sleep. It was only 4:03 am.

"Who the hell's in there?" The angry voice came from just outside my door.

"I'm Eddie Ocean. Who are you?" I asked.

"Riley Ford. You're in my hut."

I pushed aside the blanket covering the doorway and came out.

"What are you doing in my shack?" asked Riley Ford.

"Your buddies said I could use your hut until you got out of jail."

"Well, as you can see, I'm out." Riley was not very friendly. Angry is what he basically was.

"No problem. I'll gather up my things," I said.

Riley's loud voice awakened Ima, and she peeked out from Moe's box.

"Eddie, you can stay in here with me," she said as she pushed aside her door covering.

"Oh, hi, Ima. I got released from jail," said Riley.

"I can see that, Riley. Eddie meant you no disrespect. We told him he could stay in your shack."

In the presence of Ima, Riley's demeanor changed, and he became friendlier. "No problem, Ima. Is Moe in there with you?"

"No, Moe is in jail...he's doing time for flashing some young college girls. It's like a revolving door with you guys. One guy gets out of the slammer, and another gets locked up."

"What were you arrested for, Riley?" I asked.

"None of your business, kid." My prying question caused Riley's hostility to return in a flash.

"Come inside, Eddie. Good night, Riley!" Ima seemed irritated by Riley's rudeness.

I went inside to share Moe's shack with Ima. "I have to get up in about two hours, Ima. Gotta go to work for the Garbage Guys one last time, and then I'm giving Dickey Stroker my notice of resignation. After tomorrow morning I'll be returning to the sea."

"Good for you, Eddie. You're a sea captain and an ocean diver, not a dumpster diver." Ima began to spread out some raincoats across the floor near her bed. "I'm tired too, Eddie. You can lie on these raincoats. I'll see you in the morning. Good night."

"Good night, Ima."

The beep from my wristwatch alarm woke me at 6:15 am. I looked at the pager that Jill Hamm had given to me to make sure the beeping sound wasn't coming from the pager, and then, to avoid waking Ima, I quietly collected what I needed and went outside. Brownie was standing over the hibachi brewing coffee and cooking grits.

"'Morning, Brownie," I said.

His expression changed from friendly to concerned when he noticed the pager clipped to my hip. "Did the Boss give you that pager, Eddie? If you're smart you won't go to work for that mobster. That's what got Riley locked up; he got fingered for fencing stolen jewelry for the Boss. Once you join the mob, you'll never get out...only way out is dead, rolled up in a carpet and dumped in the Miami River."

"Don't worry, Brownie. This pager is from Sun 'N' Fun Sailing Charters. I got a part-time captain's job." *Brownie is such a good guy;*

*he's always looking out for other people. He's like a surrogate father figure for some of us skid rowers. It's a shame the poor fellow has those awful maladies...wish I could help the guy.*

"Well, congratulations, Captain Ocean!" said Brownie as he handed me a cup of hot coffee.

"Thanks, Brownie. You're a scholar and a gentleman. Darn, I gotta get going. Need to spend one last day in those damn dumpsters. One last time so that Dickey and Betty can find a guy to replace me." I finished my coffee and stood up. "Thanks for the coffee, Brownie. I'll have to skip the grits today. See you later."

I walked to work enjoying the beautiful morning. With the prospect of a decent job, a light was now visible at the end of my dark tunnel of despair and poverty.

After punching the time clock, I found Dickey and told him about my new captain's job. He was not upset that I was leaving—he was glad for me and reposted the HELP WANTED sign on the front gate. During my morning shift, two men came to inquire about my job, but neither one would take it after watching me grind away a few rust pockets. But then, just before the four o'clock whistle ended my final day of work inside the dumpsters, a guy with disturbingly troubled eyes and dressed in army fatigues accepted my job. He looked hungry.

"See you in the morning, soldier," I heard Dickey say to the new guy as I went into the office to collect my final pay.

After paying me, Betty gave me a hug. "We'll miss you, Eddie Ocean. You take care of yourself, kid." That was the last day of my short career in the dumpsters. *Now I have another skill to add to my resume: Engineer of Dumpster Renovations.* I chuckled as I walked out the front gate.

The pay phone on NW 8th was in use, so I continued walking toward the Miami *Post* building, and on NW 4th Street I found an unoccupied phone booth from which I could call Rosalina.

"Hi, Rosalina. Did anyone contact you about Melon Dog?"

"No luck yet, Eddie. Just a couple of pranksters. They keep calling and saying that they have Hobo. They said Hobo is Melon Dog's real name."

"Yeah, they're right. The people at Jackson Hospital call him Hobo. Pranksters? How can you tell that they are pranksters?"

"Well they're just a couple of jokers. I almost fell for their prank at first, and I was writing down their information, but when I asked for their names they told me they were Patty Whacker and Uranus Johnson. Get it? Patty Whacker…like 'nick-nack paddy whack, give the dog a bone,' and Uranus, like 'you're an anus,' lady. I hung up before they could deliver the punch line."

"Rosalina, I know them. Those are real names. They are real people."

"What? Oh my gosh! I hung up on them without getting a phone number," Rosalina said.

"Don't worry. I know where they work—they're at Jackson Memorial Hospital."

"Let's go to Jackson, Eddie. My car is in the parking garage across the street."

We were halfway to Jackson Hospital when my pager went off. "Damn, that must be my boss."

"Who? Your boss the garbage guy?" Rosalina glanced over at me.

"Oh, I didn't have time to tell you, Rosalina. Yesterday I got a job at Sun 'N' Fun sailing, but it's only part time."

"That's great! I'll take you to the marina, and then I'll go to Jackson alone to find your two friends and Melon Dog—or Hobo— whatever that dog's name is." Rosalina made a u-turn.

"Thanks, Rosalina. How will I ever repay you for all your help?" I said as Rosalina dropped me off at the curb.

"You don't owe me. I owe you, Eddie. Ciao!" She sped away as I walked toward the Sun 'N' Fun office and then went inside to find Doctor Jill Hamm talking on the phone.

"Hello, Jill," I said.

"Hold on a sec." She spoke into the phone.

"What are you doing here, Ocean?" The little troll didn't even say hello.

"You paged me, Jill?" I said as I verified the phone number on my pager. *Yes, this is Jill's number—the number for Sun 'N' Fun.*

"Oh yeah, I did page you, but just a few minutes ago I changed my mind." She went back to talking on the phone. She apparently was having an argument with her kid.

Then my pager went off again, and the same phone number was displayed. It's Sun 'N' Fun again.

"Excuse me, Jill. The pager just went off again. It's your phone number again."

"Hold on one sec, sweetie." Jill put the phone to her side and gave me a flustered look. "That's just me calling back to cancel my first page. Just two minutes ago I paged you again to cancel. You are supposed to phone in when you get paged. When you didn't call, I gave the job to Frenchy Couture."

"I don't have a phone, so I just came in to work. So are you saying you don't need me? Well, that sucks. I came all the way over here for nothing, then." I was about to leave but Jill held up her hand, like a traffic cop giving a stop signal. I stood there dumbly, waiting to see what she wanted as she continued to argue with her bratty daughter.

Suddenly she took the phone from her ear and said to me, "Do you mind? This is a personal conversation!"

"But you gave me the stop sign. I thought you were asking me to wait," I said.

She set the phone down on the desk, stood up, and shooed me out the door with a wave of her hands, just like she was sweeping a dust ball out of her office, and said, "By the way, a guy in a cheap suit was here looking for you. He had your picture and was very secretive. You better not be in any trouble, Ocean!" Then she slammed the door in my face.

From outside, I could hear her as she continued arguing with the spoiled brat on the other end of the phone line.

*What a complete asshole!* I was tempted to go back in and tell her off, but reason stopped me. Do you want to go back to work in those dumpsters, dude? I bit my tongue, deciding to leave the horrid little woman to wallow in her miserable existence; I left to get away from her cloud of negativity.

Across the waterway I saw the woman bartender at the Tiki Bar opening up for business. *Mmm, a Bloody Mary sounds good.* I walked across the marina to the tiki hut.

"Hi, miss. Can I get another one of your delicious Bloody Marys?"

"Sure, with extra Tabasco and extra veggies, right?"

"Yes please. So, you remembered me?"

"Yeah, I remember you, Captain Eddie Ocean."

"How do you know my name? I don't recall telling you."

"Yesterday a nerdy guy wearing a tan suit was in here looking for you. He looked official and had a picture of you in his briefcase. Said he needed to find Captain Eddie Ocean."

"Did he say why?"

"No. You tell me. The guy seemed kind of mysterious," she said as she put the drink and a Slim Jim in front of me.

"No Slim Jim today. I'm short on cash."

"Well then it's on the house."

I looked at her name tag: FANNIE. "Thanks, Fannie. I'll pay you back. That guy must be a bill collector from the hospital. I told the doctors that I had no insurance and no money, but they insisted that I stay overnight at Jackson Hospital. So that guy must be trying to collect the medical bill. Don't know who else would be looking for me."

"Well, Captain Ocean, are you going to be a regular customer here?" she asked.

"Probably. I took a job over there at Sun 'N' Fun." I pointed across the docks to the office. "I really need the job...but my boss is a hideous little woman and a horrible human being. Every time I see that woman I need a stiff drink to calm me down. I'm afraid she's going to make a drunk of me."

"You must be referring to Captain Jill Hamm…oh, please excuse me—my bad. *Doctor* Jill Hamm is her title. Her royal highness, the pompous, selfish queen of the Miami Marina is legend around here. Everyone except for her own mother hates that little bitch. Come to think of it, her mother probably hates her too!"

"Well, I'm glad it's not just me! I usually like most people, and most people usually like me," I said and sipped my drink. "Mmm… this is nice and spicy, just how I like." I looked at the bartender's nametag again. "Nice to meet you, Ms. Fannie."

"Yeah, I'm Fannie Licker." When she said her name, some of my drink squirted out of my nose, the hot sauce burning my sinuses as I laughed at her joke.

"Oww, that hurts! Come on, Fannie, so what's your real name?"

"I'm dead serious; my birth name is Francine Licker. People called me Franny when I was little, but in middle school some mean kids started calling me Fannie—Fannie Licker. I stopped fighting that nickname a long time ago. Now I just go with the flow."

"Well, here's to you, Miss Fannie Licker. You make the best Bloody Mary in town. Cheers!" I raised my glass, took a sip, and asked her, "May I make a local call from your phone?"

"Sure." Fannie placed a black, rotary-dial telephone in front of me, and I called Jackson to talk to Nurse Patty Whacker. She was excited. "Eddie! We have Hobo!"

"Great, Patty. Thank you so much. Where is he?"

"Uranus took him home last night. I can't have a dog at my place, so Uranus took him."

"Did a woman named Rosalina Rossi find you guys."

"Yes. She's on her way back to her office. I gave her Hobo's tag number, and she said she was going to track down the dog's owner… you know, that kid Luca."

"Good! Oh yeah, one more thing: Was a strange little guy asking for me and showing my picture around at Jackson?"

"Yeah—what's he want with you? He's a creepy little nerd."

"I think he must be a bill collector. He might as well try to get blood from a rock."

"Speaking of blood, the same guy was also over at the Vampire's house looking for you. Uranus lied…said he hadn't seen you for weeks."

"Patty, I will gladly pay off my bills if I ever put some money together, but for now I'm going over to the Miami *Post* to help Rosalina track down Luca. Thanks for all your help, Patty. How can I ever repay you guys?"

"Maybe by taking me out for a drink…or two…or three?"

"Sounds like a date. Talk to you later, Patty." I hung up the phone and paid Fannie before walking to the Miami *Post* building.

As usual, the Miami *Post* lobby was bustling with activity. The grumpy security guard must have been in a good mood because he pretended not to see me as I signed the log and then went up to Rosalina's office.

"Eddie, come on in. I thought you had to go to work at Sun 'N' Fun today? What happened?"

"So did I! My horrible boss paged me to come to work but then changed her mind and gave the job to Frenchy Couture. She wasted half my morning, but she didn't even care. She couldn't care less about anyone other than herself."

"Well there's good news…news that might cheer you up, I've got an address for the dog—Melon Dog, or Hobo—whatever the hell his name is."

"Rosalina, apparently everyone in Miami calls the dog Hobo, so I guess we should just call him Hobo too."

"Okay, well, Hobo lives at 123 Papaya Lane, unit 69. That's a rough neighborhood, Eddie."

"Well, I need to go there to see if the boy named Luca is okay."

"What about the dog?"

"I'll pick him up at Uranus's first. It's right on the way. Then I'll take Hobo home to Luca. Returning Hobo will give me an excuse to visit Luca's home." I stood up to leave.

"Let me give you a lift to Overtown." Rosalina pulled some keys out of her purse.

"Great! Let's go rescue Hobo and Luca."

Sometimes *man* is dog's best friend.

*Chapter 14*

# DESPERATELY SEEKING LUCA

Rosalina drove west on NW 8th, a route that took us directly through the heart of skid row.

"Rosalina, that's where I live, right up there under that bridge—see the box on the right?" I pointed to the top of the I-95 overpass.

"Why do you live under a bridge? Why not go to the shelter until you're back on your feet?" Rosalina asked as she leaned forward to look up through the front windshield.

"Ever been to the shelter? Crowded and nasty! Hey look, Rosalina, honk the horn. I see Ima up there. Looks like she's sketching something." I rolled down the window and waved to Ima as Rosalina tooted the horn twice.

"Ima lives up there too? That poor girl lives up there under the bridge too—in a box? That's just awful!"

Ima heard the horn and stood up to wave to us. After we passed I rolled up the window, "Yeah, you're right, skid row is no place for a young woman like Ima. I was wondering if you might give her an assignment right away—maybe a project to do before the trial of the Boss begins next week. Ima needs to get to work and get out of the ghetto ASAP."

"I should be able to find something for Ima to work on." Rosalina slowed the car as she took in the woeful sight that stretched out before us; it was skid row, the tent city.

"Look at how many tents and boxes there are out there! This is a small city," she said.

"Welcome to The Big O Skid Row. That's what the people here call this place. It *is* a city—a growing city—more people move here every day. A lot of Vietnam vets are coming home from the war and can't find work. Many end up here."

"The economists at the newspaper are calling our economic problem stagflation—stagnant unemployment combined with high inflation. The economy keeps getting worse by the day." She drove under the overpass, leaving skid row behind, and entered the Overtown section of Miami.

"Why aren't all those kids in school?" I wondered aloud and nodded toward a group of teens gathered in front of a 7-Eleven store.

"It's January 2nd. The schools are on break."

"Oh yeah, I forgot." Wow—can't believe it's already 1974. Living on the streets with no structure to my life must be causing me to lose track of time. I wish my boss would give me some work. Don't want to go back to those dumpsters.

Rosalina interrupted my thoughts, "Why are their pants falling off? Why do those guys have their pants pulled down? And what's with the sideways ball caps?"

"Rosalina, I'm afraid I might be responsible for that trend. For several days—before I found the job at the Garbage Guys—I was forced to wear pants that were way too big. They kept falling off my ass. It was embarrassing to me, but these Overtown homeboys loved my funky look. I might have inadvertently created that horrible new style."

"I think it looks awful."

"Well, at least they have colorful underwear covering their butts. It could be worse. Hey, Rosalina, pull over by that fence—up there on the left." I pointed out the Johnson residence.

Pluto was outside in the front yard, and he began barking at us when we got out of Rosalina's car.

"This is Uranus Johnson's house, and that huge beast is Pluto, but I don't see Hobo." I said just as the door of the house opened and Uranus came outside. The screen door snapped shut behind him, "Hi, Eddie. I've got Hobo inside in the kitchen."

"Thanks, Uranus. Meet my friend Rosalina Rossi."

Rosalina blushed. "Sorry I hung up on you, Uranus. No offense, but I thought you were joking about your names—you and Patty Whacker."

"Don't worry—I get that reaction to my name all the time," Uranus said with a smile as he attached a leash to Pluto's collar. "Eddie, a guy with your picture was here looking for you."

"When?"

"Two days ago. Who is he, Eddie?"

"I think he's a bill collector from Jackson Hospital."

"Been working at Jackson for seven years, Eddie, and I never saw that guy before. I never heard of a bill collector going door to door to find people, either." Uranus yanked on Pluto's leash and said, "Come, boy! Y'all come on in. Hobo's in the kitchen. Didn't want to let him outside—he might get out of the fence and run off again. That dog is too smart for his own good."

We all went inside the house. There was a young boy in the kitchen petting Hobo and trying to force a rubber chew toy into his mouth.

"Come on, Lassie. Let's play fetch," the kid said. Hobo looked agitated and barked twice.

Suddenly a voice was inside my head. "If that kid calls me Lassie one more time, I'm gonna bite the little bugger on his butt!" My sixth sense was back! It was Hobo communicating inside my head.

"Where have you been, Hobo?" I asked aloud. The dog barked three times.

"Why are you calling me 'Hobo'? Don't you recognize me? I'm Melon Dog. Where the hell have you been, Eddie?"

The kid kept pushing the rubber bone into Hobo's mouth. The dog was in a foul mood.

"We've been looking all over Miami for you, Hobo. The people in Miami call you Hobo, so we decided to call you Hobo too," I said.

The dog barked three times. "'Hobo'—that's a pretty cool name. Guess I can live with it. It's better than 'Melon Dog.' I never told you, but I always thought 'Melon Dog' was a stupid name."

"Come on, Lassie. Pluto's inside the house now, so we can play fetch in the yard." The boy tugged at Hobo's collar, trying to pull him toward the front door.

"Eddie, this kid is driving me crazy! Your friend the Anus guy kidnapped me and has kept me locked up in the kitchen with this annoying kid. I think he's the Anus's nephew. You gotta spring me from this hellhole, dude!"

"Can I take Lassie outside to play, Uncle Vampire?" the boy asked Uranus.

"That does it! Doesn't the brat know that Lassie is a girl?" Hobo lunged toward the kid with a snarl, and I caught him by the collar just before he could nip the boy on his butt.

"Calm down, boy! Let's get Hobo out of here," I said.

"It's about time, Ocean!"

I spoke to the dog and pulled him away from the boy. "Hobo, we found Luca's address. I want to take you home to see Luca."

Hobo barked at me. "Good for you, Sherlock. You do know that I live there, too; I could have taken you right to Luca's house myself."

Uranus had a puzzled look on his face. "If I didn't know better, I would think you were having an actual conversation with that dog."

"Yeah, Hobo's a real smart aleck…sometimes it seems like he can understand me, like he can read my mind," I said.

Rosalina spoke. "Eddie, I'm glad you finally found Hobo, but I need to get back to my office. Can I give you a ride somewhere?"

"Nah, we'll be fine, Rosalina. We're going in opposite directions. Thanks for everything. Gonna take Hobo to Luca's house in Liberty City. It's not far."

"Well, let me know how Luca is doing. You know my number. Give me a call." She poked around inside her purse, searching for something.

Uranus led Pluto into the kitchen, and the Rottweiler growled when he passed Hobo. The massive dog let out a deep, loud bark, and before the kitchen door was closed I could see the boy jamming the rubber bone down the Rottweiler's throat.

Hobo barked twice. "Have a nice day with the kid, Pluto, you sucka! Hope you enjoy that stinky rubber bone! Ha-ha!"

We walked Rosalina out to her car. "Ciao!" she said before driving off.

Hobo led the way as we walked toward 123 Papaya Lane in Liberty City.

"I need some grub, Eddie. Follow me!" Hobo turned left down an alley, and I followed him. He stopped at the back door of a shop, where he began barking. After a few minutes, the door opened and a guy wearing a bloodstained white apron stepped outside. He was holding a large bone with some red meat on it.

"Hello, mutt. Sit! Good dog! Now beg." Hobo followed the commands and sat on his haunches with his front paws raised up.

"Is he your dog, kid?" the butcher asked me.

"No, but I'm returning him to his master."

"I've been feeding this fellow for over a year. I call him Mr. Mutt. What's his real name?" Hobo snatched the bone.

"We call him Hobo." I watched the dog tear off red meat and gobble it down.

"Wait here, kid." The butcher went back inside and then immediately came back out with a packet. "Here, take this doggy bag for later. Scraps of beef." He handed me the meat wrapped in white butcher's paper.

"Thanks, mister. You're very kind."

The guy bent down and petted Hobo's head as the dog gnawed on the bone. "Well, I've got a customer waiting. You take care, Mr. Mutt. See you next time, kid." The man rubbed Hobo's head again and then went inside.

"That was my butcher. He's a good guy. Now, just down the block we can get dessert." I followed the dog down the block, where he stopped at another back door and barked several times. In short order, a woman came out of the shop. As soon as the door opened, I could smell fresh-baked bread.

"Well, hello, fellow. Haven't seen you for a while," she said as she stood at the door with her hands behind her back, hiding something. Hobo assumed the begging position directly in front of her.

"Good boy! Here you go." She gave him a cupcake that she had been hiding. Hobo grabbed it in his mouth, tossed his head back, and scarfed down the cupcake in three big gulps.

For the first time, the woman acknowledged my presence. "Do you want to take some cake home for your dog? He loves sponge cake."

"No thank you, ma'am. I'm worried about his weight. Maybe some bread would be better for him."

"Worried about my weight? You think I'm fat?" Hobo glared at me with angry eyes.

"I've got some two-day-old bread that's still good but will only get tossed in the trash. Wait here." The lady returned with two loaves of bread, one white and one seeded rye, both wrapped in plastic.

"Thanks. This bread looks delicious," I said.

"You two enjoy it," she said and went back inside her store.

"She's my baker. Nice lady."

"And all this time I've felt sorry for you living on the street. Seems to me that you live the life of a king out here." I said as I ate a slice of rye bread. "Mmmm, good!"

"All right, Eddie, now my mouth is dry. It's time for a drink. Follow me." Hobo went to the back door of a tavern and barked until an obese man holding a bowl full of sudsy beer emerged.

"Now, that's Fat Dude! He's my bartender."

"Hello, dog. Here you go, your favorite brew." He set the bowl in front of Hobo and patted his head as the dog lapped up the bowl of beer.

"He likes Heineken Light. Is he your dog?" asked the bartender.

"No, just hanging out with him. We call him Hobo."

"Come in and I'll buy you a beer, kid. You're over twenty-one, right?"

"Yeah, but I need to be somewhere before my horrible boss calls me in to work. I'll take a rain check." Hobo finished his beer, and the man took the bowl and went back inside the tavern.

Hobo barked twice. "Follow me. I know a short cut. Just hope that Luca's dad ain't home!"

Hobo cut down a series of side streets and took me right to 123 Papaya Lane, unit #69.

"Okay, Eddie, keep quiet. Let's see if the cruel man is inside." The dog stood in front of the door listening, with his head cocked to the side and sniffing the crack in the door near its hinges." I don't think the man is home. Let's go in."

I knocked on the door.

"The kid won't open the door. He's always afraid. Just open it up. The key is under this pot." Hobo was sniffing the bottom of a potted cactus plant beside the door.

"You're not gonna get me shot, are you, Hobo?"

"Don't worry—the man doesn't have a gun, and he's not home now anyway."

I opened the door, and the acrid odor of urine and spoiled food hit my nostrils like a spray of mace. The room was a small studio apartment littered with trash and old newspapers.

"This place is the size of a large walk-in closet," I said as Hobo ran to a door at the back of the wretched little apartment. He barked twice, and then I heard a young boy's voice coming from behind the closed door. "Dog! Dog! It's you! You came home!"

"Hello, kid, I brought your dog home. Come on out of there. I won't hurt you. I'm your friend."

"I can't, mister. I'm locked inside this closet." The lock button on the doorknob was depressed; I turned the knob and opened the closet door. Inside, a young boy was sitting on the floor in the dark with his legs crossed. He shielded his eyes from the sudden light. Hobo lunged into the closet, knocking the kid backward, and began licking his face. The kid's pants were wet with urine, and a pile of feces was in the corner.

"Did your father lock you in here?" I asked.

"Yeah, Daddy locks me in to keep me safe when leaves the house." The kid was rolling around on the floor with Hobo. Even though he seemed happy to see his dog, I noticed his inappropriately expressionless face.

"Come on out, kid. Let's clean you up. Where are your clothes?" The kid went to a dresser and took out a pair of pants and a tee-shirt. He changed into the wrinkled but much cleaner clothing.

"Can I use your phone?" I asked the boy.

"It doesn't work," he said as someone in the apartment above us began dragging furniture across the floor. I looked up at the ceiling and asked, "Who lives upstairs?"

"Ms. Bertha."

"Is she a nice lady?"

"Yes, but she doesn't like my daddy, and he doesn't like her. Daddy says she's a nosy, fat bitch."

"Stay here, Luca. I want to talk with Bertha. I'll be right back."

"How did you know my name is Luca?"

"Your dog told me."

"Dog speaks to you too?" The kid was very happy now, and for the first time he cracked a meager smile. "My dad doesn't believe that Dog can talk to people."

"I believe it, kid. We call your dog 'Hobo.'"

"Daddy won't let me give him a nice name like that. He only lets me call him 'Dog.' Daddy says I can't name Dog because some day we might have to eat him."

Aghast, I stopped in my tracks and stared at Hobo.

"It's true. The cruel man says that they might eat me."

Luca petted the dog, "Huh…Hobo? I like that name. I'll call him Hobo from now on, but don't tell my daddy."

I went up a flight of concrete steps and knocked on Bertha's door.

"Who out there?" a woman's husky voice asked.

"I'm a friend of the little boy downstairs. A friend of Luca."

"Mister, you from the social service? You that child's welfare man?"

"No, but I'm trying to help the boy. Can I use your phone?"

The door opened a crack. A heavy chain kept it from being opened more, and a black woman with a large, round face peeked out at me. Then the door was closed for a moment before opening wide, and the woman let me inside.

"The phone be on that wall." She pointed toward the kitchen.

"Thanks Bertha." I walked to the kitchen.

"How you know my name? Are you from the Po-Po?" She gave me a guarded look.

"No, Luca told me your name. He likes you—said you're a nice lady."

"I try to give that boy food when the devil is away," said the rotund woman as she followed me into the kitchen.

She stood watching me as I called Rosalina. She listened to me describe the conditions that I had discovered at Luca's home.

Bertha said, "That's putting it mildly, son. You don't know what goes on down there. You don't know the half of it."

Rosalina gasped. She was horrified by my description. "I'm gonna call the authorities, and then I'm driving over there. I want to cover this story. This is child abuse! Wait there for me, Eddie. I'm on my way!" Before I hung up the phone, Hobo began barking frantically from the apartment below.

"That devil must have come home! You best not go downstairs now, mister!" said Bertha.

The barking stopped and there was a loud yelp, a yelp of pain from Hobo. I hurtled down the concrete steps and saw Hobo outside the apartment door whimpering and licking his abdomen.

"The cruel man is back. He kicked me in the gut, and he smacked Luca's face. He smells like whiskey."

I began pounding on the locked door. "Open up, you bastard!"

The man inside responded. "I'm calling the cops. You're gonna be arrested for breaking and entering. You trespassed inside my home."

I considered trying to kick the door in but thought better of it. *I don't want to look like the bad guy when the cops arrive.*

"Luca, are you all right?" I called to him, but the boy didn't answer. "Don't worry, Luca, we're getting help."

Fifteen minutes passed, and then a patrol car pulled into the parking lot, closely followed by Rosalina's car. She got out and followed the two police officers as they approached me.

"What's the problem here?" asked a cop.

"The man living in unit #69 is abusing his son. He's in there right now with the kid, and I think he's drunk."

The cops asked the drunken man to open the door, but he refused.

"Go away. You don't have a warrant." Luca's father was slurring his speech.

"Officers, you've got to go in there." Rosalina demanded.

The two officers conversed for a moment and then told us that they couldn't break into the apartment without a search warrant.

"Ma'am, we have not witnessed any wrongdoing or abuse."

Rosalina was furious. "I'm going to contact the *Post*'s lawyers to see if they can get you a warrant, and I'm going to write a story about the abuse of this poor boy. The system has obviously failed Luca."

"If you get a good, legal warrant, I'll gladly go in and check on that kid, lady. But I don't need that guy's lawyer up my butt."

Then the other cop said to her, "He's right, lady. As far as I'm concerned, the only good lawyer is a dead lawyer."

Rosalina did not appreciate their joking and was still very worried and angry, "Eddie, tell Ima to come to my office tomorrow morning. When we get access to this apartment, I want her to sketch it. She'll capture the essence of the crime scene better than any photograph."

As the officers walked back to the patrol car, I heard one tell the other a joke:

"What do you have when 100 lawyers are buried up to their necks in sand?"

"What, Frank?"

"Not enough sand!"

## Chapter 15

# SUN 'N' FUN ON A GIBSEA 41

## THURSDAY, JANUARY 3ᴿᴰ, 1974

Hobo spent the night with me inside Moe's cardboard shack. He woke me at 6:00 am by licking my face and staring into my eyes. His voice was inside my head: "I'm hungry!"

Outside, Brownie was cooking the usual fare: grits and coffee. Hobo and I joined him. The dog gobbled up a bowl of grits as Brownie and I drank hot coffee, when suddenly my pager went off. I checked the number displayed on the screen; it was Jill calling from Sun 'N' Fun Charters.

"Brownie, I'm being called in to work. When Ima wakes up, please tell her to go see Rosalina at the Miami *Post*. They have a project for her."

"Sure, Eddie. Smooth sailing. What about the dog?"

"He can take care of himself. Just let him hang out around here. He might wander off, but he'll come back."

I walked two miles to the marina and found Jill at the dock, standing aboard a Gibsea 41-foot mono-hull sailboat. The boat's name was *Third Wish*.

"You called me, boss?"

"Well, it took you long enough, captain. I have a charter for you—a five-day, one-way coastal cruise down to Key West with a party of four. They want to snorkel dive and learn how to sail on the way down. The *Third Wish* is fully stocked and ready to go. I just finished checking her out."

"Great! When are the clients coming?" I asked.

"They're inside the office, filling out paperwork," she said. The small woman hopped onto the dock, landing on her short, stubby, bowed legs. I wondered if she had once been a gymnast. Then I thought, *Nah. She's too pampered and prissy. She would never survive the grueling training of a gymnast.*

"Look the boat over, Ocean. I'll send your party out when they complete the paperwork. Run the safety rules by them—that should only take about ten minutes, and then you can cast off."

"What are your safety rules, Jill? And where are we going, specifically, in Key West?" I asked.

Dr. Hamm looked flustered. "I'll send a printout of the safety rules with them along with your itinerary." She waved her hands in that dismissive motion and walked away grumbling to herself.

"That would be nice, doctor," I commented sarcastically.

The sailboat appeared to be well maintained and was fully stocked with provisions. I completed my check of the safety equipment and then conducted a radio check on the main VHS as well as the hand-held marine radio. On channel 16, I called the Miami *Post*. I knew that the reporters monitored the marine band radio traffic as well as the police bands, listening into the local chatter to find leads for news stories.

"Miami *Post*, Miami *Post*, Miami *Post*...this is the sailboat *Third Wish*. Come in, please."

"Hi, this is the Miami *Post*. Go ahead, *Third Wish*; switching to channel 26." It was the voice of a man.

I switched to 26 and heard the voice again. "This is Robby at the Miami *Post*. Go ahead, *Third Wish*."

"Robby, I need to leave a message for Rosalina Rossi. Tell her that Captain Eddie Ocean will be on a cruise for five days, and ask her to please help Luca and Hobo find a safe place. I will contact her when I return from the cruise."

"Is that all, captain? Over."

"Yes, thank you, Robby. Over and out."

I hung up the mic and went below deck. Each guest cabin had a suitcase placed on the bed. *Good, they've already been onboard and selected their bunks.*

I finished my inspections and waited for over fifteen minutes, but no one came out from the office. I decided to go in to see what was the delay.

"Well, it took you long enough," Jill said in a huff.

"What? You told me you would send them out to me."

"Never mind. There are four of them. Strictly landlubbers. They don't have a clue. They're in the lounge. Go read them the ship-board safety rules." She handed me a printout of the rules and a chart showing the course for me to sail and where to anchor each night. Jill shooed me away again with those stubby little arms as she wrinkled up her piggy nose to expose the oversized buckteeth.

Two middle-aged couples were sitting in the lounge. "Hi, I'm Captain Eddie Ocean. I will be your captain on this voyage. I just need to go over some safety rules, and then we can get underway." I read the rules from the printout. Just as I finished, Jill came out from her office, began strutting back and forth, and started speaking to us with great pomp and authority.

"Okay, crew. As I told you before, I am Doctor Jill Hamm, the director of Sun 'N' Fun Charters." From memory, Jill began reciting the safety rules again.

The balding gentleman interrupted her. "Doctor Hamm, Captain Eddie has already explained the rules to us."

"Well I'm not just a captain, I'm a doctor of the maritime sciences as well. I like to be very thorough, especially when it comes to safety issues." She continued her speech, and the five of us suffered through Doctor Jill's safety-first monologue. Then, at last, she was finished, and we made our way out to the sailboat, leaving Jill behind in the office.

"She sure is a bundle of laughs," whispered one of the women.

"Ma'am, that was her pleasant side…her bright side. That's how she acts in front of customers. You should see how she treats her subordinates when no customers are around. Let's get going before she crawls back out of her hole," I said as the five of us hustled down the dock and boarded the *Third Wish*.

After we had cast off the dock lines, I saw Jill out of the corner of my eye coming up the dock. I pretended not to see her and maneuvered the boat around a dock piling and out of the slip.

"She's calling us back," said one of the women.

"What? I can't hear you, ma'am," I said to the woman as I slipped *Third Wish* into neutral and revved the diesel engine to drown out Hamm's voice. I could see Jill standing on the dock screaming and waving her arms above her Brillo pad hairdo.

"Now she really looks pissed!" The woman laughed.

"She looks like an angry little chimpanzee hopping up and down on the dock," said the woman's husband as Jill ran back to her office. Suddenly her voice came over the marine radio telling me that I had forgotten the daily menu and the recipe book for the ship's galley.

"Come back now! I have all the meals planned for you!" Jill demanded angrily.

"We'll figure something out, boss. Over and out." I hung up on her and turned the radio volume down low. Faintly, I could hear her angry tirade as we motored out of the marina.

"How can you stand that egotistical, micromanaging little maniac?" asked the balding guy.

"I can't, and this is only my first cruise for her—my first assignment!"

"God help you, Captain Ocean."

We motored out of Government Cut into the Atlantic Ocean, and then I turned *Third Wish* into the wind and showed the guests how to hoist the mainsail. Once under sail I turned off the diesel engine, and we traveled south toward the Florida Keys. With only the pleasant sound of the wind and waves to be heard, everyone seemed to finally relax.

"This is wonderful!" said a woman. The foursome gathered around me at the helm as I steered the boat.

"So, now that we've escaped the wicked witch of Miami, let's get acquainted," I said. We had been in such a rush to get away from Jill that I had not even reviewed their paperwork or introduced myself properly.

"I'm Marty Fry, and this is my wife, Gabby," said the balding guy.

"I'm Sara Burns, and this is my husband, Joe."

"What do you all do?" I asked.

"My wife and I are psychologists," said Joe Burns.

"I'm a mechanical engineer and an inventor, and my wife does my patent work. She's a patent attorney," said Marty.

"Very nice! So my boss, Dr. Jill 'Maleficent' Hamm, told me that you all want to snorkel dive and learn sailing techniques as well as nautical terminology," I said as I glanced at their paperwork and steered the boat.

"Yes, I'm also a wordsmith, a fan of terminology. I just love buzz-words and jargon, especially sailing lingo. I would like to learn nautical expressions and the name of all the equipment and rigging on this sailboat," said Joe Burns.

Joe's wife looked distraught. "Joe, can't you just take a vacation and relax—just for once kick back and let your mind go numb?" The woman opened the hatch, went below deck, and then called up from below, "I don't know about you people, but I'm ready for a cocktail."

"Make mine a double," said Sara.

On day one, we enjoyed fair weather with a fresh breeze, perfect conditions for sailing, and just before sunset we anchored for the night off the coast of Pumpkin Island, near Key Largo. Each day before sunset we anchored and spent the night onboard the *Third Wish* as we worked our way south, stopping now and then to snorkel dive on the fabulous coral reefs of the Florida Keys. Our overnight stops included Islamorada and Marathon, and our final destination was in Key West, where we were scheduled to dock in a marina in the Key West Bight.

In order to teach Joe and his friends the names of the rigging and the equipment on the boat, I cut small squares from a canvas tarp and used a permanent marker to make labels. These labels were attached to various objects, lines, and rigging on the boat each evening after anchoring, to identify the equipment. All four of my students were fast learners, and soon they knew the rigging and were communicating like seasoned sailors. After the third day they were working as a team, and I sat back and watched them independently sail the *Third Wish*.

In the evenings, I eavesdropped on the group's heady, intellectual discussions concerning philosophy and politics as they sipped wine and watched the moonrise from the boat's deck. One interesting conversation that I overheard concerned my horrible boss, Dr. Jill Hamm. The psychologist couple had diagnosed Dr. Hamm as a malignant narcissistic. I laughed when they said she that she was a micromanaging little megalomaniac as well!

My enlightened passengers complimented me on my teaching technique, and I told them I was learning a lot from them as well. Joe said, "Those labels are an excellent way to teach us the rigging, Eddie. We already know this sailboat very well, and we've only been aboard a few days!"

"Well, Joe, you people catch on fast—quick learners," I replied.

"Eddie, I've been wondering about something: What is that glue that you use to attach the labels? I've noticed that the glue allows you to move the labels around so easily and then reattach them without applying more glue. And I've never seen a strong glue that does not harden or leave a residue and damage the surface that it adheres to," said Marty, the inventor.

"It's a special glue, Marty—a glue that the Whatchacallit Tribe makes. The Indians call it sticky chicle."

"The Indians? What's the Whatchacallit Tribe?"

"Yeah, my Native American friends from the Whatchacallit Village near Big Cypress. They make the glue from the sap of the Sapodilla tree mixed with oil from the musk glands of beavers and otters."

"Eddie, the glue seems to have an unusual molecular structure, a strong adhesive that stays tacky and doesn't harden like most glues. May I take a sample of that glue home?"

"Sure, Marty."

## MONDAY, JANUARY 7TH, 1974

We reached the southwest end of Key West an hour before sunset and sailed past Mallory Square. A large crowd of sun worshippers had gathered to watch the sunset. As we sailed within a few hundred feet of the seawall, the loud music and drumming entertained and excited my guests.

"This is so beautiful! We have the sun setting in the west and a carnival celebration to our east. I don't know which way to look!" Gabby said to her husband as they stood arm in arm, sipping margaritas. "Thank you for this vacation. I love you, Marty!"

We enjoyed the circus-like atmosphere of Mallory Square, complete with jugglers, acrobats, tightrope walkers, musicians, fortune-tellers, and drummers all celebrating the setting sun. I came about twice and made three passes along the docks as the sun slowly disappeared below the western horizon. Following the sun's departure, a colorful display of light illuminated the evening sky

"Red sky at night, sailor's delight!" said Sara.

"Eddie, do you actually get paid to do this job?" Gabby asked me.

"It's tough work, but someone's got to do it." I recited the old, worn-out cliché as we sailed toward the docks in the Key West Bight.

After I turned the *Third Wish* into the wind and started the diesel engine, the two couples dropped the mainsail and battened it down with the skill of seasoned sailors. Then my crew deployed the fenders and manned the dock lines as we entered the marina, and I located our designated boat slip. We docked right in front of the Half Shell Raw Bar on Margaret Street.

"That place looks interesting," Sara said as she pointed at the raw bar, a large, open-air, barn-like structure.

"The raw bar is pretty darn good, especially if you want seafood," I said. "If you can get the right table, you'll see fish swimming below your feet right under the deck while you eat! I like to feed 'em french fries."

"That would be a novel dining experience, don't you think, Sara?"

"Yes, let's try it, Joe."

"Eddie, would you join us for dinner? It's our treat," Marty Fry offered.

"Sure. Thanks, Marty."

We had a nice dinner at the Raw Bar, and before we finished, a celebrity I recognized pulled up to the restaurant riding a moped. A small entourage of people riding mopeds followed him into the parking lot, and then they all entered the restaurant. The group was seated at a long table not far from ours.

"Hey, that's Darson Caily!" I whispered.

"Darson Caily? Never heard of him. Which one is he, the tall guy with the sunglasses?" Gabby asked.

"Yeah, he's a pop music DJ. Has a TV show. Wait till those little teenyboppers spot him—they'll go nuts." I said.

Sure enough, a cute young girl with thick-braided hair spotted Darson. She breathlessly approached his table, and I heard her say that her name was Raegy.

"I'm from Jupiter, Florida. I'm eight years old, and I've been a fan of yours my whole life, Mr. Caily! Can I have an autograph and take a picture with you?" the little girl pleaded dramatically.

Soon, another young girl recognized the celebrity and ran to his table. The commotion attracted the attention of other diners as well as people walking outside of the open-air restaurant. We were seated in between Darson's table and the exit. Uh oh! This could get crazy! Suddenly, a horde of teenyboppers stampeded toward our table en route to getting a look at Darson Cailey. Luckily, we had just finished paying our check, and the others in our party followed my lead as I weaved my way through the oncoming crowd of squealing kids. We got out of the place just in time as giggling little girls swarmed Darson's table, nearly trampling us in the process. After reaching a safe spot near the front door, we stopped to look back at the frenzy. Darson was standing on top of his table with screaming teenyboppers pulling on his pant legs.

"Man! I'm glad I'm too old for that kind of pop culture hysteria," said Sara.

"Sara, I hate to admit it, but I did that groupie act at a performance by Elvis in Las Vegas. That was way back in 1965."

"That was only nine years ago! You were way past being a teeny bopper, Gabby!"

Gabby laughed and then said, "You're right—but I'm still a teeny bopper at heart. Let's get out of here!"

Youth looks forward; age looks back.

*Chapter 16*

# A HOME FOR LUCA

## KEY WEST, TUESDAY, JANUARY 9TH, 1974

After dinner, my guests collected their belongings from the *Third Wish*, left the boat, and checked into the Banyan Resort on Whitehead Street. I remained onboard and spent Monday night alone on the boat. At 8:15 Tuesday morning, a man from the marina office called to me from the dock.

"Hey buddy, you've got a call from a woman in Miami."

"Thanks, pal." I walked to the marina office and picked up the receiver. "Hello?"

It was Jill. "Ocean, the *Third Wish* is being chartered. It's a bareboat charter—no captain needed. The guy's name is Captain Rooney. He will come to your boat slip at eleven am. Check his sailing credentials, and then turn the boat over to him."

"Do I need…"

Jill interrupted me. "Oh, that geek in the cheap suit came by again yesterday. He's still looking for you. I told the guy you were in Key West."

"Why did you tell him where I was?"

"Because I don't know what trouble you've got yourself into, but I'm not about to become an accomplice by covering up for you, Ocean."

"Well, what do you want me to do here, Jill?"

"Do there? Nothing! Come back to Miami, dummy. Duh!"

"And how do you want me to get back to Miami—hitchhike?"

"I don't know. Don't they have a bus station?"

"Yeah, sure. No problem...I'll take the bus home."

The thoughtful Dr. Jill Hamm must have assumed that I had money for the bus fare. Sun 'N' Fun had not yet paid me a dime, but luckily my charter customers had given me a generous tip, and I had more than enough money to cover the ticket home and get some breakfast.

After meeting Rooney and checking his credentials, I turned the boat over to him, grabbed my backpack, and began walking toward the Greyhound bus station. The bus terminal was located on the opposite side of the island, requiring a long walk around the north end of Key West. After walking about halfway, I stopped at a mom-and-pop restaurant for breakfast. The western omelet and hot coffee filled my belly and took my mind off my resentment toward my selfish little boss lady. Walking across the beautiful tropical island paradise in the morning sunshine while listening to birds singing from the banyan trees lifted my spirits further.

With my belly full and a smile on my face, I finally reached the bus station on South Roosevelt Boulevard and purchased a one-way ticket to Miami. There was a one hour and fifteen minute window before my departure, so I walked outside and crossed Roosevelt Boulevard, where a sign was posted: SMATHERS BEACH. There, I sat cross-legged on the sand watching an attractive young woman windsurf. *She's pretty. I wonder what Little Hooters is doing this morning? Surely she must be married to Jumping Jack by now.* Bowing my head, I looked down and with my index finger, I drew a heart shape in the sand and wrote the letters E. O. + L. H. in the middle of the heart. *Wow, that's really mature, Captain Ocean! You haven't done that since elementary school, dude!* Embarrassed, I rubbed out my graphic expression of love for Little Hooters.

An hour passed, and I retuned to the bus station at exactly 11:00 am. Two Greyhounds were parked side-by-side, nose toward the curb. The idling buses spewed hot diesel fumes against my legs as I walked past them. The late morning air was turning uncomfortably hot and humid; the smell of the diesel exhaust was strong as I looked to see which bus was the non-stop express to Miami. *No not this one. This one is the local—she makes stops throughout the Keys. Here we go— the express bus to Miami.*

The door of the bus was open, so I boarded the Greyhound and handed the uninterested driver my ticket. He barely looked up from the paperback novel he was reading. "Sit where you please, kid."

The air-conditioning in the nearly empty bus was a relief from the heat and exhaust fumes outside. After walking down the aisle toward the rear, I noticed a folded copy of the Sunday Miami *Post* lying on a red-cushioned window seat, so I picked up the paper and sat down in that seat. But before reading the paper, I glanced out the window. A small man wearing a cheap tan-colored suit was looking into the windows of the local bus, and then he turned his attention to my bus, the express. *That might be the creep who's tracking me!*

Quickly, I slouched down low so he wouldn't spot me. Pretending to tie my shoe, I hid from the man and was relieved to feel the bus start moving as the driver backed out of the parking space. Peeking out as the bus pulled away I could see the man standing on his tiptoes at the curb, craning his neck as he looked into the windows of my bus. He stood there watching the bus leave the terminal for a moment, and then turned and walked back into the bus terminal. *I don't think he saw me.*

When the Greyhound was well away from the station, I sat upright in my seat. An elderly lady seated across the aisle from me had noticed my suspicious behavior, so I stuck my head between the pages and began reading the newspaper to escape her scrutiny.

*Hmm...no front-page section. Someone left only the sports pages and the local news section behind.* In the local news section, a picture of Rosalina Rossi caught my eye. Her picture was on page one of the local news above a headline: "CHILD ABUSED IN LIBERTY CITY." As the driver shifted smoothly through the gears and the bus accelerated, I took a quick peek over at the old woman. She had lost interest in me and had begun knitting, so I started reading Rosalina's report:

CHILD ABUSED IN LIBERTY CITY

On a hot summer day nine years ago, Earl Winston pitched a no-hitter in the College World Series to win the NCAA championship for Central Texas University. Later that winter, Winston was picked in the first round of the M.L.B. draft by the Los Angles Dodgers and received a $1 million signing bonus. In his first year as a pro, Winston's pitching record was 10-1 in the Triple-A league. That same year, he married his long-time high school sweetheart and former Miss Texas beauty queen, Lynn Little. Winston's storybook life and pro career came to a sudden and tragic ending the following spring, and just eleven months after his honeymoon,.

It was 1968, during spring training, that tragedy struck Earl Winston. After making the final cut and being named to the Dodgers' starting rotation, the lefty blew up his pitching arm in the final game of the pre-season. The damage to both his shoulder and elbow was so extensive that Winston was told he would never pitch pro ball again.

The fallen star's misfortunes were not yet over. That fall, Winston's son, Luca, was born, but due to complications during delivery, Winston's wife, Lynn Little, died shortly after giving birth.

Consumed with grief and deep depression, Winston turned to drugs and alcohol. His money was soon depleted, and he ended up living in poverty and relying on charity and Welfare to survive. Winston blamed his son, Luca, for the death of his beloved wife. It is now evident that Earl Winston abused his son for all seven years of the youngster's life.

Last week, under pressure from this newspaper, the local government agencies that had failed to protect Luca from seven years of abuse finally took action on the child's behalf. The Miami *Post*'s sketch artist, Ima Hooker, and I were present when Child Welfare workers and the Miami Police gained access to Earl Winston's apartment. What we discovered inside was appalling.

Earl Winston was found passed out in his bed, with the child locked inside a closet reeking of feces and urine. When aroused from his stupor, the hulking former ballplayer became combative, and four police officers were required to subdue the enraged man.

The stench inside the apartment was unbearable, and the interior of the small studio unit resembled an overflowing garbage dumpster. The filthy closet where Luca was found served both as the boy's bedroom and toilet. Luca cannot read or write and has apparently never been to any school. The only companionship Luca has ever had is a pet collie dog. We believe that neither Luca nor his dog has ever been vaccinated or received any medical care whatsoever. After an examination, medical personnel say that the boy and his dog showed signs of long-term physical abuse.

Earl Winston was arrested for child abuse and is being held in a rehab facility under house arrest. Luca is now in the custody of the Child Protection Agency. The pet collie bolted and ran off into the city before animal control workers could collar him and is still at large.

The question that we at the *Post* are asking is: How did this child, Luca, slip through the cracks of the Child Welfare System? Why did no one come forward to report the abuse? Who, in addition to his father, is to blame for the seven years of abuse endured by this young boy?

We at the *Post* intend to continue our investigation until these questions are answered and the agencies and people responsible for allowing this atrocity are exposed. We also pledge to never again let this happen to another child in the city of Miami.

Ima's sketches really brought the horrific conditions home. *Wow, that kid was even worse off than I had imagined!*

Leaning to my right, I rested my head against the glass windowpane and looked out at the Atlantic Ocean as the bus crossed the bridge north of Big Pine Key. *Thank God Luca is finally safe. Maybe they can help Luca's crazy father too—the poor guy must be one sick dude. Hobo knows how to survive on the street; he'll be fine.* The elderly lady across the aisle stopped knitting and interrupted my meandering thoughts by asking, "Sonny, are you done with that newspaper? Do you mind if I see it?" She had moved over to the aisle seat and was now sitting closer to me.

"Sure. Here you go, ma'am." I handed her the papers and began to doze off with my head gently bouncing against the glass windowpane. The head-bumping was surprisingly soothing. All the noises from my fellow passengers and the mechanical sounds coming from the speeding bus were magnified as I began to slip off into sleep. It was as if I had suddenly developed super hearing. The gentle cry of a baby from the front of the bus sounded like a whisper just an inch from my ear. The elderly lady across the aisle was flipping through the newspaper, scanning its contents. The crinkling of the paper sounded loud, like a crackling fire. Then suddenly the sound of the rustling newspaper stopped, and I was nearly asleep when the old lady let out a loud gasp.

"Oh my! Oh my!" she kept babbling to herself. "Oh my! Sonny, did you see the story about the boy and his dog? Oh my!" From within my cocoon of a haze, I realized she was addressing me.

"What? Oh yeah, real sad." Without lifting my head I spoke from a dreamy state of mind. The vibration from the hard glass window was wonderful as the A/C vent directly over my head poured cold air onto my face.

"That poor child. Well, at least Luca will be safe now." Again the sounds were distant but clear. Her voice sounded like it was a hundred miles away yet as distinct as a bell. I fell into a shallow sleep.

When I awoke, the old lady was sitting in the seat directly next to mine. I smiled over at her. Someone had put a pillow in between my head and the window and covered me up, "Where did this blanket come from?" I asked.

"Do you like it? I knitted it myself. Isn't it cozy?" she asked.

"Yes. Cozy." I was still half asleep. "And thanks for the pillow, too, ma'am."

"Your head was bumping on that window. Every time we hit a bump...*bam!* I was afraid you might get brain damage."

"Already got that...got that brain damage." Out of the corner of my eye I could see her scrutinizing me again.

"What's your name sonny?"

"I'm Eddie Ocean."

"That's a pleasant name."

"What's your name, ma'am?"

"Martha Washington, just like George's wife."

"Huh?"

"You know—George and Martha Washington. The first president."

"Oh...yeah."

"Ma'am, I know that boy personally. I know that kid that was in the news story. I know Luca and his dog Hobo, too," I said.

"Are you serious, sonny? You know Luca?"

"Yes, I really do. And the reporter—Rosalina Rossi—is a friend of mine. She did a story about me and my Native American Indian friends not long ago."

The old lady looked at me with a sympathetic smile. "Oh, I see, sonny. And I bet you're on your way to Miami to visit the reporter, Luca, and his dog too."

"That's right...well not to visit. I live in Miami...live under a bridge."

"Hmm...brain damaged you said? Hmm."

"Oh, I was only kidding about that, ma'am, but everything else is true. My brain's fine...just down on my luck at the moment. I'll get off of skid row soon."

The woman began rummaging in her purse. "Here sonny, take this." She handed me a $1 bill.

"Oh! No thanks, ma'am, I just got paid cash in Key West, but thanks for the thought."

We chatted, and she told me stories about her childhood and what it was like growing up in the early 1900s. Then she spoke of her hardships as a young mother in the 1930s and her struggles to feed her young children during the Great Depression.

"Wow, and here I am, a strong, healthy young man feeling sorry for myself. Whining to you about being down on my luck. You must think I'm a real loser."

"I feel sorry for your entire generation, sonny. During the Great Depression, even during the hardest of times, the country seemed much more civil. Even the most desperate people didn't feel a sense of being victimized. I don't recall people feeling entitled to this or entitled to that. We weren't jealous of other people's good fortune. And we 'have-nots' looked out for one another back then—at least as best we could."

The time passed quickly as we chatted, and three hours and forty minutes after our departure from Key West, the bus pulled into the Miami Greyhound bus station.

"You take care, sonny," Martha said as we parted ways.

"You too, Mrs. Washington."

Just after I got off of the bus, my pager sounded, it was Jill. I jogged four blocks out of my way to find a pay phone to call her.

"Hi Eddie, I have another boat that needs to be brought up from Key West," she said.

"What? I just got off the bus in Miami. You told me to come back on the bus."

"Damn it, Ocean! Why didn't you call me before you left?"

"I left right after we talked on the phone in the Key West marina nearly four hours ago. I took the first bus home. That's what you told me to do."

"You sure are good at screwing up my plans, Ocean. If I didn't have a request for you to captain a charter I'd fire you right now!"

"Someone requested me?"

"That's right—a chick named Katarina. A big, tough-looking, middle-aged guy named Carlos was with her—said he was her uncle. Riiiight! Her uncle! The girl looks like a supermodel, but she's a little rough around the edges. She's kind of tough."

"Katarina? Where have I heard that name recently?" I asked myself.

"Is she one of your supermodel friends from Star Island?"

"Unfortunately, I don't know any supermodels, Doc."

"Well, me and that supermodel had a little spat—she wanted to do all the talking. She insisted on having you as captain even after I told her that you are new here and not nearly my best captain! But she kept insisting on you. I'll tell you about the charter later. Right now I'm busy. I think my kid is calling on the other line." Click.

*That little troll hung up on me!*

While walking home to skid row, I slung my backpack over my right shoulder and noticed something sticking out of a side pocket.

*What? How did that get here?* I wondered as I looked at the $1 bill.

*Martha, old gal, did you put that dollar bill here? You sweet, sneaky old gal! You must really think I've got brain damage. Well, thank you anyway.*

Martha Washington's kindness brought a smile to my face, and I wondered, How did that slick old lady slip that dollar bill past me?

The hand is quicker than the eye.

# Chapter 17

# PAY IT FORWARD

By the time I arrived home it was after 6:00 pm. Brownie was up in the penthouse, cooking hot dogs on the hibachi. He greeted me as I climbed up the slope.

"Welcome home, Captain Eddie. Want a dog? Don't worry—this time I've got Ballparks, not road kill."

"Sure, Brownie, I'm starving." He handed me a long stick with a hot dog impaled on the pointed end. The dark brown skin of the plump hot dog bubbled up and sizzled.

"Yum, wow this is good! Thanks Brownie! Speaking of dogs, where's Hobo?"

"Been gone all day."

"Well, when he gets a whiff of these delicious hot dogs, he'll be home in a flash!" I said and took another bite.

"Sorry, no buns or mustard today. So tell me, Eddie, how was your trip?"

"Great trip, smooth sailing…had two real nice middle-aged couples. Had no problems till I got back home."

"Don't tell me; let me guess. Your horrible boss, right? What's her name again—Dr. Hammbones?"

"Yeah, Brownie. Dr. Hamm is not just a horrible boss; she's a horrible person—a horrible human being," I said and took from my front pocket the dollar bill that Mrs. Washington had given me and showed it to Brownie.

"Wow! Your boss, Dr. Hamm, sure pays well, Eddie! One whole dollar!" We both laughed at his joke.

"This dollar is not from Hamm. A little old lady riding the Greyhound bus gave it to me. Hamm hasn't paid me a cent yet, but In Key West I got a $50 tip from my clients. Hamm says that my paycheck for the Key West trip will come on Friday." As I spoke, I noticed handwriting on the dollar bill, and I read it aloud.

"Hey, Brownie, there's writing on this dollar bill. It says, 'Pay it forward.' The old lady must have written this." I handed him the dollar.

"Hmm…pay it forward. Never heard that expression before. Must mean to give the dollar to someone else…to pass it along."

"Yeah, that's what I was just thinking, too. But as I recall my conversation with her, I'm not so sure. She may have meant to repay a favor that you receive by doing a good deed for someone else. Pay it forward."

"Hmm…that makes sense. Well, if you're keeping that dollar for yourself, don't spend it all in one place, kid. I'm headed over to the Dive Bar. Want to come along?" Brownie handed me back the dollar bill.

"No thanks, Brownie, I'm exhausted. Might do some reading before bedtime."

"Help yourself to my paperbacks, Eddie. Catch you later."

I sat alone on an overturned paint bucket, staring at the dollar bill. *That old woman probably has less money than me. Even one dollar must have meant a lot to her. Why was she so generous to me…did she actually believe that I'm mentally challenged and that I was not just joking with her about being brain damaged?* It puzzled me that a woman as kind and sweet as Mrs. Washington could inhabit the same planet as the cold-hearted bitch, Dr. Jill Hamm.

*What can make people so different...so completely opposite?* Negative thoughts of Jill began filling my head, and reading seemed like a good distraction.

I poked my head into Brownie's cardboard shack. The place had an odd, musty smell that I couldn't identify. Twin stacks of paperback novels were in one corner. The top book on each stack interested me immediately. *Brownie, we seem to have the same taste. I've been wanting to read Aldous Huxley's* Brave New World *and also* Steppenwolf *by Hermann Hesse.*

I was about to pick up Brave New World, but an image of Brownie Shytles holding the book in front of his face with his chronic hacking cough came to mind. Then I imagined him picking at his butt before turning to the next page.

*Yuk! Poor Brownie. He has a heart of gold, but he's one repulsive dude.* Believe me, I'm no germophobe, but I couldn't bring myself to handle Brownie's books.

*Wish I could do something to help him.* I left Brownie's smelly shack wondering, *Why, dear Lord, why Brownie? Why couldn't Dr. Jill Hamm have all of those nasty afflictions? She is much more deserving.*

Outside, I sat down and leaned against the concrete wall, gazing up at the stars, looking to them as if they held the answers to my questions. The bright streetlights along I-95 made the celestial bodies in the sky above me indiscernible, but by closing my eyes I imagined the position of Orion off to the west and turned my head in that direction. *You're probably hiding right over there, Orion.* Usually Orion comforted me, but tonight I was very lonely.

*How are you doing, Little Hooters? Are you looking at the moon right now? Can you see the stars tonight? The stars that are invisible to me?* Feeling melancholy, I again looked at the dollar bill and read the phrase aloud: "Pay it forward."

Recalling all the help from others that I had already received over my short lifespan made me wonder, *What have I paid forward in return?* Even my earliest memories involved being nurtured by my family and other caring people.

In Kentucky my family sometimes traveled to Lighthouse Lake for a day of swimming. On one of those trips I remember pestering my sisters to let me have a puff of the cigarettes they secretly smoked in a secluded place. At only six or seven years old, I wanted to smoke and threatened to tell on them if they didn't give me a puff.

When they grew tired of my pestering and my threats, they told me to exhale and then deeply inhale from the cigarette that was held up to my mouth. I did and promptly turned green and felt sick after nearly choking to death.

This seemingly nasty prank was a blessing in disguise because years later, even though most of my junior high school peers pressured me to smoke, I would never touch one of those nasty cancer sticks! To this day I cannot stand the smell of tobacco and have never smoked a cigarette in my life. My sisters' nasty prank was truly a blessing in disguise, and I'm forever grateful.

When my family arrived in Roslyn, Pennsylvania from Kentucky, I was about twelve. A year later we moved across the Delaware River to southern New Jersey. My oldest siblings, Judy and Toni, had married and were living in other parts of the country. Julie, the next oldest, went to work at a large bank in Philadelphia. There she met and later married a young bank manager named Robert.

The move from Kentucky to the Northeast was a culture shock for me, but Bob, a native Philadelphian, took me under his wing. My new brother-in-law became the big brother I had never had while growing up. In my early teens, Bob took me fishing and hunting, and when I turned sixteen and got a driving permit, Bob taught me how to parallel park a car.

After I got my driver's license, Bob found an old 1959 Ford that an elderly woman-a banking customer-had for sale. The car had been sitting in her garage for years and was ugly but in excellent condition. I got it for $25. The old Ford provided me with reliable transportation for nearly four years. With a set of wheels, I became more independent and Bob and Julie soon had three sons of their own.

My sister Karen, who was next in line and closest to my age, often played with me and let me tag along with her during our early years in Kentucky. Many years later, when I was struggling to pay my way through college, Karen and her husband helped out by letting me live free of charge in their basement. With their help, I didn't have to work full time to survive and was able to go to college in the daytime and earn some spending money by repairing truck tires part time at night. Without that help, I might never have been able to finish college after my father died. *How do I pay **that** forward?*

Then my little sister, Rhonda, the youngest, came to mind. *Wish I had been a better big brother for her.* I felt sad and lonely as I looked at the gray, light-polluted night sky.

Again I looked down at the dollar bill and, for some reason, thought of my three nephews, Bobby Jr., Jeffery, and Walt. *What a handful those three ruffians are for my poor sister Julie. I should pay it forward, but how can I pay anything forward? I have nothing to give...I've lost everything!*

Then an idea came to me. My pugnacious young nephews might like to hear about my battle with the mutant crocodile / bull alligator on Crocodile Island. I decided to write them a letter describing my adventures and the epic battle with the giant croc. *That's how I can pay it forward—with a simple letter.* With a sheet of paper and a pen, I began writing down my story, titling it *Crocodile Island*.

"Hey, what's up?" Riley Ford called to me as he came up to the penthouse.

"I'm writing a letter home. How 'bout you?"

"Gotta do a job for the Boss tonight," Riley said.

"Didn't the Boss go on trial today?" I asked.

"Yeah, but business goes on. My job tonight has something to do with that trial. A witness against the Boss needs to come down with a bad case of amnesia."

"Whoa, Riley, hold on. I would rather not know about any of that mob stuff."

"Oh sure, Eddie. I could tell you all the details of our plan, but then I would have to kill you." Riley laughed, a deep belly laugh, thoroughly amused by the tired old cliché.

"That's no joke, Riley! That's why I would rather not know anything about what you're up to, dude."

Riley began looking for something, searching the ground around the hibachi grill, "Hey, Eddie, have you seen that tire iron that Brownie uses for lifting the hibachi grate? Oh, here it is. Well, I gotta go, kid. You take care, Ocean."

I finished writing my letter, folded it up, and put it in my pocket. *I'll get an envelope and a stamp in the morning.*

As I stood looking down on skid row below, a black limousine pulled over to the curb where Riley Ford was standing with the tire iron in hand. Riley walked around to the driver's side window and, after a brief conversation, he got into the back seat of the car, which then drove off toward the city.

Five minutes later, another car pulled onto skid row. *That looks like Rosalina's Datsun B-210.* The driver's door opened, and to my surprise Ima Hooker got out of the car. She looked up and waved to me, and I waved back before running down the steep concrete slope. But the incline was too steep for running safely. "Yaaaaahhhh!" When I reached the bottom I couldn't stop, lost my balance, and went sprawling face-first into the gravel, sliding on my chest. I came to a stop at Ima's feet with pebbles sticking into my face.

"Eddie, are you okay?" she asked as she set down her oversized handbag and knelt next to me to help me to my feet.

"Yeah, I'm okay. Looks like a scraped elbow is all. I'm fine," I said as I dusted myself off.

"Eddie, I came to show you something." Three disheveled guys came walking toward us and started ogling Ima. We noticed them glancing down, eyeballing her large handbag. She grabbed the bag and clutched it tightly to her chest.

"Ima, let's go up to the penthouse," I said.

"Okay." She took off her high heels, and we climbed up the slope. "You look great, Ima!"

"Thanks, Eddie. You've changed my life."

"Me? All I did was encourage you to keep sketching and then introduce you to my friend Rosalina. You should thank her, not me."

"No, you're wrong. Like I told you before, you're my knight in shining armor, Eddie. You saved my life."

"Please, Ima, stop it! Now, what did you want to show me, anyway?" Her gushing praise left me embarrassed and uncomfortable.

"This." She pulled a newspaper from the large bag and handed it to me. I began reading the headline.

"No not that one. Open it. Open to page three," she said.

On page three there was a long report about the trial of the crime boss, Tony Montana. Three of Ima's courtroom sketches were placed throughout the lengthy article.

"Your sketches are excellent Ima—beyond excellent!"

"Eddie, thanks to you, I have a room and a phone now, and my phone has been ringing off the hook. I'm getting great feedback. People want to know who I am! The big shots at the Miami *Post* came down to Rosalina's office wanting to meet me! Thank you!" She hugged me.

"No one deserves this more than you do, Ima."

"Here's where I live, and my phone number." She handed me a scrap of paper. "If you need a place to crash, give me a call."

"What I've missed most living on skid row is a good hot shower. But now I get that whenever I captain a charter boat." I looked at her address. "Oh, you live on the other side of town. That's a nice area."

"My door will always be open to you, Eddie Ocean."

"Don't worry about me. I'll be getting my own place after I pocket a couple of paychecks." I handed the newspaper back to Ima.

"No, I want you to keep that copy, Eddie."

"Thanks," I said and reached into my pocket to take out the dollar bill. I handed it to her.

"You silly goose! You don't have to pay for it!"

"It's not for the newspaper. That dollar was given to me by a kind old lady. Read what she wrote on it."

"Pay it forward. Hmm…like do a good deed for someone else in return for receiving help?"

"You're a very smart girl. It took me a while to figure that out."

Ima handed the dollar bill back to me.

"No, Ima, you keep it to remind you to pay your newfound good fortune forward."

"I'll never be able to return the favor you've done for me, Eddie." I saw a tear in her eye. Her effusive display of emotion seemed to embarrass her, and she turned her head away.

"Never let them see you cry," she mumbled softly and then said, "Well, I have an early start and a long day ahead of me tomorrow. Better get going. Are you sure you don't want to crash at my pad, Eddie?"

"No, thanks. You live across town, and I need to stay close to Sun 'N' Fun Sailing Charters in case I get called in to work. But don't you worry your pretty little head about me, Ima." I walked her to the car.

I didn't believe I'd had very much to do with Ima's recent good fortune. The editors at the Miami *Post* had simply discovered Ima's artistic skills, and with years of drawing she had honed her God-given talent.

Ima drove off into the night as I watched her taillights grow small and then disappear around a corner. That night in bed, I tried to recall all the people who had helped me survive the harsh realities of life.

Someday I might be in a better position to

Pay it forward.

*Chapter 18*

# NICKY THE KNIFE

## 5:55 AM, THURSDAY, JANUARY 10TH, 1974

The voices of Brownie and Riley woke me early. They were outside my shack, talking. The aroma of Brownie's coffee and grits warming on the hibachi beckoned me to join them, but before I could roll out of bed I heard Riley ask, "Hey Brownie, is Ocean asleep in there?"

"Probably. He always comes out as soon as he wakes up," said Brownie.

"Good. He doesn't need to know my business. Here's your tire iron. Take it before Ocean comes out."

"My tire iron? Riley, I was looking all over for that. It's my grate lifter...for the hibachi. Why did you take it?"

"Needed it for the job last night."

"What job? What did you use it for? Is this tire iron evidence in a crime? Don't ya think we should get rid of it?" Brownie's voice was becoming high-pitched.

"No need for that, Brownie boy. As it turns out I didn't have to use your tire iron after all. Hey, are you sure that Ocean is sleeping? I want to tell you 'bout last night...but I don't trust that guy," said Riley.

"Yeah, I'm sure he's sleeping or he would have come out. What did you do last night?"

Riley began speaking in a hushed voice, and I could no longer understand what he was saying, but by repositioning myself so that my head was right near the blanket-covered doorway I could once again understand the muffled conversation. Riley began recanting the events of the previous night.

"Well, last night Bouncer picks me up in the Boss's limo and drops me off on a corner in Coconut Grove. Tells me to wait. 'Wait for what?' I says, but he doesn't answer...just drives away. So I'm standing there on the corner like a schmuck, holding a tire iron... sticking out like a sore thumb! Don't even know what I'm waiting for! So's I puts the iron up the sleeve of my jacket to hide it. Didn't want to draw attention. After about five minutes, a guy driving a tricked-out '71 Pontiac G.T.O. pulls over and picks me up. When I get into the car the guy doesn't even look over at me. He just sits there staring straight ahead and then starts driving. Scary guy— thin, scrawny, with slicked-back black hair...greasy hair pulled back off a pale, pock-marked face...skin as white as snow."

"Riley, you're a big dude carrying a tire iron. How could a scrawny little pale-faced guy like that scare you?" The volume of Brownie's voice had returned to normal.

"Don't know why, but he made me nervous. It was like being in a closed-in space with evil—with the Devil. He wasn't looking at me, so I leaned forward slightly and slowly slipped the tire iron out of my sleeve...hid it beside my right leg so he would not see it. The guy still had not even looked in my direction, but then he said, 'You plan on using that on me, big guy?' Almost crapped my pants; it was something in his voice that disturbed me.

"I says to him, 'No, this tire iron is for the witness.' He didn't speak—just kept staring straight ahead at the road as he drove. He was freaking me out, so I showed him the tire iron, but he didn't look over at me. He didn't have to; it was as if he could see me out of his right ear. His thin lips tightened around his mouth to form a toothy snarl, and then he says to me, 'Good, because if you try using that tire iron on me, I will have to pluck out your eyeballs and add them to my collection.' Just then we passed under a streetlight, and for the first time I noticed a toothpick clenched in his teeth. He was using his tongue to twirl it in circles as he chewed on it. 'Got a whole jar full of eyeballs,' he says to me!"

"Jar of eyeballs? Human eyeballs? Now you're creeping me out, Riley. Who the hell was the guy?" Brownie's voice became a few octaves higher.

"Didn't know that until later. Later he told me that his name is Nikko. He's some Russian-Slovak or something. The mob calls him Nicky the Knife. Anyhoo, Nicky drives us to Coral Gables in his Goat—drives to a real high-class neighborhood and pulls over at the curb and parks right in front of a mini-mansion. I says to him, 'Don't you think this G.T.O. looks out of place, here in this fancy neighborhood?'

For the first time the evil little guy looks directly at me and says, 'You no like car? You make fun of car?' Until then, I hadn't seen his entire face. It was hideous. A long, jagged scar extended down from his hairline, across his forehead, and through his left eyebrow, ending just below his left cheekbone. Something had slashed him—slashed right through his left eye. The left eyeball was dead. A slimy, bluish film covered the dead orb."

"Shit!" said Brownie.

"Yeah! I almost shit myself when I saw that eye...that face. I begIn apologizing about saying that his car looked out of place, and he yells, 'Shut up!' Then we sIt there in silence for nearly an hour. I was going crazy inside, but I was afraid to ask him what we were doing!

"Finally at about two A.M. he opens his door and gets out. I start to follow him, but he says: 'No, you stay here. Get behind the wheel. Any problem, you honk horn once. If trouble, I meet you on next street over behind that house. That's judge's house.' He pointed to a house two lots up the street."

Brownie spoke again, "Holy crap! A judge? The judge of the Boss's trial?"

"Yeah, Judge Hollings Crown. So the Knife gets out and lights a cigarette as he stands next to the car, cool as a cucumber. I slide over into his seat, and he offers me a cig."

Brownie interrupted. "But you don't smoke."

"Took it anyway. Didn't want to insult the guy. Just puffed on it. Didn't inhale. So he's sizing up the surroundings, observing each of the large estates—probably looking for activity, waiting until people are in bed. We was parked away from the streetlight up ahead of us, but from my window I could now see what he was wearing. Penny loafers with no socks, skin-tight black jeans and a black V-neck tee-shirt. The short sleeves of the shirt were rolled all the way up to his shoulders. A pack of cigarettes was tucked in the left cuff.

"Suddenly he dropped the cigarette, smashed it with the ball of his foot, and then reached through the rear window to grab a black leather jacket from the back seat. He puts on the damn jacket and then flicks his left wrist. To my surprise, a six-inch stiletto with a white ivory handle shoots out from a concealment pouch sewn into the left cuff of the damn leather jacket. He presses a button, and a blade shoots out with a bright flash, reflecting the light of the streetlamp. He points the damn knife at me, an inch from my left eyeball, and says, 'Meet Baby.' Then he turns the stiletto sideways to show me the blade.

"'Isn't she beautiful?' he says. He's proud as hell of the damn knife. I sees the name 'Baby' carved into the ivory handle."

Brownie interrupted. "That guy sounds friggin' crazy! What did he do with the knife?"

"He puts Baby back into her hiding place. Then he opens his jacket. On the inside of the left lapel I see more steel instruments designed for slashing, pulling, tearing, and puncturing flesh—tools designed for torture and murder. Nicky checks them carefully. Satisfied that everything is in order, he reaches into his pocket and takes out a thin, tightly coiled rope and a bag of beef jerky. 'Let's get to work, big guy,' he says and then walks off toward the judge's house.

"An hour later he returns, and for the first time he seems to be in a good mood. 'Let's go get a drink,' he says with that thin, creepy smile across his pock-marked face."

"But what happened inside the judge's house?" asked Brownie.

"I didn't find that out until later, when we went to the Dive Bar. Nicky told me everything at the bar." There was a moment of silence before Riley spoke again.

"Brownie, see if Ocean is in there. Make sure he's asleep," Riley whispered.

I pretended to be sleeping, but through squinted eyes I saw Brownie pull aside the blanket covering my door, peek in at me, and then leave.

"He's fast asleep," Brownie whispered.

"Good. I trust you, Brownie, but not that guy. I don't know Ocean."

"Don't worry, Ocean's a good guy. Probably wouldn't even want to know what happened last night—but I understand."

I felt guilty for spying on Brownie after his vote of confidence, but the mobster's tale was fascinating to me.

Riley continued, "So now we get a beer at the Dive Bar and Nicky tells me what he did inside the judge's house. He says he went up the long driveway running along the side of the house. It led him to the backyard. A puppy—a beagle—yapped at him, so Nicky says 'Shhh...come here, Bentley.'"

"Bentley? How did he know the dog's name, Riley?"

"Turns out that the dog was Nicky's target all along."

"What? Why the dog?"

"Turns out the judge loves the dog. Loves the dog more than his wife and daughter, they say. The Boss's lawyer—I forget that little prick's name—but anyway his lawyer told the Boss that when he was inside the judge's chamber he saw a dozen pictures of Judge Crown with the dog and only one picture of the judge with his wife and daughter. The lawyer says that if you start the judge talking about Bentley he won't stop telling stories and bragging about how great the dog is."

Brownie spoke. "So the Boss sent Nicky the Knife after the dog? What's the point?"

"A warning to intimidate the judge. Last night at the same time, the Boss had some other guys across town threatening the two hostile witnesses that are testifying against him—scared the hell out of them at the same time Nicky was at the judge's house."

"What did Nicky do to the dog?"

"Shut up so I can tell you, Brownie. Where was I…? Oh yeah. Nicky takes out the beef jerky and starts feeding the dog. Now Bentley is wagging his tail, friendly as can be. Nicky says 'Good boy!' and hops the fence. He finds a dog-door designed to allow Bentley access to the enclosed, screened-in porch area behind the house. Nicky wriggles headfirst through the dog door, and Bentley follows him. Nicky says the sliding glass doors going into the house were armed with a sophisticated, high-tech alarm system. Nicky says that the Boss gave specific orders that Judge Crown, his wife, and his daughter would be left unharmed. Nicky was allowed to follow only one of two plans of action.

"Plan A: Place the dead dog in Judge Crown's bed. Like in that movie that came out a couple of years back called *The Godfather*. Only this time a dead dog instead of a horse's head gets put into the bed."

"That's sick!"

"So is Plan B! Plan B was to hang the dead dog with a noose around its neck on Judge Crown's front door."

"Poor dog—that's awful! I wondered what that rope and beef jerky would be used for," Brownie said in disgust.

"Apparently this is very mild violence by the Boss's standards. Anyway, because of the high-tech security system, Nicky was about to go to plan B and hang the dog on the front door when he noticed a small window near the floor in the corner of the screened porch. It was a basement window that had no security sensors or contacts because it was fixed...a window that doesn't open and close. It was left unmonitored, a major flaw in the security system!

"Nicky says he crouched down, looking through the window, and the dog came over to sniff his pocket, looking for more jerky. Nicky rubs Bentley's head, but he's not petting the dog. He says he was palpating the skull, looking for what he called the occipital protuberance."

"What's that?"

"Ha—that's what I asked. Nicky says it's the bump at the back of the skull, and it leads him to the opening in the base of the skull where the spinal cord attaches to the brain."

"Was he some kind of Russian doctor?"

"No. I found out that Nicky was a highly trained professional Russian interrogator and an expert torturer. They sent him to work for the Cato regime in Cuba. During the sixties he tortured dissidents for Cato. Said that most of the eyeballs in his collection are from Cuban dissidents. The Boss is well connected with the black-marketers on the island, and he recruited Nicky to do jobs in Miami. Snuck him out of Cuba and over to Miami."

"He's gonna kill that poor little dog, isn't he?" moaned Brownie.

"Yeah. He flicks his wrist and Baby pops out. He presses the button, and the razor-sharp blade shoots out, and then in one swift motion, snap, he severs Bentley's spinal cord just below what he called the foramen magnum."

"That's horrible!"

"He claims the dog felt no pain. He says he liked the dog, and it wasn't personal, just business. Said he would rather have killed the humans in the house."

"Those guys...those mobsters are psychopaths!" Brownie was angry now.

"Hey, Brownie, watch your mouth. Don't badmouth the Boss or his people...not smart. You wanna hear more or not?"

"Yeah, I guess you might as well finish this horror story."

"Okay. So Nicky takes a trohcar from his jacket and uses the point to cut away the caulking around the basement window. Then he pops out the glass. The window is very small, but Nicky the Knife is built like a snake. He drops the dead dog down into the basement and then slithers through the window. He says he carried the dog by the scruff of its neck over to a washing machine, where he spotted a pile of dirty laundry. He took a large bath towel and placed the dog on it, then gutted the animal. The entrails spilled out onto the towel. Nicky grasped all four corners of the towel so it held the dog like a sack. He used the towel to carry the carcass up the stairs and into the house.

"He says he passed by the doorway of a kitchen on the first floor, but then stopped and returned to look inside the kitchen. There was an enormous stainless steel refrigerator. He marveled at the size of the damn thing and pulled open the door. Greeting him was a six-pack of ice-cold Heineken beer.

"Nicky says he whispered, 'Sweet,' and placed Bentley's corpse on the granite countertop before popping open a cold brewski. Nicky says he sat sipping the beer, slowly, as he glanced around the immaculate kitchen."

"He was probably still cool as a cucumber, I bet," Brownie said.

"Because Nicky considers himself a professional, he says it's hard to admit that he secretly hoped someone would wake up for a late-night snack and join him in the kitchen. Says he wished for one of the Crowns to bumble onto his assignment. If they did, who could blame Nicky for eliminating an eyewitness? Anyway, he finished the beer. Says he was disappointed that no one had come to join his little party. Then he walks back to the refrigerator. He writes a note on a magnetized notepad sticking to the door of the fridge. Says he used his right hand—he's a lefty—in order to disguise his handwriting.

"'Judge Crown, the key word of the day is <u>mistrial.</u> Keep your mouth shut and cooperate, or the wife and kid are next!" He ripped the page off the tablet, folded it in half, and inserted it into the dog's mouth before grabbing the four corners of the towel and carrying Bentley's corpse upstairs to the second floor.

"Nicky paused at the top of the long flight of stairs. Said he stopped to listen at each door along the long hallway. From inside the door at the end of the hall, Nicky heard snoring. Quietly he opened that door and entered, closing it slowly behind him. He stood just inside the doorway. He said he needed time to allow his eyes to adjust to the dark room.

"After a moment he saw the couple in bed. Mr. and Mrs. Crown lay illuminated by the dim light of an alarm clock sitting on a shelf just above their heads. The woman wore a sleep mask with two large eyes painted on it. Nicky said it made her look cartoonish, like Betty Boop. Judge Hollingsworth Crown was lying on his back next to her with his mouth wide open and snoring, whistling like a freight train. The woman was snoring too.

"Nicky said the sight and sound of the pair disgusted him. He walked to the foot of their spacious, California king-size bed and placed the gutted dog in between them. The mess of entrails and blood soaked through the towel and stained a white comforter.

"'Mission accomplished,' Nicky whispered into the dead dog's ear. He made sure the note protruded from the animal's mouth and was visible. He says the dog looked happy like he was sleeping peacefully beside his master. Nicky returned to the bedroom door but did not exit. He stood staring at the couple as they slept next to their gutted pet, secretly hoping that they would wake up."

"He still wanted to kill them, right?" asked Brownie.

"Yeah. Nicky said that if Crown woke up and looked right at him the judge would not see him standing in the doorway because the room was too dark. Nicky says he lit a cigarette and smoked while he watched the sleeping couple. He knew he should leave, but he couldn't help himself—said he still hoped for a reason to kill them both. He fantasized about them waking up and how he would kill each one. He said he imagined that if they woke now and looked in his direction, they would only see a red, glowing ember suspended in mid-air by the doorway.

"He drew in deep on the fag. Now, in the brighter glow of the ember, he imagined that they might see his sunken, dead eye glistening blue in the light of the red ember, and then they would scream in horror after visualizing the silhouette of his pale, pock-marked face.

"Nicky says he finished the cigarette, again disappointed that they hadn't stirred. He walks over to Betty Boop and drops the cigarette butt into a half-empty water glass on the mantel just above her head. Says he leaned down and put his face just an inch above the stupid-looking mask, wanting to jam Baby into the giant eyes.

"Brownie, can you imagine waking up to find that ugly face with those high cheekbones and hooked nose staring down at you? I can picture him hovering above her, his dead eye glowing blue in the dim light of that alarm clock, his beady right eye black and glistening with hatred."

"Riley, you seem to be enjoying this nightmare." Brownie's voice sounded sad.

"Aren't you? It's no nightmare. It's a real-life horror show, dude!"

"No! It's sad and cruel, not amusing to me at all," said Brownie.

Riley continued. "Well to each his own. Nicky says the woman emitted a long, low-pitched fart, causing him to cover his nose and step back in disgust. Says it took all of his self-control to keep from plunging his razor-sharp trohcar into the hideous woman's carotid artery. Says he imagined the blood-spout shooting up and pulsating, arching up over the bed and pumping the life out of her fat neck.

"Nicky says the thought excited him so much that he almost lost control...was just about to stick her when the order from the Boss echoed through his mind: 'Don't hurt the family, Nicky—only the dog. That's an order.' Nicky restrained his homicidal desire. Says he reluctantly retreated, walking backward away from the bed, and then he left the house, taking the same route that he had used to enter.

"That's when Nicky came back to the car where I was waiting. Like I said, he was in a real good mood. He says to me, 'Mission accomplished, big guy.' I slid back over to the passenger's seat, and he got in the car.

"On the drive back to the city, Nicky popped in a cassette tape and turned the volume up high. With his Russian accent he sang along to a song. It was 'Mack the Knife.' Then he sang it in Russian, and it sounded bizarre."

"I know that song. It makes sense! Nicky the Knife probably idolizes the character in the song, Mack…Mack the Knife," Brownie said.

"Yeah, Nicky is a natural-born killer. He's a predator who loves killing and causing pain. So now we were driving and he was singing that song all the way to the Dive Bar—singing with a snarling smile plastered across his ugly face. The guy seems to be angry even when he's smiling—doesn't show even a hint of remorse or regret over cutting Bentley's spine. Then he starts flicking Baby in and out of his cuff in time to the music. It was sick!"

"Yeah, what a sicko!"

"Well, I've been up all night, Brownie. Now I need some shut-eye. I'll see you later on."

"Okay, later, Riley. I'm heading over to work at our street shop. Sleep tight, big guy."

I heard Riley rustling around inside his shack. Having no desire to see him, I waited a good ten minutes to allow him to settle into his bed before attempting to emerge from my hut.

Just as I was about to go outside, Hobo stuck his head past the blanket covering my doorway and came into my shack. I put my finger to my lips and whispered, "Shhh, Hobo," and then went outside.

*Being around Riley is bad enough, but I hope I never run into that Nicky the Knife creep.* Quietly, Hobo and I left the penthouse to get away from Riley, but I couldn't stop thinking about the poor innocent dog that Nikko had killed with his knife.

The first cut is the deepest.

# Chapter 19

# JUPITER FARMS

## 1:00 PM, THURSDAY, JANUARY 10TH, 1974

Hobo followed me to the phone booth on 8th Street and began poking around in trash littering the ground beneath a bus stop bench.

"Hobo! Get your nose out of that nasty stuff!" Even from a distance, it smelled like someone had taken a dump in the brown paper bag that Hobo was sniffing.

"Behave while I call Rosalina." To block the unpleasant sounds and the smell of the ghetto, I closed the folding glass door of the phone booth and then placed my call.

"Hi, Rosalina, guess who I found?"

"Hobo? How does he look?"

"Great! Someone must be grooming him. He's clean as a whistle."

Hobo's ears perked up. He sat facing the glass door, listening to my voice, and barked twice. "Of course I'm clean as a whistle. You should visit my beautician, Eddie; your hair could use a trim."

"I hear him barking," said Rosalina.

"Yeah, he's a real wise guy. That dog has the city of Miami twisted around his little finger...er, paw."

"Well, Luca's Aunt Lauren picked him up from Child Welfare. He's at Lauren's farm now, and I'm driving up to interview her so I can write the final chapter of Luca's story."

"That's great, Rosalina. Hey, what if you take Hobo along to visit Luca? Maybe Lauren will change her mind and take in Hobo. She might allow Luca and Hobo to stay together once she meets the dog."

"Good idea! That would be great for both of them." Hobo's ears perked up again when I mentioned Luca. "Eddie, do you want to come along too—come with me to Jupiter Farms?"

"I would love to, but I can't. What if my boss calls me in to work? Jupiter is about an hour's drive north."

"More like an hour and a half, but can't you check to see if Sun 'N' Fun is going to need you to work today?'

"Rosalina, you don't know how Doctor Jill Hamm operates her business? She's disorganized and reactionary. She does very little planning…has no leadership skills whatsoever. Most of the time she is preoccupied with her own personal problems. The lives of the Sun 'N' Fun captains revolve around the little princess's desires. We are required to report to the office within twenty minutes of her page, 24/7. She makes having a personal life hard for all of us captains." My shoulders slumped in resignation.

"Sounds like your boss is a malignant narcissist, Eddie."

"Hey, that's what the psychiatrist on my Key West charter called Dr. Hamm. After meeting her in the office before our trip he said that she had that exact personality disorder…what you just mentioned. The doc called her a malignant, narcissistic megalomaniac."

"I agree. That's the perfect clinical description of her personality type, Eddie—a self-centered, destructive force to all those around her. We have a couple of those types at the *Post*. People like her are a morale-busting wrecking ball. They make terrible leaders."

"That's for sure. Hamm has two other part-time captains besides me, and morale is very low, but we all need the money—we need to work—so we put up with the little bitch. She'll string us along for days at a time as we wait to get her call. We spend our time waiting, unable to take another part-time job and unable to venture far from the Sun 'N' Fun office to run errands!"

"You would think she'd simply have one captain at a time on standby so the others could take care of personal business."

"You'd think—but we risk being fired if we don't hop through her hoop. When she calls, we'd better be ready to drop everything and go!"

"She sounds like she's also a bully. Hey, Eddie, I have an idea! What if we forward your pager number to one of the other captains? If Doctor Jill Hamm should call you, the page will go to one of the other captains. Then you can honestly say that you didn't get her call. She might even think she misdialed your number, and she's probably such a narcissist that she won't admit to misdialing and making such a silly mistake."

"Forward her call? You can do that?"

"Sure. We do it all the time at the newspaper."

"Okay, Rosalina! Captain Frenchy Couture sure would appreciate some work. He's got a wife and two kids."

"Well, I've got your pager number, but do you know Captain Couture's pager number?" Rosalina asked.

"Yeah! His number is 305-357-9208."

"Hold on a sec…okay, I did it. Your calls are now forwarding to Couture. When we get back from the farm, I'll un-forward your pager. Where are you right now?"

"The phone booth on NW 8th Street right near the penthouse."

"Stay put. I'll pick you up in ten minutes. Have you had lunch?"

"No, we haven't eaten."

"Well, we can stop for a bite on the way to Jupiter."

"Cool!" I said. Hobo sat up in the begging position and barked three times. "Grub! Grub! Grub!"

"What's Hobo so excited about?" Rosalina asked.

"I think he's hungry—as usual."

"We'll get him some lunch soon."

"Sounds great, Rosalina."

"Ciao, Eddie. See you in ten!"

We waited at the bus stop, and when a city bus began slowing down to pick us up, I waved it on. After the bus passed, I noticed the animal control van that we had seen at Jackson Memorial stopped at a traffic light just one block away. It was headed in our direction. When Rosalina pulled over to the curb in front of us, Hobo followed me into her car just as the animal control van passed by.

"Whew! You're just in the nick of time, Rosalina. We were just about to make a run for it."

"Run for it? Why?"

"That's the animal control van. They're on the lookout for Hobo." I pointed out the van as I slid into the passenger seat.

"Let's get out of here," she said and made a u-turn.

Rosalina drove north on the interstate and, after a pit stop for some fast food, we arrived at the Indiantown Road exit in Jupiter.

"We made good time, Eddie," she said as she drove down the off-ramp onto Indiantown Road. Two miles west of the interstate she turned left onto Jupiter Farms Road.

"From here, we need to find 97th Way North. It should be 1.1 miles ahead on the left," she said as she glanced at her directions.

"There it is! Take this left," I said.

"Okay—now we're looking for Long Pond Stables. It should be on the right side," she said as she drove slowly down a bumpy dirt road.

"There, that green barn on the right—there it is! These little farmsteads are pretty cool. Looks like Luca has finally lucked out!" I said.

When we pulled up to the barn, Hobo began barking wildly.

"What's the matter, boy?" I asked, and then I heard the voices of young children coming from inside the barn. Hobo barked even louder. And then Luca came running out from the barn with a young girl following close on his heels.

"Dog! Dog!" *Luca must have heard Hobo's barking.* He cried out for Hobo as the dog jumped up against the side window, rattling the glass.

"Eddie, let him out before he breaks my window!"

Hobo ran from the car and jumped up on Luca, knocking him to the ground. The pair rolled over and over down the grassy hill in front of the barn.

"I love you, Dog!" Luca called out with joy.

"What's his name, Luca?" asked the young girl.

"Dog, his name is Dog—but now we're allowed to call him Hobo," said Luca.

Rosalina and I approached the excited children, who had hardly acknowledged our presence.

"Hi, Luca. Where's your Aunt Lauren?" asked Rosalina. Luca was still busy giggling and rolling around on the ground with Hobo.

"My mom is in the house—it's back by the pond. Follow me," said the girl.

We walked down the center aisle and out through the back of the barn, where we passed paddocks of grazing horses. The girl began skipping and galloping like a horse. Then she took us through a riding arena with jumps and barrels. We were approaching a beautiful, crystal-clear lake.

"Wow! This place is gorgeous! How many acres do you have?" Rosalina asked the girl.

"Ten acres and six horses," said the girl as she galloped and then jumped over the pole of a low jump while making the whinnying sound of a horse.

"Sorry, I forgot to ask your name, child," said Rosalina.

"I'm Katie Matthews, ma'am."

Off to the right and facing the pond was an old two-story farmhouse with a green-shingled roof.

"Cool! Is that your house?" I asked.

"Yeah, that's Katie's house, and I get to live there too!" shouted Luca, who was pretending to be a dog by hopping up and down in front of Hobo. "Ruff, ruff!"

"Wow! What a change—in Luca, I mean," whispered Rosalina.

"I know. Never saw him smile like that in Miami."

A squeaky screen door opened, and Lauren Matthews came out of the house. The wood-framed screen door snapped shut with a clap behind her, where two curious bull mastiffs peered out from behind the screen and began barking at Hobo.

Hobo stopped dead in his tracks and barked. "Whoa! Don't want to mess with those suckers! They're huge!"

Lauren reassured us. "Don't worry. My dogs just *look* scary. Those big dogs are really just lovable little pussycats."

"I hope so! Looks like they could eat us for lunch," Rosalina said nervously.

"Look, Aunt Lauren—this is my dog, Hobo." Luca was kneeling on the ground, hugging Hobo's neck.

Lauren didn't seem pleased that we had brought Hobo with us, but I sensed her agitation melting away as she stood quietly watching Luca embracing his dog.

Lauren's shoulders slumped. "Luca, I've got my hands full. We already have too many animals to care for."

Katie patted Hobo's head. "Mom, he's so cute! Can't we keep him? Please, Mom? I'll take care of him. He'll be no problem for you, I promise."

"Katie, you know we all had a talk about this—about being unable to take Luca's dog. We just can't have any more pets. Now, you and Luca get the chickens into the coop for the night and feed them while I talk to Rosalina." Lauren looked sad.

Hobo barked three times. "I can help the kids with those chickens, Eddie." He began barking rapidly and darted back and forth and from side to side in front of the chickens.

"Oh no! He's going to kill my chickens!" Lauren gasped.

"He's just herding them, ma'am. I've seen him do this before—he did it with goats," I said.

Everyone watched in amazement as the collie did his work. In a matter of minutes, Hobo had all the chickens running into the chicken coop. When the last one went in, Katie closed the door.

"Mom! Did you see that? It takes us forever to get those chickens put away!"

"Collies are herding dogs, ma'am. It's his instinct. Bet he can do that with your horses, too."

"I don't know. Horses might hurt him—kick him—but we do have six goats," said Lauren.

"Hobo is excellent with goats. He helped my Indian friends herd their goats," I said.

"That dog might be useful after all—maybe more help than trouble. Eddie, could I keep Hobo on a trial basis—maybe for a couple of days, just to see how things go?"

"Yah! Hip hip hooray!" Luca and Katie began hugging one another and jumping up and down.

"Once you see how smart that dog is, ma'am, I think you will want to keep him for good," I said.

"We shall see, Eddie. Now, Katie, would you show Mr. Ocean our horses while I talk with Rosalina."

Suddenly Hobo barked and then ran over to the fence bordering the property. On the other side was a golden retriever, and the two dogs began sniffing noses.

"Oh that's our neighbor's dog, Marley! She's a very sweet dog," Katie said.

Hobo barked twice. "She's hot! I never dated a country girl!"

Rosalina went into the farmhouse to conduct her interview. Hobo jumped the fence and got to know Marley as the kids showed me around the farm and introduced me to all the animals. After meeting the livestock, we circled the large pond twice, spotting largemouth bass, turtles, and frogs as we walked. Then the three of us climbed into a hammock that was strung between two pine trees in the front yard. As we listened to a cacophony of singing birds and noisy cicadas, we three swung gently back and forth in the hammock.

"This place is paradise. It reminds me of the Whatchacallits' Indian village in the Big Cypress Swamp," I said.

"Listen, hear that? That was a cardinal…and that one is a mockingbird." Katie began identifying the many birdsongs.

Hobo finally came back to the house with his coat full of prickly burrs.

"You sure aren't much of a country dog, city slicker," I said to him. He barked. "I'll get used to it. Did you see that babe over there! She's my new neighbor. Oh-la-la! I dig tall blondes!"

After an hour, Rosalina finished the interview and came out of the house with Lauren. By the look of their eyes, I could tell they had both been crying. Together, we all walked back to the barn and said our goodbyes, and then Rosalina and I left Long Pond Stables without Hobo. As we drove out the gate, I looked back and saw Hobo pressing up against Luca's leg. Everyone was standing in a line and waving goodbye to us.

Lauren had given Rosalina permission to publish her article, the final chapter of Luca's story. The article would be the third in a series titled "Child Abuse in Miami—How a Boy and His Dog Survived Years of Horror." The happy ending to Luca's plight was a long time coming, and on the ride back to Miami, Rosalina told me what she had learned from Lauren.

"Lauren was a substitute English teacher at Jupiter High School. Her husband, Tom, was an army reservist. Tom ran Long Pond Stables, and Lauren taught English class until Tom was called up for active duty. After Tom was deployed to Vietnam, Lauren was forced to leave her teaching job to take over the family's equestrian business. Three years ago, in 1971, Tom was killed in Vietnam. Lauren was devastated and has struggled to keep the family farm viable for three years. She is in serious debt, Eddie."

"Oh no! Are you saying she could lose the farm? So this place—this paradise for the kids and the animals—might only be temporary?"

"'Fraid so! Lauren said she would hang on as long as possible. She's going to home school Luca year round because he's completely illiterate. The seven-year-old kid is only functioning at a preschool level."

"So finally Luca is in good hands and in a good place—but it might not last? That sucks! Why is life so unfair, Rosalina?!"

"Lauren says that she'll take it a day at a time. At least for now things are good for the boy. I've been brainstorming—thinking of ways to do a fundraiser—maybe a fundraiser linked to my article. That might provided Lauren with some money, some temporary relief."

"I hope so."

"We've done all we can for now, Eddie."

"I guess so. The funny thing is that I would never have known about Luca if Hobo hadn't jumped into my boat that Sunday morning in Miami. It's almost as if Hobo was sent to us—sent to us so we could find Luca and rescue him!"

"Sent to us? 'Sent' as in 'sent by a higher power'?"

"Exactly, Rosalina!"

"Hmm, maybe. Who knows?"

God works in mysterious ways.

## Chapter 20

# MISTRIAL

### 1:10 PM, FRIDAY, JANUARY 11ᵀᴴ, 1974

Ima Hooker was sitting alone at Rosalina Rossi's desk when I walked into the office.

"Hi, Ima. How come you're not at the trial?"

"Hi, Eddie. Haven't you heard?"

"Heard what?"

"Judge Crown dismissed the case against Tony Montana. The Boss was released this morning!"

"What? Why—what happened?"

"Both witnesses against the Boss recanted their testimony. They submitted written statements claiming they had lied about the Boss's criminal activities. Both lied? What are the odds of that happening?"

"Sounds fishy to me." I was playing dumb, pretending I didn't know what the mob had done to the judge's dog and the two witnesses. The office door opened, and Rosalina entered carrying a paper bag.

"Hi Rosalina," I said. "Ima just told me the news."

"Yeah, a mistrial—what a shocker. Everyone thought they had Montana dead to rights this time." Rosalina opened the bag, slid a submarine sandwich across the desk toward Ima, and sat down at the desk.

"They must have gotten to the witnesses," Rosalina said and began unwrapping a tuna salad sandwich.

"Who got to them, Rosalina?" I continued to play dumb, knowing full well how Nikko had threatened Judge Crown's family by killing the dog, Bentley. I wondered what they had done to the two witnesses.

"The mob. The mob got to them. Somehow the mobsters must have intimidated them." Rosalina took a bite of her sandwich and noticed that I was staring at it. "Hey, Eddie, I'm sorry. I didn't know you were coming by the office or I would have brought you a sandwich from the deli too."

"Don't worry Rosalina, I'm not hungry." I lied. I was starving but didn't want to make my friends feel uncomfortable. I tried not to stare as I watched the girls eating lunch. *Yum—those sandwiches sure look good, dude!*

Rosalina set her sandwich down and used a straw to take a sip of bottled Pepsi. "What mystifies me is why Judge Crown was so acquiescent when the defense attorneys demanded a dismissal." She looked up at me. I quickly diverted my eyes from her sandwich, feeling like Hobo begging for food at the dinner table.

Ima spoke. "Yeah, I was there when that happened, and it was strange! The judge didn't even question the witnesses to find out why they had lied about the Boss. He just pounded his gavel once and said, 'Case dismissed!' All hell broke loose, and Judge Crown ran back into his chambers and closed the door.

"The prosecutors were outraged and began jumping up and down, screaming and yelling. They were running around yelling and waving their arms like a bunch of howler monkeys. The defense attorneys sprang to their feet and began cheering and patting each other on the back. Tony Montana did not seem a bit surprised. He just sat there smiling—actually it was more of a tight-lipped smirk— then he looked straight at me and winked. Here, look at my sketch of the Boss's reaction to the verdict."

I was still staring at Rosalina's sandwich, watching it disappear one bite at a time. "Look at Ima's sketches, Eddie." Rosalina motioned with her hand for Ima to show me her sketches, and I finally looked away from the tuna sandwich.

"Go to the back pages first, Eddie. I want you to see the change in Judge Crown's demeanor from the day before," Ima said as she handed me a large sketchpad.

"I've seen these. These older ones are the sketches that were printed in the newspaper," I said. "You showed me these sketches after the first day of the trial."

"Yeah, that's right. Now look at the judge's face. Notice how he looks at Montana. That's clearly a look of disdain and disgust from the judge, don't you think?" Ima had beautifully captured the demeanor of all the courtroom players. Montana seemed disinterested and bored, but his attorneys looked very worried. At the prosecution's table, the lawyers' expressions exuded confidence and determination. Crown had the look of a determined man completely in control and exuding power and authority.

Rosalina chimed in. "Judge Crown has a reputation as a hanging judge. He's a real hard-nosed magistrate who likes to hand out the maximum sentence. For him to dismiss a high-profile case so readily makes no sense to me."

"So why would the judge cave so quickly? Everyone thought it was an airtight case. What do you think, Eddie?" Ima asked.

"Bribery, maybe?" Still pretending I was clueless to the cause of the mistrial, I stood beside Rosalina's chair, watching her cut off a piece of the tuna sandwich and eat it slowly, savoring each bite.

*Damn, only one bite left.* Vicariously, I was enjoying the tuna sandwich with her. *Mmmm, it's so good!* Suddenly my stomach, which was only a couple of feet from Rosalina's right ear, made a loud rumbling sound. Rosalina looked at my belly and then up at my face and noticed me still staring at her sandwich.

"I'm stuffed. Anyone want this last piece?" she asked.

I didn't answer, but Ima said, "No, thanks. I have plenty."

"Just gonna throw it away, then." Rosalina pulled the trash can closer to her chair.

"No! No! Wait, wait! I hate wasting food, Rosalina. Maybe I can force down one bite." She handed me the chunk of sandwich and laughed.

"Okay now, back to the sketches, Eddie," said Rosalina as I slowly ate the last piece, savoring every molecule.

So I looked down at Ima's sketchpad as I ate. *Mmmm.* "Ima's right! The judge's attitude at this morning's proceedings seems to have changed drastically from the day before."

"Yeah, he looks like a ghost—pale, white, like all the blood was drained from his face. He has big, black bags under his eyes. Looks like he's terrified and hasn't slept," said Rosalina.

I bent down to get a closer look. "Yeah, I can see the fear in his eyes! That man is clearly terrified!"

"Eddie, this morning I could see that Montana was getting a kick out of Judge Crown's fear. See how he's staring straight at the judge and smirking. I didn't see the judge make eye contact with Montana all morning. Not even once! Those hard, judgmental looks of disdain from the judge were gone today. See how Crown's looking at the floor in front of the defense team? He seems to be terrified of them, too!"

Ima was right—Crown was terrified, and I knew the reason, but I wasn't about to reveal what the mob had done. That knowledge might endanger these women…might put us all in the crosshairs of the mob and Nicky the Knife.

"Well, girls, I believe in karma. Someday the Boss will get his just dues. I'm heading over to Sun 'N' Fun. Jill says I have a gig tomorrow—a special request to captain a private charter," I said.

"Oh, that reminds me, Eddie—a guy in a tan suit and carrying a briefcase was in here this morning asking about you. Said he just missed you in Key West but that he followed you back to Miami. Said he has something very important to give you." Rosalina stood up and used a paper napkin to wipe some mayo from my cheek.

"Thanks, Rosalina. I can get a little sloppy sometimes. Yeah, that's him. I saw that dorky guy at the bus terminal in Key West. He seems to be stalking me. How did he make the connection between us? How did he know we are friends?"

"He said he saw the lost dog posters and called the number—my phone number. Called me first to find out who I was and then came by the office looking for you. What's this mystery man all about, Eddie?"

"I'm afraid the guy is trying to collect my hospital bill, but he's wasting his time. You can't get blood out of a rock!"

"A bill collector chasing you across the state for a hospital bill? That seems odd. The hospital will usually write off indigent care as a loss."

*Oh my gosh! Rosalina is right! I'm an indigent—a bum! What a loser I am!* "Well, I'm not a freeloader, Rosalina. I plan on paying all my debts when I'm able to." I felt my face turning red from embarrassment.

"We know that, Eddie. Soon you'll be back on your feet, no doubt about it!" Ima put her hand on my shoulder.

"Thanks, Ima." I noticed Ima push her sandwich off to the side. "Hey Ima, aren't you gonna finish that Italian sub?"

"No. You want it? Only a couple of bites left." Ima handed me her leftovers.

"I don't mean to be a mooch, ladies. It's just that I hate wasting food. I'm not that hungry but I'll try to force this piece down, and then I'm off to see Jill." I began walking toward the door and took a bite. *Mmmm! Good!* "See you later, alligators!"

"After a while, crocodile," Ima answered with a smile.

"Ciao, Eddie. Next time I'll have a sandwich for you."

I saluted them farewell. *Yum! Good sandwich, although it could use a little spice, a few jalapeños would be nice.*

*Beggars can't be choosers.*

*Chapter 21*

# THE ICE QUEEN

When I arrived at the office of Sun 'N' Fun Charters, I found my fellow captains gathered in the employees' lounge.

"Hi, fellas!"

"Bonjour, Capitaine Eddie!" said Captain "Frenchy" Couture as he stood at a sink washing his hands. Petey and Doug nodded but barely looked up from where they sat staring down at the floor. I sensed a mood of depression in the air.

"So whose funeral is this?" I asked.

"Dr. Hamm's, I wish!" said Captain Pete.

"What has she done now, Petey boy?" I asked.

"You tell him, Doug. I'm too pissed!"

Captain Doug explained the reason for the dour mood. "Dr. Hamm assigned Petey to order new belts for the engines on three of the sailboats, so Pete gave her the list of all the parts that were needed. Then she totally screwed up his order."

Pete was angry. "Last week I spent half a day crawling around inside engine compartments, getting all the part numbers for the replacement belts and a couple of pulleys that were worn down. I gave the list to Hamm. We needed to order a dozen new belts total. The little witch must have changed my order because a few hours ago we received the shipment, and only two out of the twelve belts will fit our boats."

Frenchy chimed in. "To make matters worse, before we had discovered that Hamm screwed up Petey's order, I removed all the old belts from the *Third Wish*. The new belts don't fit her, so now I need to put the old, worn belts back onto the motor." Frenchy was using a rag to wipe black grime from his hands as he spoke.

"That micromanaging little bitch! She brags about being a doctor of the maritime sciences, but she can't even order parts for a boat motor—even when the exact part numbers are provided for her!" said Pete.

"So now we've got V-belts when we need serpentine belts. We've got belts that are too short, and we've got belts that are too long," said Doug.

"Why did she change your order, Petey?" I asked.

"Because I ordered original equipment replacement belts. Good quality belts. The cheap little brat was trying to switch my order to after-market belts just to save a few bucks. Imagine us sailing a hundred miles out to sea, caught up in a white squall when one of those crappy Chinese belts snaps and leaves us without engine power."

"Yeah, Hamm's a real piece of work. Hey guys, I know I'm not supposed to, but I'm gonna tell Eddie what happened to Hamm down in Key Largo," said Pete.

"Go ahead. Tell him, Petey. I don't care—screw Hamm and her threats," said Doug.

"Eddie, Hamm made us swear an oath not to tell this story to anyone. We're under the threat of being fired if we tell a soul, but I don't give a crap anymore!" said Pete.

"I doubt that anything that Hamm did will surprise me, Pete. The woman is just plain nasty—a real sicko! Even my friend Rosalina recognized Dr. Hamm's personality as that of a malignant narcissist."

"This is not about being nasty, it's about being incompetent. When you were down in Key West we got real busy and we were short-handed, so Dr. Hamm was forced to captain an overnight charter aboard the *Hanky-Panky*. She rarely actually works the boats, you know. Well, she ran the *Hanky-Panky* aground off Key Largo, and when the towboat came to pull her off the sandbar, she tied the towrope off on a bow cleat instead of looping around the bottom of the mast.

"Well, just before the boat came off the sandbar, a chunk of the fiberglass deck was ripped off the bow along with the cleat. The towrope was stretched tight as a banjo string, and the cleat went flying back at the towboat captain. It hit the captain, broke his arm, and knocked him down."

"If that cleat had hit his head it could have killed him!" Doug chimed in.

"Yeah, and then, when she was finally clear of the sandbar, she saw the other captain down on the deck, injured, and she panicked! She put the *Hanky-Panky* into forward drive instead of reverse and ran over the towrope. The line fouled her prop, disabling the boat again, and she began drifting toward a coral reef until the injured captain tied up alongside the *Hanky-Panky* and told the little idiot to drop her anchor.

"Another towboat was called, and they brought a diver out, but he couldn't cut the line loose. It was jammed all the way up into the stuffing box. The idiot Dr. Hamm refused a tow and kept trying to drive the boat back to shore. In the process, she mangled the fouled propeller blades and bent the propeller shaft. The stuffing box seal broke and began to leak. Now the *Hanky-Panky* was taking on water and sinking."

"Holy shit!" I said.

"The injured towboat captain sent out a Mayday call to the Coast Guard. The Coast Guard dispatched a cruiser with a pump, and they used the high-capacity pump to keep the *Hanky-Panky* afloat as she was towed into port in Key Largo."

"What a disaster! I was wondering where the *Hanky-Panky* was," I said.

"She's in Key Largo—dry-docked for two weeks. Needs eight grand worth of repairs!" said Pete.

"I'm surprised that the guys at corporate haven't fired Hamm," I said.

"Eddie, don't you know…? Hamm's rich father owns this company. Hamm's father *is* corporate. He's a New York surgeon, a real doctor; he bought Sun 'N' Fun for Jill so she could have a job after graduating with her doctorate degree from the maritime academy. Can you imagine any private company hiring that little witch? What was it that you called her—a malignant narcissist?"

"Yeah."

"She's more like a malignant tumor inside my head! With a competent and decent human being as boss, this would be a dream job— the job of a lifetime. Instead, she makes it a living hell for all of us!" said Doug.

Pete added, "I overheard her arguing with her father on the phone after the fiasco in Largo. The old man must have been telling her to stick to the office work. She was whining like a five-year-old and blaming her incompetence on a 'poorly trained' towboat captain. I heard her say, 'Daddy, I have a doctorate degree and the best training money can buy; you know that! That towboat guy probably only has a GED—a high school education at best!'"

"What an elitist little brat! She's blaming the captain she injured and almost got killed? Does that surprise anyone?" I asked rhetorically.

"So, Eddie, guess what I've been doing all morning," Doug challenged me.

"Cleaning the toilets?"

"No—she had me doing that yesterday. This morning she made me run out and buy her daughter lunch and then deliver it to the kid at the Ben Franklin Academy—the school for spoiled rotten, bratty, rich kids."

"I bet she didn't even give you any money," I said.

"Actually she did, but after I returned to the office I found out that the kid had called Hamm from the school. The brat was crying because the sub I bought for her had mayo on it. The kid hates mayo. Hamm never told me about that. She was pissed off as usual and threw a major tantrum before leaving the office—she left about an hour ago. Took the kid a new lunch."

"Eddie, do you know what new duty Hamm has assigned to me?" asked Frenchy.

"No, what?"

"Making a schedule for emptying the trash cans. She says the trash is not being emptied often enough."

"Well, at least it's not just me that Dr. Jill Hamm annoys the hell out of. I don't know how you full-time captains can take her crap all day long, five days a week," I said just as the door of the lounge swung open.

"Why are my ears burning?" Dr. Jill Hamm asked as she came into the lounge and stood glaring at us with her hands on her hips. "Don't you freeloaders have some work to do?" she said as she wrinkled up her pug nose to reveal her large buck teeth.

"Yeah, boss, we have lots to do. We need to put the old, worn-out belts back on *Third Wish* since the wrong-size replacement belts were ordered!" said Frenchy.

"Well, you can blame your friend Petey Boy for that screw-up! He should have known to order the cost-saving after-market belts. Where does he think he works? Does he think this is the Carnival Cruise Line and I'm made out of money?"

*Yeah, actually you are, you stingy little rich bitch!*

Hamm held up her stubby little arms to wave us all away. "Not you, Ocean! You come with me. The rest of you clowns, get busy!"

Hamm led me into her office, and I glanced at her framed doctorate degree, which was displayed so prominently on the wall above her desk. The document made me laugh. *Doctor of Maritime Science? Hah, she's an incompetent sailor, and a mean little bully to boot!*

"You're going to be taking that rude Hispanic supermodel, Katarina, and the older Cuban guy down to Key West. It will be a two-week cruise."

"A Hispanic supermodel? A supermodel requested me?"

"Yeah, but against my recommendation. They insisted on having you as their captain. How do you know those people?"

"I don't."

"There's something fishy going on here. So, how do they know you if you don't know them—and why did they request you if you don't even know who they are? Those Cubans scare me for some reason. They're up to something, and they're so intense."

"I have no idea why they want me as captain, Jill."

"I'm tired of all the mystery surrounding you, Ocean. First the weird little guy in the cheap suit who keeps asking about you, and now this supermodel requesting your services. And then you claiming you don't even know her? Doesn't add up, Ocean! I don't know what you're up to, but I'm going to find out. After this charter is over I'm going to re-evaluate your position with us here at Sun 'N' Fun."

"Great, boss, re-evaluating me—you're probably considering giving me a big raise, right?" My voice was dripping with sarcasm.

"Just be here at seven AM sharp, Ocean! If it were up to me, I wouldn't even be giving you this gig!" Hamm shooed me away with one hand, but before I could close the office door behind me, she called out, "Wait—Ocean!"

"What now, boss?"

"Do you wish to contribute to the Save Our Planet fund? My daughter's school, the Benjamin Franklin Academy, is fund-raising to prevent the coming of a new Ice Age. All the scientists agree that the planet is cooling due to man-made global cooling, you know."

"Me donate money? Jill you haven't even paid me for my last trip. I'm broke. Anyway, I'll donate to global cooling the day it snows in Miami!"

"Oh, so you're one of those global cooling deniers? Well, the debate is over. It's settled science, sonny boy!"

"Science is never settled unless you're like the scientists who sent Galileo to the inquisition for affirming that the earth was a sphere, not flat."

"I knew it! You *are* a climate-change denier, Ocean!"

"No, the climate has clearly changed throughout history. I love the planet. The ocean and the sky are my loves, and I hate pollution, but I'm not a scientist. I cannot give an educated opinion as to why we now have a period of cooling. I do know that there was extreme warming and cooling before mankind even existed. I know because T-Rex bones are found in abundance in Montana. Subtropical dinosaurs, reptiles, lived in Canada—and then came an Ice Age and the dawn of mankind."

"You are an idiot and a science-denier, Ocean! The entire scientific community agrees that we are the cause of global cooling! Here, take this pamphlet and educate yourself. These are articles from the major newspapers that my daughter brought home from school!" Jill handed me a pamphlet.

"Thanks, I'll read it when I get to my cardboard shack and turn on my non-existent light bulb and adjust my non-existent heating and cooling system as I contemplate the horrors of a new Ice Age." *Hmmm...living in Florida would be even more pleasant if the planet cools! But at a rate of a tenth of a degree change per decade, I'll have to wait a couple of thousand years for a cool summer in Miami.*

"Well with an attitude like yours, no wonder you live in a cardboard box. No wonder you are such a loser, Ocean!"

I left Sun 'N' Fun and stopped off at the Tiki Bar to visit Fannie.

"Hey, Fannie—how 'bout an ice cold brewski?" I pulled two quarters from my pocket. *Could my fifty cents have been better spent saving the Earth, Nahh!*

"Coming right up, Eddie!"

I sat down at the bar and began to read the global cooling pamphlets as I ate free peanuts and pretzels from a bowl.

*FROM THE N.Y. TIMES: Dated 1971*
"In the thirty years leading up to the 1970s, available temperature recordings suggested that there was a cooling trend. As a result, some scientists suggested that the current interglacial period could rapidly draw to a close, which might result in the Earth plunging into a new ice age over the next few centuries. This idea could have been reinforced by the knowledge that the smog that climatologists call 'aerosols' – emitted by human activities into the atmosphere – also caused cooling."

*FROM THE WASHINGTON POST*
"On January 11, 1970, the Washington *Post* reported that "Colder Winters Herald Dawn of New Ice Age."

*FROM THE NATIONAL SCIENCE BOARD: 1972*
"The National Science Board's Patterns and Perspectives in Environmental Science report of 1972 discussed the cyclical behavior of climate, and the understanding at the time that the planet was entering a phase of cooling after a warm period.

"Judging from the record of the past interglacial ages, the present time of high temperatures should be drawing to an end, to be followed by a long period of considerably colder temperatures leading into the next glacial age some 20,000 years from now."

"Hmm...I might be wrong after all. There is a lot of evidence here. Maybe Jill's right."
"Wrong about what?" Fannie asked.

"That man-made pollution is causing the global cooling—they say aerosols might be blocking the sun's energy."

I finished reading the last article. "Hey, Fannie, that means that soon we will all be freezing our fannies off in South Florida—no more heat! Yahoo! Here's to the new Ice Age!" I raised my glass and then took a long drink of the ice-cold beer. Here's to Vogel!

"To shorten the winter, borrow some money due in the spring."

*Chapter 22*

# KATARINA

**B**rownie was cooking dinner on the hibachi when I arrived at the penthouse just before dark.

"Yum! How did you score those little chickens?" I asked him.

"It's not chicken—it's squab."

"Squab?'

"Yeah, I call them squab. They're pigeons from downtown Miami. A guy on the street sells them real cheap. Tastes better than chicken to me—darker meat that's a little gamier.

"Well, I'm not too picky nowadays. Hey, Brownie, where is everybody?"

"Riley Ford moved out of skid row this afternoon. So why don't you take his shack—shack number three—now that it's vacant? It's better than Moe's stinky old box, plus Moe should be getting out of jail soon."

"Where's Riley moving?"

"To the flophouse apartments downtown. The Boss hired him full-time. It's Riley's reward for helping the Boss give Judge Crown an attitude adjustment." Smoke rose in spirals from the sizzling squab and enveloped Brownie's face as he stood bent over the grill, poking the meat with a long fork.

"Smells great!" I said.

I moved closer to the grill and breathed in the heavenly barbeque smoke. "Boy, I'm hungry."

"Here. Sorry—no sides." Brownie handed me a plate containing one grilled pigeon.

"Thanks!"

After we'd finished eating, Brownie and I sat on empty five-gallon paint buckets observing the humanity below. Suddenly it started raining money!

"What the hell?" I looked up to see dollar bills falling out of the sky!

"It's raining money, Eddie!" Brownie sprang to his feet. The dollar bills fluttered down from heaven like a swarm of large green butterflies. Below, people began chasing the dollars as they blew along the ground, creating chaos across skid row.

"Grab some!" I shouted. We ran around at the edge of the steep embankment, snatching bills from midair. I looked up toward the highway to see where the money was coming from. Two of the Boss's mobsters were standing at the guardrail, pouring buckets of dollar bills off the I-95 bridge, and the money pin-wheeled down onto skid row. The loud commotion alerted more people, who began emerging from tents and cardboard boxes to join the frenzy.

"Those are the Boss's men up there! The Boss must be celebrating his mistrial!" Brownie yelled.

People began screaming as they ran over to get closer to the bridge and the source of the windfall. "Tony! Tony! Tony!" they chanted in unison.

Now the Boss himself appeared, standing at the guardrail, waving down to the adoring crowd. "God bless America, and God bless the greatest justice system in the world!" he yelled to us.

"We love you, Mr. Montana!" a man with a booming voice shouted out from the crowd.

The Boss raised both arms above his head. "My good friends, that was five grand—five thousand dollars for the people who make Miami a magic city!" He brought his arms down, and with his right hand saluted the people below as the money shower came to an end. Then, just as suddenly as he had appeared, the Boss was gone.

"I've got at least twelve bucks. How much did you get?" I asked Brownie.

"Ten bucks!"

Most of the money had fluttered away just beyond our reach, due to a breeze that had carried the dollar bills away from the bridge abutment. Below, fighting broke out as people scrambled to get the last available dollars.

"Well that was really cool! Five thousand $1 bills blowing on the wind! What a sight that was!" Brownie said.

As the excitement died down, I went into my box to get some sleep while Brownie stayed up to "people watch."

*6:15 am, Saturday, January 12th, 1974*

Brownie was sleeping late and did not have the usual morning fare of coffee and grits cooking on the grill. *Hmm, that's unusual. Brownie's normally an early riser.* Since no breakfast was cooking, I decided to use some of my windfall money to grab a fast food breakfast on my way to work.

It normally took forty minutes for me to cover the two-mile walk from skid row to the Sun 'N' Fun office. *Darn, it's 6:15, that's cutting it close, dude! You're gonna have to jog if you want to stop off for breakfast.* So I jogged the first mile to make up enough time to grab an Egg McMuffin, which I ate as I walked to work. When I arrived it was 6:56 am, and Jill was waiting there to greet me.

"You're late again, Ocean!"

"What...late? You said to come at seven."

"That's right. To me, fifteen minutes early is being on time! Four minutes early is being late!"

"If you say so, boss. Where are the clients?"

"Out on the boat. I didn't like them being in my office. For some reason, that pair creeps me out."

"Is the *Third Wish* all set to sail?"

"Yeah, the Cubans are all yours, Ocean. Me and that supermodel chick are like oil and water—we just don't mix!"

"What a surprise, boss," I said in my best sarcastic voice.

"You're becoming a real wise guy, Ocean. Like I said before, I'll be re-evaluating your employment with me after the trip. You better not screw up this time!"

"It would be a tragedy to lose the honor of working for you the rest of my life, Dr. Hamm."

"Ha-ha—real funny, Ocean! Beware of those Cubans. There's something very fishy about them."

I slung my backpack over my shoulder and left the office. In the distance I saw the clients standing on the deck of the *Third Wish*. *Good Lord! No wonder Jill calls her "the supermodel"!* Standing at the bow of the *Third Wish* was a beautiful young woman. Dark, olive skin set off the brilliance of her skimpy white bikini, which barely covered her toned and curvaceous body. Straight, silky, black, shoulder-length hair glistened in the morning sun; her legs seemed abnormally long and very shapely.

The woman's slender yet muscular body moved gracefully as she untied the canvas boot covering of the mainsail. As I approached the boat, I could not take my eyes off the woman, and I failed to see a dock box three slips down from where the Third Wish was docked. My knees slammed into the box, and I fell face-first over it and onto the dock.

"Ahhh, crap!" I cried out and rolled to my side before sitting upright, not wanting to look up in fear that the young woman had seen me fall. I sat up, cross-legged on the dock pretending to be checking the combination lock on the dock box in front of me.

"That's not your box, Ocean…we all saw you fall flat on your face!" Captain Mack Berger said with a laugh. For the first time I noticed that many of the charter boat captains had come outside of their cabins to gawk at the "supermodel." *Please don't be looking at me.* Sheepishly I glanced over at the *Third Wish.* The woman had removed her sunglasses and was staring right at me with a smirk on her face. *Damn!* I got up, patted the box as if satisfied that it was securely locked, and then walked toward the boat.

"Ahoy! I'm Captain Eddie Ocean!" The woman stood perfectly still at the bow. Behind her, the burly man also stood motionless, leaning against the boom.

"Good morning!" Again I called out, but still the pair did not respond. They both just stood there staring at me, evaluating me. Now I was right below the bow and could see the woman up close. Her eyes were unusual—strangely exotic and weirdly beautiful. *What is that color?* I wondered as we made eye contact at close range.

Her eyes were a light color, but they were not blue, not green, nor brown, nor hazel. Her eyes looked gray—gray and cunning, like the eyes of a wolf! The way she stared at me without speaking was unsettling, so I looked over toward the man. His eyes were dark brown, cold, and emotionless, even more disturbing than hers.

My gaze returned to the woman, and I felt like a lamb being sized up by her wolf eyes. I imagined that the two predators could visualize my heart beating inside my chest as they stared right through me. As she stood above me on the bow of the boat with the sun behind her, there was something very familiar about her silhouette. *Where have I seen her before?*

Finally the man broke the silence. "Katarina, this must be our charter boat captain."

*Katarina!* His voice calling out the name "Katarina" made me suddenly remember them. These were the people who had rescued me from the raft and dumped me on the beach.

"Yes, sir. I'm Captain Eddie Ocean."

Finally the woman spoke. "I hope you can navigate the ocean better than you can navigate this dock." My face felt hot and began turning red as I felt it flush with embarrassment.

"Yes, ma'am. I seem to do much better on the ocean than I do on land." I hopped aboard the *Third Wish* and stood next to Katarina. She was nearly as tall as my six-foot frame, and the hulking, middle-aged man was at least six-foot four and well over 200 pounds.

"I'm Katarina Romero, and this is my uncle, Carlos Romero." I was disappointed when she lowered her sunglasses from her head to cover her eyes; her exotic gray eyes were mesmerizing. She turned her head and looked toward the office.

"Oh look! That bossy little woman is coming out again. What does she want now?" Katarina flipped her sunglasses back up onto her head, put her hands on her hips, and glared at Hamm with a furrowed brow.

To my surprise, Hamm took one look at Katarina, stopped in her tracks, and then threw her arms up in resignation before going back inside her office.

"Must not have been anything important. Let's cast off," I said.

We left the Port of Miami and sailed south toward the Florida Keys.

## 6:35 PM, SATURDAY, JANUARY 12TH, 1974

After sailing all day, I anchored the *Third Wish* in a protected cove near Islamorada. The Cubans told me they already knew how to sail and were not here for sailing lessons—they simply wanted to enjoy the boat ride. So I alone piloted the *Third Wish* south. *If these people are seasoned sailors, I wonder why they paid extra money for me to captain the boat?*

The mysterious pair seemed downright secretive and were strangely quiet, only occasionally communicating with one another in Spanish. They clearly did not like my asking them questions. Carlos went below and spent most of the day down in the galley fiddling around with a radio. Katarina stayed topside and was a feast for my eyes as she spent a few hours sunbathing and reading a paperback novel at the bow. Often, she looked up from her book and watched me working the sails. *She's checking me out…just as much as I'm gawking at her!* Even though we were flirting, Katarina did not say a word until after the *Third Wish* was anchored for the night in about fifteen feet of calm water.

"It's a beautiful evening. If you two want to take a swim, I'll make the dinner," I called down to Carlos, who was still in the galley. As charter boat captain, it was my duty to prepare dinner for my guests.

"I'll be done here in five minutes. Then you can have the galley all to yourself," Carlos said as he hid something from my view.

*Splash!* Katarina dove off the bow, and I looked down to see her swimming to the bottom in the crystal-clear water. She was down for a long time before finally popping up on the opposite side of the boat.

"Eddie, you got a tickle stick?" she asked me as she treaded water along the port side.

"Yeah, but lobsters are out of season," I informed her.

"I won't tell if you don't tell," she said as I tossed her the stick. She dove again and then resurfaced with a huge Caribbean lobster.

"Turn it loose! You can go to jail for catching that!"

She disregarded my plea and grabbed the carapace with one hand and the tail with the other. In one swift twist she ripped the lobster's tail off and threw to me.

"We need at least two more big ones!" she said and then dove underwater again.

"No! No more lobsters!" I grabbed the lobster tail and hid it in the cooler and then scanned the horizon to see if any Wild Life Patrol officers were in the area.

Carlos came up from below deck. "She won't listen to you, Captain Eddie. Since she was eight years old, nobody can tell her what to do. No one can control that girl."

"Shit! She's gonna get us all thrown in the slammer, sir!" I took my binoculars from the console and began scanning the horizon, worried about being observed by Wildlife Management vessels.

Katarina surfaced again. This time she had already ripped off the tails of two big lobsters, and she brought them onboard.

"Now you can cook us a dinner, Captain Eddie." She handed me the lobster tails, and I noticed some blood on her right hand, where she had grabbed a tail with her bare hand.

"You're cut." *Her hands must be tough as leather! I always wear gloves when catching lobsters.*

"Just a scratch. No one is around, Captain Eddie. Why are you so worried?"

"Lobsters are out of season, ma'am! We could get arrested and get a huge fine!"

"Well, now that I killed them, we can't let them go to waste. Carlos likes them boiled." She laughed at me and dove back into the sea.

The Cubans went for a swim together, and I boiled the lobster tails. Lemon-butter sauce, French bread, and a fresh salad with a bottle of white wine completed the menu. As the sun was setting below the waters of the Gulf of Mexico, the three of us ate dinner and shared the wine.

"You probably wonder why we have been so quiet, Captain Eddie—probably wondering why we don't like being asked questions or ask any questions of you. Am I right?" asked Carlos.

"Yeah, I figure it's a cultural thing—especially with me being a *gringo* and all."

"No, that's not it. Most Cubans are very social—very talkative. The fact is that we already know all about you, Captain Eddie Ocean. We probably know more about you than anyone other than yourself," said Carlos as Katarina sat quietly, staring at me with her cunning gray wolf eyes, intently observing my reaction.

"What? How do you know me?"

"That's a secret," he said.

"Well, I've figured out one thing: You're the people who rescued the dog and me from the raft and took us to the beach."

Carlos's eyes widened. "Very good! I thought you were unconscious that night. Yes, we did save your life, Eddie, and that is why we picked you as our captain for this little adventure of ours. You owe us, Eddie Ocean, you owe us your life, and we are here to collect on that debt!" The hulking man looked at me with wide, unblinking, cold, dark eyes.

"Well, what makes you think you know everything about me?" My eyes darted back and forth as I squirmed in my seat, calculating the distance from the boat to the shore. *Should I jump? Should I swim for it?*

"You're scaring him, *El Muerte*. We are not here to hurt you, Eddie, but we do need your help," said Katarina.

"*El Muerte*? That means 'the dead one,' doesn't it?" My Spanish was limited, but I tried to translate his nickname as he looked at me with cold, black eyes.

"Eddie, we are paramilitary soldiers fighting with the Cuban resistance—fighting to overthrow the Cato regime in Cuba. We work covertly with the assistance of the CIA and your government. Our destination on this voyage is not Key West; it is Cuba," he said.

"Cuba! I can't take you to Cuba! It's illegal!"

"We have it all figured out. We need to make port at a drydock near Key West. Changes to the boat and her registration must be made. They have provided Canadian passports for you and Katarina. Katarina is your Canadian wife, and I'm her uncle—just tagging along on the lovebirds' vacation."

"My wife? Canadian? Are you people insane?! Please tell me this is a joke!"

"Do I look like a joker, Eddie?" Carlos "*El Muerte*" Romero stood up and towered over me as I sat looking up at the muscular hulk. The look in his eyes caused my hair to stand on end, and the blood drained from my face.

"You're scaring him again, Carlos!"

"We will give you more details later, but we need to sail straight through to Key West. No more stopping overnight. We must sail night and day, and from now on we will help you man the boat. But we must leave at first light, so you'd better get to sleep early tonight, Captain Eddie." *El Muerte* scowled.

In a daze, I went to my bunk on the starboard stern side of the boat. Katarina's cabin was across from mine, portside and stern. Carlos took the extra large berth at the bow. During the night I got up to use the head and I noticed that *El Muerte* was not sleeping in his berth. He was sleeping outside on the deck, blocking the hatchway. *He must be guarding the exit so that I can't jump ship during the night.*

After returning to my bunk, I had just fallen back to sleep when someone woke me. "What? What is it?" I mumbled in the dark. Someone was on top of me, straddling my body, hands gripping each of my biceps.

"You are stronger than you look, Captain Eddie." It was Katarina's voice. She squeezed the muscles of my biceps; her hands were slender but very strong and callused. I looked up but couldn't make out her face in the dark. Only the white of her teeth and a glint of "eyeshine" from her gray wolf eyes reflecting the dim moonlight were visible to me.

"I want you," she whispered.

The glowing eyes came closer, and her long hair tickled my bare chest as she leaned down and kissed me hard on the lips.

Stupid was wide-awake now. *This girl is trouble! You're playing with fire, dude!*

Stupid is as stupid does.

*Chapter 23*

# THE CANADIAN GOOSE

## 10:00 AM, MONDAY, JANUARY 14ᵀᴴ, 1974

A light, misty rain was falling on the Florida Keys as we entered Safe Harbor Marina on Stock Island. The *Third Wish* would be put into the drydock just north of Key West for three days so that alterations could be made to the boat. Katarina, Carlos, and I took a taxicab down to Key West and checked into the Symington Court Hotel.

After securing our rooms, we walked down Duval Street to Sloppy Joe's Bar for lunch. As usual, Sloppy Joe's was crowded with tourists. As we weaved our way through the knots of tables and huddles of tourist dressed in colorful tropical attire, I noticed how much attention Katarina drew from the male diners. We snaked our way to the back of the pub, looking for a seat, and found an unoccupied table located adjacent to the rear bar and sat down for lunch.

Pointing to the variety of beer bottles lining a shelf above the bar I commented, "When I had my *Watermelon* boat I must have hauled a million cases of the beer over from the Bahamas to this joint.

"Hey! There's Katie." I stood and waved. *"Hello Katie!"* I yelled to her to be heard over the noisy crowd, waving my arms above my head.

"Hi, Eddie. Heard about you losing your boat—so sorry! Captain Mac Berger has been delivering the Kalik," she called out from behind the bar as she filled a glass pitcher with beer.

"Oh really, Captain Mac? I thought that Captain Harry Balz was going to take over my delivery route. What happened?"

"Harry went into business with Captain Stubby Dix...started a business right here in Key West."

"What business, Kate?"

"Sailing school. Harry Balz and Stubby Dix opened a sailing academy."

"Oh, cool! What's the school called?"

"Beating Into the Wind Extreme Sailing Academy. People say that Balz and Dix are putting out some of the finest seamen in the world."

"Well, that's great, Katie—hey, give us a pitcher of that Heineken Lite." I returned to our table and began perusing the menu until our server brought the beer and asked for our order.

"I'll try the 'Full Moon' fish sandwich," said Katarina.

I nodded my head in approval, "Good choice. I've had that several times! But today I'm going with the Sloppy Philly Cheese Steak with fries. How 'bout you, Carlos?"

"The Ernie Burger, bloody as hell, with onion rings."

We drank beer and observed the diverse crowd of people while waiting for our order to arrive.

Suddenly Carlos pushed his mug aside and placed his knapsack on the table. He opened it and took out some paperwork. "Eddie, here is your Canadian passport and some new ID cards." Carlos slid the documents across the table toward me as Katarina refilled everyone's glasses. I examined the fake credentials.

"Looks real good—how did you get my picture for this fake passport?"

"The CIA took it from the Florida DMV files. They used your driver's license photo."

"Ah-ha! I knew it! CIA! Those must be the guys who have been following me around all week. That's must be it! They got a guy in a cheap tan suit carrying a briefcase, tracking me."

"I doubt it, Eddie. If the CIA were following you, you would never have spotted them. Plus, you weren't even on their radar until we asked to recruit you just last week. The CIA didn't know who you were until we told them about you," Carlos said.

"Told them what?"

"We told them you were an experienced boat captain who owed us a favor—a big-time favor for saving your life. Told them that as a local boat captain you might be a valuable asset for our team."

Just as our food arrived, Katarina asked me, "Eddie, why do you think the CIA is tailing you?"

"I've seen a guy following me—a nerd in a suit with a briefcase. He's been asking about me all over Miami. He even followed me down here to Key West last week."

"Like Carlos said, you would not have seen him if he were a CIA agent, Eddie. You would never have spotted the guy. Carlos and I might spot a professional tail, but I doubt that you would notice them," Katarina said.

"So you think I'm a clueless boob? Well thanks a lot, Kat!" I picked up a fry and twirled it in a circle near my ear. "Maybe I'm just cuckoo, cuckoo, cuckoo! Maybe I'm just paranoid and delusional."

"No, you're not clueless, Eddie. No offense, but we're trained to spot a tail, and you're not. The CIA is really good; they use teams to switch the tail. If you noticed a man following, a woman might take his place. Someone may well be following you, but I'm sure it's not a CIA spook."

"Okay, let's get back to business," Carlos said. "The boat will be finished on Thursday. In the meantime we must act like Canadian tourists sightseeing the island. You two will play the role of happy newlyweds for a few days, and then we'll set sail for Cuba. We leave at dawn on Thursday morning." Carlos poured another beer.

"What are you having done to the *Third Wish*?" I asked.

"We're giving her a blue hull, different sails, and a new name along with a Canadian registration," Carlos said.

"What! Dr. Hamm is going to kill me!"

"Maybe. But only if the Communists in Cuba don't kill you first, kid!" Carlos said with a smirk. When he saw the look on my face he laughed, an evil-sounding chuckle.

"Killed by Communists?"

"Shut up, Carlos, you're scaring him again! Carlos is only kidding, Eddie. He's toying with you—that's his dark side coming out. That's why he is called *El Muerte*!" Katarina stared at Carlos with narrowed eyes.

"Katarina, the kid should be aware of the danger we face," insisted Carlos.

"Don't listen to him, Eddie. We're not going to let anything happen to you."

"What the hell have I gotten myself into, Katarina? What are we going to be doing in Cuba?"

"Eddie, your part will be easy. Carlos and I will do all the work. Don't you worry," Katarina said.

"What work?"

Carlos answered, "Katarina is going to charm the pants off some big shot Communist officials, and then we are going to have them deliver some special cigars to Rafael Cato." Carlos stood up. "Excuse me, I'm going to the head."

"Eddie, all you have to do is play the part of my husband, and I will be your no-good, cheating, promiscuous wife."

"That sounds like a barrel of laughs."

"Eddie, do you dance?"

"I know some disco."

"Well, before the crossing I need to teach you some Latin dances. If all goes as planned, we will be attending a few parties full of high-level dignitaries. We might need to go to some nightclubs in Havana. We need to hobnob with the Communist elites and gain their trust."

"Dance lessons? Oh great!" I said sarcastically.

"It will be fun. I thought you liked me, Eddie."

"If you weren't a revolutionary, paramilitary, anti-Communist, anti-government spy, who is likely to get me killed or tossed into a dungeon, you would be a heck of a lot more likeable, Katarina!"

"Oh, so dramatic! Put some excitement in your life, Eddie, some adventure! You only live once, *chico!*"

"I know—only live once. That's why I'm hoping my dull, boring life will at least be a long one."

Carlos returned to the table. "I paid our tab at the bar, kids—let's go," he said and tossed some money for the tip onto the table.

We spent the day touring the island. We visited the East Martello Tower as well as the historic Hemingway House and then had dinner. After dinner we returned to the hotel, where Carlos had booked a separate room for himself.

"I'm gonna watch some TV," Carlos said and went to his room. Katarina and I went to ours.

"Ready for a salsa lesson, Eddie?" Katarina asked me as she tuned in a Latin radio station.

"No, thanks. My feet ache from all the walking we did today." My excuses were of no use; Katarina insisted that we dance together, and for nearly two hours she taught me the basics of the salsa, merengue, mambo, rumba, and the bomba dances.

"How many damn dances do you Latins have?" I asked while faking a severe limp, struggling toward a chair to sit down.

"Oh, no you don't. Get up! You're doing great, *chico.*"

"What, no tango? Oh darn! Well, you might as well just kick me in the agates anyway!"

"You are an excellent dancer for a beginner! I'm very impressed," she told me as our dance marathon finally ended.

Katarina took her role-playing as my new bride very seriously and insisted that we conduct ourselves like actual newlyweds. "We must not raise any suspicions," she advised me. "Turn out the light, husband." She yanked my exhausted body down onto the bed.

*Sweet genius! This girl is gonna kill me before the Communists even get their shot!*

## 6:41 AM, THURSDAY, JANUARY 17TH, 1974

After three days of sightseeing in Key West, we returned to the dry-dock on Stock Island. The boat was back in the water and tied in a boat slip.

"Is that the *Third Wish*? She looks great!" I said. The boat looked completely different, with a blue hull, blue-striped mainsail, and her new name painted across the stern.

Carlos spoke in an angry voice. "She's not *Third Wish* anymore! Get that name *Third Wish* out of your head, Ocean. She is now the *Canadian Goose*! Get used to it!" Carlos's mood had become progressively fouler with each passing day.

"What's with him?" I whispered in Katarina's ear.

"He always gets like this just before returning to Cuba. I'm afraid he's going to be *El Muerte* from now on…*El Muerte* until this mission is over."

With me at the helm, we set sail from Stock Island under a clear blue sky, destination Havana, Cuba. Katarina had become very quiet and seemed to be growing increasingly uneasy with each passing hour. Behind dark, cold eyes the storm clouds of anger and hate were brewing in *El Muerte*'s mind. Suddenly the Cubans began speaking rapidly in Spanish.

"What are you two saying?" I asked Katarina.

"Mind the sails, Ocean. What we are saying is not your business." The dark, iniquitous look on *El Muerte*'s face terrified me, and I had to look away from his hate-filled eyes! I dared not speak again until I was spoken to.

A closed mouth gathers no foot.

## Chapter 24

# HAVANA HARBOR

Katarina and Carlos were finishing their lunch in the galley when I made one last tack to starboard. My five-hour shift of piloting the boat was ending. Katarina came up on deck to relieve me just as I finished trimming the sails.

"You're three minutes late, woman!" I faked outrage and looked down at my wristwatch.

"Boo-hoo, poor you! I'll take over now, captain. Your lunch is in the galley." She took the wheel of the *Canadian Goose* at 2:04 pm.

"Thanks, Kat. Keep her at 201 degrees south-southwest. Got a strong Gulf Stream off the starboard beam."

Constant tacking back and forth into a headwind had been required to keep the *Goose* on her course for Havana, and I was exhausted when I went below deck for lunch. I grabbed my sandwich and a bottle of water from the counter and then flopped down on the sofa near the galley. Carlos was in his cabin sitting on the edge of his bunk, cleaning a semiautomatic pistol. He saw me watching him as I ate my sandwich.

"*Qué chingados!*" He reached over and slammed his cabin door shut so I couldn't see him.

*You have a nice day too, Carlos!* I finished eating and then went into my cabin to read a book, *The History of Cuba.*

At 6:00 pm I began cooking a spaghetti dinner, and when it was ready at 6:30 I gathered the courage to knock on Carlos's door.

"Hey, Carlos, do you want to eat before you begin your shift? I made some spaghetti." When he opened his door, I noticed a hidden compartment on the far wall of his stateroom. It was a new addition to the boat. The hatch was open, and the secret compartment was full of guns. Carlos put a pistol inside and closed the hatch. When the hatch was closed, you couldn't tell there was a compartment inside the wall.

Carlos noticed my surprise at the weapons cache, "Eddie, that locker was installed on Stock Island. You keep out of there." He sat down and looked at his plate. "What, no meatballs? Is this jarred sauce? Coño!"

Carlos ate his dinner in a huff and made grunting noises of disapproval with each bite. When he finished, he went up to relieve Katarina. Her five-hour shift ended at 7:00 pm, and she came below looking beat.

"Water, water, give me water. I hate beating into the wind!" She began chugging down a bottle of spring water.

"Kat, Carlos ate his dinner, but I waited for you. He's really miserable today." I carried two plates of pasta covered with canned tomato sauce to the table.

"Thanks. My back is killing me," Katarina said and sat across from me arching and stretching her back. *Even at her worst she looks gorgeous!*

I brought a bottle of wine and a corkscrew to the table. "Maybe this will ease the pain, Katarina."

"Just what the doctor ordered."

"What's with Carlos? He's acting nasty and rude all the time now—like a different person. Today he locked himself in his cabin. He's been cleaning guns and sharpening knives all day long."

"I told you, Carlos always behaves this way whenever he returns to Cuba. Some people say he becomes transformed from Carlos Romero into *El Muerte, El Muerte* the Zombie."

"Why does that happen to him?"

"After the Communists took control of Cuba, they stole the Romero family's land and murdered Carlos's father—my grandfather. That happened in the 1950s just before I was born."

"*Your* grandfather?"

"Yes, Carlos is my uncle, the younger brother of my father, Oscar Romero. When they were both young men, their father was shot in the head right before Carlos's and his mother's eyes. It happened at the Romero family farm. My father, Oscar, was not present that day because he had become a businessman living in Havana."

"Why would they shoot a harmless old man?"

"Because he would not voluntarily surrender the farm. After murdering my grandfather, the Communists stole the farm anyway, and a week later they confiscated my father's business in Havana as well. My father, Oscar, was convicted of being a capitalist and was sent to a forced labor camp—actually a death camp. Ironically the labor camp was located very near our farmland in western Cuba, and sometimes Oscar would be forced to work his own land as a slave."

"Did they send Carlos there too?"

"No. After paying the Communists all their money, Carlos and his mother were allowed to flee to Miami. Later, Carlos returned to Cuba to fight in the Bay of Pigs invasion, and he was wounded and captured. Carlos was imprisoned and tortured in *La Cabaña* Prison in Havana for years. When we enter Havana Harbor we will sail directly past the foot of *La Cabaña* Prison, and it's very hard for Carlos to see the stone walls of the dungeon that confined him."

"His memories of that place must haunt him. What happened to your father at the labor camps?" I asked as I opened the bottle of red wine.

"First let me tell you this: My father was a very successful businessman. He owned a popular hotel and nightclub in Havana. My mother was a Ukrainian, working in Havana as a secretary at the Soviet Embassy. She was tall, blonde, and very beautiful. One night she went with some friends to my father's nightclub to dance. My father introduced himself, and I'm told it was love at first sight. They danced the night away. Six months later they were married, and a year after that I was born."

"But where are they now? What happened to them?"

"Because she was working for the Soviets and not Batista's government, my mother was given the choice of returning to Ukraine or being exiled to America. She chose Miami and took me there when I was just one year old. As I said, my father was sent to the slave labor camp, where he was beaten and starved. He lasted ten years before dying in a sugar cane field on a hot August afternoon. I'm told that the labor camp was nothing more than a concentration camp. He suffered greatly. My uncle Carlos was rescued from prison by counter-revolutionaries and brought to Miami, but not until after years of confinement and torture. Have you noticed Carlos's ears?"

"His ears? No, why? His thick hair covers them, I suppose."

"Carlos *has* no ears. A Russian interrogator cut them off and gave them to his Russian girlfriend."

"What?"

"It's true! Carlos says the Russian looks like a monster. He's missing one eye and is scary—ugly like the devil."

"Wait a minute—a Russian missing one eye? A Russian who likes to use a knife? I might have heard about this guy. I think that the guy is in Miami right now."

"I doubt it. His name is Nikko, but some call him Nicky the Knife. He lives in Havana and sometimes travels back to Russia, but never to the U.S. I'm sure they would never let the Russian into and out of the U.S."

"Nicky the Knife? That *is* the same guy! He did a job in Miami for the Boss—Tony Montana—just last week! I swear it!"

"Well, Rafael Cato does use the mob to smuggle goods in and out of Cuba. The mob once opposed Cato, but after he gained control of Cuba they allied with him. Now Cato sends mercenaries to Miami to work alongside the mob, and they spread drugs into America. The Communist mercenaries also hunt down exiled Cubans like me and Carlos. They want to kill us counter-revolutionaries, and they are suspected of the recent murder of señor Torriente, the owner of an anti-Cato radio station in Miami. Torrinte was shot while he watched TV at his home in Coral Gables."

"I read about that in the newspaper." I said.

"Maybe you're right, Eddie. Maybe they smuggled the Russian bastard into Miami to do a hit job for the Boss!"

"Katarina, should we tell Carlos that Nicky the Knife is in Miami?'

"No! No! Not until we get back home. He might turn us around and sail straight back to Miami to look for the Russian bastard. He hates Nikko and wants to kill him! He would give his own life to kill Nicky the Knife!"

"Okay, we'll keep it secret for now. Have another glass of wine, Kat. I'm gonna turn in." I poured the last of the wine into her glass.

"Carlos gave his permission for you to read his memoirs if you want to, Eddie. I think he is finally beginning to trust you."

"His memoirs? Okay."

"Wait here." She went to Carlos's cabin and came out with a binder of handwritten pages. "Here, read it in bed." She handed me the binder.

"*El Muerte*—nice title," I said.

"That memoir will explain everything, *chico*. *Buenas noches!*"

At ten minutes after eight I went to my cabin planning to read and then fall asleep for a few hours, but at 10:00 I awoke to find Katarina climbing into my bed.

"Are you sleeping in here?" I asked her.

"Yes, of course. We are suppose to be newlyweds, remember. If the Coast Guard or the crew of a Cuban gunboat should board us in the middle of the night to find us sleeping in separate cabins that would raise suspicions." She snuggled up against my back.

"Okay. That makes sense."

"Don't worry, I'll leave you alone tonight. I'm beat," she said.

Stupid seemed to have other plans as I turned to face her. "What's that?" she asked.

An hour later we eventually got some sleep.

Powerful hands gripping my shoulders and shaking me violently awakened me at 3:00 am.

"Get up, Ocean! It's your turn!" It was Carlos. He was pissed off as usual.

"Already?" It felt like I had slept for only ten minutes.

"Get your ass in gear. The *Goose* is on autopilot!"

After staggering to the helm I took the wheel and read the compass. The *Goose* was right on course, and thankfully we now had a more favorable wind, so I did not need to tack back and forth all night. It was 3:33 am when the lights of Havana in the distance sent a chill through my body and caused gooseflesh to rise on my arms and neck. I visualized a dark, stone prison cell waiting there for me. *What have you gotten yourself into, dude? There's no turning back now!*

*Should I wake Carlos and Katarina? Nah, I'll let them sleep.* With a sense of dread, I sailed toward the bright lights of Havana.

Three hours later, the sky began to lighten over the eastern horizon behind me, and now I could see land. Katarina came up from below just as I checked my watch. Six thirty-one am.

"Land ahoy," I said and pointed toward Cuba. Her face seemed to drain of blood and turn pale as she looked toward the coastline.

"Why didn't you wake us," she said and then ducked back down to wake Carlos. He came up from below cursing me, but at least now after reading his memoir, I had a much better understanding of the reason for his temperament.

"I'll take the wheel, Ocean." Carlos shoved me aside.

"Here's the chart," I said and held the navigation chart out to him.

"I know this harbor like the back of my hand." He knocked my arm away and glared at the entrance to Havana Harbor, his eyes full of hatred.

Katarina stood next to me, visibly overcome by anxiety as I examined the navigation chart.

The chart showed that Havana Harbor consisted of three separate ports. We were looking for the port at the foot of the city of Old Havana. The chart indentified that port as the *Enseñada de Atarés* Port.

"There she is, *Fortaleza de San Carlos de la Cabaña*, the gateway to Hell!" Carlos scowled and pointed to a rock-walled fortress off our port beam. My hair stood on end as I imagined the screams of the tortured political prisoners echoing through the bowels of that cold stone structure.

"*Cabrón!*" Carlos called out, sneering, and shaking a big, meaty fist at the dungeon walls.

Then we heard him mumble in a low voice, "This could be the day that I find you, Nikko...I find you and take your only eye."

After that, Carlos took in two very long, deep breaths, and then a strange calm seemed to come over him and he smiled as we passed the *La Cabaña* Prison and sailed deeper into the harbor toward an area of mooring buoys. Carlos started the diesel engine and turned the boat into the wind before dropping the mainsail. Katarina and I secured the sail to the boom. Then I went to the bow and hooked the *Canadian Goose* up to a large white mooring buoy. Carlos ran a yellow quarantine flag up to fly below the Canadian flag.

"What happens now?" I asked Carlos.

"We wait for the inspection, pay the tax, and then we get clearance to go ashore," he said.

After about twenty minutes, I saw a patrol boat leave the dock and begin to approach the *Canadian Goose*. The faces of three tanned and weathered soldiers came into view; their expressions were stern and very unfriendly. My knees went weak when I noticed that two of them held machine guns. As the patrol boat approached us, Katarina unbuttoned the top of her blouse and then tied the shirt in a knot up high, directly below her bosom.

"Give them a nice show, Katarina," said Carlos.

She walked to the bow waving to the soldiers; the muscles in her long, shapely legs drew taut as she climbed up onto the bow rail, smiling at them.

"*Hola, caballeros!*" The bright morning light illuminated her pearly white teeth; a wisp of her lustrous black hair glistened and blew across her face in the gentle breeze. *Gosh, she's beautiful!*

The distraction of Katarina's sensual performance had temporarily relieved my anxiety, but now the nervousness returned as the armed men tied the patrol boat alongside our starboard beam. Two of the men boarded us; one carried a machine gun. Carlos greeted the soldiers in Spanish, but the Cubans hardly looked at him. They couldn't take their eyes off Katarina. Then the guy in the patrol boat called out an order, and the unarmed soldier went below deck and began searching the cabins.

Everyone spoke rapidly, and I couldn't understand his or her Spanish. The soldiers kept giving me odd, curious looks as I fidgeted uncomfortably, wishing they would leave. I sensed by their glances that they were perplexed that Katarina and I were a couple. They looked me up and down, and I imagined them thinking, *You lucky S.O.B.! How the hell did you catch a beauty like her?*

The Cubans were overtly flirting with Katarina right in front of me. She pretended to be flattered by their piggish, macho, chauvinistic behavior. She put on an Oscar-winning performance by acting like an embarrassed young schoolgirl, giggling and batting her mesmerizing gray eyes at the enthralled men. She would giggle and then lean down and forward, giving the bedazzled soldiers an eyeful of her gorgeous, jiggling bosom as she laughed at their jokes.

Finally the soldiers left our boat, smiling and laughing as they waved goodbye to Katarina and untied the lines. After backing away from the *Canadian Goose*, the soldiers began hooting and hollering and patting each other on the back. One guy held his hands in front of his chest and made curvy motions with his hands.

"You sure cheered those guys up, Katarina!" I said.

"I think they liked my magnetic personality," she said with a laugh and pushed up on the bottom of her breasts to exaggerate her cleavage.

Once again I marveled at her composure under pressure and her captivating combination of beauty and brains.

Many women would rather have beauty than brains, because the average man can see better than he can think.

*Chapter 25*

# THE TROPICANA

## FRIDAY, 1:30 PM, JANUARY 18TH, 1974

"**N**ow that we are in Cuba, remember that I'm no longer your Uncle Carlos. My name is Diego Martinez, your hired charter boat captain," Carlos said as Katarina packed her suitcase in preparation to leave the boat and go to our hotel in Havana.

As charter boat captain, Carlos was required to tend to the boat and sleep onboard the *Canadian Goose* each night. He told us that he would be spending his free time on shore searching the streets of Havana, hunting for Nikko. Since we believed that Nikko was in Miami, we tried to discourage Carlos from wasting his time searching for the monster.

"Uncle, we have heard rumors that Nikko is out of the country," Katarina said, but it was no use. Carlos's sole purpose in life was vengeance. He existed only to avenge his father's murder by bringing down Rafael Cato and then killing Nicky the Knife, the Russian who had tortured him and taken his ears.

"Katarina, I will find that bastard; I will follow him to the gates of hell if I must. Now come, my dear niece—it is time for you to go. I will put you both ashore." We launched the dinghy, and Carlos took us to shore and dropped us off on the pier before returning to the sailboat.

By Judith Sipes 3

Dockside, a car immediately drove over to us. Katarina spoke Spanish with the driver for a moment, and then the elderly Cuban gentleman got out and put her suitcase into the trunk of his car. With my backpack, I hopped into the back seat.

"Sweet ride!" I said. Katarina slid into the front seat next to the driver. Our taxicab was a black 1957 Chevy Bel Air convertible. The classic car appeared to be in mint condition.

Katarina spoke to the driver in Spanish and then told me, "I asked him to put the top down. He is very proud of his car." The driver began to lower the convertible top.

I concurred. "She's a real beauty, all right. My brother in-law had one of these '57 Chevys—only his was a black hardtop."

"*Hotel Nacional de Cuba, por favor!*" Katarina said to the driver.

The driver turned and looked at us, disappointment spreading across his face. *"Que? Hotel Nacional de Cuba?"* he said and pointed at a large building not more than a hundred yards away. Katarina began speaking rapidly in Spanish.

"Eddie, that's our hotel right there—walking distance—so I asked the driver to give us a short tour of Havana before dropping us off at the hotel."

"Cool."

Kat translated for me as the driver gave us a guided tour in his classic convertible.

Up ahead I saw a nightclub. "Pull over here!" I said.

"This is the Tropicana Club. It's not open yet," Katarina said.

"Look, the ticket window is open. I'll get us a table for tonight."

"That will be fun!" she said and then asked the driver to pull over.

From the car, Katarina could see that I was struggling to communicate with the woman at the ticket window, so she came over to help out. In short order we had a pair of tickets, and Kat seemed very happy as we walked back to the car. She said, "When I told that sweet woman that we were newlyweds, she gave us a special table—it's right up front and center stage!" Katarina held the tickets up to her face and kissed them. *"Mwah!"*

After a loop around the city we pulled up to the front entrance of the Hotel Nacional de Cuba. The historic luxury hotel is located in the middle of Vedado, Havana, Cuba. It stands on a hill near the sea and offers a view of Havana Harbor. A long concrete seawall runs along the coast toward downtown Havana. The hotel had been mentioned in the history book I was reading.

"This is a very historic hotel, Katarina. It was designed by New York architects and was opened in 1930."

"I like those twin watchtowers. It's a beautiful place to honeymoon!" she said.

"My book says that the design of the hotel features a mix of architectural styles. I wonder if Brownie Shytles would like this design—this mongrel mix of architectural styles."

"Who's Brownie?"

"Oh, I forgot you don't know any of my friends. Brownie Shytles is an excellent architect, but he landed on skid row due to a lot of medical problems." A bellboy opened the car's door as Katarina paid the driver, and I handed her suitcase to the bellboy.

We checked into the hotel at 3:34 pm and went to our suite on the sixth floor. The room had a balcony that overlooked the ocean.

"Eddie, come see this view." Katarina opened the plantation shutter doors and went out onto the balcony, while I tipped the bellboy.

I joined Kat outside. "There's the *Goose*," I said and pointed off to the right toward the harbor. The mast of the *Canadian Goose* was visible, rising above some fishing boats. Carlos had removed the yellow "Q" flag and hoisted the Cuban flag up the starboard spreader. A Canadian flag was also visible flying at the stern of the boat.

"I wish Carlos could enjoy this grand hotel too," Katarina said as she gazed toward the *Goose* with a look of disappointment in her beautiful eyes. Strands of her long, silky black hair fluttered in the afternoon breeze. With my arm around her thin waist, I brushed a wisp of hair from her cheek and kissed her.

"I know you wish Carlos could be staying here, but I like being alone for a change," I said and then kissed her again.

Along the seawall, many young people had begun to gather and socialize. Some began playing bongo drums. The scene reminded me of Mallory Square in Key West.

"This place is magic, very romantic. Imagine the history. Imagine the things that have happened right here in this very room," Katarina said as she stared into my eyes. She was irresistible, so I kissed her again.

"We should get ready for dinner," she said.

"Okay. But what should I wear to the Tropicana, Kat? I don't have anything nice."

"Try these on." She took some clothing from her suitcase and tossed them onto the bed.

"You bought me an outfit?"

"Yeah. Carlos and I might seem disorganized, but we have this whole operation planned out in detail. We bought you these clothes in Miami."

To my surprise, the clothes were a perfect fit.

"How did you know my size?"

"Like I said, we know everything about you, Eddie Ocean."

The cloth of the lightweight, white linen shirt-and-pants ensemble reminded me of gauze material. The shirt was a button less pullover, and the white linen, Cuban-style pants had a drawstring that tied at my waist. A pair of black leather shoes completed the outfit.

"Do I look like an ice cream vendor? All dressed in white—all I need is a white Forage-style cap and I could sell Good Humor ice cream!" I said as I examined myself in the full-length mirror.

"Oh my gosh! You do, or maybe a milkman! You're funny, Eddie! Put on that *guayabera* shirt." Katarina laughed as I walked to the bed to get the black, Cuban-style *guayabera* shirt. I wore it unbuttoned like a jacket.

"Oh, that looks much better." The black *guayabera* covered my white shirt like a jacket and matched my shoes. Martini glasses were embroidered with brown stitching down the sides of both lapels of the *guayabera*.

"Hey, this outfit looks cool now!" I turned in front of the mirror, checking myself out.

"Mmm Mmm! *Muy guapo, señor* Ocean! Let's go!"

We went to dinner in the hotel restaurant, and because of my new outfit I noticed that I was getting a lot of attention from some of the lady diners. Of course, Katarina was also a head-turner as usual, even in her simple peasant dress. After dinner we returned to our room so that Kat could change clothes.

## 9:00 PM, FRIDAY EVENING

Katarina came out from the bathroom wearing a beautiful and very sexy dress.

"How do I look? This is a dress that I wore in competition."

"Wow! You look great! What competition?"

"Professional ballroom dancing. A few years ago, I competed for prize money. This is my Latin Rhythm dress," she said as she examined herself in a full-length mirror.

The exquisite dress stopped at mid-thigh, putting her long, well-toned legs fully on display. Thin spaghetti straps supported a tightly fitted bodice that accentuated her cleavage and went up and over her taut, elegant shoulders to criss-cross in the back. The dress had cutouts at the sides of her waist, exposing her tanned olive skin stretched tightly across her well-toned ribcage. When she moved, she glittered. A variety of small sequins and rhinestones adorning the dress made her sparkle like the surface of the sea at sunrise.

"Wow!" was all that I could say, and I flopped down in a chair with a thud. She laughed at my reaction and did a sexy dance for me in front of the mirror. That only made things worse! *Calm down, Stupid! Now is not the time!*

"I need a breath of fresh air, Kat. Tell me when you're ready to go," I said and walked out onto the balcony to watch the crowd gathered at the seawall. After about ten minutes she called me back inside, "I'm ready, Eddie spaghetti!" Katarina was visibly excited.

"You're a poet, but you just don't know it!" With my arm around her waist, we left our room and walked to the elevator. The elevator operator couldn't take his eyes off Katarina. He was practically drooling! *Take a picture, why don't you!* Katarina spoke with him in Spanish, and then she laughed.

"What did you say?" I asked.

"I asked him if he liked his job, and he said it has its ups and downs." She laughed again.

"Really? Oh brother, that's lame!"

At 10:00 pm, a taxi dropped us off at Club Tropicana, and we went inside, where a woman dressed like a showgirl escorted us to our front-row table. Then a waiter dressed like a bullfighter brought us one bottle of rum and two bottles of Coca-Cola.

"Great seats! This place is awesome!" I said as I poured us each a rum and Coke.

A full orchestra was on stage tuning their instruments; we had arrived early, and things were just getting started. At eleven o'clock a man came onto the stage and welcomed the large crowd that now filled Club Tropicana.

"What's he saying?" I asked Katarina.

"He said, 'Welcome, ladies and gentlemen. I am Ricardo, your humble host tonight.'"

The orchestra began playing, and the handsome man began singing a ballad. He sang a Spanish love song and made a lot of eye contact with Katarina as she sat smiling near the stage. Suddenly the entertainer danced over to the edge of the stage and stopped directly in front of us. He got down on his knees and extended his hand toward Katarina like a man proposing marriage as he sang the lyrics in Spanish.

"I think he likes you, Kat," I said and poured another drink.

"It's all just part of the show," she said with a red face.

Next the orchestra began playing wild Latin music, and a line of showgirls came dancing onto the stage. The lead dancer wore a bowl-shaped hat filled with fruit.

"Is that a fruit basket on her head? That's crazy," I said.

"I think she's impersonating Carmen Miranda."

At midnight the first show ended, but some of the musicians continued to play, and people began dancing in an area off to the right of the stage.

"Let's dance." Katrina stood up and began pulling my arm.

"Let me finish this drink first." I was only delaying the inevitable.

"Darn it, Eddie, that was a good song! We missed it!"

"Those people are such good dancers, Kat. I'm going to look like a fool out there."

"You are better than you think, Eddie. Besides, I can make you look like a pro."

I couldn't hold off any longer, and we walked onto the dance floor. These people seemed to be doing the salsa dance that Katarina had taught me.

"Eddie, do the salsa!" she yelled over the loud music. *Hey, I was right! It is the salsa!*

We began dancing, and it was amazing how Katarina moved in that sparkling dress. *She must be the most beautiful creature I have ever seen.* Others in the crowd seemed to share my thought as people began dancing slower so they could watch her. Some stopped dancing altogether and stood off to the side, watching the remaining dancers.

I did basic movements, but Katarina was so good she made us look like a pair of professional dancers. I noticed that only the best dancers were now left on the dance floor, as many couples began returning to their tables. *Is some kind of unofficial competition taking place?* The showgirls and performers from the show had gathered at the side of the stage and were watching the dancers down below them.

Occasionally they would point down at someone and then have a discussion among themselves. Finally the music stopped, and everyone returned to his or her table.

"You were great, Eddie!"

"Me? Didn't you notice that everyone was gawking at you?"

We sat down, and then the host, the same man who had opened with the Latin ballad, took the mic at center stage and spoke. Katarina translated for me.

"He says some of us have been selected to dance on stage with the Club Tropicana dancers."

"He says that after we dance onstage, three judges will select the best dancer, who will receive a prize."

A line of performers began streaming off the stage and into the crowd. They went to tables and selected patrons and escorted them back to the stage. No one came over to our table.

"I can't believe they didn't pick you, Katarina!" Other people must have been thinking the same thing because everyone around us was looking at Katarina with puzzled expressions on their faces. Then the host went to the microphone and spoke.

"So, now that all of our professional dancers have selected their dance partners, we shall begin!" He turned his back to the audience and faced the group of contestants who were now assembled in a line across the stage. Suddenly he turned back around to face the audience.

"Oh wait! Someone is missing! I have not made my choice…have I?" He leaped off the stage and landed right next to our table. "Do you mind, sir?" he asked me in perfect English as he extended his hand toward Katarina.

"No, sir."

Katarina smiled at me and stood up. Ricardo grabbed her by the waist and hoisted her up onto the stage, where she landed lightly and on her tiptoes, and then spun like a ballerina. Ricardo leaped back up onto the stage to join her. *Man, that dude is athletic.* The orchestra began playing, and the couples began dancing.

They danced the rumba and then the samba. *Damn, my lame-ass amateur dancing was holding Kat back! Look at her go now!* With Ricardo she was *really* putting on a show! Katarina and Ricardo were incredible dancers. People cheered and applauded their flamboyant dance moves. I began to feel a little jealous. *Jealous, Ocean…really, dude? You have known the chick for less than a week. Remember, you and Kat are just business partners…fake newlyweds. Just enjoy the fringe benefits of the job while you can, and lighten up, dude!*

The contest ended, and then one by one the competitors were introduced to the audience as they each took a bow. The judges determined the winner by the volume of the cheers and applause from the crowd. Katarina was the last one to step forward, and Club Tropicana exploded with deafening cheers and applause. I stood at the edge of the stage, jumping up and down yelling "Whooo-hooo!"

To no one's surprise, Katarina won first place; it wasn't even close. Ricardo gave her a large bouquet of flowers and then placed a tiara made of cheap costume jewelry on her head. The sparkling crown matched her dress perfectly.

"You were awesome, Kat!" I said as she returned to our table.

"That was fun! I haven't danced like that in a long time!" She was very excited and still catching her breath.

The waiter wearing the bullfighter's outfit came to our table carrying an ice bucket containing a bottle of champagne. He spoke to Katarina and then pointed up to a private box in the balcony. We both looked up to see. Smiling down at us was Rafael Cato, the Communist dictator of Cuba. He was holding a fat cigar. He moved the hand holding the cigar in a motion of salutation toward Katarina and then bowed deeply. She smiled and waved back to him.

"That's him, Eddie—the devil himself!" she said through clenched teeth, forcing a fake smile. "I hate that monster!"

"Wow, the monster sent us Dom Perignon!" I said as the matador opened the bottle of champagne.

We drank champagne and watched the second show and then danced once more before leaving the club. Exhausted and tipsy, we arrived back at our hotel at 3:57 am. Katarina dropped the flowers on the floor and flopped down on the bed as I placed the DO NOT DISTURB sign on our door. I took off my shoes and flopped down on the bed beside her. Exhausted and still fully dressed, we fell asleep quickly. We had

Danced the night away.

*Chapter 26*

# THE SPECIAL CIGAR

## SATURDAY, JANUARY 19<sup>TH</sup>, 1974

The alarm woke me at 1:00 pm, and I was hungry. Katarina lay on her back, still wearing her Latin Rhythm dress. Her tiara had fallen down to cover her eyes. Gently I removed the tiara and placed it on the nightstand and watched her sleep.

*Less than a week ago, I was sleeping in a borrowed cardboard box under the I-95 overpass. Now I'm in Cuba, staying in a five-star hotel with a beautiful young woman sleeping beside me My, how my luck has changed!*

It occurred to me that since meeting Katarina, I had hardly thought of Little Hooters. *Am I falling in love again? Falling in love with Katarina?* She moaned and began to stir.

"Hey, what time is it? My head is killing me." Katarina held her hands to her temples and rolled onto her right side to face me.

"It's one-fifteen."

"Night or day?"

"Daytime, dummy! We were up all night dancing, remember?"

"Oh yeah…Eddie, will you get me some water…please?" I stood and picked up the bouquet of flowers from the floor and then put them in a vase that was on the bathroom countertop before bringing Katarina a glass of water.

"That was quite a night, Eddie! I haven't had that much fun in a long time," she said as she sat up to drink the water.

Even hung over and disheveled, she looked beautiful, especially wearing her skimpy, sexy Latin Rhythm dress. She finished drinking and then lay down again on her side, facing me. I lay down next to her, and we gazed into one another's eyes, our faces just inches apart.

"Katarina, I think I'm falling for you, falling in love with you."

Her eyes widened, and she pulled back from me. "What? Are you crazy? You must still be drunk to say something like that!" She sat up on the edge of the bed with her back to me.

"I thought you were feeling the same way about me, Kat."

"Eddie, you don't understand." She turned her head to look at me.

"Understand what?"

"I don't have boyfriends. I'm already committed...I'm married."

"What? No you're not. Why are you saying that?" I protested as she stood up to face me.

"Eddie, I *am* married...married to the cause. Married to the counter-revolution. I don't have time for nonsense like romance or love. My only purpose is to avenge the murder of my family, but there is a good chance that my enemies will kill me first. I'm a candle flickering in the wind, a flame that might be snuffed out in an instant and burn you if we get too close." She pressed her palms to the sides of her head and groaned.

"You could fight Cato in a different way, a less dangerous way. Maybe through the media or the human rights organizations."

"I'm not complaining about the danger. I would gladly sacrifice my life to kill that monster Rafael Cato—and so would Uncle Carlos, but that's not going to happen through the media. My hatred for Cato consumes me, and until I kill him, my life is meaningless. No one including you can be a part of my life, and anyone who gets close to me is endangered!"

"I'm not afraid anymore. I just want to be with you, Kat."

"Eddie, you must not love me, and I must not love you! Loving someone makes a person weak and vulnerable!" She walked into the bathroom and closed the door just as someone began pounding on the front door of our hotel room.

"Who is it?"

"It's Carlos. Open up."

Carlos came into the room holding a fancy, hand-carved wooden box in his meaty paws. "It's already the afternoon! Did you two lovebirds just wake up? You look like hell, Eddie!" he said to me as Katarina came out of the bathroom. She had changed clothes.

"Lovebirds! No, we are just business partners, Carlos! This mission is business—just a show—an act, and don't talk so loud, *El Muerte*! You came in here like a raging bull!" she said as she held her hands over her ears.

"Calm down, Katarina. I have the cigars." Carlos opened the box and shined a little penlight onto the cigars inside. "See how the poisoned one glows. See the silver streak on that one? That's the special cigar."

"What's this all about?" I asked as we all looked at the cigar that had a silver line painted on it.

"The invisible mark can only be seen by shining this black light on it. That one is the poisoned one, Katarina," Carlos said.

"Poison? Poisoned cigar...painted with poison? What are you talking about?" I asked.

"No, the paint is not the poison. The poison is inside the cigar... mixed in the filler, not on the wrapper. That silver mark is just invisible paint." Carlos handed the marked cigar to Katarina.

"Eddie, the less you know about what we are doing, the better for you," said Katarina.

Carlos disagreed. "Katarina, if he is going to help you get the cigar to Cato, he's gonna hafta know the plan."

"I guess you're right, Carlos. Eddie we are going to try to give these cigars to Cato, if not directly to him then at least to one of his trusted generals for delivery. When Cato smokes this cigar he will have heart failure. He'll be dead within minutes, and it will appear to be a heart attack."

"Isn't giving cigars to Cato like giving ice to an Eskimo?" I said.

Carlos answered, "Yes, we thought of that, but that's why Katarina has to make this poisoned cigar a very special cigar, one that the bastard Cato will cherish."

"How do we do that, and how do we get close enough to Cato?" I asked.

"We are working on that problem with an informant we have planted within Cato's administration. I need to get busy setting up a high-level contact between Katarina and a general!" said Carlos, who then left the room in a rush.

"This is craziness, Kat! We are all gonna get killed!" I said.

"So! Finally you understand me. Finally you got it through your thick head! If we survive this mission you should stay clear of me, Eddie Ocean. Nothing good can come of us being together!"

"Kat, I never wanted to come to Cuba. I only did it to repay you for saving my life, but now things have changed. My feelings have changed, and I'm worried about you. I want to help. I want to protect you."

"See, again you make my point. Now you are weak because you have come to care about me! Your infatuation with me has made you vulnerable and weak by putting yourself in danger by wanting to protect me! You need to protect only yourself, and I only myself. We must not be distractions to one another."

"I consider my feelings for you as strength. I'm risking my life for you."

"Look, Eddie, I don't want to talk about this anymore. You just have to play the part of my dumb *gringo* husband. Just play along and follow my lead, and if we're lucky we will get out of Cuba alive and you will return home to your safe, boring life." She put the poisoned cigar back in the box.

"I'll help, but you know that I speak very little Spanish—*muy poquito*."

"Not speaking Spanish is a benefit, Eddie—it might help you keep your mouth shut and keep you out of trouble. Just smile and say these three phrases in Spanish: *comprendo*—I understand; *muy interesante*—very interesting; and *no sabía eso*—I did not know that. Now, let's get some breakfast," she said.

"Breakfast? It's lunchtime, Kat."

"Even better, let's go." Over lunch, Katarina taught me the three phrases in Spanish, and when we passed through the lobby, the clerk at the main desk called us over and handed Katarina an envelope. She opened it as we stood at the desk.

"Eddie, this is an invitation to a dinner party tonight. We need to RSVP," she said.

"Invitation from who?"

"You're not going to believe it—it's from General Rafael Cato! The dinner is to be held right here in our hotel in honor of a group of foreign diplomats."

"Bingo! We can tell Carlos that his problem of putting us in contact with Cato is solved."

Katarina asked the clerk if she could use the phone and then called Rafael Cato's office to RSVP. "We are in! It's all set!" she said as she hung up the phone and clapped her hands.

"Great! Let's get some fresh air. Let's take a walk by the water," I suggested.

It was Saturday afternoon, and people were gathering for a carnival along the seawall behind our hotel. From a row of booths lining the pathway, food was for sale, and there were games of skill and chance.

"Let me try throwing those darts. Do you know how this game works?" I asked.

Kat spoke to the vendor in Spanish and then told me, "You win the game by popping three balloons. The prize you get depends on the amount of money you wager."

"What do I need to wager to win one of those stuffed animals?"

"Five dollars," she said.

"Five dollars! Okay, I get it. It's a profit deal." I looked at the darts and could see that they had been slightly bent and were unbalanced. *Hmm…not only a profit deal but a rigged game to boot!* I needed to get three of the five darts into a balloon to win.

On my first four throws I popped two balloons.

"This is your last chance, Eddie! Can you take the pressure?" Kat said with a laugh as I prepared to toss the last dart.

*Pop!* "Bulls-eye! You won, Eddie!"

With a frown, the carny handed me a bright white teddy bear.

"Wow, that's the whitest teddy bear I've ever seen! Here you go, Kat. He's all yours." I handed her the stuffed animal.

"Yeah, he's the whitest guy on the shelf, just like you, *gringo*. Hey, that's what I'll name this little bear—Whitest!" After she mocked me again about my "yellow hair," we played a few more games before returning to our hotel room.

At 7:00 pm, Katarina came out of the bathroom dressed in a long, elegant evening gown. She had pinned her thick black hair high upon her head. She looked stunningly beautiful.

"Wow! Tonight you look like a Greek hoddess, not a Latino supermodel," I said as I put on my sportcoat.

The elevator operator took us to the rooftop courtyard of the hotel, where the dinner party was just starting. In the elevator I kissed Katarina just before the door opened.

"Good luck," I said.

"Hey, I need that lipstick!" Katarina said as she wiped the dark red makeup from my mouth and then reapplied a heavy coat to her supple lips.

As soon as we walked into the watchtower, where dinner tables had been arranged, we saw Rafael Cato standing among a group of men. He was wearing an olive-green military uniform. When he spotted us, he excused himself and left the huddle to walk over and greet us.

"You make such a lovely pair. I'm so pleased that you are able to join us tonight." Cato shook my hand and then, with great fanfare, took Katarina's hand, bowed down, and kissed the back of it.

The general said, "All night I dreamed of you dancing at Club Tropicana, my dear. When I first saw you, I did not know your name, so I decided to call you the Flamingo Princess." Cato was still grasping her hand.

"Flamingo Princess, sir?"

"Yes, because your legs are so long and beautiful, and you move so gracefully. You reminded me of a colorful, sparkling flamingo."

"Thank you, General. I'm so honored to be in the presence of such a great and historic world leader as you, sir. You are one of the great leaders of the people—a true father of Communism. You stand among the greatest leaders of our cause—those whom I most admire: Stalin, Lenin, Marx, and Mao!" It must have been very difficult for Katarina to conceal her hatred for the man, but she was clearly charming the pants off the old bastard.

"That is very flattering, my dear. But, Princess, where is your tiara tonight?" Before she could answer, he clapped his hands and looked toward the servants standing against a wall. A young man ran over, and Cato whispered in his ear, after which the man ran off.

Katarina handed the box of cigars to Cato. She had decorated the hand-carved wooden box with a bow made from a yellow strip of cloth that she had used as a hair tie the night before.

"Please accept these cigars, General. I know that these Coronas are your favorites." She handed Cato the box and bowed to him. He removed the bow, held the ribbon to his nose, and sniffed it.

"Mmm, lovely. It holds the sweet scent of my Flamingo Princess. I will wear this ribbon with pride." Cato tied the ribbon around his left wrist and then opened the box and took out a cigar.

"Ahhh, yes, the Corona *Especiales*, my favorite cigar!" Cato took one out of the box and sniffed it. Somehow Katarina knew that it was not the poisoned cigar. She reached into the box and took out the poisoned one.

"I'm pleased that you like them, General." She took the poisoned cigar and kissed it, leaving a red imprint of her lips on the fat cigar, then held the cigar out for him to see. Cato's eyes widened, and he smiled as he looked at Katarina's lip prints. Then he put the one that he was holding back into the box as she presented him with the poisoned cigar.

"From your lips to mine, Flamingo Princess." Cato put the cigar into his mouth just as the young servant returned carrying a diamond tiara. The boy handed the crown to Cato.

"This is my gift to you, Princess Katarina. The thought of your wearing that cheap tiara made of glass troubled me all night; this one is made of fine diamonds. Much more suitable for you." Cato stepped forward and placed the diamond tiara on her head. It fit perfectly around the bun of hair gathered up on the top of her head.

"Oh, General, you are too generous. I cannot accept this gift."

"Nonsense! Of course you can. You don't mind, do you, Mr. Ocean?"

"No, sir. I have the deepest respect for you and your leadership of the Party."

"Yes, Mr. Ocean, and I understand that you are also a leader in the Canadian Communist Party. Good for you, young man!" Cato said to me without taking his eyes off Katarina.

*What, me a Communist leader? Where did that come from?* Katarina was giving me a stern look, not pleased by my puzzled expression. *Okay, I know, just play along!*

"Yes sir, a leader…ahh, for a couple of years now. I used to be a capitalist, but I saw the evil in my ways. I have come to my senses, General." Now I was sure Katarina was wondering, as I was, whether Cato was going to light the poisoned cigar. With a big smile on his bearded face, he kept taking the Cohiba out of his mouth and looking at the imprint of Katarina's lips.

Cato continued to gaze at the cigar as he spoke to us. "I have enjoyed cigars for a long time. I began smoking in my early years. My father was a cigar smoker. He really appreciated a fine cigar. My father was Spanish. He originally came from a small country town in Spain. When I was a teenager in high school, about fifteen years old, I had lunch with my father, and afterward he presented me with a cigar. So it was my father who introduced me to cigars, and he also taught me to drink wine. He liked red Spanish wine." Cato sniffed the cigar again.

"Would you like me to smoke a cigar with you, sir? I usually don't smoke, but this is a special honor, General," I said.

"Yes, that would be pleasurable before dinner." Cato put the poisoned cigar back in the box and took out two others. "Princess, would you like one?" he asked Katarina.

"No thank you, General, but what's wrong with the cigar that I blessed for you, the one I kissed?" she asked.

"I will never smoke that cigar, my princess. I will have it encased in glass so that I can look at the lips of my beautiful Flamingo Princess and remember her dancing so beautifully at the Tropicana." Katarina and I looked at each other in disbelief; her kiss to make the cigar unique had backfired. None of the other cigars was poisoned; our plan was foiled!

Cato walked out from the watchtower to the edge of the railing that encircled the roof and took out a lighter; I followed him.

"Originally my cigar of choice was the Esplendido, the large Churchill-sized cigar. I would also often smoke Romeo y Julieta, H. Upmann, Bauza, Partagas, but then I found the Cohiba. It was so soft, and it was not an overly compact cigar. The Corona Especial Cohiba was easy to smoke and became my favorite." Cato lit my cigar and then lit his.

"Mmmm…smooth," I said as I took a puff. *You don't even know what you're talking about, dude! I think you smoked a Tiparillo once on the boardwalk in Atlantic City…yeah, on the boardwalk when you were about sixteen…yeah, I remember the thin cigar had a plastic tip for my mouth.*

Cato continued, "The Cohiba did not exist as a brand in Cuba until just twenty years ago, Mr. Ocean."

"Just call me Eddie, sir."

"Okay, Eddie. Twenty years ago a man who used to work for me as a bodyguard smoked a very aromatic, very nice cigar. I asked him what brand he was smoking, and he told me that it was no special brand and that it came from a friend. He had a friend who made his own cigars. I said, 'Let's find this man.'" Cato paused to take a puff and then flicked an ash over the railing. I glanced over at Katarina, who was watching us with a furrowed brow. She made a tossing motion with her arms as she inched closer to us. *The crazy girl wants me to toss Cato off the roof!*

I stepped to the side to take a position in between Cato and Katarina as he continued his story. "So I said, 'Let's find your friend the cigar maker,' and we did. I tried his cigars, and I found them so good that we kept in touch with him, and later we asked him how he made them. He explained the blend of tobacco he used and told us which leaves he used and from which tobacco plantations. He also told us about the wrappers he used, and many other things. We found a group of cigar makers, and then we set up the El Cohiba Factory. We gave the cigar makers the materials, and that was how the factory was founded. That was over twenty years ago. Now Cohiba is known all over the world!"

"You were responsible for the Cuban cigar industry, General?"

"Well, for the Cohiba cigar, yes, I suppose."

Katarina was still inching over toward us with an evil look in her eye.

"Excuse me, sir, but I'm afraid of heights." I looked down from the rooftop and backed away, pretending to be frightened. Cato laughed at me, and we moved away from the railing. Katarina stared at me with daggers in her eyes.

There came a call for the guests to be seated. To no one's surprise, I'm sure, Katarina was seated next to Rafael Cato, who sat at the head of the table. I was assigned a seat between the president of Nicaragua and an ambassador from Peru. Their wives sat across from me. To start we were served fine Russian caviar and expensive French champagne.

Everyone spoke Spanish rapidly as we enjoyed bite-size blini, Russian pancakes topped with a tiny dollop of *crème fraîche* and accompanied by caviar garnish. Without Katarina to translate for me, I was at a loss for words, so when addressed by another guest I would repeat one of my stock phrases in Spanish. That tactic seemed to work well as the other guests smiled politely, waiting for me to say more before finally breaking the awkward silence. *Hey! I'm doing pretty well with the Spanish phrases. Maybe I'll try to speak a little* more *Spanish.* The champagne was starting to affect my judgment.

The wife of the ambassador to Peru was sitting directly across the table from me, wearing a very beautiful necklace of colorful gemstones. In Spanish, I complimented her on her lovely necklace, but the reaction from the other guests seemed hostile. The president of Nicaragua said something to me that I couldn't interpret, but his voice sounded angry and harsh. Katarina gave me a hand signal to zip it, and I realized that she and Cato could hear what I was saying; she ran her index finger along her mouth again. *What? Zip it shut?*

The president of Nicaragua seemed to be waiting for me to respond to his remark as he stared at me. After taking a bite of the caviar I asked him in Spanish if he had ever before enjoyed this delicious, rare Beluga sturgeon caviar. After I asked that question I saw Katarina stand up and throw her napkin down on the table as the guests around me gasped aloud.

Sensing that I was in trouble I also stood up and said in my best Spanish, "Excuse me, I need to go outside to find the bathroom." I walked toward the exit, and Katarina stopped me by grabbing my arm and spinning me around to face her.

"You're blowing the operation! What do you think you were saying back there?" she asked.

"Why, what's wrong? I simply told that lady how beautiful her necklace was."

"No you didn't. You told her that her nose looks like a beautiful, shiny banana! What makes matters worse is that her nose does look like a banana! And then you told the president of Nicaragua that you wanted to eat the rare, delicious Beluga caviar from his ear!"

"Oh, shit."

"When you just excused yourself you said, 'Excuse me, I need to go outside to find a whore'!" I looked over at the dinner tables and saw everyone staring at us.

"I said 'whore'?"

"Yes, *whore*! How could you mix up the words *baño* and *puta*? They aren't even close! For the rest of the night, just shut up, Eddie!" She spun away and returned to her seat as I slunk out to find the bathroom.

When I returned to my seat everyone had calmed down, but they kept eyeballing me with curiosity. Later I learned that while I was in *el baño* Katarina had told Cato and his guests that I suffered from a mild case of Tourette syndrome. She said that the uncontrolled outbursts caused by my affliction only became a problem when I drank too much.

As I ate my main course, Katarina made eye contact with me and nodded toward Cato. She fiddled with her steak knife and then leaned toward Cato, her face just inches from his throat. *Don't even think about it, Kat!* I feared that she was going to slit the dictator's throat in front of the entire crowd.

Thankfully the dinner party ended without incident, and Katarina and I got out of there alive. Cato and his bodyguards escorted us down to the lobby, and at the front door, the general kissed Katarina on the cheek and then whispered something into her ear as he looked over at me. *I guess you can be pretty ballsy when you're a Communist dictator with five bodyguards, old man!* Finally Cato and his entourage left in a three-car motorcade.

"Katarina, what was that bastard saying to you?" I asked.

"He told me that you are not bad looking for a *gringo*, but that you are so dumb that I should never have children with you."

"What did you say?"

"What do you think? I agreed with him, of course!"

"Damn, I guess I made a fool of myself again!"

"Eddie, even though our plan failed, I'm now inside the monster's head. I think that I'm Rafael Cato's muse! That means we will get another shot at him; I'm sure of it, and best of all, we did not have to sacrifice our lives to kill him. We are still alive and in the game!"

Live to fight another day!

*Chapter 27*

# THE SOLID GOLD FLAMINGO

## 9:00 AM, TUESDAY, JANUARY 15TH, 1974

Katarina and I went to the front desk of the Hotel Nacional de Cuba to settle our bill and check out.

Katarina spoke Spanish with the clerk and then translated, "I told Juan that we would walk to the Old City Harbor, but he insisted that our transportation was already arranged."

"By who?" I asked.

"He says by Cato. A car awaits us outside."

Out front, a black Lincoln limosine was parked at the curb. Two burly men wearing sportcoats and dark sunglasses were standing next to the car. I recognized them as Rafael Cato's bodyguards. They opened the rear door and waved for us to come over.

"It is very kind of the general to send you, but it is just a short walk to the docks, gentlemen," Katarina told the bodygards.

"Get in!" The guy with his hand on the handle of the car door pulled aside the lapel of his coat to expose a pistol tucked inside his waistband. The strapping man was intimidating and very unfriendly, an unusual way for any man to interact with Katarina. Reluctantly we got into the back seat of the limo.

Katarina pointed her finger as the limo pulled away from the hotel. "Thank you, sir, we are just going right over there to the Old City Harbor."

"Hey, he turned the wrong way—we're going away from the harbor," I whispered to Katarina.

"Sir, we need to go to the Old City Harbor." She repeated the request, but the men did not respond.

I leaned on Katarina's shoulder and whispered in her ear, "Do you think that Cato discovered the poisoned cigar?"

"Don't know. But if so, I suggest that we don't let them take us alive," Katarina whispered back. She looked worried.

The guy in the passenger seat turned around and said, "We must make a stop at the Presidential Palace before we take you to the harbor. This won't take long."

Ahead in the distance I saw the prison that El Muerte had pointed out to us from the boat and remembered his memoir describing the torture that he had endured within its walls.

"Katarina, we are headed toward *La Cabaña* prison." I looked down to locate the door handle. "Hey, these doors have no handles on the inside," I whispered.

"That was the first thing I noticed when we got into this damn car. Something must be very wrong," she whispered.

"What's with all the whispering? Why all the secrets, comrades?" asked the driver as he looked at us in the rear-view mirror.

"Just personal matters—husband and wife squabbling," Katarina said. A smirk spread across the guy's face as he stared at us from the mirror, his eyes hidden behind the dark glasses.

To our relief, the Cubans drove past the prison and continued heading southwest and out of Havana. After about fifteen minutes we came to a town called Playa and pulled up to Cato's home. The bodyguard sitting in the passenger seat opened his door, got out, and then went into the large house, while the driver remained with us.

"You must wait here for *el presidente*," said the driver as he opened the door to let us out. In short order Cato came out from the estate wearing his olive drab military uniform. Four soldiers escorted him toward the limo.

"Sorry to cause you any delay, my lovely princess, but I could not let you and your husband leave our beautiful island without first saying goodbye." He kept one hand behind his back. Cato was hiding something from us.

"Why are you so nervous, mister?" the driver asked me. I was sweating bullets. I could tell that Katarina was nervous too, but she didn't show fear as she spoke to the general.

"General, thank you for providing us with your limo service. You are much too kind." Cato bowed and kissed the back of her hand.

"I wanted to tell you something that I have discovered about that special cigar that you gave to me Princess." Cato straightened up and looked into her eyes. *Oh shit!* I looked to the left and then to the right, trying to decide which way to run. *They must not take us alive. If we're lucky, one clean shot will kill us without too much pain.* Katarina and I looked at one another; I knew she was thinking the same thing.

"General, what did you discover about the cigar?" she asked. For the first time she looked visibly afraid and glanced over at me again. I cocked my head to signal to her that I was going to run to the right.

Cato began to slowly bring his hand from behind his back as he spoke. "After close examination with a magnifying glass, I have discovered that the impression of your lips on the cigar is very beautiful and unique, like a fingerprint. Actually a beautiful work of art that only you and you alone could ever reproduce...so beautiful. And now you have given the priceless masterpiece of your lips' impression to me." Cato touched Katarina's lips with his index finger. "So beautiful, my dear."

"I'm glad it pleases you, General."

"I have many fine works of art in my estate, but the imprint of your lips on a simple cigar is now my most prized possession. I have encased the masterpiece in glass where it now sits on my desk, available for me to look at whenever I so desire."

*Is that it? Is that all? That's why you kidnapped us?* Katarina was probably wondering the same thing. With great relief she asked Cato, "You flatter me, General. Is that the only reason you have summoned us?"

"No, there's more. After receiving such a fine gift from you, I'm required to reciprocate, my dear Flamingo Princess." Now the object that Cato had been concealing was in view as he held it out toward Katarina. It was a yellow-gold, Cuban link chain necklace with a solid gold flamingo pendant.

"This is too much, General. You have already given me the beautiful diamond tiara."

"This flamingo necklace will go nicely with your tiara, and I hope it will remind you of me when you wear it. You are welcome to return to Cuba as my special guest at any time, Miss Katarina." Again Cato bowed and kissed the back of her hand.

*She's* Mrs. *Katarina, you old fart!*

*Hey, relax, dude. A minute ago you thought you were dead meat! Putting up with a little flirting is better than getting tossed into a dungeon.*

Cato stepped behind Katarina and put the necklace around her neck. I noticed how closely he pressed against her as he closed the clasp. *You dirty old man!*

After realizing that we were not going to face a firing squad, I was beginning to relax now, but sweat had already soaked my clothes, and I felt myself tremble one last time. *Damn, this side trip was a real mindblower!* Katarina had recovered her composure as well and continued to charm the old man.

"I will never forget your kindness, General." She kissed his cheek goodbye, and we were finally allowed to leave. This time only the driver accompanied us on the ride back to the docks.

In Havana, we drove past a long line of dirty peasants standing outside of a bakery, waiting for a loaf of bread.

"Is there food rationing?" Katarina asked the driver.

"Yes, *señorita*. Due to the greedy capitalists' embargo, we have very little food for the people," he said.

"We should pull over and give that pendant to the people," I whispered.

"No, the driver would tell Cato that I gave away his gifts. We just need to get off this island and get away pronto!"

The driver kept looking at us though the rear-view mirror, so we stopped our whispering and rode in silence.

*El Muerte* was at the dock, waiting with the dinghy to take us out to our boat, but before we got to him, the soldiers from the Cuban patrol boat stopped us on the pier.

"Halt!" they yelled at us.

"Oh, no—now what!" Katarina said as they approached us carrying their machine guns.

"*Hola, señorita* Katarina! We will give you a ride out to your sailboat. Your *gringo* may come along, too." Katarina looked over at Carlos, who was sitting in the dinghy. He signaled for her to go with them.

The patrol boat got us out to our moored sailboat in a flash as Carlos followed in the small, inflatable dinghy. As he plowed through the rough water of the busy harbor, the huge man looked cartoonish. He was too big for such a little boat. It was comical to see him bouncing up and down as the dinghy was tossed up into the air by the wakes thrown off by larger vessels.

After putting us aboard the *Canadian Goose*, the Cubans roared past Carlos on their return to the dock. The large boat's wake hit Carlos, sending him three feet off his seat. Barely maintaining a hold on the tiller to keep from being flipped out of his little boat, Carlos was drenched by the wave and nearly swamped.

"*Pinche idiota!*" Carlos screamed at them and shook his fist. We could hear the soldiers laughing above the deep rumble of their powerful engines.

"Did you see what those bastards did to me?" Carlos ranted as he boarded the *Goose* dripping wet. Katarina and I tried to act upset, but we could not get the sight of him bouncing up and down in the tiny dinghy out of our minds. Suddenly we both burst into laughter.

*"Los pendejos!* You too!" he cried out.

As we sailed out of Havana Harbor, *El Muerte* was still angry, and once again he shook his fist and cursed *La Cabaña*, the prison fortress.

"I'll be back to collect my pound of flesh from you, Nikko, you Russian bastard!"

Revenge is a dish best served cold!

*Chapter 28*

# PAYDAY

## 4:30 AM, WEDNESDAY, JANUARY 16ᵀᴴ, 1974

With the Gulf Stream and the trade winds now favorable, our return voyage across the Florida Straits from Cuba to the Florida Keys required much less effort and only half the time. We pulled into the docks at Stock Island before sunrise on Wednesday and had coffee onboard the boat as we waited for the boatyard workers to arrive for the day.

"The work should only take a few hours," Carlos said as we watched the dockmaster unlock the front gate of the boatyard at 7:30 am.

"What are you having done to the boat this time?" I asked Carlos.

"We need to convert her back to the *Third Wish* and change her fake Canadian registration numbers back to her Florida registration."

"But what about the blue hull and her new blue striped sails? How do I explain those changes to my nasty little boss?"

"Those changes are an improvement—an upgrade, right? Your boss should be grateful for the free upgrades."

"Ha! Her grateful? You obviously don't know the little troll!"

"Eddie, tell your boss that she was right about my being a Latino supermodel and that it was I who demanded the changes to the boat.

Say that I wanted my photo shoot in the Keys to be done on a blue sailboat, and that I paid for the new sails and blue hull," said Katarina.

"That just might work! You're a genius, Kat! By the way, who *did* pay for all those upgrades?" I asked.

"The CIA," said Carlos.

After the boatyard workers arrived and started to work on *Third Wish*, we walked to a diner across the street to have breakfast. Three and a half hours later, the boat was finished, and we set sail for Miami.

## 11:00 AM, FRIDAY, JANUARY 18TH, 1974

We sailed into Miami Marina and docked the boat in the slip that was assigned to *Third Wish* at Fun 'N' Sun Sailing Charters. Within minutes of our tying her up, Dr. Jill Hamm came running down the dock, screaming and waving her arms.

"That is a private dock! You are trespassing! Get out of that slip before I call security!"

"Chill out, Jill! This is the *Third Wish*." I hopped onto the dock, and Hamm's eyes narrowed as she recognized me. She seemed confused.

"Whose boat is this, Ocean? Where is *Third Wish?*"

"I told you, this *is Third Wish!*"

"What the hell have you done now, Ocean, you screw-up!" Now she was hopping mad as she ran around the boat looking at the hull and sails.

"We needed to make some changes for Katarina's photo shoot."

"Changes? I did not authorize work to be done on this boat. You must have cost me a fortune, Ocean! You're fired!"

"Jill, don't worry. Katarina Romero's modeling agency covered the cost of the work. It's expensed to her photo shoot budget. Don't you see? In addition to the charter fee, you got a free overhaul! Isn't that great Jill?"

"No, that's not great! I did not authorize the work! You should have checked in with me first! You're fired, Ocean! Get off company property! I'm going inside to call the police!" Jill went to the office as we gathered our belongings and then walked off the dock.

"I can't believe that woman! What a little bitch!" said Katarina.

"Yeah, but she's doing me a favor by firing me. That micromanaging little troll is sucking the life out of me, sucking the life out of everybody who works at Sun 'N' Fun!"

"Well, I'm sorry. Can we give you a ride somewhere, Eddie?" Katarina asked.

"Yeah—will you drop me off at the Miami *Post*?"

"Sure. Let's go." Carlos drove, and Katarina and I sat in the backseat and said our farewells.

"When will I see you again, Kat?"

"I'll stay in touch, Eddie, but remember what I told you in Cuba— we'll only be friends." Carlos pulled over at the curb in front of the *Post*, and I kissed Katarina before getting out of the car.

It was noon when I pressed the button and rode the elevator up to Rosalina's office. I was already missing Kat and remembered her dressed in the Latin Rhythm dress, joking with the Cuban elevator operator. *I can't believe they still have elevator operators in Cuba.* Rosalina's office door was wide open, and she and Ima Hooker were eating sandwiches at Rosalina's desk.

"Every time I come here, you gals are just loafing around eating. Don't you ever work?" I teased them and walked in.

"Eddie!" they both called out simultaneously and in harmony.

"I just got back from a charter to Key West."

"How was your trip, Eddie?" asked Rosalina.

"Boring! Just a Latin chick and her uncle, a pair of real dullards." *Hmm...Quick thinking, dude. You might make a decent spy after all!*

"Well, we have a lot of news to tell you, Eddie, and I'm afraid it's mostly bad news," said Rosalina. I looked down at the sandwich she was holding. *Yum, a Cuban medianoche. I wonder if she is going to finish the whole thing this time?*

Rosalina put the sandwich down and said, "Lauren Matthews is being evicted, and the bank is foreclosing on Long Pond Farm. They have thirty days to move. We don't know where she and the kids will go or what will happen to all those animals. What a shame."

The news shocked me. "That's awful. I had no idea! That poor woman has been through hell and back! I'm beginning to wonder if Luca will ever have a stable home or family life." I flopped down in a chair. The midnight sandwich was no longer so appealing; I had lost my appetite. "Those poor kids!"

"Now for the really bad news, Eddie. Maybe you should tell him, Ima."

"Really bad? What news could be any worse?" I looked at Ima.

"Brownie Shytles is dying. He's been put into a hospice...sent there to die," Ima said.

"I suspected something was wrong with him. The morning of my charter cruise, Brownie didn't get out of bed to cook breakfast. That was very unusual," I said.

"It was probably later that night that they took him to Jackson Hospital. They say that without a major bowel operation he will soon die. He will bleed to death...internally, I think," said Rosalina.

"His shack was a mess—so full of blood, vomit, and excrement that John Dumas had to burn it down. I don't think Brownie will last much longer," said Ima.

I stood up. "I've gotta go see him!"

"I'm still on my break. Let me give you a lift in my car," said Ima.

"You have a car now?"

"Oh yeah, I didn't tell you, Eddie. I bought a used car!" said Ima.

"Finally some good news! So now you have a job, an apartment, and a car. You've come a long way, Ms. Ima Hooker!"

Ima dropped me in front of the hospice, and I went inside. Three beds were lined up along the wall in Brownie Shytles's hospice room.

He was lying on his back in the bed closest to the window. The other two beds were empty. When I saw Brownie lying in his bed, I didn't even recognize him. The skin covering his gaunt face was stretched tight, yellow and paper-thin. The whites of his eyes were yellow and sunken in.

"Hi, Brownie."

He looked over at me with his mouth agape. His breathing was raspy and labored. He made a grunting noise—a greeting, I supposed.

There was a cup containing ice on a table next to his bed. "Here, Brownie." I put some ice chips into his open mouth, and he seemed to savor the cold, wet shavings.

"I was hoping you would come...don't have much time left," he whispered. I could barely understand his words. I sat on the edge of the unoccupied bed next to him.

"I'm all alone. No one will stay in this room with me—they said I'm too disgusting. They demanded a different room," he mumbled as I gave him more ice chips.

Brownie was lonely and afraid, so I decided to tell him about my adventure in Cuba to take his mind off his suffering. "Brownie, if I tell you about my trip to Cuba, you must agree not to tell anyone else. What you are about to hear is top secret. Do you understand me, Brownie?"

"Yeah, Eddie, I'll take it to my grave—and that will be soon," he said, panting; speaking took great effort.

"After I was shipwrecked on Christmas, the people who rescued me from the ocean were Cuban exiles. Two counter-revolutionaries. They recruited me to help them with an undercover mission to Cuba. They are trying to assassinate Rafael Cato!"

I told Brownie in detail about Katarina, *El Muerte*, and our encounter with Cato in Cuba. Brownie seemed to come to life as the plot thickened, especially at the part when Cato took the poisoned cigar from Katarina.

"Did he smoke the cigar in front of you?" Brownie asked.

"No, Cato wouldn't smoke the poisoned cigar. He saved it because Katarina's lip prints were on it." Brownie seemed to have gained strength, and life came back into his eyes. Wide-eyed, he continued to listen to my tale.

"So that's it, Brownie. In the end our plan failed, but at least we got out of Cuba alive!"

Just as I concluded the story, a nurse came into the room. "Visiting hours are over, sir," she said.

"Okay, Nurse." I stood up and asked her, "Ma'am, is there a doctor whom I could talk to about Mr. Shytles's condition?"

"No, no doctors are here at the moment."

"Can we speak outside, then?" I asked her after saying goodbye to Brownie.

We spoke in the hallway. "Maybe you can help me, ma'am. I want to know what can be done to save Brownie. I know that he needs a major operation or he will die," I said.

"Yes, I'm afraid so. The reports that I have seen recommend a bowel resection and a colostomy initially. That operation needs to be followed by a series of reconstructive operations. The cost of the surgeries and follow-up patient care would be exorbitant, I'm afraid—tens of thousands of dollars."

"Tens of thousands, you've got to be kidding!" I was going to ask about setting up a payment plan but realized that I had only thirty bucks in my pocket and was out of work again! "Well, thanks, ma'am. I'd better get to work to earn some money then."

I left the hospice and walked to the Garbage Guys. The HELP WANTED sign had been reposted on the fence. *Thank God, the dumpster job is still available!*

I went into the office, and Betty agreed to let me start work immediately. With grinder in hand, I climbed into a hot, stinky dumpster and went to work. I started work at two thirty, which meant that I would get paid for about an hour and a half of pay before closing time.

"Hey, fella, are you Mr. Ocean?" I was startled by the voice and looked up to see the guy in the cheap suit looking down at me as I sat on the floor of the dumpster holding my grinder.

"Why?" I asked and set the grinder down.

The balding man covered his nose with a blue handkerchief to shield it from the odor. "I know that you're Mr. Eddie Ocean, sir, I have a picture of you. I've been searching for you—searching for weeks now. We need to talk about a financial matter of great importance."

"I'm not permitted to take breaks, sir." I picked up the grinder and started working on a large pocket of rust.

The man yelled to be heard over the loud noise caused by my grinding. "Okay, I'll wait until closing time."

After working for about ten minutes, I stopped and peeked out from the dumpster to see if the guy had left. I wanted to get a drink of water from the hose, but the guy was sitting at the employees' outdoor lunch table adjacent to the water spigot. He was reading a newspaper and showed no signs of leaving, so I continued grinding away the rust pockets. *Great! I'm trying to earn some money to help out Brownie, and now this geek is about to hand me a big, fat hospital bill of my own!*

Every so often I peeked over the edge of the dumpster to see if the bill collector had given up and gone away. I was dying of thirst. No such luck—now he was looking inside his briefcase. The quitting time buzzer sounded, and I peeked out of the dumpster again. This time the guy was looking directly at me. Damn! I ducked back down but realized there was nowhere to hide, so I climbed out of my hellhole and walked toward him. *However much it is I owe, let's get the unpleasantness over with.*

"Okay, what's this all about, mister?" I asked as I took a drink and then washed myself off with the hose near the picnic table.

"You are going to like what I have to tell you—you'll like what I have for you, Mr. Ocean. You should not have been avoiding me for the past two weeks."

I sat down at the picnic table as he took out some paperwork from his briefcase. *Oh boy, here it comes—a big, fat bill!*

"Mr. Ocean, I work for the Harbinger Trust Fund of New York City."

"I knew it! That's a collection agency, right?" I asked as he handed me a document.

"No, sir, we are not a collection agency. We are a highly regarded international banking and investment firm. It has been most difficult to serve you with these papers." *Serve me with papers! Ha, I knew it!*

"Since your home address is listed as 'at large,' and we could not locate you for some time, the money owed to you was deposited into a trust fund at our institution. I was assigned to locate you and give you access to your account and the funds."

"Did you say money *owed to me*...access to *my* funds? What are you talking about, sir? I'm broke...dirt poor. This is clearly a case of mistaken identity."

"I think not, Mr. Ocean. Aren't you the gentleman who designed the very popular Kroc line of rubber footwear and also the person who was the first to cut your hair in the popular mullet hair style?"

"Well, yes, I guess so. But it wasn't actually me; a giant, mutant bull crocodile was responsible for making those changes to my appearance. And against my will, I might add!"

"Well, a company can't possibly pay royalties to a crocodile, can they?"

"Royalties?" For the first time I looked at the papers the man had handed to me. They were two checks made out to me! *What? These are checks...$100,500.00 and $25,000! This is a prank!*

"Excuse me, sir, you look very familiar." *I think I recognize this guy from that TV show.* "Aren't you Allen Funt? Am I on *Candid Camera*?" *I wonder if I'll be paid for my appearance on the show?*

"Mr. Ocean, do you believe that a famous man like Allen Funt, the host of *Candid Camera*, would track you down for over two weeks just to play a joke on you?"

"No, guess not." *Could these checks be legit?* I stood up and tilted my head back to get some fresh air. The sky began spinning, and then everything went black.

"Get him some water. He's been in the dumpster without water for hours. He's probably just dehydrated." Dickey's voice woke me. He and the nerd were standing over me as I lay on my back, my hand still clutching my cashier's checks, albeit limply now. Above me, their faces were framed by a clear blue sky and puffy white clouds. I looked down at the checks again. *Oh my God, they are for real!* Finally I was able to sit upright and drink some more water.

"Mr. Ocean, I suggest that you deposit those checks immediately into a local bank account. Since they're from out of state, they will take about a week to clear. Now, before I leave, I just need you to sign here." The guy gave me a form to sign as we sat down at the picnic table.

"Thank you sir!" I returned the form. "And thank you for being so persistent!"

"You were a tough one to track down kid. I'm afraid that Electronic banking is the wave of the future...when that happens they won't pay gumshoes like me to fly around looking for you guys and I'll go the way of the dinosaur." The man stood and put the paperwork into his briefcase.

I looked up and asked, "What's your name, mister?"

"Dactyl...Terry Dactyl."

"Thanks for everything, Mr. Dactyl."

"Just doing my job, young man. Now, after you open a bank account, call this number and give them your routing and account number. Any future royalty payments will then go directly into your account." He handed me his business card.

"*Future* payments?" I felt dizzy again.

"Hey! He passed out again!" Dickey Stroker's voice sounded as if it were a thousand miles away. I did not want to wake up to find out that it was all just a dream.

*Thirty minutes ago I was adding up my pay...one and a half hours equals $2.00 + 1.00 for a total of $3.00! Now I'm holding checks worth $125,500! My bad luck has finally changed for the better!*

After sprinting half a mile to the Bank of Miami, I arrived there at 4:40 pm. *Great—twenty minutes until closing time!* A young, attractive blonde woman stood at the teller's window.

"Hello. How can I help you?" Her name tag identified her as Miss Julie.

"Hi, Miss Julie. I need to open an account and deposit these checks," I said as I gave her my cashier's checks. She examined them and then looked up at me with a quizzical expression. The large sums caused her to do a double-take and she flipped both checks over to look at the back.

"You will have to talk with a bank manager about opening an account and depositing these checks, sir," she said as she leaned forward and looked down suspiciously at my feet. Suddenly she took a step backward and wrinkled up her nose. I realized that I reeked of the odor of garbage and sweat; my clothes were stained and filthy.

"Have a seat over there, please." Julie pointed to some leather chairs, and after a brief wait, a young man wearing a suit came over to me.

"Hello, sir, let's go to my office." He turned and then led me to it. "My name is Mr. Hatley. Please have a seat." He shook my hand before sitting down behind his desk. "What can I do for you today?"

"My name is Eddie Ocean, sir, and I need to open a checking account. Sorry about my appearance. I just came here from work." I slid the checks across the desk to him.

"Oh I see! You just came from work—and where do you work, Mr. Ocean?" he asked as he looked at my cashier's checks.

"I work at the Garbage Guys over on NW Eighth Street, but it's only a temporary job."

"Uh-huh—so it's only a temporary job. Well, by the amount of these checks, I see that those garbage guys must pay pretty well!"

After seeing the large sum of the checks, the same look of skepticism and disbelief that Julie had expressed earlier now crossed Mr. Hatley's face.

"They pay me almost double the minimum wage now," I said with pride.

"Double the minimum wage, huh? Well listen, Eddie, I grew up on the streets of Philadelphia, and I've seen and heard every hustle and scam known to mankind! So do you really expect to pass these cashier's checks by me...at my bank?" Hatley held the $100,500 check up toward the fluorescent lights. He appeared to be trying to see through it.

"Sir, that check is legit. Call the Harbinger Investment firm and check it out."

"Eddie, you look like a nice kid. Let's pretend you never came into the bank, and I won't have to call Juan over." He pointed at the armed guard near the front door.

"Mr. Hatley, those checks are good, I assure you."

"Okay then, here's the deal, kid. If I make a Long Distance call to New York only to find out that these checks are forgeries, I will be forced to have you arrested for attempted bank fraud. The Harbinger will be aware that you possess forged checks, and at that point I will not be able to help you kid...so this is your last chance to back out of your scam."

"Go ahead and call New York, sir. Please call." Hatley seemed surprised by my confidence. He picked up his telephone and began to dial the telephone number imprinted on my checks.

He seemed annoyed as he began his conversation, but the expression on his face softened as the person at the other end spoke to him. Finally Mr. Hatley spoke again. "Yes, sir! No, thank you very much sir!" Mr. Hatley hung up the phone and actually smiled at me. "So the checks are good...so, Mr. Ocean...you are some sort of eccentric inventor who prefers to live at large on the streets of Miami, or so they say."

"Well not by choice, sir. I won't be on the streets for long now."

"Well, the Bank of Miami will be honored to take care of all your banking needs, Mr. Ocean. I'll open your account today, but it will take a week for these out-of-state funds to clear."

I had thought a cashier's check would clear more quickly, especially after it had been verified by the institution that issued it...but who was I to look a gift horse in the mouth? *An hour ago I thought I was dodging a bill collector—and now I have $125,500...and the promise of more to come!*

Mr. Hatley helped me open my checking account, and then he deposit my checks for me. Afterward, I went home to skid row with my bank deposit slip and new checkbook tucked in my back pocket. Every few blocks I stopped and took the deposit slip out of my pocket to look at it again. *Wow this is real; I have $125,500!*

Up at the penthouse I was cooking some canned beans and coffee for dinner when I saw a young boy with a backpack following a middle-aged man walking across the open field below. They were headed toward the Addicts' Village, a very bad section of skid row. The man had caught my attention because he was carrying a long stick over his shoulder with a red sack tied to the end. He had the classic look of a Depression-era hobo, and with the towheaded little boy following him, the pair looked like they had walked off the canvas of a Norman Rockwell painting. *Hey, mister—don't take the kid over there!* The man and the boy were walking into the section occupied by desperate drug addicts and crooks. *Some of those guys will cut your throat for a dime, mister!*

"Hey you!" I called down to them and waved for them to come up to the penthouse. They hesitated but then began coming up the slope.

The kid got to the top well ahead of the man. "Do you live up here, mister?" he asked as he looked inside my cardboard box.

"Yeah, kid. You should stick close to your dad. Some people around here are not very nice. That is your dad that's with you, right?"

"Yeah. We lost our house. I had my own room and a backyard, but they made us sell our house at a sheriff's sale." The kid's shoulders slumped; he seemed both sad and angry as he kicked an empty tin can down the embankment. "My mom ran off with an insurance salesman, and we had to take my dog to the pound. The guy at the dog pound put Copper in a cage!"

The man made it to the top of the embankment and greeted me. "Hi, my name is Olsen, and this is my son, Rocky," he said as we shook hands. Rocky spotted the food and walked over to the hibachi, where he stood staring down at the beans.

"Rocky said that you lost your house, Mr. Olsen."

"Yeah, I'm an auto mechanic…had my own garage, but we went belly-up. I'm a very good mechanic but not much of a businessman. We just lost our house last week…been surviving by doing odd jobs and auto repair work at a couple of local gas stations, but I'm not making enough to support us."

Rocky was still looking at the beans cooking on the grill when he said, "I told my dad not to worry about money. When I play baseball for the Detroit Tigers, we'll have plenty of money, and a big house, too." The kid looked hungry.

"Mr. Olsen, will you guys join me for dinner? I only have beans."

"Sure, thank you, kid. I have a pack of hot dogs. We've been eating them cold, but I'll throw the rest of them on your grill if you'd like."

As we ate our meager meal of hotdogs and beans, I gave Olsen a list of skid row dos and don'ts. "Those areas where the people are living in parked cars are your type of people, family types, but stay out of that area, the place that you were headed to earlier." I pointed to an area off to the right, where trash and empty whiskey bottles surrounded shabby tents and cardboard boxes.

"We'll only be staying here for a couple of days, just until I find full-time work," Olsen said as he used his fork to cut the hot dog that was in his bowl of baked beans.

"Good luck, Mr. Olsen. Jobs are scarce these days. The only work I could find was inside a garbage dumpster. This economy is a bitch."

"I just need a chance to show my stuff," Olsen said.

I stood up and walked over to Riley Ford's shack. "This shack is available. It's unoccupied. Do you want to use it?" I smacked the side of the cardboard box.

"Cool! It's a fort!" said Rocky.

Mr. Olsen and the kid went inside the shack to check it out and then came back outside. "Thanks, kid! This is like the Hilton compared to where Rocky and I have been sleeping lately!"

Before bedtime Rocky sat with me while his dad put Riley's shack in order. The kid was a baseball nut. He told me about his favorite baseball players. He knew their ages, heights, weights, strengths, and weakness, and he could recite all of their statistics.

"Check this out, Mr. Eddie!" Rocky handed me a baseball card that he took from his backpack. "That 's Al Kaline. He's my favorite player. That's who I would be if I had a choice. Someday I want to be like Al Kaline. I will be playing right field for the Detroit Tigers." He stood up and ran to his right and then jumped into the air, pretending to catch a fly ball.

"Did you know that the Tigers almost got into the World Series a year ago, but they lost to those crappy Oakland As." Rocky and I talked about baseball and his dog for nearly an hour. "I used to have dogs when we owned our house. My favorite dog was a cocker spaniel named Copper. He was really smart."

"Rocky, I bet you'd like Hobo," I said.

"Who's Hobo?"

"A very smart little collie that I know."

"That's a cool name—Hobo. Hey, Mr. Eddie! I just realized something: We're hobos, aren't we? Hey, Dad, are we hobos?" Rocky called out.

"No, of course not! We are not hobos, Rocky; we are just in between jobs. Your bed is ready!"

I told Rocky a few stories about my sailing adventures with Hobo, but I left out Hobo's encounter with the giant croc on Crocodile Island, fearing that the kid might have nightmares.

Rocky was getting tired. So was I. "Well, kid, you've worn me out. I gotta get some shut-eye now."

"Okay, goodnight, Mr. Ocean." Rocky went to join his father, and I went into my shack.

After lighting a candle, I looked at my checkbook one more time, and it seemed very odd to be lying in a cardboard box on skid row with a $125,500.00 bank deposit slip in my hand. *The cash should be available next Friday, they said—Friday the 25th. Yippee!*

As I was falling off to sleep, I made plans about what I would do with all the money. *I will get a sailboat…I'll get one even bigger and better than* Third Wish. *Yah-hoo, this cash will put me back into the charter business!*

That night, vivid dreams of sailing my new boat came. In one dream I sailed to the Whatchacallit Indian Village to show off my new boat to my Native American friends. *I especially want Jumping Jack and Little Hooters to see my new boat!*

Morning came, and I woke up early to begin cooking grits and making coffee. The aroma of strong coffee roused Mr. Olsen and Rocky; they joined me for breakfast. After we ate the grits and drank the coffee, I walked to work. I hated the dumpster grinding job, but Dickey was backlogged with work, and I wanted to repay his kindness by giving him a helping hand one last time.

Dickey was disappointed that I was quitting again, and he tried to dissuade me. "The pressure cleaning job might be opening up. Are you interested in that job, Eddie?"

"Thanks but no thanks, Dickey. I think my luck has finally changed for the better. Soon I'll be back sailing on the high seas again."

Dickey reposted the HELP WANTED sign on the front gate as I climbed into a stinky dumpster, promising myself, *This will be the last time, dude, I swear.*

At the end of the workday, I returned to skid row to find that Rocky and his dad were gone. Inside my shack I found a baseball card on top of my pillow. On the front of the card was a photo of Al Kaline posing in his batting stance. It was a different Al Kaline baseball card, not the one Rocky had shown me the night before.

*Thanks, kid. This card probably meant a lot to you.*

Something was scribbled on the card. At the bottom of the card Rocky had written in cursive across Al Kaline's legs. "For my new friend Eddie Ocean from the future right fielder of the Detroit Tigers, Rocky Olsen."

I pinned the card on the inside wall of my cardboard shack. *There is nothing like being young and filled with grand hopes and dreams. Good luck, Rocky!*

## FRIDAY, JANUARY 25TH, 1974

I got to the bank at 8:50 am and waited for the guard to open the doors. Julie was at her window when I went inside.

"Hi, Miss Julie. Have my checks cleared?"

She remembered me. "Hello, Mr. Ocean. Let me check on that. Yes, $125,500 is available in your account! You are in the money! Do you need any cash back today?"

"Cash back! Yahoo! This is too good to be true. I was expecting bad news…expecting something to go wrong, some kind of delay!" I said and pounded excitedly on the countertop. People looked at me like I was crazy. "How about $50 cash, Julie?"

"Sure. Will two twenties and a ten do?"

I took out my checkbook, wrote a check to cash, and Julie handed me the money.

"Perfect! I'm going boat-shopping today!"

It felt like I was walking on air as I went to the yacht broker's office at the Miami Marina. A salesman there provided me with a list of sailboats currently offered for sale. Some of the boats were located out of state, and many were located outside of the country, but a few of the local listings looked interesting to me. I put check marks next to five local listings.

"That 44-foot Beneteau that you checked off is right here in the Miami Marina. Want to take a look at her?" the salesman asked.

"You bet!"

The sailboat was a cruiser, just what I was looking for, and in excellent condition. Her name was *Orion*. *That must be an omen; she's named after my good friend Orion, the hunter of the night sky!*

"What are they asking?"

"Eighty-nine thousand," he said.

*Damn that's a good price; she's only a couple of years old!* "That seems a bit high," I said as I started the negotiation.

"Because of the poor economy, she has already been reduced three times, Mr. Ocean. The original asking price was $124,000. The owner is very motivated. If you do a little shopping, I think that you will find out that $89,000 is more than fair. Would you like a sea trial?"

"Absolutely!" I was excited and eager to sail her.

The boat was 44 feet, bow to stern, a two-year-old French-made Beneteau. We took her out of Government Cut and into the ocean. With a stiff southeasterly breeze, this was my kind of test drive. The Beneteau went through the choppy Atlantic Ocean with ease. *She cuts through the waves like a hot knife going through butter! Hope the broker hasn't noticed how excited I am.*

"She is fast!" I said to the yacht broker. Compared to the heavy wooden *Watermelon* boat, *Orion* caught the wind, heeled over, and then seemed to fly over the waves. Her ride was much smoother as the lighter fiberglass hull cut through the waves instead of pounding forward like the *Watermelon*, and she was nearly twice as long as the *Watermelon*.

"How many does she sleep?" I asked.

"She has three estate cabins that sleep two in each, and then a pair of bunk beds on the starboard side. That's a total of eight berths." *Let's see now…I could charter up to three couples at a time! That might generate some serious income!*

"Mr. Ocean, *Orion* is also equipped with the latest state-of-the-art electronics including a Loran radio-navigation system and radar."

"I could have used radar on Christmas when that freighter ran me down in the *Watermelon*."

"I read about your accident in the paper. That wouldn't have happened if you'd had radar."

We returned to port, and I was in love with *Orion*. "Well, what do you think of her, Mr. Ocean? I doubt you'll find anything close to *Orion* for the price."

"I really like her, sir, but she's the first boat I've looked at, and I try to never buy on impulse or on first sight. It's kind of a rule I have."

"Well, I'll show you the other two sailboats that are docked here, but for the value, they don't compare to *Orion*, Mr. Ocean. If you're a serious buyer, I suggest that you move fast. *Orion* won't be on the market for long." *He's right! But stick to your rule, dude. Sleep on it.*

After seeing the other two sailboats that were offered, I told the broker that I was interested only in *Orion* and that I would be in touch with him. Then I left the marina and went for lunch at a nearby steakhouse. The big, juicy T-bone steak and baked potato loaded with butter was the most delicious meal that I had enjoyed since eating Morning Wood's "wet-oven" roasted pork that had been prepared for me in the Whatchacallit Indian Village. After lunch I went to visit Rosalina and found her at her desk, typing like a madwoman.

"Hey Rosalina…what, no lounging around eating sandwiches today? You're actually working for a change? That typewriter sounds like a machine gun!"

"Very funny, Eddie, I'm doing a follow-up story on Luca. It's a very sad story. Lauren Matthews has been served the eviction notice. She has to find a new home and leave Long Pond Farm."

"That's terrible, Rosalina! Where's Ima?"

"She's out at the farm drawing sketches for my article."

"Wouldn't taking photos be faster and easier?"

"Sure, but Ima's sketches capture the inner emotions of her subjects. She shows their inner turmoil and feelings like no photographer can."

"You're right, Rosalina. I think she does that by how she draws their eyes."

"Yeah, and the expression lines on their faces, too," she said.

"Well, Rosalina, I have a bit of good news for a change. I think I've found my dream boat; she's a real beauty. I'm probably going to buy the *Orion* tomorrow morning."

"How can you do that? Did you inherit some money or something?"

"You might say that."

"Well, congratulations, Eddie! You can take Ima and me for a sunset cruise sometime."

"That will be my maiden voyage, Rosalina. You can count on it!"

"Sorry, Eddie, but I'm up against a deadline—need to get this piece written."

"Okay, I'll leave you to your work. I'm gonna head over to check on Brownie Shytles."

In Brownie's room at the hospice, a large bouquet of tulips were in a vase on the table. I read the attached note. *These flowers are from Ima Hooker...she must have brought Brownie that gift as well.* A gift-wrapped box was sitting on one of the unoccupied beds. When I went to Brownie's bedside I thought he was sleeping, but I couldn't wake him, and his breathing was erratic.

A nurse passing by the doorway saw me shaking Brownie's arm. "That's no use, kid. He's in a coma. He's beginning the Cheyne-Stokes respiration syndrome. He probably won't make it through the night. Do you know of any relatives we should notify?" the nurse asked me as she listened to Brownie's heart with a stethoscope.

"No, I think the poor guy is all alone in the world, ma'am. I want to take him to the hospital."

"Mr. Shytles is a DNR—that means do not resuscitate, and you don't have the legal standing to take custody of him or move him anyway."

"You're just gonna let him die, then?"

"That's what he came here for. He came to the hospice to die. I'm sorry. We have tried to make him as comfortable as possible."

I sat down in a chair and sat helplessly watching Brownie struggling to breathe...watching him die. I tilted my head back and felt sleep envelop my weary body.

*Why Brownie? He's such a great guy! If there were any justice in this world it would be Dr. Jill Hamm lying in that bed, not Brownie. I guess it's true...*

Nice guys finish last.

*Chapter 29*

# CHIEF TYEE

## SOME TIME DURING THE NIGHT OF SATURDAY, JANUARY 26TH, 1974

Brownie Shytles stood in front of an easel with a laser pointer as he addressed the crowd of architects and engineers. Trim and fit, Brownie was dressed in an expensive tailor-made suit, and he looked ten years younger than the last time I had seen him in the hospice. From the back of the room I watched Brownie explain his ground-breaking architectural engineering design, a new technology that would make high-rise buildings and other structures virtually earth-quake proof.

"As you can see, the weight-bearing pilings of the building's structure are mounted on Teflon disks, which are in turn topped by high damping rubber bearings." The red laser dot moved in a circle around an area at the bottom of the blueprint, and although I had no clue what Brownie was talking about, the crowd of engineers seemed to be enthralled by his lecture.

A man in the front row stood up to ask a question. "Mr. Shytles, what is the maximum magnitude earthquake that you believe a structure built with your earthquake resistant foundation could withstand?"

"I'm glad you asked me that question. It segues into the demonstration that I have arranged for you. You will see that my design has the potential to withstand an 8.5 magnitude quake."

The crowd gasped.

"Mr. Shytles, sir, 8.5? That means that your buildings could be built virtually earthquake-proof, not just -resistant! How is that possible?"

"Come, let me demonstrate." Brownie led everyone outside to the parking lot and stood before a platform on which two identical 22-foot-high structures had been constructed side by side. They were replicas of a seventy-three-story high-rise building in L.A.

"This is a shake-table. The twin seventy-three-story structures on the shake-table are identical other than the fact that the one to your right stands atop my anti-earthquake-engineered footings." He picked up a control and turned a dial that caused the shake-table to begin to vibrate.

"This shaking is equivalent to a magnitude 2 earthquake." Both structures vibrated equally.

"They're both shaking. I see no difference between them," said a skeptic in the front row.

"That's right. My design has not come into play yet. Now lets try a mag 4." The building on the left began to visibly shake and sway from side to side, but the one on the right continued to vibrate at the same rate as before.

"And now a mag 6.5." The crowd groaned as the structure on the left broke apart at the eighth floor and the tower fell to the ground, narrowly missing the other standing structure.

"Now 7.5!" Brownie shouted, turned the dial, and the structure trembled and seemed to slide slightly from side to side but remained standing. A murmur went through the crowd.

"Shall I try a 9.0, ladies and gentlemen? Everyone please step back. Step away from the table, sir!" Brownie chided the skeptic at the front of the crowd. The remaining structure began to break at the tenth floor but did not fall down.

"Okay, 9.5!" The shake-table vibrated like a paint mixing machine, and the structure cracked in half and fell. Beams and cross supports that landed on top of the shake-table were thrown off by its violent gyrations and landed at the feet of the crowd. People jumped back to avoid being hit. Then they began to cheer and applaud.

"Bravo! Mr. Shytles, your design is virtually earthquake proof! The highest magnitude quake on record was the 9.5 magnitude recorded in 1960, the one that devastated the city of Kanamori, Chile, and killed over 5,700 people!"

Suddenly Brownie began to weep, but his were not tears of joy. He seemed very sad, not happy about his successful architectural design. "Yes, I know. I was in that earthquake. My family was in that quake," he said.

Someone began pulling on my arm. "What do you want?" I asked of my unknown assailant.

"You fell asleep in the chair. We let you spend the night since your friend is dying, but you will have to say your goodbyes now." I opened my eyes to see a nurse standing over me. Brownie was lying in his bed. He already looked dead, but he was still breathing erratically.

It had all been just a dream! The dream of Brownie's demonstration had been so vivid and realistic; it seemed more like a vision than a dream.

The nurse began taking Brownie's blood pressure as she spoke. "It's a miracle that he made it through the night. Mr. Shytles must have a strong will to live," she said and then listened to his chest with her stethoscope.

After finishing her exam the nurse stood upright and said, "I don't understand how he can still be alive. He doesn't want to give up the fight. He doesn't want to let go."

"Brownie's one of the kindest people I have ever known, ma'am. I wish he would let go now and stop suffering. He will certainly go to a better place than this," I said and stood up.

The nurse was about to leave the room but stopped and pointed at the gift sitting on the unoccupied bed. "Aren't you going to open your present?"

"That's a gift for Brownie. It's from Ima Hooker."

"No, it's from Brownie. Brownie asked me to wrap it up and give it to Eddie Ocean—that's you, right?"

"Yes, ma'am. I'm Ocean." I was still groggy from sleep as I walked over to the bed to see the gift and read the note.

To: Eddie Ocean. From: Brownie.

*What the hell—why a gift for me?*

I ripped off the wrapping paper and opened the box. "What are all these things?" I asked as I looked at the instruments inside.

"Those are Brownie's drafting and architecture tools. He said he wanted to give them to you because someday you might meet someone on your charter boat who needs them." When I looked at Brownie's gaunt face, a tear welled up in my eye.

"What's this?" I asked as I noticed a folded dollar bill under the slide ruler.

The nurse leaned forward to see. "Must have been the only money he had left, I guess. That's sad—only one dollar to his name. He left it for you, I guess." She stood beside me, peering into the box.

"Who are these people?" I asked and showed her a small photo of Brownie hugging a woman and a young girl.

"That's Brownie with his wife and daughter. Before he slipped into a coma, he told me many things about his life—a deathbed confession, he called it. But Mr. Shytles had very little bad to confess—he was a very good and kind man, as you said."

I didn't even recognize Brownie in the photograph. He was healthy and handsome, with a twinkle in his eye. "I didn't know

Brownie had a family. He never mentioned them to me." I was perplexed as I examined the attractive woman's face. Her cheek was pressed against her young daughter's cheek.

"You mean Brownie never told you what happened to his family? It's one of the saddest stories I've ever heard!"

"No, what happened?"

"His family was killed in South America."

"Killed? How?"

"They were vacationing in Chile. Brownie was off studying some of the local, ancient architecture in the city of Kanamori when an earthquake struck. His wife and daughter were killed when their hotel collapsed on them during the quake. Brownie helped dig their crushed bodies out of the rubble with his bare hands, and for two years after the tragedy, Brownie drifted around South America in an alcohol- and drug-induced stupor.

"When his money ran out, Brownie returned to the US and entered rehab to recover and began working again. He said he would dedicate his life to designing buildings that would not collapse in an earthquake. But then, before he could complete his work, he fell ill from the damage done by parasites and alcoholism. He lost his job. He told me his greatest regret in life was never completing his earthquake-proof design."

"That story is just too bizarre ma'am...this can't be happening... this can't be true!"

"What are you talking about?"

"Well, last night as I slept in that chair, I had a dream about Brownie. Brownie had perfected his design. I even saw it work on a scale model high-rise building...I saw the blueprints...saw detailed drawings in my dream! How could I dream about those things when this is the first time I have ever heard of them?" *Was my dream actually another vision into the past? Wait, no—this time I was seeing into the future! Last night ancient spirits must have been messing around inside my head again.*

When I put the photo back into the box, I noticed writing on the single dollar bill. *Pay it forward! Hey, this is Mrs. Washington's dollar! I gave it to Ima, and Ima must have given the dollar to Brownie!* Now it had come full circle and was back in my hands.

"Pay it forward?" I repeated aloud. "I don't feel so good, ma'am."

"Sit down, Eddie. I'll get you some water." The nurse fed me water like I was a little baby boy sitting in a highchair. My head was spinning as I stared at the dollar. *Brownie, such a talented man... leaving this world with only one dollar to his name.*

The hospice nursing station was a beehive of activity as the morning shift employees began relieving the graveyard shift. I was hoping to set up a meeting with the yacht broker to make an offer to buy the *Orion*, but as I stood at the nurses' station trying to get someone's attention, it seemed as though I were invisible.

"Hello? Hello? Hi, miss." Everyone ignored me. The night shift wanted to get the hell out of the hospice, and those reporting for the day shift looked like they needed a dose of strong coffee. Suddenly I heard a man's voice yelling at me.

"Sun Chaser Eddie Ocean! What do we have to do to get through to you, paint you a picture—draw you a map?" The voice had a familiar accent. I turned to see who was speaking, but nobody was near me. I looked around the area, bewildered, and then I noticed on the far side of the room a very old man with long white hair was sitting in a wheelchair. His face was weathered and creased with a thousand wrinkles; he stared directly at me with his mouth agape and saucer-sized eyes wide.

"Can I help you, Mr. Ocean?" Finally someone at the nursing station had noticed me, and I turned back around to face the desk.

"Yes, ma'am. May I use your phone?"

"You're supposed to use the payphone." The nurse pointed to a payphone on the wall near the old man. "But I'll let you use this phone if you make it quick."

"Great—should only take a minute for me to set an appointment," I said.

*"Pay it forward!"* Now the old man was screaming loudly, but to my surprise no one paid any attention to the crazy old coot.

"Who is that old man with the long white hair?" I asked the nurse as she slid the phone closer to me.

She craned her neck to see who I was referring to and then said, "Oh, that's Chief Tyee. He was brought to us from the Seminole Reservation up in Hollywood, Florida." *Ah, that's it...that's the accent... Native American.*

"Why does he keep yelling at me like a madman? And how does he know my name?"

"Yelling? Chief Tyee has not spoken a word in three years. He had a stroke and is aphasic." The nurse gave me an odd look like *I* was the madman.

"She can't hear me, wasichu! Did you not learn anything from your vision? Did you not learn that if that architect dies, his design will die with him? His earthquake-resistant technology will be lost for many years if he goes to the afterlife. His powerful magic will be lost until someone else in the future has his vision. Mr. Shytles's designs will save thousands of lives, but only if he lives."

The loud, angry voice filled my head, and I realized it was audible only to me. I turned to look at the old man. His expression had not changed. *You are creeping me out, old man!*

"You must pay it forward, Sun Chaser Eddie Ocean!" The chief's mouth had not moved, but his angry eyes darted from side to side. The old man's wrinkled mouth remained agape as his demands echoed out from that dark hole. *The ancient spirits are back in my head again! I have been in denial. All along I have known what they expect me to do with my newfound fortune, but my dream of having a sailboat has caused me to deny that reality.*

I picked up the phone, but instead of calling the yacht broker, I called Nurse Patty Whacker at Jackson Hospital.

"Patty, it's Eddie Ocean. I need your help. Brownie Shytles was a patient in the ICU a short time ago. His surgery was canceled due to lack of insurance. They must still have all his records and his consent forms on file. We need to find his medical records and then get him into emergency surgery, fast! I just hope it's not too late."

"I'm familiar with Brownie's case, Eddie. He was denied indigent coverage—refused treatment because he still drinks too much," Patty told me.

"Patty, I've got the money to pay—I can pay cash. Find out how much it will take to get him on the OR schedule and then send an ambulance to pick him up at the hospice."

"The last time this issue of payment arose, administration said they would require a deposit of at least $50,000."

"Holy crap, $50,000! Okay, no worry. Brownie will have a check for $50,000 when he arrives at Jackson. Please make sure they take good care of him, Patty."

"Are you coming with him?"

"No. I have another important matter to attend to."

I took out my checkbook and wrote a check to Jackson Hospital for $50,000 and then gave it to the charge nurse. "Ma'am, if you have any questions about Mr. Shytles being transferred, call nurse Patty Whacker at Jackson Memorial at this number. All the paperwork and his consent forms were signed weeks ago," I said as I handed the check to the nurse.

"Fifty thousand dollars! You are a true saint, Mr. Ocean." The middle-aged nurse looked wide-eyed at the check.

"You give me too much credit, ma'am. The damn voices in my head made me do it. I was gonna use that money to buy my dream boat. Don't know if I would have done the right thing of my own volition. It was the old man's damn voice!"

"Son, you sound angry and cynical. I don't think you should be bitter for having a moral compass. You should feel blessed for receiving spiritual guidance—guidance from that 'voice,' as you call it."

"If you say so, ma'am. May I make one more phone call, please?"
I asked.

"Mr. Ocean, you may make as many calls as you want."

I had not given up my hope of getting the *Orion*. My plan was to call the yacht broker and work out a deal. Even though I no longer had enough money to buy the sailboat outright, I had most of the money that was needed. As I stood looking down at the telephone, I planned on what to say to the yacht salesman while I calculated how much money I had left in my account: *$125,500 minus $50,000—that leaves me with $75,500! I might still get that sailboat after all! Maybe the seller will let me make payments on the remaining balance!*

Excited, I turned away from the phone and walked toward the door. Chief Tyee was still sitting frozen in his wheelchair like a corpse with rigor mortis. He couldn't move, but his eyes followed me as I passed by him, and a crooked smile crossed his face. Then I heard his voice again, it had a slightly different accent this time and was gentle yet powerful.

"Broad is the path, but narrow is the way."

*Chapter 30*

# A DAY AT THE FARM

Outside the hospice, a city bus was approaching from the west as I stood at the crosswalk. *If I wait for this darn traffic light to change, I'm sure to miss my ride. Go for it, dude!* I did a little chicken hop to time the flow of the oncoming traffic before darting into the street. The driver of a dump truck blasted his air horn and shook his fist at me as I ran across the road in front of him and then dodged another eastbound vehicle.

After weaving my way through the morning rush hour traffic and across the busy street, I ran down the block toward the bus stop as the bus roared past me. With a loud hiss and a groan from its air brakes, the bus stopped at the curb up ahead, and I took my place at the end of the line of nightshift hospice workers heading home for the day. While I waited my turn to board the bus, an ambulance with its lights flashing and siren wailing sped past and stopped in front of the hospice. *Good luck, Brownie.*

"You almost got yourself killed crossing that street, kid!" the bus driver said to me as I dropped two quarters into the money slot.

"Had to catch your bus, sir. This is a big day for me; today I will buy the sailboat of my dreams."

"Oh, yeah? Well, good luck, kid. The Miami Marina will be the fourth stop." The driver turned to the woman who was next in line after me as I chose a seat directly behind the driver.

"Fare, lady!" he said. She giggled and put money into the slot.

Because the ride would be short, I sat in the front row of the bus by the window, and the woman took the seat beside me. She kept smiling and looking at the reflection of the bus driver's face in the large, rectangular mirror above his head, and he kept glancing back at her with a smile of his own. When the woman realized that I had noticed the middle-aged pair flirting like teenagers, she leaned over and whispered to me, "Isn't he handsome?"

"I guess he's all right," I said. Actually the guy did not look attractive to me whatsoever.

"He's not only handsome, he is *so* romantic. Every time I board his bus he calls me 'Fair Lady'!" she said and twirled a lock of hair with her finger. I did a double-take to see if she was joking, but she wasn't.

"This is your stop, kid," the driver said as he gave the infatuated woman a big toothy smile from the rear-view mirror.

I hopped off the bus and jogged toward the yacht broker's office, feeling like I was on top of the world. I would have regretted it for the rest of my life if I had not helped Brownie get medical treatment.

It felt good to do the right thing. Moored in the distance I saw the *Orion*. *Wow, she's a real beauty! This is great; I've helped Brownie and I'll still get my boat. I can have my cake and eat it too!* Up ahead I saw the broker's office, and I slowed down to a walk so that when I arrived I wouldn't be out of breath. *Don't want to look to anxious... need to negotiate, dude.* When I was within about fifty yards of the yacht broker's office, the door opened, and to my surprise Dr. Jill Hamm came outside.

"What the hell is she doing here?" I said aloud to no one in particular. Hamm paused for a moment when she saw me coming up the sidewalk. She turned toward me, waved, and then laughed before turning and walking off toward Sun 'N' Fun Charters.

The yacht broker was sitting at his desk doing paperwork when I entered his office.

"Hello, sir. I'm here to make a deal for the *Orion*." The broker looked up with a sheepish grin.

"Uh-oh," he mumbled and then stood up. "Hello, Mr. Ocean. I'm afraid *Orion* has been sold. I warned you not to procrastinate. *Orion* was a real bargain—a steal!"

My heart sank. "You got to be kidding me, mister! I left a message for you on your answering machine! I said I was coming to make you an offer!"

"Yes, I got your message, Mr. Ocean. You wanted to finance a balance of $10,000, but I'm afraid that the other buyer paid cash on the barrelhead, and she got here ahead of you, kid. First come, first served."

"She?"

"Yes. Dr. Jill Hamm, the director of Sun 'N' Fun, just bought the Orion for her company's fleet of sailboats. We just closed the deal not more than five minutes ago. Would you like to take a second look at the other two boats that are for sale, Mr. Ocean?"

"No! I'm too upset right now, dude! I'll be in touch." I went outside, stood in the middle of the sidewalk, and screamed at the heavens. "When will you bastards cut me a break? What more can I do to please you?"

People stopped and stared at me, a homeless lunatic ranting and raging at the heavens! I must have been frightening to them.

"This is not right! This is not fair!" *Calm down. You need a drink, dude!* After a few more minutes of venting, I walked over to the Tiki Bar.

Fannie Licker was tending bar. "Hi, Fannie. Give me a Bloody Mary. Make it a double with meat and extra veggies."

"You look like you just lost your best friend, Eddie," she said as she made my drink.

"I'm glad you said that to me, Fannie. What you said helps put what just happened into perspective."

"How so?"

"Well, the reason I'm bummed out is because my dream boat, the sailboat *Orion*, was just sold out from under me. I got here too late—but the business that caused my delay may have saved a good friend's life."

"I don't get it."

"When you said, 'You look like you just lost your best friend,' you reminded me of what's really important."

"Still don't get it."

"What's more important, Fannie, saving a friend's life or getting a new boat?" Fannie's simple comments about my losing my best friend was making me feel better.

"Okay, I see. Eddie, another boat will come along, but good friends are hard to come by—right?" Fannie placed the Bloody Mary containing a Slim Jim, celery sticks, and carrots in front of me.

"Oh, wait!" She took back the drink and added extra Tabasco sauce. "There you go, just how you like them, Eddie, hot and saucy with extra veggies."

"Thanks! Fannie, you're not going to believe who bought my boat! It was that little witch, Dr. Hamm!"

"I hate that evil little woman. Everybody in the marina hates her. She is a spoiled little rich bitch!"

"The guys at Sun 'N' Fun say her rich daddy in New York buys her anything she wants. He's probably the one who paid for *Orion*," I said.

"Probably. Her father owns Sun 'N' Fun. He bought the company just so the little brat would be able to have a job. If he didn't own Sun 'N' Fun, she would have been fired long ago. Hamm has wrecked two of their boats so far—ran 'em onto reefs down in the Keys. Oh, excuse me, Eddie." Fannie went to take care of another customer.

I finished my Bloody Mary breakfast and put money on the bar. "Fannie, keep the change and have a great day. I'm off to see Rosalina Rossi."

"Take care, Eddie. I'll keep my eyes and ears open for you—for boat sales."

After hopping onto a crowded northbound bus at Biscayne Boulevard, I sat next to a young guy who seemed to be about my age.

"How they hanging, dude?" the guy said as I took my seat.

"Up in a bunch. I'm having a bad day. Thought I was getting a boat today, but things didn't work out."

"Too bad. I'm looking for a job. You know anyone who's hiring?" he asked me.

"Jobs are scarce. Try the Garbage Guys over on Eighth Street," I said.

"Yeah, unemployment has really skyrocketed, but if I were president I would end unemployment altogether," he said.

"Really? How would you do that?"

"Easy. I would take all the women who are out of work and put them on one island, and then take all the men who are out of work and put them on a different island. It's that simple!"

"Huh? How does that put the people to work?" I asked.

"Because everyone will be busy building boats to get to the other island!" he said.

"Ha! That's a good one, dude! Hey, this is my stop. Check out the Garbage Guys, ask for Dickey Stroker—he's the foreman," I said as I got off the bus and went into the *Post* building.

The nasty security guard at the Miami *Post* was on duty at the front door of the newspaper. He scowled but waved me through the security checkpoint. "It's the middle of the day, punk! Get a job!"

Rosalina was at her desk with Ima, working on the follow-up story about Luca, when I arrived.

"Hey, do you guys know how to end unemployment?" I asked as I walked in and then told them the joke. Rosalina didn't laugh, but Ima chuckled.

"That's really lame, Eddie," said Rosalina.

"I thought it was funny," I said.

"Eddie, Rosalina is right—that joke was pretty darn lame. Come here and have a look at our story. This is only the proof," Ima said and stepped back so I could see the papers strewn across the desk.

The story was very well written, and Ima's sketches really brought the article to life. The look in Luca's eyes was haunting. When I finished reading, I looked at the sketches of Lauren standing forlornly with the kids and began choking up with emotion.

"Excuse me...need some water." Embarrassed, I rushed out of the room. *You're acting like a little girl, dude!* At the water cooler I regained my composure and then went back into the office.

"Sorry, ladies, but that article is a real tear-jerker." The girls seemed very pleased by my emotional reaction to their story.

"There's more bad news, Eddie. Problems have recently come up that I haven't reported in my article," said Rosalina.

"Oh no! What else could go wrong?"

"Lauren's tractor broke down, and she was cited and fined by the county for not removing or composting a big manure pile. Then one of her mastiffs bit a man from the sheriff's office when he came to deliver her the eviction papers. The county might take her dog, and Lauren's afraid they might kill the dog and sue her."

"And I thought I had troubles."

"Eddie, we're going up to Long Pond Farm after lunch. Want to come?" Rosalina asked.

"Sure. At the moment, my schedule is wide open."

We ate subs in the office, and this time I had money to buy my own sandwich. After eating lunch, we left for Jupiter.

"Get a job, you long-haired punk!" the guard said to me as we passed him to leave the building.

"Don't mind him. That guy's got serious issues," Rosalina said and patted my back. We crossed the street and got into Rosalina's car; then she drove out of the parking garage.

"I need gas," Rosalina said as she pulled into a gas station located just before the I-95 entrance ramp.

"It's self-serve, Rosalina. I'll pump the gas." While I pumped the gas I saw Mr. Olsen standing in the bay of the garage. He seemed to be arguing with another man.

"Hey, Mr. Olsen!" When I called to him, Rocky's sun-bleached white head popped out from the middle of a stack of tires.

"Hey, Dad, it's Eddie Ocean!" Mr. Olsen waved but continued arguing with the man as Rocky came running out of the garage toward the car.

"Hi, Rocky. What are you doing here?"

"My dad just finished working on that car, but the guy doesn't want to pay him," Rocky said as Mr. Olsen walked over to join us.

"Hi, Mr. Olsen."

"Hi, Eddie. The owner of the gas station just stiffed me for twenty bucks. I fixed that car in less than half the estimated time for the repair, so the guy says I don't deserve the full fee—says the job was too easy for me to get paid so much."

As I looked at Olsen's greasy coveralls, I suddenly had a brainstorm. "Hey, Mr. Olsen, want another job? If I paid you, could you fix a farm tractor?"

"I can fix almost anything if I can get the parts," he said as Rosalina and Ima got out of the car to see what was going on. After the ladies met my new friends, it was settled: Rocky and Mr. Olsen would come with us to Long Pond Farm to see if Lauren's tractor could be repaired.

It was 2:30 pm when we pulled up in front of the barn at Long Pond Farm. The two bullmastiffs came running out of the barn howling and barking.

"Don't worry. Those dogs are harmless. Good boy, Buzz! Good girl, Lila!" I said and grabbed Buzz's massive blockhead with two hands and shook it, sending striations of slobber over my pants legs and shoes.

"These dogs are awesome! I bet I could ride them!" Rocky said and grabbed Buzz around the neck as Lila used her wide, fat tongue to slime his face.

Lauren Mathews came up to the barn riding a handsome palomino horse at a gallop. She was wearing bibbed coveralls over a western-style shirt with cowgirl boots and a brown western hat. The fit woman jumped off the horse and led him by the reins into the barn to un-tack him.

"Welcome," she called to us as Katie and Luca came down a ladder from the hayloft.

We all walked into the barn. "Where's Hobo?" I asked Lauren.

"He's probably visiting his girlfriend next door. She's a golden lab; they've got a thing going on. Well, who's this handsome young lad?"

"This is Rocky and his dad, Mr. Olsen. Mr. Olsen this is Lauren Matthews, Katie, and Luca." Rosalina introduced them.

"Lauren, Mr. Olsen is a mechanic. He might be able to fix your tractor," I said.

"I'm afraid I don't have money for that right now," she said.

"Let's worry about that later," I said. Mr. Olsen and I walked to the tractor, which was parked behind the barn in front of big pile of manure. The kids ran off toward the lake to play.

"Katie, be back in time for your chores!" Lauren called out as the three women walked toward the farmhouse.

"Hey, Eddie, is Lauren single? She's a real looker!" Olsen asked as he began inspecting the John Deere tractor.

"She's a widow. Hey, let me hold that for you. Mr. Olsen, I was wondering, why do you go by *Mr.* Olsen anyway, sir?"

"Don't like my first name, kid—it's Humperdinck, Humperdinck Olsen."

*Pssst* I was trying to stifle a laugh, but I wasn't having much luck. "Sorry, sir."

Mr. Olsen worked rapidly and seemed to know exactly what he was doing. Nothing about the machine seemed to confound or stump him. "She's got a leaking fuel line, cracked hydraulic hose, a loose throttle linkage, dirty fuel filters, and a gasket on the motor is leaking some oil."

"Darn, that's a lot of work."

"Nah! This tractor is in good condition. I can get her running right now but I'll need to get new filters, a gasket, and a new hose eventually. All told, once I have the parts, this project is only about a three-hour job." Olsen took off the fuel filter housing and cleaned the filter element with a brush and diesel fuel as I watched.

"Okay, get up there and see if she'll start now," he said. I climbed into the seat, turned the key, and the engine started on the first try!

"Yahoo! Damn, you're good, Mr. Olsen!"

Olsen stood below, looking up at me with a big smile. "Do you know how to operate one of these tractors Eddie?"

"Hell, no!" I said as I gazed at all the levers and handles.

"Come on down. I'll do it. I grew up on a farm in Kentucky. Let me take her." Olsen began scooping up manure with the tractor and loading it into the hopper of a manure spreader. He handled the machine with great precision and made short work of the first load. Then he hitched the spreader to the tractor's tow hitch and began spreading the manure in the pasture. After four loads and within less than an hour, the pile of manure was gone. Olsen shut off the tractor and climbed down as I brought him a glass of water from the barn.

"Have a drink." Olsen was standing beside the tractor drinking water when two horses walked over to us and began nuzzling him, trying to see what was in his cup. Olsen let one horse lick the plastic cup, and the horse seemed disappointed that there was water in it.

"He must have been hoping for a cold beer," I said as Olsen picked up the palomino's left front foot. "That one's name is Frost," I added.

"Hello, Mr. Frost," Olsen said as he examined the horse's hoof. "Eddie, this handsome fellow needs to be re-shod. This front shoe is loose. It's falling off, and that's dangerous because those nails could puncture his sole or his frog."

"How do you know so much about horses?" I asked.

"We had some on the farm in Kentucky. I used to do all my own horseshoeing, but that was many years ago," Olsen said.

"Really? You're a blacksmith too? Hey, I saw some blacksmith tools in the barn."

"Get me a halter and a lead rope. I'll fix this guy up in a jiffy," Olsen said as he checked Frost's other hooves.

I got a halter and a rope from the barn, and then Olsen led Frost into the back of the barn and cross-tied the palomino in the center aisle. Olsen effortlessly pulled off all the horse's shoes and then used long-handled nippers and a curved knife to trim all four hooves.

"Frost is done. Bring me that sorrel gelding with the star."

"His name is Sebastian," I said.

One by one, Olsen trimmed all the horses' overgrown hooves and then brushed them down until their coats were shiny. "When Lauren gets some new horseshoes for these guys, I'll nail em on," he said as he wiped sweat from his forehead. I began to sweep up all the hoof shavings from the concrete aisle of the barn.

"Oh my! Look at this place! Look at what you guys have done! The manure is gone, and the horses' feet look great!" Lauren said as all three women came walking into the barn.

"Mr. Olsen did it. I did little more than watch him work, ma'am," I said.

Lauren ran over, hugged Mr. Olsen, and gave him a kiss on the cheek, but then pulled back, embarrassed by her aggressiveness. The couple stood fidgeting awkwardly and looking at the ground as Ima, Rosalina, and I smiled at one another. *Looks like this could be the start of a romance!* I think we all had the same thought.

Finally Olsen spoke up. "Ma'am, I made a list of parts that you need for that tractor. They should not be very expensive, and the labor should take me only a few hours. Also, if you get two sets of number 3 size horseshoes, two sets of number 4s, and four double Os for the little pony, I can come back and shoe all of your animals."

"You are a wonderful man, Mr. Olsen!" Lauren said. Olsen's face began turning bright red.

"I would come back tomorrow, but I don't have a car—don't have any transportation at the moment, ma'am."

"Mr. Olsen, I can pick you up and bring you back to the farm tomorrow after lunchtime. Where in Miami are you and Rocky staying?" Ima asked.

Olsen began stammering. I figured he was embarrassed to let Lauren Matthews know that he and his boy were homeless and living on the streets, so I intervened.

"Mr. Olsen, didn't you say you needed to go to a motel for a couple of days?"

"Ah what...a motel?" Olsen looked confused.

Lauren's eyes widened. "Motel? Nonsense. There's a nice little one-bedroom apartment with bunk beds inside my barn. It's vacant. I had it rented out to the Davises—a pair of real chiselers who stiffed me for a month's rent. They ran off with a couple hundred dollars worth of my equipment when they found out about my eviction notice."

"Stay here? That's a great idea! Mr. Olsen, don't you think that Rocky would love staying at the farm for a couple of days?" I asked.

"My kids would love having another playmate!" Lauren added.

"We can't take advantage of you like that, ma'am. I can't afford a one-bedroom apartment right now—not even for just a couple of days." Olsen looked down and wiped his grimy hands with an orange rag.

"Take advantage of *me*! You must be kidding! It's the other way around, sir. You just did hundreds of dollars' worth of work for me this afternoon!"

"Well, I guess I could earn my keep, ma'am, thank you."

"Then it's settled. You and Rocky are staying. Let me show you the apartment." The pair walked to the apartment at the front of the barn.

"They look like a match made in heaven," said Ima.

We left Rocky and his dad at Long Pond Farm and drove back to Miami. While she drove, Rosalina informed me about what the women had been discussing. Long Pond Farm was going to be sold at a public auction in just two weeks, and Lauren was going to start selling off the livestock and her farm equipment.

"Lauren is waiting until after the weekend to tell the children. She's afraid of how Katie and Luca will react to the news that they need to move to an apartment and the animals will be sold.

"Lauren plans on keeping Hobo because he's small, but all the other animals have to go," Rosalina said as she turned onto the on-ramp to I-95.

"And just when Luca finally seemed to be happy—what a shame. Those kids are going to be devastated," I said.

You don't know what you've got till it's gone.

## Chapter 31

# MONEY WELL SPENT

**W**e returned to Rosalina's office at 7:05 pm. As Ima and I got a drink at the water cooler, Rosalina began checking her messages.

"Eddie, nurse Patty Whacker left a message for you. She said that Brownie Shytles's emergency surgery was performed but that he is in critical condition and still unconscious. They've put him in the Surgical Intensive Care Unit at Jackson Hospital."

"That's great—at least now he has a fighting chance. Maybe I'll visit him in the morning, if they'll let me," I said.

Ima tossed a cone-shaped paper cup into the trash can and asked me, "Do you want to crash at my place tonight, Eddie?"

"Nah, but thanks, Ima. I need to get a change of clothes. I'm pretty ripe from the day at the farm."

"Plus Ima, we have to work late tonight, remember," Rosalina put in. "We have a midnight deadline. Luca's story hits the presses at midnight."

After leaving Rosalina's office, I went out to Biscayne Boulevard and stopped at a newsstand to buy a newspaper before catching a bus home.

"Sir, I'll take the paper and a pack of spearmint gum."

"That will be sixty-five cents, kid."

After paying the man, I jogged to the bus stop and stood under the streetlight, thumbing through the Help Wanted classifieds. *Where have all the jobs gone?*

*Honk! Honk!* The blast from a car horn interrupted my thought.

"Get in!" a woman's voice demanded. When I looked up from the newspaper I saw Katarina sitting behind the wheel of a black 1967 Chevrolet Corvette convertible with the top down. Even though the sun had set, she was wearing large, round sunglasses with dark lenses. Her black hair glistened in the amber light of the streetlamp, and she looked stunning. She really could be a supermodel!

"Get in, Eddie! I'm hungry!" she yelled over the rumble of the small-block V-8 engine.

I tucked my newspaper under my arm and hopped over the door and into the convertible. "Hi, Katarina! What are you doing in this part of town?" I asked.

"Slumming!" She revved the powerful engine, popped the clutch, and with tires squealing sped off down the street. From the side mirror I could see two black streaks etched into the pavement beneath a grey cloud of smoke from burnt rubber.

"I'm hungry!" Katarina repeated. She was not in the mood for conversation as she drove like a maniac through the streets of Miami. The wind felt good as it blew through my hair, and in silence we raced toward Little Havana. *She sure gets cranky when she's hungry.* Up ahead, the sign on Versailles Cuban Restaurant came into view, and I realized that Versailles was Katarina's destination.

"I love this place! Last time I was here, I was with Nick Dagger and my Indian friends," I said as the Corvette screeched to a halt in a parking space next to a red Ferrari.

Katarina turned off the motor and looked at me. "Did you say Nick Dagger? *The* Nick Dagger of the Tumbling Stones?" Finally Katarina's interest was piqued.

"Yeah, Nick's a cool dude, and Kylie Simon was very nice, too."

"*The* Kylie Simon? Kylie Simon the singer?" Katarina asked me as we walked into the restaurant and found a table.

"Yeah, I met them through Versace, the Italian designer."

"Versace too?" Katarina raised her sunglasses up onto her head and leaned closer to stare into my eyes. Her cunning, grey, wolf-like eyes were penetrating, and I looked away.

"No, look at me. I want to see if you're joking," she said just as a waiter handed us two menus.

"Coffee?" he asked.

"Yes please, coffee *con leche*," I said. The waiter was about to walk away but stopped for some reason and looked me up and down suspiciously. Then he turned to Katarina and spoke Spanish. Whatever he said made her laugh.

"What did he say that was so funny?"

"He told me not to let you order black beans because they make you fart too much." She giggled again. "That was pretty rude. Why the heck would he say that, Eddie?"

"That waiter must have recognized me from my last visit here. He must have remembered my Whatchacallit Indian friends."

"Well, did you fart too much?" Katarina started laughing again.

"No, not me. It was my Whatchacallit friends. It's the custom of my Indian friends to pass gas and to belch loudly as a way to express their appreciation for a good meal. The last time we ate at Versailles, my warrior friends really enjoyed the huge feast provided to us by Versace and Dagger. They let everyone in the restaurant know how much they enjoyed their breakfast. Even Nick Dagger joined the copious display of flatulence and belching. I thought it was funny, but the other diners were horrified, and Kylie Simon and Versace were totally embarrassed. Kylie was really pissed off at Nick Dagger for acting immature."

"You amaze me, Eddie. Never before have I heard of a homeless guy living in a box who hangs out with superstars, jet setters, and farting Whatchacallit people. What the hell, man! You're crazy!"

After getting some coffee and food in her belly, Katarina was more sociable, and she told me that she wanted me to return to Cuba with her to play the role of her Canadian husband once more.

"So that's what this is all about! That's why you found me—to ask for a favor. And just when I thought you actually missed me," I said.

"I did miss you, Eddie. You're a lot of fun. You're my boy toy."

"Wow, your toy—thanks a lot, Kat."

"Rafael Cato has invited us to a celebration of the Cuban Revolution. On this trip we will fly into Cuba as Cato's special guests. Do you know what that means, Eddie? It means I'll get another shot at taking that Commie bastard out, but the trip will be very dangerous." Katarina's clear, grey eyes sparkled with excitement. The thought of danger seemed to turn her on, and I have to admit that my life back in the States had seemed a bit dull after playing her dangerous spy game inside Communist Cuba.

"Okay, I'll go. I'll do it! I'll do it for you, Kat." *My God, she's even more gorgeous when she's all excited! How can I say no to a woman like this? Plus, I miss her.*

After dinner we walked out to the car. "Is this your Corvette?" I asked.

"No, it's the FBI's. It was confiscated from one of Tony Montana's lieutenants—it had a kilo of coke in the trunk. Sometimes we get to play with the FBI's toys," she said as she hopped into the car without opening the door. We sped off toward the southeast.

"Hey, you're heading toward Coral Gables, and I live near Overtown."

"I'm still hungry," Katarina said as she turned a corner way too fast, causing the tires to squeal.

Katarina parked the car and raised the convertible top.

"Is this your crib?" I asked.

"Yeah. Let's go." Katarina went to a third floor apartment and unlocked three sets of deadbolts before opening the door. The one-bedroom apartment was immaculate but Spartan, with minimal furnishings. I noticed that there were no personal memorabilia or even personal pictures.

"Hey, your fridge is completely empty," I said and closed the refrigerator door. The freezer contained nothing except for two trays of ice cubes. "You must eat out a lot, Kat," I said as I sucked on an ice cube.

"Yeah I really need to do some shopping, but right now I'm still hungry!" She grabbed a handful of my shirt just below the collar and kissed me hard on the lips.

It was 5:00 am when my wristwatch alarm went off, and I rolled over to see Katarina lying on her back with a pillow covering her face.

"I'm hungry, Kat," I said. She pulled the pillow off her face and looked over at me.

"Are you trying to kill me, Ocean?"

"No, I mean my stomach is hungry."

"Oh, okay. After I shower, let's get breakfast at Wolfie's and then go for a jog on Miami Beach." Katarina rolled to her side, and I looked into her exotic eyes. I wanted to see if she had any real feelings for me whatsoever, so I decided to test her. *I'll tell her I have a girlfriend.*

"Katarina, I met a girl. I think I might be falling for her." Katarina looked at me, and her expression hardened. For a split second a look of jealousy flashed across her face, or maybe it was anger, but then it was gone.

"Oh? So why should I care, Ocean? I told you we would never be more than friends. Good luck with the bitch." She went into the bathroom, and I heard the shower running.

I was watching TV when Katarina opened the bathroom door wearing a skimpy black bikini bathing suit that exposed most of her olive-brown body and long, shapely legs. A white towel was wrapped high on her head to cover her thick, wet head of hair.

"You look like a smoking hot café latte with a dollop of whipped cream on top." *My God, she's gorgeous! So this is what you get when you cross a Cuban with a Ukrainian, eh?* I got up and walked over to her.

"Hey! What are you doing?" She let out a squeal as I picked her up and carried her across the threshold of the bathroom and over to the bed.

"I'm still hungry." I said, and I tossed her into the air. She squealed as she landed with one big bounce on the bed.

"What about your little girlfriend?" she asked.

"We've only had two dates. I don't even know if her feelings for me are the same as mine, Kat. I'm definitely still available." Violently, she pushed me down on the bed and then ripped the towel off her head and threw it across the room. An hour later we left for breakfast.

After breakfast at Wolfie's, we went across Collins Avenue to the beach. Several people were jogging, and some more were swimming for exercise. After walking a short distance, we stopped beneath the arch of a tall, curved coconut palm and kissed.

"I can't believe we live here. This is paradise," Katarina said.

"I agree. I'm living the street life in paradise, Kat." With my arm around her waist we watched the semi-circular dome of the bright sun break above the horizon. The deep orange semicircle shimmered like a glob of liquid sitting atop the ocean's surface.

"Looks just like that sunny side-up egg I had for breakfast," I said.

"Yeah, you ate too much. Let's burn off some of those calories," Katarina said and then ran off down the beach. I chased after her.

"Hey, I thought we were gonna jog!" I whined as I sprinted at full speed to catch up to her.

After an intense three-mile run, Katarina drove me to the hospital. This time she drove fast but not like an insane maniac.

"Eddie, I'll be in touch with you to give you the details of our trip to Cuba." She dropped me at the curb in front of the hospital, and with a squeal of her tires she was gone, leaving me standing in a cloud of the gray smoke. *That girl's dangerous. She's a real wildcat! Yeah, dude, a gorgeous wild Kat who's liable to get you killed!*

"Who the hell was that, Eddie? That chick is smoking hot, bro!" The Vampire, Uranus Johnson, called to me from the front door of the hospital.

"That was Katarina Romero. She's one crazy girl!"

"I want to meet that chick sometime. Eddie, you come to see Brownie, bro? Come on with me."

Vampire walked me to the SICU, but the nurses weren't going to allow me to go into the intensive care unit. Only family members of the patients were permitted inside. Disappointed, I was about to leave the hospital, but Vampire saved the day.

"Eddie, put on this lab coat. We'll pretend that you're a new phlebotomist and that I'm showing you around for your first day." He handed me a long white coat. "Luckily, I actually do have a request to draw blood from Brownie Shytles. I'll take my time doing it so you can visit with him."

"You're a genius, Uranus!" We walked into the SICU, but the nurses at the nursing station weren't fooled. They were on to our little ploy.

"Vampire, you know we just saw you with your friend trying to get in here only five minutes ago!"

"Who, my friend? You mean this guy? He's my new assistant— must have been someone who looks like him." The nurse smiled and played along with the game, so we went to Brownie's bedside, where a pretty, redheaded, freckle-faced nurse dressed in white pants and a white top was attending to him.

Brownie had tubes going into his nose and mouth and was lying on his back. Color had returned to his face, and he seemed to have already gained a little bit of weight. Even though he was unconscious, he looked better than I had ever seen him look before. *His organs must be functioning once again.*

"The doctors say that your friend is going to be okay. They think he's going to make it. The doctors have induced the coma for his benefit, but they plan on waking him up tomorrow morning," said the nurse.

I looked at Brownie's serene face. "When Brownie wakes up, he's gonna wonder how he got here—how he got admitted to the hospital, and how he was able to get the operation. Will you tell him that all his friends on skid row were able to put some money together? And please tell him not to worry about his medical bills."

"Sure, Eddie, I'll tell him your little white lie. But everyone here knows that you gave him the money. The ambulance guys spilled the beans when they brought Mr. Shytles here with your check pinned to his patient gown. But if you don't want Brownie to know it was your money, I'll tell him your story."

"Thanks, ma'am. I just don't want Brownie feeling obligated to me for the rest of his life. He has a very important task to complete. He has an architectural design that he needs to perfect."

"That's very magnanimous of you, Eddie Ocean."

Vampire finished taking the blood sample and said, "We gotta go, Eddie. Say bye-bye to the pretty nurse."

We left the SICU and stood waiting for the elevator. "Eddie, are you gonna let me meet that hot chick who drives the Corvette?"

"Oh, Katarina? Don't waste your time, Vamp. That girl keeps her heart in a lockbox. She believes that to care about someone makes a person vulnerable and weak. She's afraid to love because she's afraid that love will only make her weak and unhappy. She's afraid of putting someone she loves in jeopardy. The girl lives a very dangerous life, dude."

"Dangerous life? What is she, a race car driver or something?"

"Or something. Anyway, it's not serious between Katarina and me. She calls me her boy toy."

"Well, if that wild Kat is too much for you to handle, bro, give your good friend the Vampire a call!"

"Will do, brother!"

I left the hospital that day but returned three days later to visit Brownie. His condition was now listed as stable, and he had been transferred out of the SICU to a room on the fifth floor. When I went in, he was sitting up in his bed reading an architectural magazine.

"Welcome back from the dead, Brownie."

"Eddie, you tell the guys over on skid row that I'll repay them someday. I'm getting my résumé in order, and I'm going to finish my earthquake project if it's the last thing that I ever do in life. Soon I'll be able to pay everyone back, every last penny," Brownie said as I helped him walk to the bathroom.

"You look ten years younger, Brownie. I'm glad to see you doing so well, but now, my friend, I'm afraid I've got to leave you."

## MONDAY, APRIL 1ST, 1974

Today the sky is clear and the morning air is cool and refreshing. I'm sitting outside my cardboard box making this entry in my secret diary. The aroma of coffee and grits warming on the hibachi is pleasant and fills me with the sense that something good is in store for me today, and for the first time in over a year I have some money to my name.

Over two weeks have passed since my rendezvous with Katarina, and I haven't heard from her since. Katarina is exciting and beautiful, but she has a cold heart, a toughness that I feel will never allow her to love someone.

A wisp of cool air just filled my nostrils with the smell of strong coffee. The aroma makes me think of Brownie. I miss eating breakfast with that stinky little dude; the guy has a heart of gold. Now my thoughts are focused on Luca and Hobo. What will become of them now that Long Pond Farm was auctioned off last week? I wonder who bought the farm?

I decided to take a trip downtown to visit Rosalina to find out the answers to these questions and to discover where Luca had gone.

After dousing the hot coals with water, I walked to the bus stop near skid row singing the song "Street Life," but I stopped my warbling when I approached a man sitting on the bus stop bench.

He said, "You waiting for the northbound E bus, kid? Because it just left."

"No, I'm catching the F—I'm going downtown." While I was waiting for the bus, a big Cadillac Eldorado convertible passed by traveling on the opposite side of the street. The car drew my attention because of its huge size. "Awesome! That Caddy is more like a land yacht than a car!" I said to the stranger and pointed at the big white convertible.

"That's an El Dorado. Hey, it's coming back around," said the guy just as the big Caddy made a sudden u-turn and came back toward us. The car stopped at the curb directly in front of me.

"Hey, mister, you need a ride?" I couldn't believe my eyes: John Dumas was behind the wheel, dressed in a tropical shirt and smoking a fat cigar.

"Hey John, where have you been? I thought you left town!"

"Get in, Eddie. Where you headed? I'll give you a ride. Does your friend need a lift too?"

"No, thanks. I'm going in the other direction—north to Opa Locka—but nice wheels, dude!" said the stranger sitting on the bench.

I got into the big Caddy and sat in the white leather passenger seat. "Man, this is comfort, like sitting in a Castro Convertible reclining chair!"

"Tilt her way back like mine. Where you headed, Eddie?"

"I'm going to the Miami *Post*, John. Where have you been hanging out lately?"

On the drive, John told me that he had run into Riley Ford one night and that Riley treated him to dinner at the Forge restaurant.

"Yeah, Eddie, you probably knew that Riley was a wiseguy for the Boss for the past couple of years…well, he finally got his big break. One night the Boss assigned Riley to go with a gangster named Nicky the Knife to do an important job. After that job the Boss said that Riley was a made man…he's a bigshot with the mob now."

"Is Nicky the Knife still here in Miami?" I asked.

"I guess so, but he wasn't with us at the Forge. The Forge was incredible, like a gaudy palace, and John knew everybody in the damn place. The bigshots treated John with respect, Eddie. I couldn't believe it!"

*I gotta find out where Nikko is.* "John, do you know where Nicky the Knife hangs out?"

"No, I've never seen the guy. Heard he's real creepy, though. So anyhoo, Riley bought me a big steak dinner, and when we finished eating, he pulled a big wad of cash out of his pocket, paid the check, and then dropped a hundred-dollar bill on the table as a tip! A hundred bucks just like it was a ten! You ever been to the Forge, Eddie? Its over on 41st, Miami Beach."

"No, but I heard some clients talking about that place on a charter once—four wealthy, middle-aged people. They loved the food," I said.

"The Forge is full of money-makers—all the movers and shakers. The upper crust of society hangs out there. Mobsters, businessmen, lawyers, politicians, and hookers all rubbing elbows and swapping spit. After dinner Riley took me to the bar for some drinks, and this older Asian woman dressed to the nines started flirting with me from across the bar. She was covered with more ice than Mt. McKinley."

"Covered in ice?"

"Yeah, that means diamonds, dummy. So anyhoo, I buy her a drink, and she invites me over. Next thing I know, I'm waking up in her bed in a mini-mansion right on Miami Beach. Now, I know she's twenty years older than me, maybe she's sixty, but she's still not a bad-looking gal for her age, and I've always had a thing for Asian women."

"John, are telling me that you've become a gigolo?"

"I might have been playing the gigolo at first, but I've come to realize that Phat Ho is a special lady. No kidding, that's her name, Phat Ho, and I care a lot about the old gal now. I love being with her, and it's not just for her money anymore."

"Did she buy you this car and that watch?" I noticed the gold Rolex on John's wrist.

"Yeah, at first Phat was just buying me gifts all the time, but now I earn my own money. She set me up in my own business. I had my eye on a barbershop that was for sale downtown. Eddie, did I ever tell you that years ago I was a barber?"

"I don't think so."

"Well, Phat Ho said that a barbershop was too blasé and out-dated for Miami and not a money-maker. So instead she rented a big space for me on US1 in Coconut Grove, and we set up a unisex hair boutique. My salon is called the Carriage Trade Salon. Eddie, can you believe it—I'm the owner of the Carriage Trade Beauty Salon. I have four stylists—three chicks and a guy...well, I think he's a guy. Anyhoo, we're making a ton of money now!"

Two blocks ahead, the Miami *Post* building was coming up on the right side. "John you should visit Brownie at Jackson Hospital. He's doing real good."

"I've visited him twice already, but now he's gone. Eddie, didn't you hear?"

"Hear what?" I asked as John pulled to the curb.

"Brownie was discharged and left town. He took a job with a big-time high-rise builder in Los Angeles. He's already in L.A."

"That's great! Sorry I didn't get to say goodbye. So now I must be the only one left living on skid row from our little band of misfits!"

"Well, I guess you are, Eddie. Moe Lester was tossed in the loony bin. I visited him, too. He looks healthier and all cleaned up, but the poor guy has a screw loose."

"I thought Moe was in jail. Well, maybe in the sanitarium he can get some mental help."

"No parking, mister! Get that pimpmobile outta here before I have it towed!" The nasty security guard had come out to make John move his car, so I got out of the big Caddy and slammed the massive door shut. "You take care, John."

"You too, Eddie. Stop by the Carriage Trade, and I'll give you a free trim. You sure as hell need one, brother!" John said before driving off and flipping a bird at the angry guard.

*Wow, I really will be the last loser to leave skid row. I gotta get a boat to live on and pronto!*

"You're just a cheap pimp! Get a job, you bum!" The security guard taunted me as he followed me toward the elevators.

As usual, Rosalina and Ima were busy at work in her office. "Hello, girls."

"Hi, Eddie. We have big news for you! Tell him, Ima," said Rosalina.

"I'm engaged." Ima held out her left hand to show me a huge diamond ring."

"Wow, engaged? Engaged to whom? I didn't even know you had someone special, Ima."

"We had to keep it secret. He's the public defender for the District Attorney's office."

"You mean Attorney Richard Normous, the tall, blond guy I've seen in your courtroom sketches?"

"Yes, I'm engaged to Dick! Dick is my fiancé. Isn't he handsome?" Ima showed me a photograph of them standing together on the beach. "Dick knows about my past, and he doesn't care. He loves me, Eddie!"

"Eddie, can you handle some more good news?" Rosalina chimed in.

"I'll try."

"Lauren Matthews and Mr. Olsen are also engaged. No surprise there—I saw that one coming a mile away."

"That was fast, but what about the farm? Wasn't the farm sold last week?" I asked.

"No, didn't you hear? Ima got her fiancé, Dick Normous, to do a pro bono for them. He got them an extension on the eviction notice. They have one more week left on their extension, and the radio station fundraisers have collected over $22,000 for the Save Luca's Farm fund."

"That's awesome, but how much do they need to keep the farm?"

"Ninety-five thousand, five hundred!"

"What? Wow, that's a lot!" I was stunned.

"I know, Eddie. They'll never make it," said Ima.

I pulled my checkbok from my back pocket and looked at my balance. *Hmm, I have $73,500.06 left in my account. Dude, this can't be a mere coincidence, can it? The amount of money in my account is the exact amount that is needed to save Long Pond Farm!*

"Rosalina, add this on your calculator: $73,500.06 plus $22,000. Isn't that 95,500.06?" *I can't believe this is happening to me again! It's an omen!*

"Yes, that's right, why?'

"The money that Luca needs to keep his home is exactly equal to the amount of money that I have left in my bank account—well, with a six-cent surplus. How is that possible?" I asked.

"Ah, I don't understand. What are you saying?" Rosalina looked down at the calculator, confused.

"Don't you see Rosalina? The ancients—the spirits—entrusted me with this money to help Luca; I've only been a custodian, the money has never really been mine. I finally see the truth." I held out my checkbook. "This money is meant for Luca. Why else would it add up—right down to the last penny?"

"Eddie, sit down, you look pale. Are you lightheaded again?"

I sat down, visibly shaken by the revelation.

Rosalina tried to comfort me, "I know that you're upset about them losing the farm. Everyone is upset, especially after my article about Luca ran in the *Post*, but Eddie, you can't singlehandedly save the world."

"She's right, Eddie. You already gave away all of that money to save Brownie's life. Things will eventually work out for Luca, too," Ima said and ran her fingers through my hair.

"Rosalina, would you let me borrow that pen—and lend me one dollar?"

"Sure, Eddie." After Rosalina handed me a dollar, I took out my checkbook and wrote a check to the Save Luca's Farm Fund for $95,499.00. Then with a paperclip I attached the dollar bill to my check.

"Rosalina, please give my check and this one dollar bill to the fundraisers for me."

"Sure, but what's with the dollar bill? Why not write the check for the entire amount?"

"I want to keep my bank account open. By paying this way, I'll have a balance of $1.06 left in my bank account."

Ima began to cry, and then she hugged me.

"Don't worry, Ima. It's not so bad. I've got three tens in my pocket—thirty bucks."

"Eddie, do you want a job here at the newspaper? I could pull a few strings for you." Rosalina told me that she could get me a job at the newspaper loading trucks at the shipping dock, but I declined her offer because I knew that when Katarina called me I would have to be available to leave immediately for Cuba. I thanked Rosalina and left the office, my hopes for owning a sailboat shattered once more.

Downstairs, the sourpuss security guard scowled and yelled at me as I passed. "Get a job and a haircut, hippie!"

This time I didn't ignore the obnoxious man. Instead I walked over to him, got in his face, and said, "What are you gonna do about it, rent-a-cop?"

His face turned bright red with anger. "I'm gonna give you an attitude adjustment, punk!" He reached out to grab me by the throat, and I put a wristlock on his right arm and drove him down to his knees. *"Aaaaaah!"* he cried out in pain.

"Now beg, you crotchety old bastard! Beg and I won't break your arm!"

"Ahhh, let go! Okay, okay, please, please, I give up, kid! Ahhh, my elbow—my shoulder!" I let him go, and the guard stood up and began shaking his right arm. When I turned around to leave, a crowd of onlookers started cheering and clapping.

"It's about time someone put that bully in his place!" A guy yelled from the crowd. "Way to go kid!" The guard picked up his telephone.

*Looks like the old fart might be calling the cops. You'd better get out of here, dude. You could use a drink!* After riding a bus to the marina I went to the Tiki Hut Bar. Fannie Licker was on duty.

"Hi, Fannie. Gimme a cold brewski, *por favor.*"

After Fannie brought me an ice-cold mug of draft beer, her phone rang.

"Tiki Hut Bar!" she answered and then stood very still staring down at the receiver with a furrowed brow.

"What's the matter, Fannie?"

"Ah, it's for you, Eddie. It's Dr. Hamm!"

"What? Jill Hamm? That bitch fired me. Here, gimme that phone. Hello?"

"Hi, Ocean. I saw you go into the Tiki Bar. Look, I've got a problem. We just bought a beautiful 44-foot Beneteau, and now I'm one captain short. Want to run a charter for me on the *Orion?*"

"Sure! I need the money." I swallowed my pride for the chance to captain the *Orion* and make some money.

"Come on over to the office, I'll give you the details." She hung up.

"Fannie, Dr. Hamm wants me to captain a charter."

"You're not gonna do it for her, are you? After how she treated you!"

"I need to do it." After guzzling my beer I walked over to Sun 'N' Fun and went inside.

"Ha-ha, you sucker! *April fool!* You are such a loser, Ocean! I would never let you on one of my boats again; you're not a team player, Ocean! Ho-ho-ho. Ohh my God, you should see the look on your face right now!" The evil little woman was literally jumping up and down behind the counter, her Brillo pad hair pulsating as she jumped up and down, mocking me.

"Screw you, Hamm!" I walked back to the tiki bar, pissed off and embarrassed over falling for Hamm's cruel trick.

"Fannie, it was just an April fool's joke! Hamm's not giving me a gig. I need another beer."

"What an evil little bitch! I shouldn't have let you go over there. I knew something was fishy!" Fannie said as she filled my mug.

A guy walked in and sat several chairs down from us and then called out, "Hey Fannie, a vodka martinus for me!"

"Do you mean a martini, professor?" she asked.

"No, but I do plan on having more than one today."

Fannie gave him an odd look and then began making his drink directly in front of me.

"Who's the weirdo?" I whispered.

"That's professor Edward, an anthropologist from the University of Miami. He's a real pompous ass. Thinks he knows everything and everyone else is stupid."

"Hey, Fannie, can you turn the volume up on that TV?" The professor pointed to the TV as a news report showing videos of several earthquake disasters came on the screen. Suddenly Brownie Shytles's face filled the TV screen.

"Hey, Fannie! Brownie's on TV. Look!" Amazed, I stood up and listened to the reporter.

Master architect Mr. 'Brownie' Shytles, whose family died tragically in a South American earthquake several years ago, has dedicated his life to designing earthquake-resistant buildings. Mr. Shytles has developed an innovative new building foundation that was just tested yesterday outside of the engineering department at UCLA. Twin scale model replicas of the seventy-three-story U.S. Bank Tower were tested on a device called a shake-table. Yesterday, the group of industry-leading engineers, architects, and geological scientists in attendance proclaimed Mr. Shytles's design a momentous success. The following film is the video replay of Mr. Shytles's shake-table demonstration.

Playing out before my eyes was a replay of the vision that I'd had of Brownie's lecture. He was giving his shake-table demonstration, and every detail, right down to Brownie's words and his tailored business suit, was identical to my vision. My hand was shaking as I took a long drink of beer.

"You look like you've just seen a ghost, Eddie. Don't you think that the report was good news?" Fannie said as she used a towel to wipe up the beer that had sloshed over the rim of my mug.

"Sure, Fannie. I was just surprised to see Brownie on the TV, I guess." *She will never believe your "vision" story, dude.*

"Eddie, that's great for Brownie, but now you're broke again," Fannie said as she topped off my beer. She knew the story.

"Maybe so, but my money was well spent!"

Sometimes it's better to live simply, so that others may simply live.

# Chapter 32

# KIDNAPPED

The afternoon was lovely, and with so much on my mind I decided to walk home from the Tiki Bar rather than ride the bus. After traveling about halfway to skid row I came upon a street vendor selling paella at the entrance to a small park. Atop the vendor's cart, yellow rice loaded with seafood and chicken filled a large metal wok. *That looks delicious.*

"Give me one bowl of paella and a Pepsi, please." After ordering, I took my lunch into the park and sat down at a picnic table to eat. Three squirrels and dozens of birds began gathering around my table, begging for a handout.

I used a plastic spoon to flick yellow rice toward the critters, and they squabbled over my offerings. One fat, bossy, gray squirrel got the lion's share. "Welcome, my little friends. Thanks for not leaving me to eat all alone." When I got down to the bottom of the bowl of paella, there were a few clams that had an odd, although not a bad, flavor, so I ate them. After finishing my lunch, I tossed the Styrofoam container into a trash barrel, and the bossy squirrel jumped in head-first after it and started gnawing on the container.

"No wonder you're so fat, squirrel!" I took the last swig of Pepsi, belched loudly, and tossed the empty can into the barrel, narrowly missing the hyperactive gray squirrel, who protested loudly as I continued walking home.

For the rest of the afternoon I stayed up in the penthouse reading a cheesy paperback romance novel, the only book available, before turning in early for the night. At about midnight I woke up with my stomach on fire and went outside to vomit. My body felt hot all over, my head throbbed, and I had severe abdominal cramps. *That paella was tainted! I've got food poisoning…better go to the hospital. You will never make it that far dude!*

Wishing that Little Hooters were there to take care of me, I lay alone inside my cardboard box suffering badly. At about three o'clock in the morning, I was finally able to sleep, but my fever brought on a vivid dream, maybe a hallucination. Little Hooters was standing over me, nursing me back to health. *My sweet Little Hooters, I have missed you so badly.* Little Hooters wiped my forehead with a cool, wet washcloth and told me, "It's no use, Eddie. I cannot save you this time. I'm so sorry, you are dying!" And then she began to cry. The crying face morphed into Katarina's face looming above me.

*Don't cry for me, Kat. I've had a good life,* I said, and then her face dissolved into a mist and she was gone. Feeling the urge to vomit, I crawled out of the shack but collapsed just outside the doorway. Suddenly I found myself standing on top of the I-95 overpass, looking down at my prone body below. With a pool of vomit in front of my pale white face, my body rested just outside the entrance to my shack.

*Have I died?* A bright, white light flashed, blinding me temporality, so I closed my eyes. When I opened them, I found myself sailing in the ocean on a sunny day. *Hey, this boat is the* Orion! There was a stiff, fresh breeze, and I trimmed the sails to gain speed. *Wow, she's fast!*

Three dolphins appeared and began jumping and playing in my bow wake. *Hello old friends! Good to see you again,* I greeted them, and they responded with excited squeaks and chirps. Then seabirds of every feather began following my sailboat. They greeted me with a deafening cacophony of birdcalls. *Welcome, my fine-feathered friends!* Off my portside beam, a giant sea turtle with a welcoming smile across his big green beak surfaced as my boat raced past. A long, jagged scratch marred the top of his rock-hard shell. *Hey, it's you, Mister Turtle. The last time we met you broke my prop, sending me adrift to Crocodile Island, sending me off on a series of great adventures. Thank you for that, Mr. Turtle!*

Suddenly, without any setting of the sun, it was pitch black. Darkness surrounded my boat, and all the animals were gone as I sailed alone into the dead of night. *The ancient spirits are gathering for their nighttime councils, I see.* Constellations began appearing in the aphotic night sky above.

A powerful voice boomed down from the heavens: "Sun Chaser Eddie Ocean, you are not dreaming; you are having a vision, a look into your future. This is our gift to you for having served us well. You have passed all the trials and tribulations and have completed your task of saving Luca. You have brought honor to yourself and the ancestors by helping many others in need along the way."

The omnipotent voice was painfully loud. I covered my ears with my hands to muffle its intensity. Then a young woman appeared, standing at the bow of my sailboat. She stood with her back to me, looking out into the blackness ahead of the boat.

"Hello! Who are you?" I called out to her. In the darkness I could not see her features, only her silhouette and her long hair trailing behind her, floating gently on the stiff breeze. Slowly, she began turning toward me, but before I could see her face there came a loud clap of thunder, so loud it caused me more unbearable pain, and I was forced to cover my ears again and look down toward the deck.

**Boom! Boom! Boom!** The noise thundered three more times, and suddenly the vision was over. Now there was only a voice, a loud but definitely mortal voice.

"Get up, Eddie Ocean, get up!" **Boom! Boom! Boom!** I opened my eyes, turned my head skyward, and saw Carlos *"El Muerte"* Romero standing over me, pounding on the outside wall of my cardboard shack.

"Get up, Eddie, get up! The Russian butcher has kidnapped Katarina!"

"What? Where's the boat? Where am I?" My stomach was erupting like a volcano as I rose to my knees, stood up, and then pushed past Carlos to vomit off the embankment. My projectile vomiting came in waves and lasted for several minutes while Carlos berated me for being drunk. I could barely stand and nearly fell forward down the steep slope. *What was he saying to me?* Finally my stomach settled down, and I drank some water.

"Katarina is in great danger, and now you are a useless drunk, hung-over and sick!" Carlos was screaming.

"I'm not drunk...got food poisoning." My voice was soft and weak.

"Did you hear me, Eddie? The CIA says that Nicky the Knife has kidnapped Katarina...he's taken her to Cuba!" I was starting to regain my senses, and I looked at Carlos's face. Never before had I seen the look of panic and fear in *El Muerte's* black eyes.

"Do you know what that Russian might do to Katarina? He might do much worse than this!" Carlos yelled and then lifted the hair that covered his temples. Where there should have been ears, there were only two holes going into his head.

"The Russian cut off my ears and gave them to his girlfriend! Imagine what he might do to Katarina!"

"What can I do, Carlos?" The adrenaline surging through me at the thought of Katarina being tortured and butchered by Nicky the Knife was bringing me back to life.

"Snap out of it—drink more water. I need you to help me take a fast-boat to Cuba. We must go there to find Katarina. We will take two of our best special-force operators and rescue Katarina from the butcher. We must go now! My car is down below." The look of fear and panic on Carlos's face was unsettling. I grabbed my backpack and stumbled down the slope.

With tires squealing, Carlos took off toward the city. "First, we must stop off at Katarina's apartment to collect her passport and IDs. From Cuba we will take her to our safe house in the Cayman Islands. If she has been harmed, we'll return to Cuba to kill more of the Communist bastards," Carlos said as he drove the car at break-neck speed.

"Hey, why are you heading downtown? Katarina lives near Coconut Grove. I was at her apartment last week," I said.

"No, Katarina lives on Brickel Ave. She must have taken you to our safe house in the Grove, not to her apartment." Carlos said as he whipped the car around a corner.

"Safe house?" *So that's why the place looked so sparse, so unlived in… so cold and vacant. Why would Kat not want me to see her apartment?*

"We're here!" Carlos shouted as the car screeched to a halt. He ran up a flight of steps to the second floor with me following close on his heels. Carlos used a key to open Katarina's apartment, and we went inside.

"Where's the bathroom?" Feeling like I might vomit again I went into the bathroom and stood hunched over the toilet but only suffered from a series of dry heaves. On top of the toilet tank was a bouquet of fresh flowers. *That's a good sign. These flowers look no more than a day old. Katarina must have been here yesterday.* A clear shower curtain adorned with images of jumping blue dolphins covered the bathtub; I pulled it aside. On a ledge surrounding the tub, there was a yellow rubber ducky and a plastic bottle of bubble bath that was covered with pink, heart-shaped bubbles. *Seriously, Kat? Bubble baths…a rubber ducky!* I went to the sink to splash cold water on my sweaty face and found myself standing on a red, heart-shaped shag throw rug. After splashing my face and taking a drink I looked at my reflection in the mirror.

*What's this?* Someone had written on the mirror when it was fogged by steam. *Maybe it's a message left for us by Katarina!* After leaning close to the glass, I breathed heavily out from my mouth to re-fog the mirror, and more letters become visible as well as a drawing. In the middle of a large heart shape that had been traced by a finger, I saw the letters K.T. + E.O.

*Katarina must have drawn this after getting out of a hot shower.* I closed my eyes and imagined her standing in front of the mirror, with her hair wrapped up in a towel that stood tall atop her head. *This is the same childish doodle that I drew in the sand on the beach in Key West! Is it possible? Does Kat secretly love me? Has she been hiding her feelings for me all this time?* When I came out of the bathroom, Carlos was digging through Katarina's bedroom closet.

"I'm in here, Eddie. Check those dresser drawers over there," he demanded.

When I entered the bedroom, I froze in my tracks. I could not believe my eyes. Katarina's bedroom was decorated like that of a young girl. *This is not what I expected. That cold, sterile, safe house that she pretended was home better fits her personality. This stuff can't belong to Kat!* Many sweet and sentimental knickknacks and memorabilia were placed all about her room. Ticket stubs from movies and plays had been used as bookmarks in the books of poetry and romance that lined a small wooden bookcase. She had a movie poster of the film *The Way We Were* thumbtacked to the wall. *That's the corny film that I saw with Patty. I can't imagine Kat sitting through that mushy film without laughing out loud. Apparently she liked it!* Befuddled, I stared at the smiling faces of Robert Redford and Barbra Streisand.

I turned toward the bed. *Look at that, dude. That's Whitest!*

Sitting on Katarina's bed, leaning back against a pillow, was Whitest, the little white teddy bear I had won for Kat in Cuba. She had made a red vest for him, and in yellow thread, *Eddie* was embroidered in cursive across the front of the little vest. She not only had kept the teddy bear, she had even made him a red vest!

On her long dresser were two framed photographs, one at each end. I picked up the nearest picture. That's us! It was a photo of Katarina dancing with me at the Tropicana. She was wearing that sexy Latin Rhythm dress. *She is so beautiful.* I put it down and went to see the other picture. It was a shot of us standing near the seawall outside our hotel in Cuba. *What's this red smudge?*

I picked up the picture to get a closer look and recognized Katarina's lip prints in red lipstick on the glass frame. Just above the sunglasses clipped to my shirt collar the faint impression her lips were visible. *She kissed the left side of my chest. She kissed my heart! Does Katarina secretly love me?*

"Come on, Eddie, I got her passport—let's go!" Carlos rushed toward the door.

I began to follow him out but then stopped short. "Wait, Carlos!" I went back and grabbed the teddybear, Whitest, and also the picture with Katarina's lip prints and shoved them into my backpack.

*You really had me fooled, Ms. Katarina Romero! Beneath that gorgeous, cold exoskeleton—underneath that hard, tough ice façade, you hide your tender heart! Katarina, now I know you* are *capable of heartfelt love!*

"We have no time to waste, Ocean!"

"Okay, Carlos, let's go! Let's go find Katarina!"

## THE END

www.ingramcontent.com/pod-product-compliance
Lightning Source LLC
Chambersburg PA
CBHW030013180626
46810CB00001B/21